Praise for Jill McGown

DEATH IN THE FAMILY

"Complex . . . Intense . . . Engrossing . . . McGown conjures up an abundant array of suspects . . . with credible motives . . . [with] clever and often ironic [writing] style smoothly s[witching between] these characters."

SCENE OF CRIME

"Convincing characters and a deft plot make for another intelligent procedural."
—*Chicago Tribune*

PICTURE OF INNOCENCE

"[A] fantastically intricate murder plot . . . It's a pleasure watching McGown's wheels of justice grind."
—*Kirkus Reviews*

VERDICT UNSAFE

"A cleverly constructed, realistic courtroom drama that keeps you totally involved."
—ANNE PERRY

MURDER AT THE OLD VICARAGE

"A first-rate mystery . . . A spider's-web of a tale . . . Fiendishly clever."
—*The Washington Post*

By Jill McGown

RECORD OF SIN
AN EVIL HOUR
THE STALKING HORSE
MURDER MOVIE

THE LLOYD AND HILL MYSTERIES

A PERFECT MATCH
MURDER AT THE OLD VICARAGE
GONE TO HER DEATH
THE MURDERS OF MRS. AUSTIN AND MRS. BEALE
THE OTHER WOMAN
MURDER . . . NOW AND THEN
A SHRED OF EVIDENCE
VERDICT UNSAFE
PICTURE OF INNOCENCE
PLOTS AND ERRORS
SCENE OF CRIME
DEATH IN THE FAMILY

DEATH IN THE FAMILY

JILL McGOWN

FAWCETT

BALLANTINE BOOKS • NEW YORK

A Fawcett Book
Published by The Random House Publishing Group
Copyright © 2003 by Jill McGown

All rights reserved under International and Pan-American Copyright Conventions. Published in the United States by The Random House Publishing Group, a division of Random House, Inc., New York.

Fawcett is a registered trademark and the Fawcett colophon is a trademark of Random House, Inc.

www.ballantinebooks.com

ISBN 0-345-45849-4

Manufactured in the United States of America

First Hardcover Edition: February 2003
First Mass Market Edition: May 2004

OPM 10 9 8 7 6 5 4 3 2 1

CHAPTER ONE

Judy Hill had never been afraid of another person in her life. In her childhood and adolescence, there had been no cause for fear, but not even in her twenty-odd-year career as a police officer had she ever been truly afraid of someone else. She had found herself in potentially violent situations; she had even been injured in the line of duty. She had dealt with aggressive drunks and the odd deeply disturbing psychopath, but she had always had complete confidence in her own ability to deal with whatever and whoever crossed her path. Until now.

And the monster who had achieved what no rapist or murderer had yet managed was toothless, helpless, asleep . . . and barely two hours old.

"Charlotte," said Lloyd, sitting down on the bed.

Predictably, they had been unable to agree on a name; Judy thought that they had considered everything from Abigail to Zoë and back again, but she couldn't remember them discussing Charlotte. Names were very important to Lloyd, since he had been given one that so appalled him that everyone called him by his surname, and he was worried about inflicting that trauma on the baby. "That's nice," she said.

"Yes? I thought of it when her head appeared. She looks like a Charlotte."

Judy nodded. "She does. Of course she's got French

blood. What about a middle name?" She smiled. "We could always name her after you." Lloyd's French grandmother had been responsible for his awful name, which he said made him sound like a cross between a stripper and a potato. "Just put an extra *e* on the end."

"We could," he agreed. "Over your dead body."

She laughed. "How about after your grandmother?"

"Charlotte Françoise," he murmured, then shook his head. "No—no one would ever get it right. If people can't even use apostrophes, there's no point in expecting them to cope with a cedilla. And she might not like it. Make it plain Frances, and you've got a deal."

"As long as you promise not to go on about people spelling it *c-i-s* at the end, because they will."

"Done. Other people won't have much call to spell her middle name, anyway. Charlotte might go on about it, though, if she takes after me." He looked at her, his head to one side. "Charlotte Frances Lloyd. Yes. I like that. Perhaps she looks like Grandma Pritchard—that might have been what suggested a French name in the first place." He bent closer and scrutinized her. "Does she look like either of us, do you think?"

"Well, given that she's bald and blue-eyed . . ."

"Very funny. I think she'll have brown eyes like you. And she's pretty well bound to have dark hair. And she's definitely got your jawline."

"She hasn't *got* a jawline."

"Can I hold her?"

Judy was only too pleased to pass the tiny, fragile bundle to Lloyd, who had at least been through this before and presumably knew a little more than she did about the whole alarming thing, and watch him as he cradled his brand-new daughter.

It had been a long labor, and bearable only because Lloyd was there. Judy had seriously doubted that he would be; Barbara, the mother of his other two children—both adults now—had not been accorded the same measure of support. He had conveniently been too deeply involved in police business to be present at the births and hadn't even seen either Peter or Linda until they had been in the world for several more hours than Charlotte had. But he had been there for Judy, and he had even made her laugh, something she would have thought impossible in her imaginings of what it was going to be like. "Wouldn't it have been easier just to go through with the wedding?" he'd asked her, at the height of the discomfort.

Charlotte had decided to announce her imminent arrival two days before what should have been their wedding day. For her timing Judy was indebted to her, because getting married while looking like a barrage balloon had not been her choice. In a supreme act of selflessness, she had gone along with Lloyd's oddly conventional desire—given that he was usually anything but conventional—to be married before the baby was born, but Charlotte had obviously inherited her mother's sense of style and had vetoed that. Besides, it had been snowing when Lloyd had driven her to the Malworth maternity unit in the early hours of the morning, and the forecast had been for more of the same; she wouldn't have liked to get married on a cold, snowy day. Having a baby was different—she was glad she'd had a winter baby and hadn't had to carry all that extra weight through the summer.

"So how was it for you?" she asked.

"Embarrassing—I had to keep apologizing for you."

"I didn't swear, did I?"

"Not half."

Judy would seek confirmation of that; Lloyd could tell her anything and get away with it. She couldn't remember what she'd done. "I suppose you were glad it took forever. I think you were frightened you might have to deliver her."

"People do not deliver babies. Pregnant women are delivered *of* babies."

"Whatever. *And* you were frightened you'd faint." She grinned. "You didn't, did you?"

He smiled, then shook his head slightly, and she could see him blink away a tear before he spoke again. "Tom was right," he said, his accent more Welsh than it had been, as it was when he was emotional. "It was the most amazing thing."

Tom Finch was Lloyd's detective sergeant and a friend of theirs; he had enthused throughout Judy's pregnancy about the joys of watching a birth, much to Lloyd's discomfort.

"I wish—" Lloyd began, and broke off. "Sorry."

She smiled, guessing the rest. "Don't be silly. Just don't go telling Barbara you wish you'd been there."

"No. I'm not quite that tactless." He smiled down at Charlotte. "Will she resent having an old bald bloke as her father, do you think?"

"Fifty isn't old."

"Fifty-one. As good as. And she can't resent anything yet. But I'll be nearly seventy when she comes of age."

"And I'll be fifty-nine." Judy shrugged a little. "I suppose we just have to wait and see if it bothers her. Not a lot we can do about it."

"Linda rang," said Lloyd, in a not-unconnected diversion. "She sends her best wishes and congratulations."

"Does that mean she's really come to terms with it, or is she just putting a brave face on it?"

Lloyd shook his head. "I think it means that curiosity about her half sister has won out over disapproval of her father having done such a thing at his time of life. She even says she's going to come to the wedding—assuming we ever get round to it again."

Judy ignored that. They had agreed no guests on account of her condition, but she didn't have that excuse anymore. So not only would she have to go through all that buildup again, but this time the day would be complete with relatives and friends and a wedding reception, because Lloyd had missed out on all of that first time round; his marriage to Barbara had been done on a shoe-string, with only the closest of relatives in attendance. This time, he wanted to do things in style. Still—at least Judy could wait until her hormones were all back in the right place, so she put the thought of marriage to the back of her mind. "Have you spoken to Barbara?" she asked. "I mean—she should be told that you've got another daughter, shouldn't she?"

"Linda said she'd tell her. And, chickenhearted as I am, I thought that sounded like a splendid idea. I tried to get in touch with Peter, but I think he and his wife are away skiing or something. My father says we're to bring her to see him as soon as she's old enough. Did your mum ring you?"

"Yes—she and Dad are coming tomorrow."

"It'll be nice to see them again."

Judy hesitated a little before she spoke again. "My mother offered to stay for a couple of weeks and help—would you mind if she did?"

"No, of course not."

It seemed genuine. Judy hadn't been sure how he would feel—would he want them to be a cozy threesome in the first few weeks of the baby's life? But if he did, he wasn't betraying it, and she thought that now, with his emotions so near the surface, he might not be as adept as he usually was at acting. She wanted her mother there. Anyone, really, who knew something about babies and would be there all the time. No matter how many health visitors and midwives came, she knew she wouldn't feel sanguine about being responsible for this new person.

Lloyd sat back a little and looked at the baby, and then at her, with another little smile. "We've been pretty clever, haven't we?"

Judy nodded, trying not to show the sheer panic that welled up whenever she thought about the future. Pretty clever or pretty stupid. One or the other.

"You'll like Ian. You really will."

Kayleigh looked dully at the picture of the school's founder that hung on the wall behind the head's desk.

"I like Dad."

She had thought, when she was interrupted in the middle of lessons to be told that her mother was on the phone, that she was ringing to tell her that her dad was home, that everything was back to normal. He and her mother had split up in June, and he didn't know about Alexandra; that was why she hadn't been able to see him since then, so that he wouldn't find out that she was having the baby after all, because he had wanted her to have a termination. Alexandra had been born just before Christmas, so she hadn't even seen him then.

But he had come to Dean's trial, and they had all gone for meals and things—he and her mother had seemed to be getting on all right, and Kayleigh had hoped they might reconsider the split. It was all her fault, and the least she could do was try to get them back together. She had written to him, suggested that he go to see her mother to try to change her mind, and she had thought, just for a few moments, that it had worked. But instead of that her mother was telling her that she had some new man.

"Of course you do, and you can see him anytime you want now; I've told you that. But he's still lodging with his friends—once he's found a place of his own, we'll sort something out. Maybe you could spend Easter with him." Her mother paused for a moment. "But you'll like Ian, too."

It was while Kayleigh was seeing Dean that her mother had started talking about Ian—she had met him at the place where she worked. Kayleigh remembered how she had felt with Dean and wondered if her mother felt like that with Ian. Had she got pregnant, too? Was that why she was doing this?

There was a silence before her mother spoke. "No, nothing like that," she said. "We just know we're right for each other." Another pause. "Do you remember your real father, Kayleigh?"

Kayleigh frowned. No one knew who her real father was. Not even her real mother, as far as Kayleigh was aware. "No," she said, puzzled. "How could I?"

"Not your natural father." Her mother gave a little laugh. "I meant Richard."

Oh, Richard. Yes, Kayleigh remembered him, even though he had died when she was four and a half years old. She just had trouble thinking of him as her father; Richard and her mother had adopted her, but Phil was her father, as far as she was concerned. Richard had died in a car accident; all she had known was that one day he was there and then he'd gone, like everyone else in her life.

"Yes. Just."

"Ian's quite like him to look at. Tall and dark, and slim. And he's like him in other ways, too. He's very kind and easy to get along with. I feel about him the way I did about Richard, and I honestly never thought I'd feel like that again. You'll like him, too; I'm sure you will."

Kayleigh didn't speak.

"Ian's quite a bit younger than Phil. And he knows all about computers, so you'll like that."

Phil was a bit overweight, a bit thin on top, and almost fifty; this new model was closer to her mother's age, had sleeker looks, and came with an extensive knowledge of computers. Her mother was selling him to her and went on selling him to her for the next fifteen minutes before finally hanging up.

Kayleigh went back to the lesson from which she had been plucked and wondered what had happened to Dean; they were sentencing him today.

The handcuffs were removed, and Dean Fletcher pulled his hands back, rubbing his wrists. The bolts were shot home, the door was deadlocked, and he tried to get into something approaching a comfortable position, not easy with his knees jammed as they were against the wall of the prison van cell.

Dean had spent virtually all his twenty-four years doing things calculated to land him behind bars, so imprisonment was not a new experience. He had stolen from cars, shoplifted, broken and entered, caused affrays, carried offensive weapons, committed actual bodily harm, absconded from custody, made off without paying . . . all good clean criminality, and his fellow passengers would have no problem with any of that. But this time was different, and he knew only too well what lay ahead of him, having endured months of it in the remand center before he'd even been found guilty.

They had put him in the van cell nearest the guard, something they had never done before, and when they took on the last prisoner being collected from the court Dean discovered its significance.

"Is that the peedie in there?"

The guard said he didn't know, but the prisoner clearly did, and Dean could only listen as he loudly informed the two occupants who were already on board and endure the obscenities now directed at him, rather than at the guard as they had been before, hoping that they were all bound for destinations other than his. It wasn't fair. Because he *wasn't* a pedophile. He wasn't.

The van pulled out, picking its way through the heavy traffic, stopping and starting at traffic lights, bearing Dean through the sleet and snow of London back to the remand center to await his transfer to the prison to which he had been committed for eighteen months. It could, he knew, have been worse, but right now it seemed like a life sentence.

He had been messing around on the Internet, and they had started chatting. In the short messages that had been exchanged, she had called herself Jennifer Archer and had said that she was an eighteen-year-old student. They had talked about records and TV shows—all the usual sort of stuff. Nothing heavy, nothing suggestive, just chat. When they had moved on to private chat, he had discovered that she wasn't in New Zealand or Zanzibar but right there in London, and over the next few nights they had exchanged messages, which had rapidly become a lot more personal, and very promising. He had asked her to meet him, and she had agreed.

The prosecutor had made out that Dean made a habit of finding young girls on the Net; he had said that it was the first and only time he'd met someone this way, but he could see that the jury didn't believe him.

"You didn't consider this a somewhat juvenile way to pass the time?"

"Yes, but it was just a bit of fun."

"Oh, so you do consider it juvenile?"

"Yes."

"And you knew that juveniles often used 'chat rooms,' didn't you? You were specifically on the lookout for a juvenile, weren't you?"

His solicitor had advised him to plead guilty because that way the girl wouldn't have to give evidence and he might get a shorter sentence, but he couldn't do that. He had pleaded not guilty on the grounds that he had believed her to be sixteen or over and had had reasonable grounds for this belief, which was nothing but the plain truth. His solicitor had pointed out that he was lucky—if he had been a month older, even that defense would have gone out the window. Luckier still that he hadn't arranged to meet her a week earlier, or the judge really would have had a life sentence at his disposal.

That first evening, they had walked along the river for a bit, but the evening was chilly and he had suggested going for a drink. She had said why didn't they just buy a bottle of something and drink it in his camper van? She had been a bit nervous when they got back to the camper, said she'd changed her mind, but after she'd had a few drinks the evening had progressed as he hoped it would. Afterward, she wouldn't let him drive her all the way home, just told him to stop the camper on a street corner. They had exchanged mobile numbers, and she had left.

They had met•several times during the next three months, but he had never met any of her friends and she had never met his; she never took him home or came to the flat that he shared with a couple of other mates. It was always in his old beat-up camper. He thought at first that she was just looking for a bit of rough, a bit of excitement, and sex in the camper was part of it, that she would have been ashamed to introduce him to her upmarket friends. He'd even thought she must be married or something, far from thinking she was underage. But it had become much more than just a sexual adventure, despite the way it had started, despite the way it was conducted.

He had . . . well . . . fallen for her. Really fallen for her. Head over heels. She was so unlike any of the girls that he'd ever been with before. The whole thing felt like a dream now, like something he'd imagined, but hiding away from everyone, cocooned in the camper, he had felt so . . . so privileged, he supposed, that someone like her was choosing to spend her time with him. He knew she wasn't telling him everything and that she was a bit screwed up about things in general, but he felt as though she needed him, needed to be with him, and that had been good. Better than good. And the truth was that he would have done anything for her. Anything. That was why he had just gone along with her wish to keep it all just between them.

It had seemed special. Until the night that she hadn't turned up and he had gone home alone. He had thought then that she'd made it up with her real boyfriend or gone back to her husband or off on her travels or come to her senses—whatever. That it hadn't been special for her after all. He had been hurt but not surprised. He had known he could never hang on to her and had been trying to resign himself to never seeing her again.

Next day, he'd had a visit from the police, asking him about someone called Kayleigh Scott, inviting him to go to the police station and answer some questions. He said he'd never heard of her and then slowly became aware that whoever she was, she was thirteen years old and they suspected him of having had sex with her. Even then it hadn't clicked; he had genuinely believed they had the wrong man, was even laughing and joking about it—the first of many mistakes he made. But it had seemed ridiculous—what would he want with a thirteen-year-old girl? He had even let them search the camper. It wasn't until the details emerged of when and where he was supposed to have met her that he realized they were talking about Jennifer.

In a panic, and foolishly, he had continued to deny it,

said that she was making it all up, and they had let him go. They'd searched the flat and had even taken his computer away, to try to find child porn, he supposed. The others had thrown him out of the flat after the search and he had had to live in the camper, but that apart, he had thought that it was all over. Then, three months after the investigation had begun, they told him they had found DNA evidence of her presence on the bedding that they had removed from the camper. He knew there was no way he could bluff his way out of it any longer, finally told the truth, and was charged.

The magistrate had said that in view of the youth of the victim and the prolonged nature of the alleged abuse, they felt that the case should be referred to the Crown Court. Everyone knew there was a long backlog of cases and that it wouldn't be heard for months, so the magistrates gave him bail despite the opposition of the police. But the very idea of being charged with a sex offense appalled Dean, and he had done what he had so often done before and gone on the run. And, as they had always done before, the police caught him. That time, he was remanded in custody, and that was where he had been ever since.

The van was pulling into a prison yard, and one of the prisoners was taken off, shouting a parting obscenity. Dean crossed his fingers, hoping against hope that the others would be taken off, but they weren't. He knew the prison vans' routes by now; they were all, he and the other two, bound for the same place.

Dean had seen her again in court, when all his lies, all the unfunny jokes about underage sex, jumping bail, everything he had said and done, came back to haunt him. He could see the jury's faces, and he knew he didn't stand a chance as the prosecution hammered home the fact that she had been twelve years old when he, a couple of months short of his twenty-fourth birthday, had found her in the chat room.

"Does it seem likely to you," the prosecution counsel had asked them, "that the defendant could possibly have believed her to be a grown woman of eighteen?"

It didn't seem likely or possible to the jury, apparently. And Dean didn't blame them—there she was in court, her long fair hair demurely plaited, her eyes wide with innocent alarm, her thin frame and her sober school uniform adding to the effect. That had not been the way she had looked when he had been seeing her.

He looked different himself, and he knew the jury wouldn't be getting a favorable impression. The expensive haircut had grown out along with most of the blond dye; he hadn't been sleeping, and he had, unlike most people in institutions, lost weight; eating wasn't something you felt much like doing after someone had spit in your food.

Guilty, they had said after less than an hour's deliberation, and he had been back this morning for sentencing. And he was lucky again, apparently—given that he'd already served almost six months on remand, with full remission he could be out by the spring. With good luck like this, Dean didn't want ever to have bad luck.

The other two were still amusing themselves by calling him names, and Dean knew that the first chance they got they'd do worse than that. He'd be as ready as the next man to beat the shit out of anyone who sexually abused children, but when you were talking about a girl who was fashionably skinny, who wore designer gear, who smoked and drank, who told you, in her privately educated accent, that she was on a gap year before reading European politics at university, and who had passed puberty, a pedophile wouldn't have wanted to know. But his fellow passengers weren't to know that.

Nor was the jury; according to her, she had told him
her real name and how old she was right from the start,
had carried on chatting to him on the Internet just for a
laugh, and had gone to meet him believing him to be a
boy of her own age. When she had tried to leave, he had
persuaded her to stay and have a drink with him.

"Did the defendant drink much that first night?"

"No. He just kept giving the bottle to me."

She hadn't let him keep pace with her, had kept reminding him that he had to drive her home. But she told
the court that she hadn't liked the vodka and had drunk
it only because she was so nervous and it had helped her
relax. Then he kissed her, she said, and she "quite liked
it," so she let him do what she called "the other things."

"And did the defendant say anything to you afterward?"

"He said not to tell anyone or he could get into
trouble."

"You saw him a number of times after that, didn't
you? Why?"

"Because he was nice. And he gave me presents for letting him do it. CDs and things."

Yes, he'd given her presents—he'd even bought some
of them. It didn't seem right, nicking stuff to give to a
classy girl like that. But it wasn't the way she was making
it sound.

"But in the end, you told your mother about it. Why?"

"Because I knew he shouldn't be doing these things
with me."

His barrister—a woman, because his solicitor thought
that might look better—tried to make Kayleigh retract
all of that when she cross-examined, but she wouldn't
and got so distressed by the questioning that they had
had to adjourn to let her recover.

So prison it was, but prison was the least of Dean's

worries, despite the dangers inherent in being locked up with violent men of violent views; the very worst part of all was that his name was now on the sex offenders' register and would stay there for the next ten years. It would only take some pervert to do something awful for the police to drag Dean in for questioning, putting him right in the firing line when frightened parents and local skinheads, united in outrage, came looking for blood.

The van arrived, and he heard the others' cells being unlocked as he waited. Then it was his turn to put his hands back through the opening in the door, to have the handcuffs put on again, to have the door unlocked, and to get up, stiff and sore from the uncomfortable and alarming journey, to be led into the prison, where the handcuffs were once again removed.

He was taken to the holding room prior to being stripped and searched and given his prison uniform and number; as he walked in, one of his fellow prisoners shot out a foot and Dean ended up sprawled on the floor. He was getting to his feet when the other turned and an expertly aimed kick hit its target.

"Oh, was that you I tripped over?" he said as Dean doubled up in agony. "Didn't see you down there."

A prison officer pulled him to his feet, choosing to regard the whole thing as an accident, and that was when the pain, the humiliation, the sheer injustice of it all overwhelmed Dean.

"Ah, now look what you've done," said the first man. "You've made him cry."

Jerry smoked, so they took their coffee out into the lobby, where the long low tables were surrounded by studded leather sofas and furnished with huge ceramic ashtrays.

Jerry lit his cigar and opened his briefcase, putting a

ring binder on the table. "So there it is, Ian. What do you think?"

Ian picked up the ring binder, looked at the glossy brochure, at the job description, at the spectacular views of the Sydney Harbour Bridge and the Opera House. "It looks like a great job. But I don't know, Jerry. I'm used to being my own boss."

Jerry held his hands wide. "You would be your own boss. All right, technically you'd be working for me, but I won't be there, will I? That's why I want you to go. You'd make your own hours, your own decisions—you'd hire and fire whoever you wanted."

Ian looked at the brochure again. "It looks like a beautiful city."

"Believe me, Ian, it is. And it's got everything you could want, plus sunshine. You wouldn't regret it. Not for one minute."

Ian smiled. "Then why aren't you going there yourself?"

"My business commitments—that's all. I can't be in two places at once, and most of my business is in Europe. But Australasia is important, and I need a presence in that part of the world. I haven't offered it to anyone else—you were my first choice."

Ian could see that it would be a great place to live, but everyone he knew was here. He didn't want to go to the other side of the world, however good the weather, whatever the opportunity. He shook his head. "I don't think so, Jerry. Thanks, and all that, but—"

Jerry drained his brandy glass. "I don't understand why you aren't jumping at it. You're not getting any younger, you know. Opportunities like this don't come along every day at your age."

Ian smiled. "I'm thirty-eight, not sixty-eight."

"But you're not twenty-eight, either. You know this is a great job—and you'd love it. So would Theresa."

"Maybe." Ian motioned toward Jerry's empty glass, going to the bar when he nodded.

"Give them my room number!" Jerry called after him.

Ian raised a hand in acknowledgment. He could, of course, have summoned a member of the staff to bring the drinks, but he wanted time to think. He'd have to explain to Jerry what the problem was, or he would think he was mad. It didn't seem right, telling Jerry before he'd even told Theresa, but Jerry knew that he could snap his fingers and a dozen whiz kids would come running; he deserved an explanation for Ian's lukewarm reaction.

He returned and set down the drinks. "The thing is," he said, "Theresa wouldn't be coming with me."

Jerry's eyebrows rose, but he didn't sound too surprised. "Have you split up? When did that happen?"

Ian took a sip of his beer. "It hasn't happened yet. But it's going to. I've met someone else."

"Whoever she is, Theresa's worth ten of her. She gave up her career so that she could keep you in food—I hope you're remembering that."

"Look—I know what Theresa's done for me, and I'm grateful. She knows that. But . . . well, this has been in the cards for a long time now. Meeting Lesley just made it happen, that's all."

"So what's she like, this Lesley?"

"A couple of years younger than I am, small, slim—blond. Full of energy and commitment."

He realized as he was describing Lesley that if it was true that men always went for the same kind of woman, he was the exception that proved the rule. Theresa was almost Lesley's exact opposite.

"And it's happened just like that? You've met someone you fancy, and twelve years with Theresa count for nothing?"

He had known this would be worse than telling

Theresa herself. "No, not just like that. Things haven't been all that hot between me and Theresa for a long time—I don't think it'll come as much of a shock to her. Probably more of a relief."

Jerry sat back. "How did you meet this Lesley?"

"I wish you'd stop calling her 'this Lesley' like that. I met her when I did that work for the charity that employed me to oversee their new computer installation. She's a director there."

"Oh, yes. And you were working on that for—what? All of a month?"

Ian could feel the waves of disapproval from across the table and felt obliged to defend himself and Lesley. "Sometimes you don't need any time. You just know. We knew. As soon as we met."

Jerry looked less than impressed. "But that was last April! You mean you've been cheating on Theresa all that time?"

"No! Well . . . yes, if you want to put it like that. Something happened that made it difficult at the time. But we're telling them today, so this is a bad time for your offer to have come along."

"Them? This Lesley has a husband, I take it?"

"No. She's a widow. She's telling her daughter today. Look—there were reasons why we couldn't say anything before now."

"None of my business."

"No. But the bottom line is that I can't drop everything and go to Australia at a moment's notice."

"I'm not asking you to drop everything! And it isn't a moment's notice—you've got until the end of February to make up your mind." He shrugged. "You seem to have made up your mind about ditching Theresa in half that time, so this should be a doddle."

Ian felt himself flush slightly. Put like that, his protests did seem a little hollow.

"And maybe Lesley would like the idea."

Ian was sure she wouldn't, but at least Jerry had stopped calling her "this" Lesley.

"I'm sure she'd prefer it to living on your somewhat erratic income," Jerry went on. "She might not be as supportive as Theresa."

"She doesn't need my income," Ian muttered.

"Oh, she's a *rich* widow? And it was love at first sight. How fortunate. No wonder you can turn a great job down without even considering it."

Ian ignored him; Jerry and he had been friends since childhood, and he knew Lesley's money hadn't been the lure—if it had, Ian would have gone in with Jerry in the first place and be able to wine and dine people at five-star hotels in London as a matter of course, like he did. But Ian supposed that it did mean that he was able to turn down opportunities he might once have jumped at. Besides, he was certain that Lesley would hate the idea. He said as much to Jerry.

"Talk to her," said Jerry. "See what she thinks. Take the stuff with you."

Ian put the ring binder in his briefcase. He would talk to Lesley. And she would say no, because she would have no reason to say yes; her life was here. And once Lesley had said no, not even Jerry, the ultimate salesman, would be able to talk her into it.

"Keep the change."

Phil walked up the driveway, his hands thrust deep into the pockets of his jacket, his head down against the snow-filled gust of wind, wishing he had worn a coat and hat. His thinning hair was no protection against the elements, and the wind was whistling through the jacket. It might have a designer label, but it didn't keep you warm. He made the shelter of the porch and turned to look at the garden.

Even in these conditions, he liked the way he'd got it now; it looked good all year round, with the little fountain surrounded by pebbles, slate blue and shiny in the wet snow. It wasn't on, of course, but even switched off, even today, it gave him considerable satisfaction. All the gardening programs on the telly had given him the urge to do it, and taking up DIY landscape gardening at forty-seven wasn't easy. It had taken him all spring, but he'd got it right in the end. Lesley had protested that they could hire a professional to do it, that there were horses for courses, that she wouldn't get a landscape gardener to do her accounts, all that stuff. But Phil had wanted to do it himself, and he had. He had promised Kayleigh he would build a summerhouse with a sundeck this year, and he had been looking forward to that.

And she seemed to think that it might still happen; she had begged him to see Lesley again, talk to her. So here he was, with the excuse of having been to hear sentence passed on Dean Fletcher.

Lesley opened the front door, looking at him a little suspiciously as he told her why he was there and expressed some surprise that she wasn't in court.

"I knew whatever sentence they gave him wouldn't be enough. I felt I could do without being made to feel even angrier."

If it had been up to Lesley, Dean wouldn't have been given any sentence at all; she had been all for letting the whole thing pass, as usual. Phil didn't say any of that. The last thing he wanted was to start a row.

"Come in quickly, if you're coming in. It's freezing."

Phil closed the door and hung up his wet jacket as he told her what had happened in court.

"So he'll be back out before we know where we are,"
she said. "What if he comes looking for Kayleigh when
he does get out?"

"Then he'd go back to prison. And how would he find
her if you're moving away?"

Lesley had decided that she and Kayleigh were moving
out of London once the court case was over. Throughout
Phil and Lesley's years together, they had been constantly
on the move, because Lesley's answer to problems was to
move away from them. He had argued that it was bad
for Kayleigh to keep taking her away from what she
knew, but all he had achieved was the boarding school
solution; that way, Lesley had countered, it wouldn't
really matter if they moved, because Kayleigh's friends
would be at the school and that would give her the stability she needed.

"Besides," Phil added, "they've put him on the sex offenders' register. He won't be allowed even to contact
Kayleigh."

"You've got great faith in the system." She headed for
the sitting room. "Perhaps I should take her out of boarding school, have her where I can keep an eye on her."

Phil sighed. More upheaval. But it would be foolish to
argue on two counts: one, he would much rather Kayleigh
was at home, wherever that was going to be, because
that way he could visit her whenever he liked, and two,
he wouldn't win. "Well, I'm all for that," he said. "But
not because I think he'll come anywhere near Kayleigh."
He followed Lesley down the hallway. "I just think she'd
be happier at home."

He was glad to be back in the centrally heated warmth
of what he still thought of as his own sitting room rather
than the stuffy but chilly courtroom or the wet and miserable streets or even the very pleasant room in a friend's
house in which he was currently living, having never

quite given up hope of Lesley changing her mind. His friend was glad of the extra cash, and Phil didn't want to do anything more final about finding a place to live.

"And we can't change what's happened," he went on, "so I think we should all try to get on with our lives." He took a breath and said what he had really come to say. "I'd like us to be doing it as a family. Kayleigh wants us to get back together, and so do I."

"That's not possible."

"Why not? We've put worse than this behind us."

He prepared himself for her reaction to that, because even allusions to what had been the worst time in either of their lives, jointly or severally, were not encouraged. But Lesley didn't seem to have noticed.

"Because it's over."

He knew that, really. His problem was working out *why* it was over. In June, just after they had finally gone to the police about Fletcher, Lesley had told him that she wanted him to leave, and he still had no idea why. It made no sense. They were happy. All of them. He and Lesley had seen Kayleigh through the worst of this business as they had seen her through everything, always, and they had done it together. All right, there were rows, but they blew over. They were a unit. A family.

He hadn't known how to respond. If he had done something to which Lesley had taken exception, he could have defended himself or apologized or begged forgiveness. But he hadn't; all she had said when he had asked was that she didn't want their relationship to go on. He had left in the hope that time and distance would heal whatever wound had been opened by their recent problems.

"But I thought you were happy."

"I wasn't unhappy." She gave a short sigh. "The fact is . . . there's someone else."

At last, something he understood, even if he didn't like it. It didn't surprise him that she had met someone else; they had been apart a long time. "Who?" His voice was dull as he asked the question and he hadn't really expected a response, but he got one.

"Ian Waring."

Ian Waring? Was he supposed to know who Ian Waring was? He frowned, then remembered, his eyes widening slightly. "The guy who did the computers?"

"Yes."

Waring lived in Stansfield and had been commuting to London every day while he worked on the computer system. Phil had called him the computer commuter, and Lesley had almost always jokingly referred to him as CC; for a moment, his name hadn't meant anything to Phil. He had known she got on well with Waring, but he'd only been there a few weeks and it had never occurred to Phil that there was any more to it than that. She must have been seeing him ever since.

"I would have told you at the time, but all the business with Kayleigh blew up and I thought you might get angry and tell her. I didn't want her to know about Ian until the case was finished, in case it upset her."

"And you don't think it'll upset her now?" At last, his bewilderment was giving way to the good old-fashioned anger that Lesley had rightly assumed would have been his reaction. "This is the last thing she needs right now, Lesley!"

"I think I'm the best judge of that."

"Well, I don't! She's just been through a very difficult time, and not content with whipping away the only stability she's ever known, you're replacing it with someone she's never even met!"

"*I'm* her stability. It's not really your concern, Phil."

He jumped up. "Not my concern? Not my *concern*?

She's been my concern since she was five years old!" He tried hard to calm down, to control the temper that he lost so easily, and he sat down again. It was easier to keep the lid on things sitting down. And getting angry wouldn't help. Lesley had made up her mind. He listened, without comment, as Lesley told him her plans. Waring would be moving in until they had decided where they wanted to go; she didn't know, obviously, how long it would take to sell the house.

"What about visits?" Lesley had asked him not to go to the school, and now he understood why. She didn't want Kayleigh's new classmates getting to know him as her dad only to find him being replaced by Ian Waring. And Lesley had said that Kayleigh could spend time with Phil on the holidays, but Christmas had been a washout; she had taken Kayleigh away on holiday. Apart from the week of the court case, he hadn't seen her since July, and letters and phone calls just weren't the same. "I think she needs to know she's still got me if she needs me," he said. "That she can come to me anytime, or ask me to come to her."

"She does know that. You told her yourself last week. And I told her, too—we can sort all that out. We can arrange something for Easter—she's not on holiday until then anyway, and I think she needs any time she's at home in the meantime to get to know Ian. He's telling Theresa today, so he'll be here quite soon."

At least she understood that Kayleigh would have to get to know Waring; she didn't think that it would work just by magic.

"She'll be very disappointed. She thought we might get back together." He got up to go. "Tell her I'll let her know my address as soon as I've got somewhere permanent."

Lesley came with him to the door, and he put his jacket

back on, stepping out into the chilly air. "When are you telling her about Waring?" he asked.

"I spoke to her this morning."

Phil frowned, looked at the clock in the hallway. "How? You couldn't have got there and back today unless you left in the middle of the—" His mouth fell open. "You phoned her, didn't you! You phoned and told her she'd find this man installed when she got home. Sometimes I just can't *believe* how insensitive you are!"

"I thought Kayleigh would prefer it that way. And I think you're being a little melodramatic."

"You phoned her, and then just left her in that godforsaken place to brood about it on her own!"

Lesley sighed. "It's not Dotheboys Hall. And she's a lot more resilient than you think. She understands the situation."

"Does she? Well, if you're not going to see her, I am!"

"No, you're not. You'd only upset her."

"And how are you going to stop me?"

"By ringing the school and telling them that I don't want them to let you see her. So it would be a wasted journey."

She would do it. And the school wouldn't go against whatever she decreed. He had no rights, no comeback. If he wasn't careful, she could cut him out of Kayleigh's life altogether. He shook his head and turned to go.

"I've still got a lot of your things here. What do you want me to do with them?"

He turned back and looked at her—sweetly reasonable, shivering slightly in the sleety wind, as unmoved as if she were replacing a faulty washing machine rather than the man Kayleigh thought of as her father—and told her what she could do with them.

"I don't think there's any need to be crude. And I do want to know what you want done with them."

He looked at the fountain and the pebbles. She had let him do that, knowing all the time that she was going to do this to him. Let him make plans with Kayleigh for the summerhouse, knowing that she was going to move him out to make room for Ian.

Oh, Lesley would give anyone her money and her time; she was generous in every respect except the one that mattered. She was blithely ripping apart his world, Kayleigh's world, some other woman's world, and she didn't care, as long as she got what she wanted. She really didn't care. He put down the suitcase and scooped up some of the bigger pebbles. "Sell them to pay for a glazier!" he roared.

Lesley ran next door for help while he was venting his anger; he had never hit anyone in his life, but a lot of ornaments and dinner plates had gone west when Lesley had caused his temper to snap. He had never done it quite so spectacularly before, and he had smashed almost all of the windows before two of his neighbors manhandled him out of the driveway and onto the pavement, whereupon Lesley locked the gate and went back inside.

He shook the two men off and walked away, no less angry for his bit of vandalism but grimly satisfied that she had, if only temporarily, lost her bloody serenity.

"It's been confirmed that it's a World War Two unexploded bomb, sir. The army want us to evacuate these three streets."

Tom Finch looked at the map and groaned. All residential streets. "How soon?" he asked.

"Within the hour."

"And how long do they think it's going to take to make the bomb safe?"

"Impossible to say."

So he had to assume that these people might need overnight accommodation. And it was cold—they'd need somewhere with heating, and hot food and drinks would have to be available. The media would have to know what was going on. And the other emergency services should be put on standby in case of accident or injury. But first things first. They had to know who they were evacuating and if they had special needs. Babies, pets, old people, disabled people, pregnant women. Some of them might have to have medical assistance.

Tom ran a hand over hair that was once again springing into tight blond curls now that he was letting what his wife called his SS cut grow out. He blew out his cheeks and plunged in. "OK. Get the troops to do a door-to-door, warning the householders—"

"Can I just stop you there, Tom?"

Now what? It seemed to Tom that every time he opened his mouth, the instructor found something to criticize.

"You don't have troops, Tom. The army has troops. You have officers."

Tom sighed. "I know it's sexist to call women girls, and I know it's sexist even to call them women in the police force—"

"Service."

"Service," Tom repeated, through his teeth. "But what's wrong with *troops*? It's what everyone says—it's more natural."

"You're not trying to win an Oscar, Tom. You're trying to pass your inspector's exam. The army's involved in this exercise— using the word *troops* could be confusing."

"I'm talking to another copper!"

"You're talking to a colleague. In these scenarios, if at no other time in your career, you call senior officers sir— not guv or boss—you call junior officers by their rank and surname, and when you are talking about them, they are all officers or colleagues. Not lads, girls, mates, WPCs, cops, coppers, troops, or anything else."

"Right." Tom sighed deeply. In September, for the second time, he had passed Part I, but that was a written exam, just to find out if you knew the law, basically, and he did. But Part II tested your managerial skills, and that had been his downfall last time. His managerial skills were all right as far as they went, but they didn't, apparently, go far enough. He wasn't smooth enough for them. If you asked him, this exam was designed to turn out homogenized middle managers who went by the book, rather than real men and women who could instinctively perform in a real, unpredictable job.

"That's as may be," Judy had said when he'd been sounding off about it. "But it's the only way you're going to become an inspector—then you can be as real as you like, so long as you get the job done and don't tread on too many toes."

And he really did want to be an inspector. So now, on his rest day, every week, he was doing the training that Judy had advised him to take. But he wasn't convinced that he was cut out for inspectordom. Every other scenario seemed to be someone complaining about something. PCs miffed because they hadn't got a job they were after, women complaining that they weren't being given a fair crack of the whip by their sergeants, members of the public complaining that someone had given them cheek. If that was what being an inspector was all about, they could keep it.

The instructor smiled. "It's part of the job. In real life you probably wouldn't get fourteen situations like that to deal with in the space of two and a half hours. But you might in the exam. And if you handle them well, you'll pass. It's as simple as that."

"And are you saying I'd fail because I'd used the word *troops*?"

"No. I'm saying you'll lose points. You have to get seventy-five percent to pass—that's a high target. So everything that can lose you points should be ironed out now, so that you're giving yourself the best chance you can."

So they began again until, at last, it was time to leave the fictional Sandford and the terminally politically correct Westshire police service and return to reality. Tom got into his car and checked his mobile phone, where he found a text message from Lloyd, which read: "Girl, as promised. Mother and baby both gorgeous." Then another one that just read: "Charlotte Frances."

He smiled. He'd had a call first thing saying that Saturday's wedding was off, the birth was on, and Lloyd was going to be there for the main event, despite his belief that he would pass out cold. He tapped out his reply:

Gr8 2 no CF & J OK. R U OK?

A few moments later he got a reply that confirmed that Lloyd was his usual self.

1st r8, m8, ta—& is it NE 1der U can't spell?

"I'll clear out now, if you like."

Theresa shrugged. Ian's revelation hadn't come as a surprise; she had known for months that there must be someone else, someone he'd met when he was working in London, because he went back there every chance he got. Or invented reasons to go; today he'd said he was meeting Jerry, but the last she'd heard, Jerry was in Australia, setting up a branch of his company down there. At first, it hadn't occurred to her that it was anything but work, but then, unlikely though it seemed, she had had to conclude that Ian was seeing someone else. She was surprised that he had taken this long to tell her; she had thought he would be more straightforward than that.

"And you can stay here as long as you like. I mean . . . I expect we should sell it eventually, but there's absolutely no hurry from my point of view."

In the sixties, Ian's father had been a woodsman employed by Stansfield Development Corporation, the body that oversaw the rapidly expanding industrial new town and was hanging on to as much of its natural forest as it could. The secluded woodland cottage had come with the job; Ian had taken over the tenancy on his father's retirement, and he and Theresa had bought it at a considerable discount in the late eighties when home ownership had been the government's flagship policy. They had paid off the mortgage, and the house was worth a great deal more than they had paid for it; even with her joint ownership, he would get a reasonable profit, and Ian never had any spare money. Whenever he made it, he managed to spend it, so why was there no hurry?

"Oh, yes," she said, remembering, smiling a little. "She's rich, isn't she?"

"Her husband left her very well off."

"She's rich."

He smiled a little, too. "All right. Yes. She's rich."

They had both known that their relationship had run its course; Theresa wasn't going to pretend indignation or hurt that she didn't feel. But though she knew Lesley Newton only as a name that Ian had mentioned, she was puzzled. Lesley didn't really seem Ian's type. He was a fish-and-chips man, and she organized and attended high-powered charity functions where every other face was famous. And the secretiveness just wasn't Ian's style. "Why didn't you tell me before?" Theresa asked.

"Before what?"

"Before you started sleeping with her. Or at least once you had. Why meet in secret for months and months?"

Ian looked a little sheepish. "She had some sort of problem with her daughter. She wanted me to wait until it was resolved, and I—well, I preferred waiting here to living in some London flat."

Theresa smiled again. "She's got a problem daughter?"

"No! No—I don't think so. Just the usual teenage angst thing, I imagine. And whatever it was, it's all sorted out now."

Trusting Ian. "But you don't know what it was?"

"No—well, it's none of my business, really."

"Have you met the daughter?"

"No, not yet."

Theresa shook her head. "Oh, Ian."

"What does that mean?"

"Are you sure you know what you're letting yourself in for?"

"Look—other women would be screaming at me and throwing my clothes out of the window. Not telling me to watch my step."

"I'm the discarded lover, and I should act like it?"

"Instead of like my mother, yes!"

She felt like his mother. Ian was jumping feetfirst into something he knew nothing about. "Why would I do that? I'm very fond of you, and I *do* think you should watch your step. I don't like the sound of unspecified crises with teenage daughters who haven't even met you yet."

An electronic rendition of the "William Tell Overture" broke the silence that followed her statement, and Ian spoke briefly and cryptically to someone on his mobile, then looked at her.

"That was Lesley. She—she's in a bit of a state. Her ex

threw a bit of a wobbly when he found out about me. She wants me to go there tonight."

"Does she? And is that what you're going to do?"

Ian looked distinctly uncomfortable. "I suppose so."

"How are you going to get there? The last train's in five minutes."

"I'll drive, of course."

She smiled. "Make the most of it. Driving it in London won't be much fun." The Alfa Romeo Spyder had been Ian's present to himself when his business had finally made some real money; it had cost twice as much as her van. "What about the postcrisis teenage daughter? Won't your arrival precipitate another crisis?"

"I wondered about that, but Lesley says she's away at school."

"And she knows, does she, that you'll be there when she comes home again?"

"Lesley told her today."

"Oh."

"I wish you'd stop doing that!"

Theresa affected a look of total innocence. "Doing what?"

"Sitting there looking all-knowing." He got up. "Anyway, I mean it, about staying here as long as you like. And if you want to carry on living here, I'm sure we can come to some arrangement about money."

"No, I'll find somewhere smaller." She had never liked living in the middle of a wood all that much.

"I was thinking about the business."

"All I need for the business is the van and a telephone. I don't need this house. It's too big for two people, never mind one."

She had started the ironing business to help out the finances, because in the beginning Ian's income all had to be plowed back into the business; he needed a lot of time to build up a client list, and he had to cover his running expenses in the meantime. Her academic career was costing, rather than making, money, because research made money only if it was commercial, and hers wasn't.

Ironing had occurred to her because, perversely, she hated doing it; other people felt much like she did about it and might pay to have it done—that had been her reasoning. And that if she was being paid to do it, she might hate it less. The start-up costs were low, and the tentative ad she had placed in the local paper had produced more interest than she had imagined it would.

She had operated out of a one-bedroom flat before she'd moved in with Phil, and that was when she had had to accommodate clothes hanging up all over the place; now she employed other people to do the ironing. She did the collections and deliveries and was considering employing someone to do that so that she could get back to her real job. The one-bedroom flat would be perfectly viable again, but she could afford better than that; she thought she might look at one of those big luxury flats on Byford Road. They had room to breathe, and a spare bedroom wouldn't go wrong.

"I'm sorry," Ian said.

"There's no need to be. One of us was bound to do this sooner or later."

But she was glad that it was Ian who would have to deal with any guilt that was going around; she could sit back and feel virtuous.

Lloyd let himself into what he still thought of as Judy's flat, even though he had now officially moved in and given up his own, much to Judy's sorrow. It had been in the old village of Stansfield—not really a village, not now, but a part of the new town of Stansfield that belonged to a century three hundred years removed from the one that most of it inhabited. Judy was very fond of the village and had always loved his flat for reasons that escaped Lloyd, but it was too small for the three of them.

He liked the sound of that phrase, but it was with some apprehension that he looked at the new pram, at the large pile of small clothes. Charlotte wouldn't need anything until she was about two at this rate, he thought, having received knit garments of all sorts and sizes from both of her aunts. He could knit, too, though he had never vouchsafed that even to Judy. Knitting had been a Lloyd family hobby, and as a child he had watched his big sisters, fascinated by the fact that they could make what looked like a ball of colored string turn into a piece of material.

With the disregard for convention that characterized the Lloyds, his sister Megan had, as soon as he was old enough to hold them, given him knitting needles, wool, and the necessary instructions. And after a few false starts he, too, was making material. A long, thin, grubby, slightly holey strip of material, which he gave to the next-door neighbor's dog as a scarf, but he ate it. Lloyd's next attempt was a real scarf, using two balls of wool of different colors. He gave that one to his mother, who hadn't worn it but at least had refrained from eating it; it was, he had felt, a significant step.

Once he'd got the hang of scarves, he'd had a go at most things: woolly hats with pom-poms, mittens, a pair of socks for himself that had to be the most uncomfortable things he had ever worn, even a sweater for Melly, which she had also worn, thereby showing her deep loyalty to her little brother. But in the end, he really was quite good at knitting—not like Megan, whose needles were simply a blur from which the garment appeared before your eyes, but not at all bad. At around puberty, he grew self-conscious about this talent and laid down his needles forever.

But that had been another world; no TV, at least not one of their own, until he was about nine. No Internet, no PlayStation, no multiplexes or E-mails or mobile phones or any of the other wonders that preteens and everyone else these days had to amuse themselves with. Knitting had been a way to pass the time.

He smiled. It might be fun to knit again. He'd thought about it when the baby clothes had arrived from Charlotte's aunts, but it hardly seemed sensible to add to them. He could knit something for Judy, assuming he could find out in advance what she would like. Covertly, of course. Which wouldn't be too difficult, because he had volunteered to stay at home and look after the baby full-time when he got his early retirement. Part of him rather liked that idea, and part of him dreaded it. But he'd offered, so he would just have to deal with it.

He had left both Judy and Charlotte sleeping off their exhausting day. They were being kept in for a few days, Charlotte having arrived twenty-eight days earlier than forecast. She wasn't classed as premature, but they wanted to be certain that everything was in good working order with both her and Judy. So far, there seemed to be no problems. He had forgotten how often babies slept and just how loud they were when it was time to eat. Crying, eating, and sleeping, that was all they did. He smiled, remembering his son Peter's baffled acceptance that his little sister had very little entertainment value.

Judy felt much the same as Peter had, Lloyd was sure, and she hadn't enjoyed her first attempts at breast-feeding, but, for the moment at least, she was determined to try, the midwife having convinced her of the benefits. Barbara had breast-fed Peter and bottle-fed Linda; it seemed to Lloyd that it had made no difference, but he had thought it politic not to pass this advice on to Judy while she was trying to persuade Charlotte to stop exercising her lungs and start feeding. He laid a bet with himself that Judy would give up within the month. She was trying to do everything the way the so-called experts told her it should be done, but he suspected that as soon as she got used to the idea of being a mother her own wishes would assert themselves again. Judy couldn't stay too unselfish for long.

Judy had been joined by another new mother, and on his way out of the maternity unit he had been joined by a very merry young man who beamed at him and informed him that he was the father of a baby girl.

Lloyd congratulated him and added, with considerable pride, "So am I."

"Are you?" The young man belatedly tried to disguise the surprise.

"Oh, yes. Charlotte Frances—six pounds and half an ounce. She was a touch early."

"Emma Jane. Eight pounds, four ounces. It's our second—the first was a boy, so I was really hoping this would be a girl. She was quick—I nearly had to deliver her myself."

Lloyd didn't bother correcting him. No one ever cared, anyway.

"Nina started about four o'clock this afternoon, and I was driving her here in all that snow. And she was panicking a bit, and I'm saying, 'Don't worry; we've got ages yet—Dominic took five hours to arrive.' And we get here, and the next thing I know we're in the delivery room, and this perfectly beautiful baby girl is there. I'm not kidding—the whole thing took about seventy minutes from start to finish."

Judy would be envious, Lloyd had thought as he congratulated the young man again. "I'm afraid Charlotte took a lot longer than that to come into the world," he had said, his mind on one piece of information the young man had given him. "You're not driving home, are you?"

"What? Oh—I forgot about that. I've been celebrating."

"Yes, I rather thought you had. I'll give you a lift if you like."

"Oh, no, I wouldn't want to put you to the trouble."

"Well, let's put it this way. Either I give you a lift, or you get a taxi. Because you're certainly not driving. And I should warn you that I'm a policeman."

"Oh." His eyes widened a little. "Yes. Right. Thanks. Yes. It's wonderful, isn't it, watching them being born?"

"Wonderful," Lloyd had agreed, steering him toward the car park.

Lloyd had been told about the miraculously short labor and Emma's matchless beauty at least another four times before being instructed to pull up outside a detached house on one of Malworth's new private housing estates. They always looked a little like toy houses to Lloyd, their architecture aping that of much grander houses, their rooms numerous only because they were tiny.

"That was very kind of you," his passenger said, opening the door. "And . . . thank you. Yes. Very kind. My name's Crawford. Roger Crawford." He offered his hand.

"Lloyd. Don't mention it."

"Yes. Very kind." He got out, then turned and beamed at Lloyd again. "It's wonderful, isn't it, watching them—"

"Wonderful. Bye." Lloyd leaned over and pulled the door shut before Crawford started again, then watched as he made his unsteady way up his snow-covered driveway to his front door, turning and waving as he opened it. Then Lloyd had made his way through freshly falling snow to Malworth High Street and the flat above the greengrocer's shop that he should now start thinking of as his flat, pondering the wonder of childbirth.

It *was* wonderful, though during the birth itself he had used the trick he used at postmortem examinations; he'd squinted slightly, to make his eyes blur, so that he couldn't really see what was going on. But he hadn't lied when he'd told Judy that it had been amazing, because it was Judy who had amazed him. Judy, who got panicky if she had to change offices, so fond was she of what she knew and understood, had gone through with the pregnancy when he was certain that she would choose to have a termination and had been so determined to do everything naturally despite her dread of the whole thing that it made him emotional every time he thought about it.

She had looked very carefully at all the pain-relief methods open to her and had decided to use none of them, except possibly gas and air. Everything else, she said, sounded worse than putting up with the pain, some of them seemed plain silly, and some of them could affect the baby, which was quite definitely out. And Judy had stuck to her decision, even when the going got really tough.

When the contractions were coming every couple of minutes and going on for almost as long, she had abandoned the music they had suggested she bring with her and had got him to talk to her instead, because, she had said, that made her feel better than any music could ever make her feel. And she could never know how good that had made *him* feel.

Not that anyone present at the actual birth would have guessed that they were as close then as they had ever been, because by then she had indeed been swearing. At first, it was at nature, for having devised this method of procreation; next, it had been at men in general, for getting all of the pleasure and none of the pain; but finally, and for some considerable time, it had been at him in particular, for having made her pregnant in the first place.

He was glad her mother was going to be here for a while. Judy would be much more relaxed. And he was looking forward to seeing Judy's parents again; he liked them both, but he got on particularly well with her now-retired university-lecturer father, who thought the world of Judy and never actually said so, at least not to her. Judy was just like him.

It was still early evening, but Lloyd had been up since three in the morning and he was too tired for his usual nightcap. Uncomfortably aware that this might well be his permanent state for the next twelve months or so, he went to bed, looking reflectively at the cot in the nursery as he passed the door.

Charlotte had a twin, of sorts. Another little girl, born on the eighth of January, in the same year, in the same place. Emma Jane Crawford and Charlotte Frances Lloyd. He wondered about astrology, how alike or how different the two of them would be. He wondered about fate, what would happen to them, how they would live their respective lives. And he wondered what the world would be like when *they* had been around for fifty years. What would the mid-twenty-first century be like? Would anyone at all still knit, never mind four-year-old boys? Barring illness or accident, Emma Crawford's father would very probably find out one day; Lloyd would find out only if he lived to be a hundred.

It was a sobering thought and one that might have been worthy of closer examination, but by the time he had thought it, he was asleep.

CHAPTER TWO

Eight o'clock on Friday morning, Ian should have been tucking into his boiled eggs, reading the paper, listening to the radio. Instead, he was going through the motions of arguing with Lesley, because it made him feel less of a wimp. The argument had been going on for days, and tomorrow being the last day of February, Lesley had launched an all-out offensive.

"But have you really thought about what it means?" he said. "Leaving our families, and our friends . . ."

"I thought *we* were going to be a family."

"You know what I mean! Don't split straws." He supposed they would be a family, eventually, but it wouldn't be easy if Lesley insisted on moving every time something happened that upset her. He had known that she wasn't going to stay in London even though it meant giving up her work with the charity, but she hadn't even sold the London house before they had left, largely because of Phil's window-breaking session, and had moved at the end of January to, of all places, Malworth.

She had liked the sound of Bartonshire when Ian had talked about it, and so he had found himself almost back where he had started. But Stansfield was a little too cheap and cheerfully working-class for Lesley; they had moved to the Riverside area of Malworth, where the houses cost the earth, and now, barely a month later, she wanted to move again.

Kayleigh had just started at the local private school as a day pupil. It would be very disruptive for her, he'd said, when Lesley had first suggested that he should, after all, take Jerry up on his offer, but she had said that Kayleigh hadn't been there long enough for it to be disruptive. He had usually given in by this point in an argument, because whatever Lesley wanted Lesley got and there was a limit to how much breath he was prepared to waste. But packing up and going to Australia just because she didn't like Kayleigh being friends with this girl? It seemed to him to be an overreaction that really did have to be discussed. So they had discussed it, every day for the last week.

"Why do you want to take her away? I don't think it's anything to worry about. She's only known her a month. It's probably just a crush, or something."

Kayleigh had only just met Andrea when Lesley had started worrying about it. And on Kayleigh's birthday, when Kayleigh had gone to bed and they were finally on their own, she had hit him with Australia.

"I think it's more than just a crush. Andrea's three years older than Kayleigh, and you have to admit that it's a bit unusual, a seventeen-year-old wanting to hang around with someone who's just turned fourteen. Kayleigh's over there so often she might as well move in. And you know what they were like at Kayleigh's party."

Yes, he knew that she and Andrea had spent the entire time together, with Kayleigh blithely ignoring her other guests, but they had just been talking, listening to music, doing the things that teenage girls did. Andrea was a young seventeen-year-old, despite her expertise with small babies; Ian honestly couldn't see the problem. And he wasn't convinced that the attachment was that way round.

"We don't know that she *does* want to hang around with Kayleigh. Kayleigh wants to hang around with her—Andrea might just not know how to shake her off without hurting her feelings."

It was sometimes very hard to believe that Kayleigh had been adopted; she was very like Lesley in a lot of ways. It really wouldn't matter whether Andrea wanted her around or not; if Kayleigh wanted to be in her company, then that's the way it would be, whatever Andrea's wishes.

"Did she look as though she wanted to shake her off?"

Ian gave a little nod, conceding the point. "OK—but I don't see how it merits flying off to the ends of the earth. As soon as an eligible male appears on the horizon, Andrea will lose interest in Kayleigh."

"Possibly. But you don't know Kayleigh all that well." Lesley put down the piece of toast at which she had been nibbling for the last fifteen minutes.

No wonder she was skinny, Ian thought. She never ate. Just lived off nervous energy. He loved Lesley; he loved her drive and enthusiasm, her generosity, and her earnest desire to make the world a better place. But sometimes he thought wistfully of Theresa, who took things as they came, who did what she had to do to make her own world work and gave what she could when asked to help other people's worlds work a little better, who ate three meals a day, and who *relaxed* from time to time. Lesley never relaxed.

And it seemed to Ian that Lesley's concern for Kayleigh was sometimes misdirected, that Kayleigh would do better with someone like Theresa, who would be less concerned and more aware. Lesley sometimes seemed to regard bringing up Kayleigh as just another project, as just something else that needed doing in a world full of deserving causes. He felt a little guilty as he thought that, because she was right; he didn't know Kayleigh very well. Certainly not well enough to sit in judgment on Lesley's handling of her.

"Then tell me about her."

"She's . . ." Lesley sighed. "She's inclined to get too involved, too wrapped up in things. Sometimes it's hobbies, sometimes it's causes, and sometimes it's people. She tires of them eventually, but right now it's Andrea. She never sees anyone else; she never talks about anyone else—she's wearing the same sort of clothes, buying the same sort of music, reading the same sort of magazines—she's even had her hair cut like Andrea's. She's practically turning into her."

Kayleigh had more money in the bank than he had ever had, and Lesley's policy was to allow her to spend it as she chose: shopping trips to London, where everything was charged to Lesley's accounts at various expensive establishments, were a regular thing, and shopping on the Internet, using Lesley's charge card, was positively encouraged. Kayleigh's desire to dress like Andrea had at least curbed the spending, which Ian thought was no bad thing.

"Going to Australia isn't going to solve anything."

"It'll get her away from Andrea."

"But you said she would tire of her anyway. And that's just this immediate problem." Ian shook his head. "If it is a problem. She'll still be the same person—if she's given to doing this, then she'll just find someone or something to get involved with there. She'll be chaining herself to kangaroos or something." It was an attempt at a joke, at putting the whole thing into perspective, but it didn't work. "I wouldn't worry about it, Lesley. I'm no expert, but kids that age feel things very intensely."

"I know. And I'm sure she will grow out of it. But . . . it's different this time."

"How?"

There was a moment before she spoke. "Because," she said slowly, "I know this is going to sound silly, but . . . I think it's reciprocated. I think there's something—I don't know, something *unhealthy* about it."

"Unhealthy?" Ian pushed his half-eaten egg away. It was giving him indigestion trying to eat and argue at the same time, and the egg was cold now, anyway. "How do you mean, unhealthy? Do you think this girl's a lesbian or something?"

Lesley made an impatient noise. "I don't know, and I don't care. That's not what I'm talking about."

If Ian thought he had grasped anything about this sudden about-turn over Australia, it was that Lesley was worried that Andrea might have designs on Kayleigh, but apparently he'd got that wrong, too. "Then what *are* you talking about?"

"I just don't like it. I think it could become destructive, and I believe we have to split them up."

"By going to Australia?"

"By going as far away as possible, and that is Australia, if you don't fancy the South Pole."

That was *her* attempt at a joke; Ian smiled. "There are places I'd rather go. America, maybe."

"I know. But I'd rather Kayleigh didn't know we're moving because of Andrea, and since you were offered the job before she'd even met her, Australia seems the perfect solution."

"It's a bit drastic."

She smiled, caught his hand. "It isn't a two-month journey by steerage. We'd just be a long-haul flight away from Britain. And it's not as if we're using our life savings to get there—we can come back for visits, or bring people over to see us. If we hate it, we can just come home again."

True. The world was really quite a small place, especially if you had the money to make it so, and Lesley had. And she wouldn't think twice about paying for anyone at all to come and visit, about funding as many visits home as anyone wanted. Which would be fine, if they all liked living there. But it wouldn't be just as simple as she made out if the reverse were to be the case; if she hated it, they would come home, and if Kayleigh hated it, they might come home, but if *he* hated it . . . he would come home on his own.

"So will you ring Jerry? Please?"

Oh, yes. He would ring Jerry. Of course he would ring Jerry. What choice did he have? And Jerry was, of course, delighted that he had changed his mind, even if it was at the very last moment. Ian had made the call at breakfast time, and by lunchtime a date in July had been set for the job to start and Lesley was ringing estate agents.

The fine rain that had fallen all morning, that had quietly drenched those gathered at the graveside, still misted the windows of the bungalow where John Russell's friends, family, and colleagues had gathered after the funeral, custom and practice having won out over the wishes of the deceased that his passing should be marked with nothing more than the bare necessities.

Five days ago, with no warning of any sort, a heart attack had killed him; Judy and her mother, the two people who had loved him most, poured drinks and handed round food, trying to behave as if nothing of any great moment had happened, trying to accede to his wishes with the same sort of determination that Judy had shown when she was having the baby, and it was breaking Lloyd's heart to watch them.

The Russells had indeed come to see the baby, which

was a blessing; Lloyd didn't think Judy could have borne it if her father had died before he'd had a chance to see his only granddaughter. John had gone back after a couple of days; despite his retirement, he was still working part-time as a lecturer and was standing in for an absent colleague. Judy's mother had stayed on, as promised, and had made Judy's transition to motherhood as painless as possible. When Judy felt able to fly solo, her mother had gone back to London, and until the moment it had happened there had been no indication that anything was wrong.

The service had been spare and severe. No music, no flowers, by order of the deceased. No eulogy. Just prayers for his soul. Lloyd had had many a boozy philosophical discussion with John and had tried to find out what made this intelligent, thoughtful man believe in the concept of soul, of an afterlife, of God. He hadn't been conspicuously religious, hadn't even been a churchgoer, but he had believed, something Lloyd had never found possible.

And, contrary as John Russell could be, he had also thought that once people were dead, there was no point in making a song and dance about it. And no point in grieving; if he was right and the deceased had gone to a better place, then the grief was misplaced; if Lloyd was right and life simply ceased, then of necessity this could not be something that bothered the dead, so whom would the mourners be grieving for? Funerals, as far as John was concerned, had two purposes. One was to provide a dignified exit from the world, and the other was to commend the soul of the deceased to God. And that, he had said—in written instructions—was all that his funeral was to do.

But he had missed the point. Lloyd looked at the

groups of stiffly uncomfortable people who sipped their drinks and nibbled at the food that Judy and her mother had spent all morning preparing, and shook his head slightly. He had been to a number of Russell gatherings, both here and in the university flat they had lived in before John's retirement, and they had without exception been warm, inviting, friendly affairs, where no one felt out of place or in the way. Now, everyone did. It wasn't right. It certainly wasn't how John Russell would have wanted it to be.

Linda and her boyfriend were there; she smiled sympathetically at him as he caught her eye. The last time he had seen her had been when she had come to see her new half sister, and neither of them could have imagined that this would be the setting for their next meeting. She had lodged with the Russells when she had first come to London and had been as fond of Judy's father as Lloyd had been, but, like everyone else, she was, Lloyd knew, sneaking looks at the time, wondering how long etiquette demanded that you stay.

And damn it, Lloyd thought, it just wasn't good enough. He stood up. "Would it be all right if . . . if I said a few words?" he asked, employing what Judy called his pithead Welsh accent.

John Russell's academic colleagues, his fishermen friends, his students, his neighbors, his family, all looked at Lloyd, their faces apprehensive, fearing that a bad day was about to get worse.

"I know that most of you would be a lot better at this than me. You're used to giving talks and . . . and . . . that sort of thing. And . . . well, I know that John didn't want anyone making speeches about him or anything." He paused and took a breath. "But it seems to me there's something that needs to be said, so here goes."

His audience shifted slightly. Linda gave him a con-
spiratorial nod of encouragement, but he didn't dare
look at Judy or her mother.

"When I met Judy's dad, he told me his name was John
Russell and not to call him Jack. I wouldn't even *tell* him
my first name, so we had something in common from the
start."

Some polite smiles.

"And . . . and we found we had a lot in common,
really. But we argued about everything, all the same—
from whether soccer was a better game than rugby to
whether or not there was a God. He was the rugby man,
as it happens, not me."

More dutiful smiles.

"And he was the God man." Lloyd paused for a moment. "Well, he knows now which of us was right about
God. And . . . well, it seems to me that if *he* was right,
and he's looking down on us right now, then he knows
that he was wrong about funerals, because they're not
just for the person in the coffin. So . . ." He licked his lips
slightly, took another breath. "So I've still got a bone to
pick with him, wherever he is. And . . ." Now he warmed
to his theme, growing bolder. "Well, all right, *he* didn't
want hymns, but maybe we did. Maybe a hymn or
two would have . . . I don't know . . . made it all a bit
easier on us. Singing, music, all that . . . well, it's a release, isn't it?"

Some real alarm on the faces now, as he had expected,
when they realized they were listening to a Welshman
talking about the therapeutic effects of singing; they
were, Lloyd knew, all entertaining the horrifying thought
that a son of the Land of Song was going to lead them in
impromptu, unaccompanied hymn singing, which was
exactly what he wanted them to think. He had no idea

how this was going down with Judy and her mother, and he didn't dare find out.

"And," he went on, earnestly, diffidently, "one time, when we were arguing the toss about heaven and all that, we got round to funerals, and John told me that he would really like jazz played at his." For the first time, he looked at Judy's mother. "But he didn't put that in the instructions, so no one knew but me. Still . . . there's no reason why we can't have some now, is there?"

Judy's mother shook her head, smiling a little.

Lloyd walked to the CD player. "John didn't want anyone to come to his funeral." He selected a CD from the rack, sliding it in. "But everyone came, all the same." He turned back to face them. "And . . . well . . . I think that's because we all wanted to let Judy and her mother know what we felt about him." He looked down at his feet, then up again. "We'll all miss him, whether he wanted us to or not," he concluded as the softly defiant notes of jazz piano, satisfactorily on cue, filled the room. "It's as simple as that."

"Hear, hear," someone said.

"I certainly will," said someone else. "I remember when I came to the university . . ."

Lloyd sat down amid the buzz of conversation that his words and the ice-breaking music had released and got a tiny wink from Linda. But he still hadn't checked out Judy's reaction; now he took a genuinely nervous deep breath and looked at her. She was giving him the Look, but she was smiling.

A result, as Tom Finch would say.

Phil Roddam looked round his furnished flat and tried to address himself to his immediate problem, which was to get a job. What was left of his money wouldn't last forever, and someone, somewhere, must want a chartered accountant. He didn't much care where he went; now that he was back in Britain, he had automatically headed for London, since that was where he had theoretically lived at the last count, but he had no reason now to live here, and he was very used to changing employers, thanks to the nomadic Lesley.

When he'd left Lesley with her shattered windows, he had gone back to his friend's house and during a sleepless night had decided to do what he had been going to do when he left the university but hadn't, what he had been going to do before he got married but hadn't, what he had been going to do when he got divorced but hadn't, because then he had met Lesley, and once again it had been shelved. He was going to see the world.

Why not? Lesley had made it clear that any arrangements with Kayleigh would have to wait until the Easter break, and he had no reason not to spend his money how he pleased, no ties, no family to think of, unless you counted his aunt Jean in Worthing, and she wouldn't mind what he did with his money, having plenty of her own.

When he was twenty, he would have taken off with no more than the economy-class plane fare to his first destination, but now he wanted to do it comfortably, so he was going to sell everything he owned, cash in insurance policies and premium bonds; the money raised, plus his savings, would finance his travels.

It had taken him just ten days to rid himself of his job, his car, his memberships in expensive clubs, anything and everything that cost him money or was worth money, and take off with his credit card and a healthy bank balance. He had been away for four weeks; he had seen a lot of the world in some style, and he had enjoyed it, though maybe not as much as he would have done when he was twenty, not as much as he would have done if

Lesley and Kayleigh had been with him, and not as much as he had hoped. It hadn't taken his mind off his troubles.

And when he had come back, a week ago, it was to find that Lesley had moved away and the neighbors, if they knew where she had gone, weren't about to tell the mad window breaker. It was the same story at the charity where she had worked; they had no idea where she'd moved to, according to the young woman he spoke to. He'd tried everything he could think of; Waring had been self-employed, so there was no one Phil knew to ask about him. He was a computer man, but if he had a Web site, Phil hadn't been able to find it.

He hoped Kayleigh was happy and for all he knew she was, but that was the problem. He *didn't* know. Poor little Kayleigh had had too much disruption in her life, and all he wanted was to know where they were, so he could write to her, telephone her now and then, have her with him for weekends. It occurred to him then that he might look at seaside towns for jobs; she'd like that. He could surprise his aunt Jean and set up home in Worthing, like she had. A bit chilly, though, in the winter. Devon or Cornwall, maybe, or even the Channel Islands. You didn't have to be a millionaire; you could work for one. Millionaires needed accountants.

Kayleigh's school wouldn't tell him anything at all; they didn't give out personal information, they said. They did finally tell him that Kayleigh was no longer a pupil, so Lesley had probably made good her intention of having her at home; she was unlikely to have changed schools for any other reason. But home, of course, had Waring in it now, and Kayleigh might be having trouble adjusting.

He frowned and couldn't believe that it hadn't occurred to him before now. Lesley had commandeered someone else's man. He knew nothing about Mrs. Waring beyond the fact of her existence and that she and Waring had lived in Stansfield; Lesley had mentioned her first name, but he couldn't remember it now. He didn't know if there were children, but if there were, presumably Waring was paying his wife some sort of maintenance. If so, she would know where he was now.

He almost ran all the way to the library, breathlessly demanding to know where the phone books were as soon as he got inside the doors. The Bartonshire phone book had not been overlooked, vandalized, or stolen, and in it he found I. J. Waring. Of course, Mrs. Waring might have moved away, or it might be a different Waring. His Waring might not even *be* in the phone book. Back out on the street, he rang the number, and it was answered by a machine.

"Hi—sorry I can't come to the phone, but if you leave a message, I'll ring you back."

"Oh," said Phil, after the tone. "Yes. Er . . . my name is Phil Roddam," he began, and then realized he hadn't the faintest idea what he was going to say. He'd imagined some feedback, and now he was having to make a speech. He should have thought it out before he rang, but he hadn't, so he just had to get on with it.

"Look—I hope I've got the right number. If not, just ignore this. But if you're Mrs. Ian Waring, and your husband—well, that is . . ." He ran a hand round his collar and then just took a run at it. "If your husband left for pastures new in January to set up home with someone called Lesley Newton, could you please ring me?" He gave her his mobile number. "It's important, or I wouldn't—well . . ." His voice trailed off as he ran out of words to explain the situation. "It's important," he concluded. "Thank you."

Right, he thought. Of course she'll ring you. She always rings inarticulate raving lunatics who leave messages on her answering machine.

They were in the burger bar at the leisure center. They had it to themselves; they often did at this time in the afternoon. The staff were mopping the floor, cleaning the tables, getting ready for the keep-fit fanatics who would drive straight from work to pump iron or swim or run on a treadmill, then wolf down hamburgers and chips before getting back into their cars to go home. It seemed to Kayleigh that if they cycled to work and skipped the hamburgers, they would keep just as fit, save a great deal of money, and do the planet a favor while they were at it.

She pushed away her half-eaten burger and pierced the paper carton of orange juice with a straw. Andrea was doing more justice to her burger, and Kayleigh thought she'd better wait until she'd finished eating before she told her.

She and Andrea had met in the junior section of the leisure center gym; Kayleigh was trying to build up her weight, and Andrea just liked keeping fit. It was Kayleigh's doctor—or, rather, her mum's doctor, a Harley Street man, of course—who thought she needed to put on weight. Personally, she thought it was nonsense; she could throw the javelin farther than anyone else at the school and do more sit-ups. She was a lot stronger than she looked. But she liked coming to the gym and she liked weight training, so she used her doctor's concern as an excuse to come here rather than get on with her homework.

It had been Andrea who had started up the initial conversation. She had been hired as a mother's helper and was so excited and pleased about it that she had had to talk to someone.

"It's the first time I've had just the one to look

after—there were five after me at home. And then I worked in a nursery for a bit on Saturday mornings. I looked after them all, from babies to toddlers. But I loved my babies best."

Kayleigh thought she would like being one of Andrea's babies and had said so; Andrea had been tickled about that. And she was easy to talk to; it was like having a sister, she supposed. Andrea drove a car; it wasn't her car, it belonged to the lady she worked for, but it was for Andrea's use, and that seemed terribly glamorous to Kayleigh.

She waited until Andrea had finished eating before she told her.

"Australia?" Andrea repeated. "But how? When? How long have you known?"

"He was offered the job in January. But he said he didn't want to go—so did she. And the first I knew of it was when I got home from school today. She said he'd changed his mind. So—" Kayleigh shrugged. "She says we're going."

"But you *can't*! What are you going to do?"

"I don't know." Kayleigh felt utterly miserable. "I wish I knew where Phil was."

"Could he help—I mean, after what happened? Would your mum listen to him?"

Andrea knew about Phil's window-breaking act—she disapproved, Kayleigh thought, though she had never said so. And Kayleigh knew that he shouldn't have done it, but she understood how he had felt. What he had done was all Andrea knew about him; if she met him, she would like him, Kayleigh was sure, even if he did break things when he got angry. But he had gone off traveling, and they had moved before he had come back.

And she had thought she would hate not living in London, but she really had enjoyed the last few weeks. The school was all right, and it was good to be able to leave it when lessons were over. She could talk to Andrea, tell her anything, everything. She didn't judge her or give her good advice. Andrea was a bit like Phil, really. Kayleigh had always been able to talk to him in a way that she had never been able to talk to her mother. But it was better with Andrea, because she didn't tell her off like Phil sometimes did.

"My mum tried to ring where he used to work, but they don't exist anymore, so we've lost touch with him."

"How long was he going to be away for?"

"He said a month. He sent postcards, but that was always from where he had just been, so my mum couldn't get in touch with him to tell him we were moving, and he doesn't know where we are."

There was a silence, then, which Andrea finally broke. "Do you ever think about your real mum and dad?"

Kayleigh nodded, shrugged a little. "He could be anyone. But I remember her. Just."

Andrea's eyes widened. "I always thought you meant you were adopted when you were a baby. How old were you?"

"I was four when I was adopted." It wasn't a memory that she had of her mother, not really. Just an impression, a feeling. A presence that she had known had suddenly no longer been there. She couldn't even put it into words in her head, never mind pictures. "She abandoned me when I was two and a half."

Andrea was openmouthed. "I don't know how anyone could do that. I mean, if you were a tiny baby, and she was panicking . . . but if she'd had you all that time, what would make her abandon you?"

"I don't know. She just left me with a neighbor and vanished." She had never really told anyone about her background before; she'd told Dean some of it but not all. Somehow, with Andrea, it just seemed natural to tell her.

"Have you seen her since?"

Kayleigh shook her head.

"Ah, well." Andrea used the tone of voice she used to soothe the baby. "Maybe something happened to her."

"No. The police found her. But she gave me up for adoption."

"Do you know what happened to her after that?"

"She died. I think she took an overdose or something."

"Oh, poor you. It must be awful, knowing you were abandoned like that."

Not really. Not knowing who her father was, that was what Kayleigh found difficult. She wasn't that bothered about her mother having abandoned her. And right now she wished her adoptive mother would abandon her, too, and go to Australia without her.

Theresa listened to the message, a slight frown on her face. She was glad the machine had taken the call—it gave her time to consider how to approach him.

She had been out viewing a prospective home, as the estate agent called it. A flat in Byford Road had finally come on the market, and she had gone to see it, would probably make an offer for it. The fleeting thought that had formulated the night Ian told her about Lesley Newton had somehow become a goal, and she hadn't looked at any other properties at all.

This house, surrounded by woodland and quite unlike the rest of Stansfield's modern housing, was one that would sell for a lot of money, and it shouldn't be a drain on Ian's resources—that had been her conscious thought. But her subconscious had had a different opinion. It wasn't that she was desperate to live either in a flat or on Byford Road; it was whatever part of her, buried so deep that she had truly been unaware of its existence, wanted to get its own back. Being specific about what she wanted provided an excuse to make Ian wait until she was good and ready to move, because she didn't suppose he would want this informal arrangement going on forever, however guilty he felt.

She made herself a cup of tea and sat by the phone, wondering what Phil Roddam wanted. Only one way to find out. "Hi," she said when he answered. "My name's Theresa Black—you left a message on my answering machine."

There was a little silence. "Oh," he said. "Right. I suppose Mrs. Waring doesn't live there anymore."

"She never did. There isn't a Mrs. Waring. I lived with Ian Waring until he went off to pastures new, as you put it."

Another silence. "Do you have children?"

"No." Puzzled, she waited to hear why he wanted to know.

"Well—the house you're living in . . . is it yours?"

Her dark eyebrows lifted slightly. "Is that any of your business?"

"Oh—oh, God. No. No—look, I didn't mean to . . . that is, I—oh, hell."

Theresa laughed. "What exactly do you want to know?"

She heard him take a breath. "I want to know where Lesley is living."

"And how does that relate to whether or not I own this house or have children?"

"It doesn't. It was just that—well, I thought if your ex-partner was paying half the mortgage, or had to pay maintenance or something, then you must be in touch with him. Do you know where he's living? Is he still with Lesley?"

At least that explained his interest in her personal affairs. "Yes," she said, a little warily. "I do know where he's living, and he is still with her."

"Can you give me their address? Lesley seems to have sworn people to secrecy."

"Well . . ."

She heard a sigh. "Oh, please, not you as well. Just their phone number will do."

Theresa thought about how Ian had gone rushing to Lesley's aid after this man had thrown a wobbly, as he had put it. In Ian-speak, that could mean anything from using four-letter words to brandishing a meat cleaver.

"Is Lesley scared of you?"

He laughed. Really laughed. "I don't think Lesley's scared of anyone. Least of all me. One day she just said, 'By the way, Phil, you *are* the weakest link—good-bye.' And that was that."

"Then why does she want to keep her address secret?"

"Well . . . I went back to see if we couldn't try again—that's when I found out that she'd been having an affair for months. I'm afraid I took it rather badly. I expect she thinks I'll do it again."

Theresa frowned. Perhaps it *was* the meat cleaver. "Do what again?"

"I broke some windows. I'm not proud of it—I just . . . well, I lost my temper, and I tend to break things when I do that."

"Did you hurt anyone?"

"No! She was outside with me. There was no one inside. I wouldn't have done it if it had been going to hurt anyone." There was a pause. "I'd have taken a sledgehammer to the ornamental fountain instead."

Theresa smiled. "I have to say I can see why she might not want you to come calling again."

"I don't want to call on her. I just want to talk to

Kayleigh, ask her if she's happy. I've only seen her once since July, and I couldn't talk to her properly then, because Lesley was there all the time."

Of course—Kayleigh must be the problem daughter. Theresa's eyebrows rose slightly; she had assumed the girl would have a middle-class, upmarket name. Perhaps she had misheard. "Kayleigh?" she repeated. "As in the old pop song?"

"Yes. Not Lesley's choice—Kayleigh was adopted. She tried to change it, but Kayleigh is just as formidable as Lesley herself, and was even when she was four years old. She just shook her head and said her name was Kayleigh Scott and that's the way it stayed. She kept both her names, despite the adoption."

"Adopted? But surely you have the same rights as any other father—"

"No—I'm not her adopted father. He died. But I brought her up, and I don't want to lose contact with her."

Theresa wasn't at all sure what to do, an unusual state for her to be in.

"You're my only hope," Phil Roddam said, into the silence.

"Do you have any reason to think that she *is* unhappy?"

"No, but I've no reason to assume that she's happy. I know she wasn't asked what she thought about Ian moving in."

"I kind of got the impression that Ian didn't have much say in the matter, either." Theresa decided that she liked the sound of Phil Roddam, but she didn't think she could go against Lesley's wishes. "I honestly don't think I can give you their phone number, but if you give me your address, I can ask Ian to let Kayleigh know where you are. Will that do?"

"That's kind of you. Thank you."

*   *   *

Tom Finch came out of the bathroom to see Liz looking in on Charlotte, who was in her carry-cot in their room.

"Is she making you broody?" he whispered.

Liz smiled and shook her head, leaving the door ajar, then checked the other bedrooms in which their own children slept just as soundly, before heading downstairs. "No. Two's quite enough." She turned to look at him as she reached the hallway. "Why? Is she making *you* broody?"

"No," he laughed. "I agree. We've got all that out of the way now."

In the living room, he flopped down on the armchair. The bag stuffed with all the things babies had to take around with them was on the sofa, bringing back memories; it was hard to believe all that belonged to someone who had been around for only two months. It was a reminder that babies cost a fortune, as he told Liz.

But they would have more money, of course, if he passed Part II. He'd passed the mock one that his instructor had held—he had tried very hard to remember to be what they thought of as professional and correct, and he had even managed to keep his cool during one scenario that had really got to him. He would never have thought that playacting could become so real, but it did.

Liz ruffled the blond curls that were now almost back to their full glory, much to his and everyone else's relief. "You've got your worrying about Part Two face on."

"I don't think I can go through all this again, Liz. If I fail this time, I think you're stuck with a career sergeant."

"Then I'll just have to divorce you. I expected a super-intendent's pension at the very least." She sat down, and picked up the remote control, putting on the early evening news. "Stop worrying. Just wait and see how it goes."

"But we could do with the extra money." He was getting morose now, convincing himself that he had failed before he even took it. Of course, as a DI he would still find himself working odd hours, so even if he passed, there might be problems. Liz would want him to go into uniform, work regular hours, and that wasn't what he had in mind at all.

But worrying about passing or failing was useless; he would just have to take it, then wait and see.

Dean Fletcher had been in prison twice before, and at this point in previous stays he had been confident of early release. But this time he was a sex offender, and the statistics for the granting of parole, like everything else in this place, went against him. Despite that, he had made an application and hoped fervently that he might, just might, be able to start crossing the days off, because he had been a model prisoner and had stayed, as far as was possible, out of trouble. It hadn't been entirely possible, because this time all the minor irritations of being locked up were eclipsed by the ever-present fear of trouble finding him.

His trouble had come in dribs and drabs to start with, like the business in the holding room. Random violence, arbitrary malice. The real punishment had arrived in the form of three of them administering a beating while the sole prison officer on duty on their landing was dealing with a not-unrelated disturbance elsewhere. Dean had told the prison medical staff that he had fallen downstairs. They had pretended to believe him but had mentioned Rule 43. Dean didn't want that.

Rule 43—actually, Dean had discovered, Rule 45, but no one called it that—was a desperate measure that he had been advised not to take. And he had been right to stick it out, because after that beating things had improved; the word presumably had gone out that he had got what was coming to him and to lay off him unless he stepped out of line. He was warily and wearily treading that line every minute of every day of every week he was in here, and he wanted out.

But even then, he wouldn't be a free man, not for ten long years, maybe never again. And that was what Dean was finding hardest to forgive.

Judy hadn't left Charlotte in anyone's care except her mother's, until today. It was a foretaste of what was to come between when she returned to work and when Lloyd got early retirement, and she wasn't sure how she felt about it.

Half of her felt certain that almost anyone else in the world was better equipped to look after a baby than she was, especially since anyone could feed her; Judy had, as Lloyd had irritatingly predicted, given up trying to breast-feed. Neither she nor Charlotte seemed able to get the hang of it, really.

Judy had thought that today would be difficult enough without a baby in tow, and Charlotte had, thankfully, been entirely happy to be handed over to Liz Finch, who, having had two of her own, was Judy's first choice of baby-sitter. Indeed, Liz had been her only choice; she wouldn't have trusted Charlotte to anyone else. If Liz hadn't been available, there would have been no option but to take Charlotte to the funeral. As it was, she had fallen blissfully asleep in Liz's arms; like Lloyd, being awake at that time in the morning wasn't for her.

But Judy would be back at work at the beginning of July, and she really would have to start thinking very seriously about child care, find someone she trusted. Liz, unfortunately, wasn't at home anymore now that her children were both at school, or she would have been happy to look after Charlotte. It had been sheer luck that the funeral had been on Liz's day off—or so she had said; Judy had a suspicion that the day off had been engineered, just to help out. The Finches were like that.

People were beginning to leave now, and the day that had begun with everyone tense and uncomfortable had, thanks to Lloyd, turned into one where people felt relaxed and even happy, glad to have known her father.

She would miss him, miss his unfailing support. He had known, even as he had given Judy away to Michael on her wedding day, that her heart was with Lloyd and had gone out of his way to cultivate Lloyd's friendship, to find out what made him tick. She and her father had never spoken about it; she had never told him how she felt about Lloyd, and he had never told her his feelings about her mistaken marriage; he had just made sure that she knew he was on her side, whatever she chose to do in the end.

When everyone had gone, the family spent some time together, but eventually she and Lloyd had to leave; her mother declined the offer to come back with them, assuring them that she would be perfectly all right on her own. Judy's uncle had been with her mother until the funeral, but he had had to get back to work. Judy didn't like leaving her mother there alone, but she was adamant.

"I have to get used to it sometime," she said. "It might as well be now."

The rain that had fallen on London all day still flecked the windscreen as Lloyd drove off.

"Pity you don't wear a flat cap," Judy said.

"Why?"

"You could have twisted it."

Lloyd laughed.

"One of the neighbors told me how brave he thought

you were, getting up and speaking in front of all these clever lecturers."

"I thought the boy from the valleys would go down quite well. A few 'ums' and 'ahs' and false starts. Doesn't do to upstage professionals—let them feel superior, and they'll respond much more readily."

Judy pulled a face. Even her mother, while she knew a lot of it had been acting, had thought that he had been genuinely nervous; it had taken Judy herself twenty years to know when it was *all* an act, and then only if it wasn't for her benefit. And she still couldn't be sure what was real and what was invented. "Did he really say he would like to have jazz played at his funeral?" she asked.

"Well . . ." Lloyd pursed his lips. "Not in so many words."

Judy sighed. "Or—to put it another way—he never said any such thing?"

"That would be a fair assessment of the situation." He took his eyes from the road for a second to glance at her. "It worked, though. Didn't it?"

Oh, yes. It had worked. She smiled, a little reluctantly. "Thank you for rescuing us."

"Anytime."

Lloyd pulled in at a service station to fill up with petrol, and for the first time that day Judy was entirely alone. Her emotions, all over the place since Charlotte was born, were even more mixed than they had been on the journey down. There was sadness, obviously, because she would miss her father dreadfully; the funeral had made her realize that she really wasn't going to see him anymore and that Charlotte would never have any memories of him. But now there was worry, because her mother had never lived alone and Judy didn't know how she would cope. And relief, that the funeral was over.

She had known to expect all of that, of course; but the

feeling of freedom—strange and welcome after being answerable to a small tyrant for the last fifty-one days—was unexpected, and it came with a price. Guilt, because she felt like that at all, and because it had been her father's funeral that had brought it about, and because she knew she wanted to be her own boss again, to get back to work and let someone else change nappies and give feeds. And that gave rise to a new fear, the fear that she didn't love Charlotte enough.

Lloyd emerged from the shop and got back into the car, handing her a bar of chocolate. "It's quite normal, you know," he said.

She sighed. "What is?" She knew perfectly well what he was talking about. He always seemed to know exactly what she was thinking.

"Wanting to send them back."

She smiled. "I don't really. It's just that when you haven't had an unbroken night's sleep for weeks and it seems all you're doing is running round in circles, washing clothes, sterilizing bottles, and wiping bottoms, a day off is a reminder that there is another world out there."

"You're just feeling it more because of your dad. Eat the chocolate. It'll make you feel better."

Lloyd was a great believer in food at times of emotional upheaval. "But it's not just that," she said. "It *was* nice being able to talk to people who talked back, but—" She broke off, worried about telling even Lloyd how she felt. But if she couldn't tell him, she couldn't tell anyone. "It's more that I feel as though *I'm* looking after her for someone else. As though she isn't mine at all." She looked at him. "I shouldn't feel like that, should I?"

Lloyd shrugged. "I don't think you can say that people should or shouldn't feel anything. You feel the way you feel, and that's all there is to it."

"But it's not normal."

"Who says? At the moment, she's a small animal who needs to eat and sleep and have everything done for her." He smiled. "There isn't much to work with. But you'll be amazed how quickly things change; believe me, you will."

"But what if *I* don't change?"

He smiled again. "Do you actively dislike her?"

"No, of course not! I just—I just feel kind of detached from her. I don't seem to have much of a maternal instinct."

"And what was it your mother told you about that?"

Judy sighed. "That you didn't need instinct as long as you used your common sense."

"Quite. And you've got plenty of that." He leaned over and kissed her. "Usually."

Lloyd could always make her feel better. But his facility for lying, so ably demonstrated at the funeral, was one of the reasons she had backed away from marriage, even from living together, until now. Not because she thought for one moment that he would lie to her maliciously—she knew he would never do that—but because she knew that her emotions could be manipulated as smoothly and deliberately as he had manipulated his audience this afternoon. That's what he was doing now; for all she knew he had been deeply disturbed by what she had said.

A car hooted, trying to get in to the pump, and Lloyd waved an apology, started the engine.

"Besides," Lloyd was saying as he pulled out onto the road, "instinct isn't all that it's cracked up to be. Look at lemmings and cliffs. Moths and naked flames. Penguins and low-flying aircraft, rabbits and car headlights—"

"Penguins and low-flying aircraft?"

"Penguins crane their necks to look up at planes flying overhead and fall over backward as a result."

She shook her head. "Are you making that up?"

"No! They do. Or so they say—I think someone's disproved it now."

Judy smiled and closed her eyes. He and the truth might be fair-weather friends, but he was good at rescuing people, and she let him rescue her now, as she drifted off to sleep.

"Not to mention the would-be husbands of black widow spiders," he was saying. "Insects and Venus flytraps. Giant pandas and increasingly scarce bamboo shoots. . . ."

CHAPTER THREE

"I just said I was borrowing a van from a friend. It wasn't a lie. You are still my friend, aren't you?"

Theresa smiled. "Why are you borrowing the van at all?"

Ian looked decidedly shifty. "Because we need clothes and crockery and things, even if it is just for a month, and it's a lot more than we can fit into Lesley's old Audi."

"*Old* Audi?" That surprised Theresa, given that all she really knew about Lesley was that she was wealthy.

"Oh, yes. About five years old. She spends money on everyone but herself."

Wealthy and saintly, thought Theresa, a little bitchily. That's nice. It was mid-June, early morning, they were in the high-tech kitchen of the flat she had so stubbornly set her sights on, and on this beautiful day the balcony windows were open to admit a warm, gentle breeze. Theresa felt that she should be happier than she was, but she still hadn't really adjusted to living alone. She had thought the move might help, that it had been the familiar surroundings without Ian in them that made her lonely, but it hadn't been. She just *was* lonely.

Still . . . the rooms were as spacious and comfortable as she had thought they would be, and she had plans for her new home. Once she'd got it decorated to her own taste, things would be better, she was sure. But the plans would have to wait until the cottage was sold; in the meantime, she had furnished it with some stuff from the cottage. She hadn't had room for it all, which, as it turned out, was just as well.

At the beginning of April, she had been telephoned by Ian, who had stiffly and formally asked her if she would help him and Lesley out. They were on the move again, apparently, but the people who had bought their house in Malworth had just informed them that they were having to move out of their house a month earlier than planned, and Ian and Lesley, unwilling to pass up their own sale, needed a stopgap for half of June and two weeks in July. And since Theresa was going to be moving out of the cottage . . .

Thus the cottage had had to be taken off the market, and today Ian and Lesley were moving in.

During that phone call, Theresa had asked why they were selling up not two months after they had arrived in Malworth, but Ian hadn't answered her. Lesley, presumably, had been monitoring his end of the conversation, and he was clearly not permitted to divulge any more than Theresa needed to know. She had asked if he had passed on Phil Roddam's request and had been told that it wasn't possible.

The next phone call had been last night, when he'd called her "mate" and asked if he could borrow the van; he would leave her his car in exchange, he said, so that she wasn't without transport. It would only be for a couple of hours. She had agreed, providing she had the van back before eleven, which was when she would be going out to do her collections and deliveries. And she had every intention of getting to the bottom of all of this.

"No," she said. "I mean why are you borrowing the van rather than getting someone to do it for you? A DIY removal doesn't seem to me to be Lesley's style. And you must have had removal people booked for the rest of your stuff—why not ask them to do it?"

He looked shifty. "Because this way I could see you. Talk to you. Properly."

Theresa raised her eyebrows. "And why did you want to see me and talk to me properly? Is the angst-ridden teenage daughter proving too much for you?"

"No. Kayleigh's fine. We get on all right."

Theresa switched on the kettle and spooned coffee into mugs. "Why didn't you give her Phil's address?"

"Oh, it's 'Phil,' is it?" he said, suddenly on the defensive. "I didn't realize you were that friendly."

"Jealousy doesn't suit you, Ian." But his reaction wasn't prompted by jealousy; she knew that. It meant that she was on the right trail, that he was unhappy about something and it was something to do with Phil Roddam. "And, yes, you get to know someone quite well when he's ringing you up every week, begging you to give him a break."

"You haven't told him where Lesley is, have you?"

"No, but it would hardly matter if I had, since you're moving out again. Is that why you're moving? Because he's bound to track Lesley down soon, so she has to keep one jump ahead of him?"

"No, of course it isn't."

She made the coffee, wondering about the secrecy. She had only spoken to the man on the phone, but she liked him. Ian's reaction to her familiarity with him suggested that his guilt— because he was, undoubtedly, looking for some sort of absolution from her—was centered on Phil, which made no sense if Phil had done something dreadful and deserved to be cut off from communication with Kayleigh. But she asked anyway, just in case. "Was he violent or something?"

"Not as far as I'm aware. No—I'm sure he wasn't.

He's got a bit of a temper, but I'm sure he isn't violent, not like that. I told you that he caused a bit of trouble when Lesley told him about us. . . ."

"I know about the windows. But she hasn't excommunicated him because of that, has she? It's not Kayleigh's fault. Stopping him even writing to her seems a bit over-the-top."

"She thought that Kayleigh would be better off in the countryside, that's all. It had nothing to do with Phil. He was away when we moved and she couldn't get in touch with him."

"But he's back now. So why all the secrecy about where she's living?" She handed him his coffee and walked through to the sitting room, turning as he came in behind her. "And why is she moving again?" When she got no reply, she came right out with what was bothering her. "Did he sexually abuse Kayleigh—is that what it is?"

Ian looked appalled. "Oh, no—you mustn't think that. No. Lesley says he's great with Kayleigh."

"Then why is she doing this?"

"She had no intention of keeping the address secret, not to start with." Ian sat down, his face troubled. "She meant Kayleigh and Phil to see each other. But then this move came up, and she thought he might make difficulties."

"How could he make difficulties?"

"With Kayleigh. She doesn't want to go, and Phil would take her side. Lesley is very anxious to leave, and she wants it all to go as smoothly as possible."

"Which brings me to my next question." Theresa blew absently at the steam rising from her coffee mug. "Why would it make any difference to him where you are? It's not as though you live all that close to him now. Where are you moving to? Or is that a state secret?"

Now he went pink. "Australia," he muttered into his coffee.

Theresa's eyes grew wide. "I'm sorry? I thought you said Australia."

He looked at her over his mug.

"Australia, Ian? *Australia?*"

"Jerry offered me a very good job the day I met him in London."

Oh. He really had met Jerry in London—Theresa had been convinced that was a lie, since she had been told nothing of the conversation and she usually was. Now she knew why; she had been cheated out of a new life in Australia. Not that she cared, but Ian had obviously thought that she might.

"I turned him down originally, but Lesley was desperate to move, and since I'd been offered this job, we decided I should take it."

"*We* decided?"

He looked down, not meeting her gaze.

"And why is she desperate to move? You've only *been* in Malworth five minutes."

Ian looked distinctly uncomfortable now. "Because of Kayleigh. She . . . she's in a relationship that bothers Lesley. Really bothers her."

"Does that make yet another person who won't be allowed to communicate with Kayleigh?"

"I suppose so," he muttered, and looked at his watch. "Oh—it's almost half past seven. I'd better get going or I'll be cutting getting the van back to you very fine."

Then Theresa realized what was happening, what it was that Ian was finding difficult to live with. It wasn't the time that was hastening his departure; it was that she was about to put two and two together, and unfortunately for him, she just had.

"She's taking Kayleigh to Australia without even *telling* Phil?"

"Yes, well, like I said . . . she thinks he would make difficulties."

"I'll bet he would! Ian—that's not right; you know it's not!"

Ian held his hands up. "Save your breath. You're not going to say anything that I haven't already said to Lesley. She's adamant—and she does have right on her side."

"Right?"

"OK, the law," Ian amended. "Phil has no blood or legal connection with Kayleigh, and there's nothing to stop her doing what she's doing."

"He brought her up from when she was five years old! And what about Kayleigh herself? No wonder she's crisis-prone! What does she think about it?"

"She hasn't said much—she thinks we've lost touch with Phil accidentally. And we did, to start with. I've said as much as I can to Lesley—it's not really any of my business."

"It'll be your business once you're stuck in the outback with Kayleigh having a crisis."

"It's Sydney, not the outback."

"Oh, it's Sydney, is it? So much for the good country air."

"I'm sure she'll be out-of-doors a great deal more than she would be here. It's a great place for kids."

"Like you'd know."

"I'm certain that Kayleigh will love it. It's me I'm not so sure about."

She shook her head. "So why are you going there?"

He ignored her. "And Lesley says she'll tell Phil once we're there. There'll be no problem about him coming to visit her, or anything like that. Lesley would pay his fare."

"Oh, no. No problem at all. Everyone's got the time to hop on a plane to Sydney every other weekend."

Ian stood up. "I've got to go, Theresa. I'll bring the van back by eleven."

Today was the day they were moving out, because the new people were moving in on Monday.

And today was the day that Kayleigh was going to put into action the plan that she had spent weeks perfecting. Things could go wrong; she knew that. She might even have to abandon the whole idea. But nothing had gone wrong yet.

The removal men were just finishing, taking out the last of the stuff that was going with them to Australia to put it in storage. There wasn't all that much, but what was going tended to be large, heavy, or fragile or all three, in the case of her mother's grand piano. The rest of it was books, records, photographs, family heirlooms, that sort of thing, a portrait of Kayleigh herself that her mother had had painted when she was five, a portrait of her mother and Richard. The house had been sold complete with the furniture; only what they needed on a daily basis was being taken to the one in Stansfield.

Her mother hadn't liked having to move into Ian's cottage; it meant his talking to Theresa, for one thing, and she didn't really like him doing that. She was right not to like it, because if you asked Kayleigh, Ian sometimes wished he'd never left Theresa. Kayleigh could have told him that he would, because her mother took a lot of getting used to. But it was either that or letting the sale fall through, and her mother certainly didn't want that to happen, so it was the lesser of two evils as far as she was concerned.

And it had been when she and her mother had gone with Ian to the cottage to see what was what and how much they would need to take with them—her mother, practiced in the art of moving house, had no intention of

taking more to the cottage than was strictly necessary—
that Kayleigh had seen how she could achieve her goal.

Ian was borrowing a van to take the stuff to Stansfield
and was going to be pushed for time if he didn't get back
with it soon, because they had to load it up, drive to the
cottage, unload it, and get it back to his friend by eleven
o'clock and it was a twenty-five-minute drive from the
Riverside area of Malworth to Stansfield. It was exactly
sixteen miles door-to-door; her mother, of course, had
checked even that.

Her mother hadn't understood why he wouldn't just
get the removal people to take it, but he said it was a
waste of money and she had humored him, like she always did with other people about small, unimportant
things. But with anything that really mattered it was a
different story.

The removal van drove away, and as Kayleigh
watched, a small white van pulled up and Ian got out,
waving to her.

"He's here!" she called up to her mother.

"About time!"

"Thank you all for coming in so early," said the assistant
chief constable.

Tom glanced at Lloyd. Gatherings of the clan were always viewed with deep suspicion, and this meeting of
CID personnel of the rank of inspector and above was in
order to unveil the restructuring on which the top brass
had been laboring for almost eighteen months, or at least
that part of it that concerned the Criminal Investigation
Department. Rumors had been flying about during all of
that time, and Tom had even more interest in what was
really going to happen than he might have, because he
had, thanks to Judy's insistence that he go on the training
course, passed his inspector's exam. Not that he was an

inspector yet, but as he was a potential inspector this meeting concerned him, because now he was going to find out what opportunities were likely to be available.

"I have no wish to open up old wounds," the ACC went on, "but as most of you know, Bartonshire Police Service suffered a setback a couple of years ago when it was discovered that one of our divisions had, not to put too fine a point on it, fostered corrupt officers running their own corrupt system, albeit with what they believed were good intentions. . . ."

Tom blew out his cheeks a little. The ACC was famous for never using one word when thirty would do. He listened with half an ear to a minute reexamination of the old wounds that the ACC didn't want to open up.

Tom supposed if a uniform inspector's job was made available by the restructuring he would have to apply for it. It would please Liz, and, he reluctantly admitted to himself, it would add valuable experience in other fields to his CV, if he sought further promotion in the future. Besides, it looked bad if you didn't go after what was available, in or out of uniform. But Bob Sandwell said he'd heard CID jobs would be created within the new structure and Bob was always right, so Tom was very hopeful.

"And as a result, Stansfield, as our largest divisional headquarters, bore the brunt, and has since then been policing all serious crime. This, of course, is far from ideal, as resources are considerably stretched. . . ."

"Tell me about it," muttered Lloyd. "Especially when you second half the bloody staff to work on projects that are a total waste of time and money."

Tom smiled. Judy was on the last few weeks of her maternity leave, but she was still on attachment to the LINKS project, which, despite her gloomy predictions, was running its course. They wouldn't be told this morning whether or not the Local Information Networked Knowledge System would be adopted, but Judy and her colleagues had produced their final recommendations, which were favorable. The firm belief was that it would be too expensive and that the idea would be scrapped or, at best, adopted in a modified form. Bob Sandwell said he thought it would go ahead as originally envisaged, and on the strength of that Tom had invested ten pounds at ten to one when the inevitable book had been opened on the outcome.

"The idea of setting up a serious-crime squad at this HQ was mooted and discussed at considerable length and in great depth."

Tom gave the ACC his full attention. This was his chance.

"However . . ."

Tom's head dropped. The dreaded word. However, it wasn't going to happen; the ACC didn't need to use any more words after that first one, but he was, of course, using a great many. Tom could see a future full of settling disputes between colleagues and smoothing the ruffled feathers of the public stretching before him, interspersed with getting old ladies and injured dogs out of potentially hazardous situations while remembering not to call anyone mate. The serious-crime squad had been his one hope, and for once, Bob Sandwell had got it wrong.

He could probably kiss his tenner good-bye, too.

Judy had never got used to changing nappies. It wasn't something she was put on this earth to do. But then, she had had to get used to a lot worse than dirty nappies in her time, and she had never let that put her off. Removing nappies full of pee and poo did have the edge over autopsies, but only just. The nappies smelled better.

She smiled as Charlotte, now clean and fresh, lying on

her tummy and wearing nothing, lifted her head, pushing herself up on sturdy little arms.

"Your daddy would have had to do that if he hadn't had to go to a silly old meeting." Judy got out of nappy fatigues every time she could, and Lloyd was usually entirely willing to do his bit, she had to admit, despite her prenatal misgivings about his dedication to fatherhood. And the silly old meeting would, with luck, confirm when he would be able to leave work and swap places with her.

"Ba-ba-ba," said Charlotte.

"Da-da," said Judy. "Daddy. Da-da."

Part of her, a very tiny part, was almost enjoying this now, the part of her that knew so much had happened in the last five months that she would miss an awful lot by going back to work. She had seen Charlotte's first smile—at least, the first one she had bestowed on her. Charlotte might have been secretly smiling to herself for days before that, for all Judy knew. She had heard her first laugh and was working on getting her to produce her first word, or at least coincidentally produce a couple of syllables that could be construed as a word. But a much larger part was longing to use her brain again for something other than conversing with Charlotte.

"Ba-ba-ba-ba."

"Really?"

"Ga-ga-ga."

"Who are you calling ga-ga?"

Charlotte was varying the noises occasionally now, but usually it was just "ba-ba-ba." Now she rolled over onto her back, a newly acquired skill, and Judy picked up a plastic ball, rolling it gently over Charlotte's tummy, tickling her, laughing with her when she giggled her captivating baby giggle. Lloyd had said that things would change, and they had. Judy felt that there was some communication now, even if it was gobbledygook, though she did still feel a little as though someone would come and take Charlotte back to whomever she really belonged to.

Charlotte's plump little hands held the ball, and she sucked it reflectively for a few moments, then let it go. It rolled gently off her tummy and onto the bath towel on which she was lying. Judy picked it up, put it back on her tummy. Charlotte held it and let it go again. When they had done it for the third time, Judy knew it wasn't coincidence—she and Charlotte were playing a game. A real game. She felt inordinately proud of both Charlotte and herself and wished Lloyd had been there.

"According to my book, you shouldn't be doing that for at least another month. You must be a very advanced baby. When your daddy comes home, we'll show him this game, won't we?"

"Da-da-da."

Judy's eyebrows rose. "Yes," she said. "Da-da."

"Ba-ba-ba."

"OK, have it your way. When your ba-ba-ba comes home." Judy tickled her again, and Charlotte squealed.

"Ba-ba-ba-ba. Ba-ba." Charlotte's voice rose. "Ba-ba-ba! Ba-ba-ba-ba!"

"What's that about? What *is* a ba-ba-ba? Do you want your donkey?"

The soft toy had a bell inside that Charlotte loved to hear, but she hadn't worked out how to make the noise yet. In a way, that was even better than if she had, because it delighted her so; it wouldn't be quite the same if she knew to expect it.

Charlotte took the donkey in her hands and let it go, but it just sat there on her chest.

"That won't roll," Judy advised her. "Donkeys don't roll."

"Ba-ba-ba-ba-ba."

"Well, that is one argument, but I think the facts speak for themselves. Donkeys don't roll." Judy picked up the donkey, shook it, made the bell ring. Made Charlotte laugh. "You," she said, holding it out.

Charlotte took the donkey, let it go, and it sat on her chest. "Ba-ba-ba," she said.

"Ball?" Judy picked up the donkey, gave Charlotte the ball, and the game began again. Over and over and over again. "I thought you were supposed to have a short attention span," she complained. "I think we should get your nice new nappy on now, get you fed and dressed, and go for a walk in the sunshine. Do you fancy that?"

"Ba-ba-ba."

"That's what you always say."

The taxi swept left into St. Pancras, and Phil thrust a fiver into the driver's hands, ran up the steps, found a free window in the booking hall, bought his ticket, rushed out to the platforms, and found the station devoid of trains. Had he missed it? It was supposed to be leaving at 8:35 and it must be almost that now, but he didn't think it was later than that. He couldn't see a clock—there must be a clock, for God's sake. He had sold the Rolex watch that Lesley had given him to help finance his travels; the cheap replacement that he had bought had, ironically enough, been stolen, and he hadn't bothered getting another one. Men with no responsibilities didn't need watches, he'd told himself.

Finally, he located the clock, high above his head. A huge old-fashioned clock set into the wall and designed to be seen only by passengers who were getting off trains, which seemed less than useful to Phil, but perhaps the Victorians knew why they had put it there. It wasn't quite twenty-five to nine, so where was his train? The arrivals screen informed him that the train due in from Nottingham was running thirty-two minutes late, and he sank down onto one of the metal benches, resigned to a long wait, as other trains, going to other places, arrived and left.

Tight-lipped and angry, he strained to hear the virtually incomprehensible announcements that echoed in the Gothic arches of the building, competing with the din of starlings, then gave it up as a bad job. The screen would tell him what he needed to know.

Australia. He had known that Lesley was trying to stop him from finding something out, but this was completely out of the blue. Thank God Theresa had rung him. She had said they weren't going for another month, but he wasn't going to waste any time. If he had a month to work on her, he would use every minute of it.

It had been a very long time since he'd been on a train in Britain. He'd used a few foreign ones in his travels, but before he'd sold the car he had driven everywhere. The trains bound for other destinations were more or less as he remembered them; he hadn't been expecting the little turbo train that finally arrived in from Nottingham, looking out of place in a station built for big, macho steam engines pulling endless carriages, and accustomed, in the more recent past, to long and lean Intercity express trains with diesel-power cars at either end. The turbo looked as though it had escaped from someone's train set. Even the bloody trains had been emasculated, Phil thought. Maybe Lesley was running the service.

He stood impatiently at the barrier while the train was being serviced, as though getting onto it early would make it leave sooner. As soon as the gate opened, he practically sprinted down the platform and claimed one of the seats, which he found rather too small for his comfortable frame. At three minutes past nine, it pulled out

of St. Pancras and Phil relaxed just a little, now that he
was under way.

He had no idea where he was going when he got there,
but he knew it was the only house in a road called Brook
Way and he would get a taxi.

Lloyd stifled a yawn and sneaked a look at his watch. It
was just after five past nine—was that all? He felt as
though he'd been here for hours. He had been up until
three in the morning—not because of Charlotte, who
now was much more grown-up than he was and had
slept all night for weeks now—but because he had wanted
to finish the jigsaw that Judy had bought him as a
joke birthday present and which he had started at mid-
night. He would blame Charlotte, however, if anyone
remarked on his lack of alertness.

Having given an exhaustive discourse on why a serious-
crime squad was not thought to be viable, the ACC finally got around to telling them what they actually
intended doing.

"It has been decided that Bartonshire will be split into
three divisions. The west of the county will constitute A
Division, with its headquarters at Barton's Highgrove
Street station, and the east will be split once again into
the two historic divisions of B Division at Stansfield and
C Division at Malworth. Malworth will be extended
from its traditional boundaries to cover roughly the same
area as Stansfield, with a more-or-less-equal distribution
of urban and rural policing."

A murmur immediately rose from his audience. Malworth, the seat of the corruption, had lost its divisional
headquarters status some time ago, having been deemed
to cover too small an area, and the station itself had had
no CID for over a year; everyone had assumed that it
would be swallowed up by whatever setup the reorgani-

zation produced. And everyone had been wrong. Except
Bob Sandwell, of course. Lloyd glanced over at him and
smiled.

"Each division, which will be run by a uniform superintendent, will have a CID headed up by a detective chief
inspector, assisted by a detective inspector . . ."

No need for "up," Lloyd thought. You would get a lot
more said in a lot less time if you didn't use unnecessary
buzzwords.

". . . and whatever the establishment agreed upon, it
may not reflect actual staffing levels for some time, but it
should spread the load more evenly."

Stansfield's CID was currently headed by Detective Superintendent Case, who, unlike Lloyd, had already had
his early retirement confirmed. Judy's promotion and sec-
ondment, everyone had again assumed, had been with a
view to retiring Lloyd and putting her in charge of the re-
organized Stansfield CID, whatever form it took. But
Malworth had to be staffed now, and it didn't just mean
that there was a CID opportunity for Tom, whose de-
meanor had changed from one of resignation to one of
anticipation and whose eagerness to leave the meeting
and put in an immediate application was practically tangible; it apparently meant that they would no longer
have one DCI too many, because the ACC was now announcing that there would be no more staff cutting. And
that meant that his early retirement had just been knocked
on the head, as Tom would say.

It was a blow. Judy would no longer be looking for
someone who could take care of Charlotte on a temporary basis; she would now be having to consider
long-term care. But, honest with himself as ever, Lloyd
acknowledged that it was also something of a relief. He
had begun to regret his offer as soon as it had been made,
because though he did his best to disguise it, he was of

the old school, and the idea of Judy working while he stayed at home had offended the male chauvinist sensibilities that he tried very hard to ignore.

But, he thought, as the meeting broke up and he and Tom went out into the warm, breezy day, heading for Tom's car, that was strictly between him and his heart. Truthfulness, in Lloyd's opinion, was strictly for self-consumption.

The bus labored up the hill toward the bus station, and Dean tensed up a little. He almost hadn't got on it; he had walked up and down Marylebone Road, arguing with himself, as the small crowd of people waiting for the buses grew. It was, quite simply, the very last thing he should be doing. But he had to do it.

He almost hadn't phoned her, either. He had received a letter in prison that simply read: "Please, please, please phone me. Jennifer Archer," and a mobile phone number. At first he'd simply crumpled it up and thrown it on the floor. Why would he want to phone someone who had screwed up his life? Then, after a few minutes' contemplation, he had picked it up, smoothed it out, and just stared at it.

She had used the alias she had denied ever using, so that no one would confiscate the letter, since he was supposed to have no contact with her. And just whom would he be speaking to, if he phoned her? The girl he'd made love to, fallen in love with, or the one who had lied about everything in the witness-box? If he didn't ring her, he would never know, and he knew that would bother him.

He had carried the note around with him for days, but when he had finally had enough money to buy a phone card and the chance to use the phone, he hadn't taken it. He hadn't thrown the note away, though, and every now and then he would take it out and read it and wonder why she wanted him to ring her.

So the next time he did ring her, and what she had said had astounded him, made him think long and hard. Then he had got his release date and had requested a calendar so that he could indeed begin crossing off the days until the glorious day when he stepped through the gate, never so welcome.

As promised, the bus pulled into Stansfield at exactly 9:15, according to the big clock in the bus station, and he was walking quickly through the pedestrianized center of the town, following Kayleigh's directions, glad that his route was taking him away from the square, brick-built building that housed the police station, toward the other side of the town.

The hotel that she had told him to look out for was on his left, on the corner of the wide walkway he was on and the dual carriageway of the main road, running at right angles to the walkway. Across that road was a bus stop used by the local buses, and, beyond the Stansfield Civic Centre behind it was the wood through which there was a path to his destination.

He was just a mile away from risking the precious, fragile freedom that he had so recently regained. He could turn back. But he didn't.

Ian drove the van up the short driveway to the cottage and wondered whether it made more sense to park at the front door or in the garage.

The garage, he decided. It would make unloading a little more awkward, but it did mean that the bulk of his load—destined, as it was, for the kitchen and the bedrooms—could be taken through the connecting door to the utility room, and that would be quicker than having to take the packing cases down the hallway to the kitchen and the stairs.

He unlocked the garage and the adjoining door, then came back out to the van. He hadn't expected the sudden lurch that his heart gave as he saw it sitting there, for all the world as though Theresa were still here and his life had not taken the rather unnerving turn that it had. Indeed, he hadn't ever officially moved out of the cottage; he had removed his personal goods and chattels, such as they were, but Lesley's itchy feet meant that he had never got to the stage of altering his address on the various pieces of paper that characterized one's life; as far as officialdom was concerned this was still where he lived, and he sincerely wished that it were.

He and Theresa hadn't been unhappy; they had just become too used to each other. For the last two years they had been more like brother and sister than lovers. Not bored with each other, not really—he had always enjoyed Theresa's company. She was quick and clever and fun to be with. The spark had gone, that was all; they had simply been marking time until one or the other of them called it a day, and it had happened to be him.

But there was a part of him buried deep in his heart or his mind or his soul—wherever it was that a man kept his conscience—that wouldn't be fooled into believing that and refused to stay silent any longer. *You know,* it said. *You know that you wish Theresa was still here, that you had never met Lesley.*

No, he argued. He didn't want to leave Lesley. She had shaken him out of his inertia, given him a new direction; life with her was exciting and different.

But you liked the inertia. And your life would be much simpler if you hadn't met her. It would be the life you used to live, the dull, uneventful life you want to live again. And you wouldn't be on your way to Australia.

He backed the van into the garage and then found that unloading wasn't just awkward; it was impossible: the packing cases wouldn't go through the narrow connecting door. He drove out again and backed up to the front of the cottage, got out, unlocked the front door, and opened it wide. Maybe, he thought as he opened the van's rear doors and reached for the first packing case, maybe he could persuade Lesley that Stansfield was far enough away from Andrea and they could all just move into the cottage.

But now he wasn't even fooling himself, never mind his conscience.

CHAPTER FOUR

There had been too much stuff for the little van; while Ian went off to the cottage, her mother had crossly filled her car up with the overflow, complaining as she did so that if they had got the removal firm to do it none of this would be necessary.

Now she was looking for something, picking things up, checking under furniture, in drawers, in coat pockets.

Kayleigh, who had been ready to leave for some time, wearing the jeans and sweatshirt that her mother had decreed was the right gear for unloading vans—giving adequate protection from possible cuts and bruises—was sitting on the sofa, a small case packed with what she would most immediately need, and watched the search without apparent interest.

"Kayleigh? Did Ian give you the keys?"

Kayleigh frowned. "Which keys?"

"The house keys."

"No."

"Well, where are they?" Her mother came over. "Stand up, dear. You might be sitting on them."

Kayleigh knew she wasn't sitting on them, but she stood up as requested. Her mother lifted the cushions, felt down the sides of the chair. "I don't understand," she said. "I thought they were on the hook."

"Maybe Ian took them with him by mistake."

Her mother looked perplexed. "Why would he have been using them in the first place?" she asked.

Kayleigh shrugged.

"Oh, it's too bad!" said her mother. "What am I supposed to do now? I can't lock up, and I can't ring him."

"Why not?"

"You know why not! She had the number transferred."

Her mother had taken that personally, but Theresa ran a business—she wanted to keep the number, naturally.

"Why can't you ring him on his mobile?"

"He's left it somewhere, and he doesn't know where. It's probably in his car, but he didn't tell me he couldn't find it until it was too late to do anything about it."

Because he had lent his car to the friend whose van he'd borrowed. What with one thing and another, Ian was losing a lot of brownie points today. Kayleigh had found that she did like him; he was, as her mother had assured her, a likable man. But Kayleigh knew that his heart wasn't in this move to Australia, and so did her mother.

"Can't you just use the Yale lock?"

"No, it's too vulnerable. All the stuff here belongs to the new people now, and the removal van's been standing outside the door all morning—every burglar in the area knows the house is going to be empty. I have to lock up properly." She threw her hands up in the air, a gesture of impatience with the world that Kayleigh knew well. "Oh, why does everything have to go wrong at the last minute? If these people had just stuck to the date they agreed . . ."

If these people had stuck to the date, if Ian kept his phone clipped to his person like her mother did, if other people always put the keys back on the hook that she had had put up for the purpose . . .

But life, Kayleigh was glad to say, wasn't like that, and

as far as she was concerned, everything had gone according to plan.

Lloyd's car had been off the road for a couple of days; Tom had given him a lift to the meeting and was now taking him to pick it up, but for the moment he was waiting in the car while Lloyd broke the news about his non-retirement to Judy. He had thought it best to do that as soon as possible, in view of how fast word got round. He didn't want her hearing it from someone else.

"Well?" he said as Lloyd got back into the car. "How did she take it?"

"Pragmatically. How else?"

Tom grinned. "Let's see," he said. "I remember asking you before—it means dealing with things as they are, and not as you'd like them to be, right?"

"Right. She's going to see what she thinks of the nursery Liz mentioned—the one that takes babies under six months. She thought she might try leaving Charlotte there for a day while she's still on maternity leave and see how they both got on with that. But I think she's in two minds about the whole thing, especially now."

"It's only natural," said Tom. "Do you think there's a chance she won't go back to work?" Liz had intended going back when she had their first, but when it came to it, she had decided to stay at home.

"Only if she feels there's no alternative. She was very interested to hear about Malworth."

"Do you know how they're going to do it, guv? I mean, are they going to advertise, or what?"

After the meeting, Lloyd had had a brief chat with the ACC in the car park, and Tom was hopeful that he might get some inside information.

"I think they're hoping to recruit from within the force,

but I don't know that for certain. All I really know is that I'm to head Stansfield CID—officially, at last."

Lloyd had been acting head of Stansfield CID at least twice; it was time he got to run it his way, Tom thought.

"And I suspect that Judy will get Malworth if she wants it, whoever else they interview. She'll have some say in who her DI is to be."

Tom smiled, then shook his head. "Bob Sandwell's bound to apply," he said. Bob had been acting DI for months, and he'd been waiting over a year for a vacancy. It wasn't likely that Judy would recommend Tom over Bob, even if he and Liz had become close friends with Lloyd and Judy during Judy's pregnancy, Liz being someone whose advice Judy trusted. *Especially* since they were friends, he amended; she wouldn't want to look as though she was playing favorites. And Bob had, of course, been right about the CID vacancies, proving that he was a better detective than Tom into the bargain. "I think I'd better be pragmatic, too," he said.

He came into the outskirts of Stansfield and left the main road to enter the maze of roads that constituted the industrial estate, down one of which operated the one-man outfit that Lloyd used for car maintenance. Tom could never remember which road it was; they were all called after industrial pioneers, and he had a tendency to get his McAdams and Telfords and Brunels confused. "Which one is it, again?" he asked.

"Crompton Court."

Tom frowned. "What did he do, then?"

"What did who do?"

"Crompton." When he got a puzzled silence, he made his request clearer. "You know—like Telford built bridges or canals or whatever it was; what did Crompton do to get famous?" He'd got unfamous again as far as Tom was concerned.

"I think he was the one who produced the spinning mule. And I don't know what that was, before you ask, but I know they called it the mule because it used bits of the spinning jenny and bits of some other textile machinery."

Tom frowned as he kept an eye out for Crompton Road. "Why does that mean it was called the mule?"

"It was a sort of pun. Because jenny is another name for an ass, and the offspring of an ass and a horse is a mule."

"I'll bet that had them rolling in the aisles. Why was the other one called a jenny, anyway?"

Lloyd sighed melodramatically. "It had something to do with Hargreaves's daughter's spinning wheel overturning—it gave him the idea, and his daughter's name was Jenny. Second on the right," he instructed. "May I ask why on earth you want to know all this?"

Tom indicated the turn into Crompton Court. "Because," he said, "if I do get the promotion, I'm going to have to hold my own with all these fast-track graduates, and if they ever taught me all that stuff at school, I wasn't listening."

Lloyd laughed. "And you think they were?"

"Well, they've got degrees in something."

"Probably in corporate strategy and information technology. I really don't think you have to bone up on the industrial revolution. And—that's it on your left—you might not have to be pragmatic, either, because I think Bob's more interested in duty inspector. Talk to him about it—he won't mind."

"When's it all going off, guv?"

Lloyd sighed again and looked pained. "I take it you are asking me when I think that the posts will be advertised. And the answer is I don't know." He got out and bent down to speak to Tom. "You can get back to the main road more quickly if you turn right out of here and go along Arkwright Way," he said. "Eighteenth-century inventor and factory owner, industrialized the cotton industry."

Tom grinned and hooted as he left, already composing his CV.

Judy was walking through Riverside Park to the Riverside Nursery, whose very name proclaimed just how much it was likely to cost.

Malworth had two public parks, linked by the river Andwell; one was on the other side of the new bypass that cut through the town and was run-down and bleak, like Parkside itself, the area beyond it. The Riverside area had an altogether grander park, overlooked by opulent houses. Riverside was the jewel in Malworth's crown; it had had its town houses preserved, and the new development on Bridge Street included luxury flats and high-class businesses. The Riverside Nursery in Andwell House was one such business.

She was having to rethink everything now that Lloyd wasn't going to be at home after all. Turning Charlotte over to strangers was going to be difficult enough when she had thought it would be only for a few weeks; long-term was bothering her. She wasn't at all sure why, because it was still the case that anyone who looked after babies for a living would be far more knowledgeable than she was.

It might, she thought, have something to do with her father dying like he had, with no warning, no illness, nothing. She blinked away the tears that still came to her eyes whenever she thought of him; Lloyd said that when his mother had died, he had thought he would never be able to think of her again without the sadness, but that it really did pass, and Judy hoped he was right, because she knew her father would disapprove of the tears. But it had been so sudden, so unexpected.

He had been in his late sixties, which was much too young, but that sort of thing sometimes happened to people younger than that. And what if it happened to her or Lloyd? The plain truth was that no one knew how long they had to go. It could be fifty years or five minutes. She and Lloyd were what the maternity unit had rather unflatteringly called elderly parents, and if Charlotte's time with either of them was, heaven forbid, unduly curtailed, Judy didn't want her to have spent it being farmed out to strangers.

And, Judy thought, the even plainer truth was that she had meant it to be Lloyd, and not her, with whom Charlotte spent her time. Selfish, as ever. And it *was* selfish, she supposed, wanting to go back to work. But then, you could just as easily argue that it was selfish *not* wanting to go back. Bartonshire Constabulary had invested a lot of money and time in her; they expected an operational detective chief inspector for their trouble. Not someone who wanted to stay at home and look after her baby.

"What do you think?" she asked Charlotte. "Would you like being in a nursery with people who know what they're doing looking after you?"

Charlotte blew a raspberry.

"Oh. Not keen, huh? But you didn't really give yourself time to consider the idea, did you? There'll be other babies there—you'll be able to network. The assistant chief constable is very strong on networking. Making the right contacts. I'm sure you'll be very good at that."

"Ba-ba-ba-ba."

"How about 'Ma-ma-ma-ma'? That's me. Mama. You say it."

"Ba-ba-ba."

"Baba. That's you." She bent down and put her face

close to Charlotte's. "You baba. Me Mama. Other one Dada."

Charlotte caught her nose.

With some difficulty, Judy persuaded her to let go and straightened up. "And the thing is, if I had to do this forever, I'd go ga-ga. You said so yourself, this morning. And you don't want a ga-ga mama. You really don't."

She carried on toward the nursery, talking to Charlotte, while Charlotte tried to hit the toys strung across the pram, shouting with delight when she accidentally succeeded and they spun round.

Judy rather liked having the excuse of a baby for talking out loud; it helped her to think. And she had decided the first time she took Charlotte to visit Liz Finch that it would be on foot—she wasn't popping her into a car every time she took her somewhere. They would both benefit from the fresh air, and she, with her post-Charlotte figure, would benefit from the exercise. And she had been right; she was almost back to her fighting weight. But Lloyd had discovered that if you wanted to get Charlotte to sleep, then driving her round in the car worked every time, just like it did with her mother, he had added, in a dig at Judy's tendency to drop off when Lloyd was at the wheel.

"And it's all very nice when you're like this," Judy went on. "You're a very cheerful baby, by and large, but you'll be teething any day now. And that hurts a bit, so you won't like it, and you'll probably cry a lot. Don't worry—you won't remember a thing about it; take it from me. But your mama and dada will. And I think I'd rather have some time off from that if possible. I think I'd rather be running Malworth CID, where almost no one will be teething. You do understand, don't you?"

"Ba-ba-ba."

"So you say, but you might be like your dada, and say whatever you think will produce the reaction you want."

She had considered a child minder, rather than a nursery, on the grounds that they didn't cost as much and it might be more personal care, but she wasn't too keen on that, even before she had looked into it properly. She had asked Charlotte's opinion and had felt that the "ba-ba-ba" was at best noncommittal.

They could afford a nanny of sorts, just about. Judy didn't really like the idea of someone living in, but she supposed it would be all right if she picked her very carefully. That, of course, meant more house hunting, which had been put on hold recently. She wasn't looking forward to that, either.

And she wasn't particularly looking forward to the rearranged wedding day; Saturday, the first of August, at Stansfield Registry Office, with a reception that was going to cost the earth. He had chosen Stansfield for the nuptials because that's where all their friends were and, he had added, they would probably be living there by then. Judy felt sheer dread at the idea of practically the whole of Stansfield Police Station turning out to watch her tie the knot and she really did find it very hard to be unselfish, but she was going along with what Lloyd wanted, mainly because she had realized just how much he wanted it—enough to reveal, after years of keeping it secret, his name to everyone who knew him.

He had told her once that he had changed it by deed poll, but that, of course, hadn't been true. Not only hadn't he done that, he had never changed it at all; all his official documents carried his full name, as she had found out when they had originally given notice of their intention to marry. She had discovered at the same time that he had a perfectly good middle name that he could have used if he had wanted, but he hadn't, so part of him was proud of this unusual, if embarrassing, French first name, and she could understand that. But telling everyone what it was . . . that would, she knew, be giving him sleepless nights. And since getting married was that important to him, she had given in over the wedding arrangements and let him have his extravagant head.

She could see the nursery, and she stopped walking, crouching down so that she was on Charlotte's level. "It's like this, kid," she said. "Your choices are relatively inexpensive child minder, more expensive nursery, second-division nanny, which is all we can really afford, but I expect we'd both like her better than a premier-division one anyway, or a ga-ga mama. Which of the above would you prefer?"

Various people came and went from the nursery as Judy watched. A woman not much younger than her, pushing a twin buggy. She looked tired; Judy wasn't in the least surprised. As they passed, one of the twins started to cry, and so, of course, did the other. And why were they crying? Because the woman was leaving them at this nursery? Because she was abandoning them to their fate with strangers, instead of looking after them herself like she should be doing?

Don't be ridiculous, Judy told herself. Babies cry. The thought that Charlotte might have been twins horrified her, because that would have been more than her common sense could have coped with.

A blonde passed them, an expensive fashion statement pushing a pram that had seen better days, and Judy watched as the blonde pushed open the door of the nursery and went in. There was nothing wrong with that, she told herself. If she chose to spend her money on child care and clothes for herself rather than a pram, that was perfectly reasonable. Logical, even. She would need the pram for only a few months—why buy a brand-new one?

Though Judy suspected the clothes would no longer be fashionable this time next week, so the argument probably fell down there.

She couldn't *believe* that she was mentally tutting at someone because she hadn't spent money on her baby's transport. But Judy knew that she wasn't, not really. She was transferring her own guilt. Worrying about what other people would think of her. She wanted to pursue her career instead of being with Charlotte, that was the top and bottom of it. For all she knew, that girl had no option but to work; she was very probably a single mother. Judy didn't have to work—Lloyd was perfectly capable of providing for her and Charlotte.

A young man, carrying a baby from his car. Judy wondered about him. A widower? Someone whose wife just up and left him holding the baby? A working couple, and he was the one for whom it was least inconvenient? Perhaps they took it in turns to drop the baby off, like taking it in turns to drink or drive. A man whose wife was in having the next one? She was being a lot more charitable about him than she had been about the young woman, she realized. For some reason men with children to look after always seemed heroic.

One by one, the customers—clients? whatever they were—left, and the girl nodded to Judy as she walked back the way she had come. Judy almost asked her what she thought of the place but didn't. And she wasn't going to find out about it standing outside and clocking the other customers, which was what she had been doing for the last ten minutes. The minirush seemed to be over now, so this was probably a good time to go in for a chat.

"Let's have a look inside, then. We don't have to commit ourselves, do we?"

At half past ten, having spent thirty minutes in the nursery, talking to the woman who ran it, meeting a couple of the girls who looked after babies, having morning coffee and biscuits, Judy and Charlotte left. It was a pleasant place, with all sorts of things to stimulate infant minds. The girls seemed to know what they were doing, their charges seemed happy, and the boss woman had all the right qualifications. Charlotte had smiled and laughed and said "ba-ba-ba" to everyone she had met; Judy felt that she could leave her there right now and Charlotte wouldn't care.

But Judy would. She sighed. She didn't want Charlotte saying her first word to a stranger or taking her first steps in a smart, state-of-the-art nursery. She wanted her baby to be in her own home, with someone she lived with, wherever and whoever that was going to be.

"Looks like we're down to a so-so nanny or ga-ga mama. What do you think?"

"Ma-ma-ma."

Judy stared at her. My God, she *was* just like her father.

"Lesley?" Ian called upstairs. "I'm just going to take the van back. I'll be as quick as I can. It's only a five-minute trip."

He set off for Byford Road, wondering how all this had happened to him. The brook that ran alongside the road looked pretty, after the wet spring that had caused it to flood more than once; the water seemed to have been revitalized, moving briskly and busily over the stones. A solitary figure stood on the bridge, watching it, as Ian drove past. With its backdrop of trees, the scene looked like a painting.

The woodland that his father had managed for so many years was tended by council workers now, rather than the casual labor that his father had employed. But these itinerant workers—Gypsies, most of them—had made a better job of it. Or perhaps, he thought, people were just more considerate of their surroundings then. Or perhaps there simply weren't as many people, so not as many antisocial ones.

The wood, shifting in the now-stiff breeze, still looked good, particularly in autumn, when it turned to red and gold, but it was difficult to appreciate it when he knew that the little clearing where he had played as a boy was now little more than an unofficial garbage dump. The council removed the rubbish from time to time, but it always happened again. There was a perfectly good disposal center where people could take unwanted items, but that was too much like hard work. Easier just to dump it in the clearing. You couldn't see the pile of rubbish from the road; it was when you were enjoying a walk through the wood that you found yourself looking at it.

He turned right out of Brook Way and negotiated the miniroundabouts that guarded the entrances to the center of Stansfield, waiting to see what the black cab approaching on the roundabout was going to do, since its driver was signaling left but hadn't taken the left turn up to the town center. The cab came straight over, and Ian, glancing in his mirror, saw it take the next left turn into Brook Way. He wasn't going up to the town, either; he drove along the main road and turned left into Byford Road, where Theresa had her flat. Even that seemed wrong, because she didn't seem to him to be entirely at home there. Six months ago, none of this had happened, and he wished with all his heart that it never had.

It was twenty to eleven when he pulled into the garage area, where his Alfa sat waiting for him. Up in the flat, they swapped keys once more, and Theresa looked at him, her head to one side.

"You said you borrowed the van so you could speak to me properly. But you didn't, did you?"

No. Ian looked down at his feet.

"Come on. Out with it."

He took a deep breath. "I think I've made a terrible mistake, Theresa."

Phil got out of the cab and walked up the driveway of the cottage. He could see her car in the garage; presumably she was in. He went along the path to the front door, his hand poised to ring the bell; then he withdrew it. If she saw him on the doorstep, the door would be closed again; perhaps he could get in some other way.

The garage seemed to have been built onto the cottage—he walked back along the path, stepping as noiselessly as he could onto the graveled driveway, and almost tiptoed between the Audi and the wall, toward what looked like a connecting door. He shook his head when he glanced into the car, piled to the roof with bundles and boxes—she had no rear vision at all. And she'd just parked it and got out, leaving the keys, her bag, everything in it. All right, the house was in the middle of a wood, but she was a strange mixture, Lesley; she seemed to be concerned about everyone but herself. If that had been someone else's car, it would be locked, the garage would be locked, and there would be nothing of value left in it to be stolen. But her own car—well, that was unimportant. And yet, despite the apparent selflessness, she always got her own way.

If the door was locked, he might try ringing the front door bell, just in case she allowed him in. But if he couldn't get in that way, he would get in some way, because she wasn't going to get away with this, not without listening to what he had to say. He would get in if he had to break the door down. But he didn't have to break it down; the door opened into a dark, windowless utility room, with a washing machine and a freezer and various other bits and pieces, lit only by the faint shaded light from the open kitchen door.

"Lesley?" he shouted, moving farther into the room. "Lesley! Are you here?"

Dean had followed the path through the woods to where it forked; the right fork, Kayleigh had told him, took you to the rear of the cottage; the left fork took you to Brook Way Bridge. He had taken the left fork and was now standing on the bridge, watching the water as it danced and gurgled beneath him. He had been there a long time, looking up when vehicles passed on Brook Way, the inspired name of the road that ran alongside the brook, keeping an eye on the one-track road that branched off it, the official road to the cottage.

He had seen a van leave by that side road and drive past him; that must be the van they had borrowed to move their stuff, he had reasoned. Kayleigh had said it had to be back with its owner before eleven. A few minutes later, he had seen a black cab sweep past him going the opposite way; he had expected it to carry on along Brook Way, but it had taken the turn to the cottage. The taxi had left after a moment and had come back toward him, empty, its hire light on.

He had seen a postman cycle up the side road and back down again, and now, he saw a man walk down it and come along Brook Way toward him. As he drew closer, Dean swore to himself and turned his back, looking down at the stream. Because if Dean could recognize him, then he could recognize Dean, and that was the very last thing Dean wanted.

But that must mean that she was on her own now.

"Even if you left her, things couldn't go back the way they were," said Theresa.

"I know. I don't think I'd want them to—and I'm sure you wouldn't."

"No," she agreed. She wasn't so crazy about her new life, but she hadn't been that fond of the old one. It just took a while, getting back into some sort of social groove, after all these years.

"And I don't want to leave her. But I don't want to go to Australia, either."

"Then why are you going?"

He moved his shoulders in a disconsolate shrug.

Theresa tried another tack. "So it's just Australia. If you weren't going to Australia, you would be happy. Yes?"

He looked into the middle distance for some moments, which was all the answer she needed.

"I don't know," he said, at last. "I just feel as though I've been taken over. Australia might be what's making me feel like that. But . . ." He looked at her then. "But I think I felt like this even before Australia was an issue."

Theresa felt more like his mother than ever. It wasn't everyone who had to put up with their ex-partners unburdening themselves about their current partners. "Then why on earth did you agree to it?" she asked.

"I don't know. Lesley is . . . very forceful."

"She bullied you into it."

"No!" Then, less emphatically, "No."

"Is that 'no' in its affirmative sense? The sense in which you used it when she said you should take the job? You knew it wasn't working out with her, and yet here you are, Australia-bound. Why?"

"Because she's really worried about Kayleigh. She genuinely wants to get her away, but without Kayleigh realizing that she's doing it on purpose. And I'm the one who's been offered the job in Australia, so she needs me to go through with it. And . . . well, because I couldn't think of enough good reasons why not."

"Why are you telling me this, Ian? What are you expecting me to do? Give you a note for Lesley? 'Please excuse Ian from going to Australia, as he has a bad cold'? If you really don't want to go, then you have to tell her, and tell Jerry." She'd have to get started on her round soon; she had to pick up from her ladies, and if she was late leaving, it put the whole schedule out. "And then you have to work out whether you want to go anywhere with her."

"I do! That is . . . I really want to be with her. But it doesn't seem to matter what I say. We do what she thinks we should do. I just—" He sighed, shrugged.

Theresa shook her head. "Well, the remedy's in your own hands. I must say I thought you had more backbone than that."

That wasn't strictly true; Ian had never had much gumption, really. Theresa had simply never had the desire to tell him what to do or how to live his life, and before that his father had allowed him to do exactly what he wanted, so in a way he was only now finding out that he *could* be bullied.

It was almost five to eleven, and time she was on her way. "Sorry, Ian. I have to go."

They walked down to the garage area; Theresa opened the van door and got in as Ian made to get into his car, but he straightened up again.

"Maybe I will tell her we're not going anywhere," he said. "We can live in the cottage, pay you for your half."

Theresa closed the van door as he drove past her, and shook her head again. If she knew Ian, he would like the idea of having Lesley and Kayleigh living in his bolt-hole even less than he liked the idea of Australia. And even if he did go and lay the law down to Lesley, it wouldn't be because he wanted to; it would be because she, Theresa, had told him to. And the problem with that was that he didn't know how to be forceful; he would probably just create an atmosphere and end up going to Australia anyway.

She hadn't told him that she had rung Phil; she would have if his name had cropped up, but it didn't. She'd tell him later, because she supposed—a little reluctantly—that they ought to know that he would be getting in touch, because he had been furious when she'd told him about Australia.

Lloyd stared at the petrol gauge. Stu, for such he liked to be known, had said that he'd given the car a good long run to make sure it was all right, and it hadn't occurred to Lloyd to check the petrol. He would have thought that Stu would have done that, but evidently Stu had not, and now Lloyd was slowly, gently, inexorably, slowing to a halt. On a dual carriageway, with traffic behind him. He put on his hazard lights and coasted down what turned out to be a slight incline, offering up thanks to whoever or whatever ordained these things that he was going to be able to turn off into a business park where at least the car wouldn't be a danger to other road users.

But it was miles from a petrol station. He got out with a sigh, took the empty petrol can out of the boot, and locked the car, walking back toward the main road. Once there, he had a long haul, but he hadn't seen a taxi and he had no idea about these little shuttle buses. If either of these modes of transport appeared, he would take it. He walked on, turning every now and then to check the vehicles behind him. And this, it appeared, was his lucky day; not only had he been saved from a life of house-husbandry, but within one minute of leaving his car the gods sent him, not a taxi or a bus, but a patrol car, which he flagged down to the surprise of its two occupants.

The one on the passenger side rolled down the window. "Sir?"

"It's . . ." Lloyd thought hard, and the name came to him. Today he really had been touched by angels. "It's Harker, isn't it? Eddie Harker?"

"Yes, sir," said the young man, looking wary.

"Any chance of a lift to a petrol station, Eddie?" He held the petrol can aloft. "It's a long story. Don't ask."

Harker opened the rear door, and the driver, Lloyd could see as he got in the back, was Don Rogers, whom he'd known for years, so no feats of memory required. "Don," he said, by way of greeting, and got a nod back.

"The Brook Way roundabout service station's nearest, I reckon," Don said, pulling away.

En route, Lloyd listened with half an ear to the messages on the radio until the one that made them all sit up.

"Can someone take a treble nine at Brook Way Cottage, Stansfield? We have a report of a woman found with severe head wounds, believed dead, but an ambulance is on its way."

"That's us," said Rogers. "We're practically there already. You'll have to come along for the ride, sir."

Harker informed Control that they were on their way.

"Thank you, six-four-one. The area car is also responding. The informant gave his name as Ian Waring—described the victim as his girlfriend, says he found her like that. No other information."

Lloyd would never have admitted it in a million years, but he was enjoying himself hugely. It had been a very long time since he had answered an emergency call with the siren whooping and the blue lights flashing, and they were in a race with the area car; it was making him feel like Charlotte did when her donkey's bell rang. And Don

Rogers was an exhilarating driver; two minutes later, at five past eleven, the car was sweeping round the roundabout, past the service station, heading up Brook Way. No other cars in sight. They had won.

The area car appeared just as their vehicle took the turnoff, and caught them up as they approached the cottage. A yellow Alfa Romeo sports car was parked in front of the house, off the driveway; the garage was empty. The front door stood open, and a man lay on the gravel beside one of the brick columns that supported the porch. The cars stopped, and everyone got out; Rogers was attending to the man on the ground, Harker was telling Control that they had a second injured party in need of medical assistance, and the other two went inside in search of the woman about whom the call had been made.

"His pulse is very weak," said Rogers. "Can you tell me your name?"

"Ian." He coughed.

Lloyd crouched down by the man, who was in considerable pain and swimming in and out of consciousness. His clothes were bloodstained, and his leg was clearly broken; two trails of disturbed gravel led from where he lay back toward the garage, suggesting that a vehicle had come out from the garage and run him down. Lloyd could see blood on the pale sole of the man's shoe, and he frowned, not convinced that any of the blood was actually his. He bent his head as the man's eyes opened and he tried to speak.

"Intruder—man . . ."

"All right, Ian, you just hang on," said Rogers. "Talk to me, Ian. Ian—can you hear me? Do you know your other name, Ian?"

But he closed his eyes, and despite all efforts to keep him awake, he lost consciousness.

One of the constables came to the door of the cottage. "Sir, there's a dead woman here, all right. She's been battered to death, by the looks of things. And she's still warm."

Lloyd stood up. "Tell them we need the whole shooting match here. And tell them to inform acting DI Sandwell that we'll need an incident room set up."

"And find out where the bloody ambulance is!" shouted Rogers. "Or we'll lose this one as well."

CHAPTER FIVE

Judy had strolled back along Bridge Street, window-shopping for a wedding outfit in Malworth's expensive boutiques. If she was having to go through with this wedding, she might at least get something worth having out of it, as she had informed Charlotte. "Not that your dada isn't worth having," she had added. "But I still don't see why we have to get married. If you ask me, marriage just complicates things."

Now she was entering the park, pulling the pram carefully up the steps to the footbridge over the river, and bumping it down the steps at the other side, an activity that Charlotte found very diverting. Judy liked having the whole place virtually to herself; the regular dog walkers and joggers tended to be early-morning or early-evening users, and mid-morning on a weekday was quiet and peaceful. By the time the school holidays came, the public park would be full of picnickers, organized and disorganized games, walkers, cyclists, cross-country runners, staged open-air events, and everything else, but today, on this sunny, breezy Friday morning, it was quiet.

The only other people she could see were a long way off; an old couple sitting on a bench, looking toward the river, two women strolling through the gardens, an artist doing a watercolor of a statue, his paper weighted down, and, setting a baby in a carry-cot onto folding wheels, a girl in a gray sweatshirt and black jeans, even younger than the ones who worked at the nursery. She walked off, wheeling the baby along the path by the river, disappearing behind the weeping willows that trailed their branches in the water.

The park had something for everyone; Judy turned back to Charlotte. "Do you think you need a garden, Charlotte?"

Charlotte blinked at her solemnly.

"Your dada does. He says children should have gardens—he says his father had a strawberry patch in his garden and you should have one, too, so you can pick them and eat them while they're warm from the sun, he says. I don't think he knows the first thing about growing strawberries, though. And I know I don't."

Charlotte gave a little contented sigh.

"I think you'd like having this park to play in. If you want to pick strawberries, we could go to one of these pick-your-own places, couldn't we? You'd like that. He says it wouldn't be the same, but I think it means that at least you'll be guaranteed some strawberries to pick. Of course, I'm not romantic, not like him. You'll find that out."

She carried on chatting as she strolled in the sunshine, stopping as another park user, a solitary woman, approached. Talking to Charlotte was all very well, but until she was a little older it could be regarded as eccentric by a passerby. Judy smiled and issued the standard park greeting, which varied only with the weather: "Lovely day!"

But the woman, lost in her own thoughts, just looked at Judy vaguely and passed on.

Once she was out of earshot, Judy carried on. "There's a toddlers' playground somewhere—shall we go and look at it? It might give me an idea of what to expect."

She wheeled Charlotte along to the fingerpost to find out which way she should be heading and spent some time examining its many fingers before finding it. "This way," she said, maneuvering the pram with the same lack of expertise as that with which she maneuvered a car.

Charlotte smiled at her—laughed at her? Judy smiled back, but the smile froze on her lips as she heard the scream. It seemed to come from the direction in which she had just walked, and Judy, moving as quickly as she could with the pram, retraced her steps and saw the girl she had seen earlier, standing under the willow tree, by the pram, her hands to her mouth. The old couple were making their way toward her, but the ladies in the garden were too far away to have heard the scream, and the artist had apparently left, because he was nowhere to be seen now. Judy got there first.

"She's gone!" the girl said. "The baby's gone!"

"Did you see anyone near the pram?" Judy automatically checked the time, and it was seven minutes past eleven; she had seen the girl with the baby not five minutes ago, so it had to have happened very recently. The woman who had passed her—where was she? Judy looked round, but there was no sign of her now.

Judy showed her ID and asked the couple if they had seen the woman, but they hadn't, and neither had the girl, who stood there, clutching a mobile phone, saying she had only left the baby for a moment. The man went up the steps to the bridge to see if he could see anyone on Bridge Street answering the woman's description but came back, shaking his head.

Judy stared at the empty pram, and the thought that it might have been Charlotte jolted her system; she didn't know if it was her maternal instinct kicking in at last or just the reaction of anyone who had care and control of someone helpless and trusting to the thought that a moment's inattention could lead to this, but she felt physically sick and had to get herself under control, marshal her thoughts.

"Have you rung the police?"

"No—I . . ." The girl looked at the phone in her hand. "I was just getting the phone for—" She broke off. "No."

Judy took out her own mobile phone. "What's your name?"

"Andrea Merry."

"And you're the baby's mother?" Judy was dialing 999 as she spoke.

"No, I'm just the nanny. The baby's name is Emma. Emma Jane Crawford."

For the second time in as many moments, Judy was stunned into noncomprehension. Emma Jane Crawford? That was Charlotte's twin; it must be. She and Lloyd talked about her often; he always used her full name like that. Judy had got to know Emma's mother in the maternity unit, and Lloyd had met her father; she felt as though they were personal friends.

"How old is she?" Judy asked, hoping, irrationally, that the answer would prove that it was some other baby of the same name, some baby who didn't share her birthday with Charlotte, whose parents she and Lloyd didn't know.

"Just over five months."

It *was* Charlotte's twin. Judy had to work hard to be professional about the whole thing as she told the emergency operator she wanted the police.

"And what was Emma wearing?" she asked the girl.

"A Winnie-the-Pooh all-in-one."

Judy reported the incident, then set about getting details, which would at least save some time.

"You didn't see anything, Andrea? Someone running off?"

"No—nothing."

"Where were you when it happened?"

"I realized I'd left my mobile phone in the car, so I went back to get it. I left Emma in the shade, under the tree."

"Where's your car?"

"On the Bridge Street car park. I went shopping with her, so I just left the car there and walked here."

The Bridge Street car park was a few hundred yards along from the footbridge; most Riverside Park users left their cars in the grassed area marked off in the park itself.

Judy looked at her in frank dismay. "You went back to the car park and left the baby on her own?"

"Yes—well, it was quicker without the pram. I didn't want to take it apart again, and I didn't want to bump Emma all the way up the steps and back down the other side twice. I was only gone a couple of minutes."

Judy had to remind herself that it wasn't her job to apportion blame, just to find out as much as she could. And even that wasn't her job, strictly speaking. She was a witness, not an investigating officer.

"How long were you back at the car?"

"Just long enough to pick up the phone. I came straight back."

It could have been the woman Judy saw, but it needn't have been. Anyone could have been walking along the street or crossing the bridge, seen the pram, and just taken Emma from it. It would have taken only a few seconds to be back on the road, merging with the Friday morning shoppers. It would have taken Andrea two minutes at least to get to the car and back.

The Bridge Street car park was big and busy, serving

the main shopping area and the supermarket. "Did anyone stop and watch you as you got Emma out of your
car? Or follow you when you left? Did you see anyone
when you went back to your car?"

The girl shook her head in a blanket answer to all these
questions, which didn't surprise Judy. People would be
busy loading and unloading cars, finding money for the
ticket machine, unlikely to be taking any notice of Andrea and Emma, and Andrea wouldn't have taken any
notice of them.

"But it's only just happened," she said. "She can't have
got far."

"She?" Judy pounced on that. "I thought you didn't
see anything?"

"I meant Emma."

Of course she did. Judy told herself to be rational
about this, stop jumping down the girl's throat, but she
didn't feel rational. She felt scared and sad. Someone was
going to have to tell Nina Crawford what had happened,
and Judy was deeply thankful that she was not officially
in charge. She would gladly leave that to someone else.

A hope, faint and fleeting, that it had been Nina who
had seen Emma, alone and unguarded, and had removed
her from the so-called nanny's so-called care was born in
Judy, just to die again. Nina would have wheeled the
pram away, not snatched the baby from it. And she
would have told Andrea, however angry she was with
her, what she was doing. Because no one would wish that
suffering on anyone. Though Judy wasn't convinced that
Andrea *was* suffering.

And now a nanny was being very firmly crossed off
Judy's range of options, which left just one.

Dean had pulled the car off the road onto the grass and
scrambled out, jumping the brook and missing his foot-

ing as he landed, slipping into the shallow water. He had hauled himself out and, dripping wet, had made his way toward the wood, trying to put as much distance between himself and that car as he could, as fast as he could.

He had seen a handful of kids swinging from the branches of a tree, and they had seen him. Woods were not Dean's natural habitat; if it had been London, there would have been crowds of people and he could have lost himself in moments simply by going into a shop or dodging down a side street. All he could do here was plunge off the track and into cover, which was what he had done.

But it was, he had soon discovered, dense cover; he had felt thin branches whip against his face and arms but had gone deeper and deeper in before glancing behind as he ran, and had been relieved to see nothing but bushes and trees. He had turned back to look where he was going, but it was too late to stop himself pitching headlong to the ground, as something had tripped him up, and he had landed with a bone-jarring thud.

Now he opened his eyes, unsure of what had happened, and tried to assess the damage. He could smell the moist earth, could feel his heart pounding with the exertion and the fear, could hear birdsong high above. When he opened his eyes, he could see the long-dead leaves, moss, and twigs on which he lay and, when he ran his tongue over numbed lips, could even taste them. He wiped the dirt from his mouth and sat up slowly. All his senses, it seemed, were more or less in working order, but something hurt like hell. His chest, he thought.

He put out a hand, but the act of putting his weight on it hurt his chest even more, and he lay back down again with a groan. After a few moments, he tried again, this time prepared for the pain, and got himself into a sitting position. His jeans were torn, and his shoe had come off; he looked round, a little hopelessly, for his missing trainer and was surprised, in this alien landscape, to spot it lying almost hidden in a clump of greenery to which he could not put a name, if it had one. And now he could see, spilling out from the base of its tree, the thick, low branch that had brought him down.

Getting to his feet was difficult and painful but not, he discovered, impossible. He straddled the branch, putting his wet trainer back onto his wet foot again, and leaned back against the tree to recover from the effort. Think, Dean, he told himself. It won't hurt to think. Where are you going from here?

Those kids hadn't followed him, he was sure of that, but he was deep in a part of the wood he didn't know at all; he had no idea how to get to the path that would take him back to town, no idea even in which direction he had been running. From the elevated position of the bus station he had seen that the wood almost encircled the center of the town, stretching out in all directions, dotted with roads and housing estates; if he found a path and started walking, he could come out miles away from the town center.

And if he was going to get back to London, the bus station was his only option; hitching a lift was out, unless Stansfield people were given to stopping for wet, blood-stained strangers. He looked down at himself, at his bare arms scratched and cut, and wasn't sure that anyone would even let him on a bus in this state. He could, he supposed, wait until it was dark, when he would have dried off and the bloodstains—helped by the water— wouldn't be so noticeable, but that was almost twelve hours away.

He couldn't stay in here for twelve hours. And he had a horrible feeling that he would never get out in the dark.

He had to start walking in any direction and keep walking until he found a road. There would be something—road signs, something—to tell him how to get back to the bus station. He would have to think of a story that would account for the state he was in, that was all.

But he'd wait awhile. Until the pain wore off a bit.

One for sorrow, two for joy, thought Phil as a pair of magpies flew down onto the track, then back up again to the roof of the station building.

Not much joy here, he thought as he paced the platform. The train back to London wasn't due until midday, and he would have preferred to have been less conspicuously waiting for it, but the station buffet had apparently closed down and the waiting room was being refurbished. He kept glancing across to the entrance, expecting the police to appear at any minute. Even if the trains were running on time, they had half an hour to work out where he'd be.

Another magpie swooped down onto the hanging basket suspended from a high station lamp standard and away again. One of the pair he'd just seen? Or a third? Phil looked across at the newly painted ticket office on the other side of the rails and could see the two magpies, still busily darting to and fro, while the third wheeled off into the scaffolding where a bridge over the lines was being built to replace the damp, dingy, uneven tunnel under the tracks that Phil had just used. How did the rhyme go on? One for sorrow, two for joy . . . three for a girl.

He sat down on a strange metal frame with a hinged plastic shelf on which it was just possible to perch, much like the magpies. Once, he'd imagined his life taking the path that most people's lives took; courtship, marriage, children. The courtship and marriage had happened, no children. Just an acrimonious divorce, and then a solitary existence for two years until he had met Lesley. And she had come complete with a little girl. Kayleigh, a bright and mischievous five-year-old with whom Phil had had an instant rapport. Suddenly he had a family.

And everything had been fine until Dean Fletcher came along. Well, Phil amended, perhaps not fine, but at least they had all been together. He frowned a little. Had he really seen Fletcher when he was leaving the cottage? No, he thought, he couldn't have. Even if Fletcher was out of prison, how could he know where Kayleigh was? Young men with cropped dyed blond hair all looked pretty much alike.

A flash of black and white, and another magpie made its appearance, its eye caught by the sun glinting off the track; it landed right in front of Phil, strutting along the sleepers before flying off to join the one on the scaffolding. Two pairs made four, Phil thought. Four magpies. Three for a girl, four for a boy, he thought sadly.

Just over four years ago, he and Lesley had had a little boy, unplanned, but no less welcome for that. Luke, whose short life had brought both joy and sorrow and whose name Phil had spoken this morning for the first time in years, had come and gone within six months, and their lives would never be the same again.

Three more magpies suddenly flew up from the tall hedgerow that skirted the car park behind the station. His two pairs still chattered to one another on the scaffolding and the roof, so that made seven in all. Five for silver, six for gold, Phil thought.

Seven for a secret never to be told.

Judy's description of the woman who had walked past her in the park had been printed out, and in the park Tom handed it out to his team.

"We don't have much to go on," he began. "DCI Hill will be helping compile a photofit when the photofit guy gets here, and we're getting a photograph of Emma printed out, but the description will have to do for now. Superintendent McArthur is heading the investigation, and anything you get that may be relevant should be phoned through to the incident room immediately. If anyone saw a woman answering that description anywhere at all, we need a statement."

The park had no surveillance cameras; in well-behaved Malworth, very few people wanted to deface its statues or destroy its flower beds. Even pickpockets seemed to go elsewhere, as a rule. Criminal activity in the park had increased, of course, like everywhere else, and CCTV was on the Council agenda, but it had not yet been installed.

"And if anyone thinks they actually know who she is, do not—repeat: not—go charging off to interview her. If she is the abductor and she has baby Emma, she needs very careful handling—report back and await instructions."

Tom thought that his time might be better spent walking round the Riverside area with Judy, trying to spot the woman, and McArthur had agreed. Judy was, after all, the only person who knew exactly who she was looking for, and until the public appeals bore fruit they had nothing concrete to go on. If it had been a spur-of-the-moment abduction, the woman might have abandoned the baby and be walking around in a daze. If the baby had been abandoned, they had to find her fast, and this might be the way to do it. Teams of officers would be combing the park for the same reason, and the first team was arriving now, piling out of the van, pulling on the orange jackets that would make them easy to spot if anyone had any information to impart.

If it hadn't been Judy who had seen her, Tom would

have been skeptical of this lone, preoccupied female whom no one else had even noticed, would have thought the witness was perhaps seeking a moment of glory. But it was Judy, and this woman existed.

And then there was the artist. Everyone had seen him, but he had been too far away for them to have any real description at all, save that Judy and the female half of the old couple believed that he had a beard. They had established that the child was not the subject of a custody battle, so a male kidnapper was unlikely, but not unheard of. Everyone who was in the park was being asked about both of these people.

"If anyone thinks they have seen this woman, it's important to find out if they saw her alone or carrying a baby, and whether or not she was with another person or people. If they saw her with a man, we want a description—and we'd be very interested in what, if anything, he was carrying. The man we want to interview is probably carrying a wooden case with artists' equipment in it."

Tom walked down to where Judy, absently jiggling the pram, was talking to Superintendent McArthur, an unknown quantity, having just arrived in Bartonshire last month to take charge at Malworth. He was big, dark-haired, good-looking, the kind of man who suited the uniform. Tom imagined he worked out. And he wasn't much older than Tom himself. One of the fast-track lot, he was Scottish, apparently, but he spoke with the accentless tones of one who had been privately educated.

"Someone's just found a Winnie-the-Pooh all-in-one stuffed into a rubbish bin outside a shop on Bridge Street," Judy told him.

"Which means she's changed the baby's clothes," McArthur said. "This could have been planned. She's probably miles away by now."

Tom nodded. "But my idea's still worth a try, sir. Isn't it?"

"Anything's worth a try."

A few minutes later, Tom and Judy began their apparently pleasant and aimless stroll with Charlotte around Riverside, walking along Bridge Street, the long street that led to the traffic-bearing bridge over the river, its mock-Victorian street furniture designed to blend in with the real Victorian architecture.

Tom was pushing the pram, pulling faces at Charlotte, making her smile sleepily, while Judy scrutinized every other female on the street. Until now, Charlotte had slept through most of the excitement, apparently; Tom thought about his own children, neither of whom had seemed to sleep at all before their first birthdays, and asked Judy if she realized how lucky she was with the placid and cheerful Charlotte. Why he and Liz were putting themselves through it again he wasn't sure, but the baby they had assured each other in February they didn't want and had immediately set about trying to conceive was due in late December.

"Oh, yes," Judy said. "Don't forget who her father is—I was expecting the worst."

Tom smiled. Lloyd's fuse was short, and few people who knew him had escaped his sharp tongue when something—often something of no real importance—sparked off his quick temper, which was almost always restored as soon as it had been lost, but he could do a lot of emotional damage in those few minutes. Judy's influence had, Tom thought, made him less inclined to do that, so maybe it wasn't luck; perhaps it was her influence that worked with Charlotte. "I think you must just be a natural, Judy," he said.

"I hope I am, because I don't think I'm going to be able to go back to work."

Tom didn't want to hear that. "Why?"

"Because I had finally decided that a nanny was the only option." She sighed. "And then this happened. How can I trust Charlotte to someone who might just decide to walk off and leave her?"

"Come on, Judy. She's a seventeen-year-old kid—she's not a nanny, whatever she calls herself. She's a mother's helper."

"Nina Crawford trusted her."

Mrs. Crawford didn't go out to work; she had three-year-old Dominic to look after as well as Emma. She had employed Andrea purely to help her out and, when the wet spring had finally given way to sunshine, had been pleased when Andrea had suggested taking Emma to the park. It had been an established routine; Tom felt a little sorry for Andrea.

"These girls at that nursery aren't much older than Andrea," Judy went on. "They're not responsible enough to be left in charge of babies."

"Oh, I don't know about that. I think most of them are. Especially the ones that work in nurseries. And . . . for what it's worth, I think Andrea was very unlucky."

"Unlucky? She was more concerned about phoning her friends than she was about looking after Emma."

"She was still desperately unlucky." Tom leaned over the pram and spun one of Charlotte's toys for her. Charlotte, wide awake now, shouted until he hit another one.

"She'll make you do that for hours," Judy warned him. "Her games are interminable."

"That's OK." Tom patiently played the game as he walked along, rather enjoying it. After a few moments, he tried again. "It was a one-in-a-million chance that Emma was snatched. It really was."

"Huh?"

"It's not what you'd call frequent, is it? Have you ever dealt with a baby snatch before?"

"No. But that's not the point." As she talked, Judy was looking at every one of the lunchtime shoppers who were milling round the boutiques and cafés of Riverside. "She should have been where she was paid to be—with Emma."

Tom stopped walking. "I think you're being a bit hard on her."

Judy took her eyes off the passersby to look at Tom. "Why are you defending her?" she demanded.

Tom shrugged and carried on pushing, mainly because Charlotte was volubly objecting to the unscheduled halt. "Because it would take her a couple of minutes to nip back to the car park. My mother once forgot she'd taken me shopping with her. Went home and left me outside a shop in the pram. In Liverpool."

"She *didn't*!"

Tom grinned at Judy's horrified expression. "She did. She went racing back, and there I was, perfectly happy. I'd been there for half an hour."

"That was over thirty years ago. Times have changed."

It was *always* different thirty years ago, Tom thought. In thirty years, they would be saying that it was different thirty years ago. "All I'm saying is that it was very bad luck that the only person who saw the baby unattended was someone who stole her. Most people would have just kept an eye on her until Andrea came back, and told her off for leaving her. Or at worst, would have ignored it, and walked on."

"And that excuses what she did?"

"No. I just think the outcome was a bit much, considering what she actually did. Like . . ." He searched to find a suitable analogy. "Like when driving without due

care causes a fatal accident. It doesn't make it dangerous
driving, does it?"

"You wouldn't want the driver as a chauffeur, though,
would you?"

The scene-of-crime people had bagged up a large cat-
shaped cast-iron doorstop that weighed about six
pounds and showed all the signs of having inflicted the
terrible injuries on the woman who lay dead on the floor
of the utility room. The rough, dull surface of the cast
iron was unlikely to produce fingerprints, but these days
they could coax prints off surfaces once thought impossible, so Lloyd was keeping his fingers crossed.

Freddie, the pathologist they were lucky to have working on their doorstep, and a longtime friend of Lloyd,
began his in situ examination. Lloyd, aware that Freddie
preferred to work at the scene without being interrupted
by questions, left him to it and went through the kitchen,
where the floor was marked with blood that had come
off someone's shoes; chalk circles indicated that they had
been examined. There had been blood on one of Waring's shoes; he had probably left the footprints himself, but there was a chance that it was the murderer.

The marks continued down the hallway, as did Lloyd,
but they carried on to the front door, where one of the
scene-of-crime officers was working, whereas Lloyd
turned left into the sitting room. The photographer was
taking shots of the overturned occasional table, the
smashed mirror hanging crookedly on the wall, and the
glass splinters that littered the carpet.

Lloyd would normally at this stage be interviewing
the person who had reported the crime, but not this time;
Ian Waring was in the accident and emergency unit at
Barton General, and he was the one who had reportedly
called the police. The hospital had confirmed Lloyd's

supposition that the blood on Waring's clothes was not his own; Waring's most serious injuries, they said, were internal, and the fractures to his leg and foot had not punctured the skin. The injuries were consistent with his having been hit by a vehicle and crushed against the brick column.

They were currently attempting to stabilize his condition in order that they might operate, but the operation itself would be touch and go and a great deal would depend on the patient's ability to survive it. The prognosis was not particularly hopeful; he might not regain consciousness.

They had found a mobile phone lying underneath Waring when the paramedics had moved him; last number redial had produced the emergency operator. The phone had blood on it, blood that again had not come from Ian Waring, and that constituted a little puzzle, in Lloyd's opinion.

And he would normally be talking to the neighbors, but not this time, he thought, as he left the sitting room and went upstairs, because there were none. He would be inquiring into the background of the victims, checking for diaries, letters—anything that would give him a clue as to why a woman had died and a man had been severely injured. Not this time, he discovered, because this house had nothing of that sort to yield; it had been cleared of anything personal. The bookshelves were empty, the drawers, the cupboards, all cleared. The packing cases were being gone through, but so far nothing of any use had been found.

And, usually, he would have had the tireless Tom Finch to do what he would doubtless call the legwork, having been brought up on TV cop shows, but he had been sent to Malworth to join the huge team mobilized to investigate a baby snatch that had just taken place.

Lloyd hadn't been prepared for the lurch his heart had given when Bob Sandwell told him that a baby had been stolen in Malworth; for a dreadful moment, he had been aware of only one baby in Malworth. But someone else was having to cope with that terrible worry, and he couldn't help feeling grateful for that.

He was a sergeant short at the moment, because Bob was acting DI and had gone to the hospital to find out what he could about Waring and the incident in Malworth required more immediate manpower than the murder, so, for the moment, his sole CID assistance was the ever-reliable DC Alan Marshall. If a murder team turned out to be necessary, it would be assembled from all the divisions, but sometimes murder wasn't that difficult to solve.

Marshall was amiable, Scottish, and dogged, but he didn't have Tom Finch's sharp observation powers or Bob Sandwell's uncanny ability to find out what they needed to know. Sandwell always seemed to know just who to ask and what to ask, which was why he was the man to go to if you wanted all the latest gossip. If anyone at Barton General had found out anything at all about Ian Waring, Bob would get to hear about it—apart from anything else, his sister was a staff nurse there, and he had acquired a lot of useful information that way.

The Alfa Romeo parked outside the front door belonged to Ian Waring, and the address held by the DVLA, his bank, and everyone else was this cottage, so that seemed to indicate that they were in the process of moving out. Lloyd had already assumed that; the lack of personal belongings suggested that they had already been removed and that only the things that were needed until the last moment were being packed today.

Some of the cases were in the bedrooms, some in the kitchen—each had been packed with what you would expect from these rooms and had been closed, ready for transport. But the one in the utility room had not been closed and had clothes in it; it seemed likely to Lloyd that the victim had removed them from the washing machine and was packing them in the carton when she was killed. The contents of the packing case had spilled out when it had been overturned and were splashed with the blood that had gone everywhere. That meant that her attacker would almost certainly also have been splashed, which was, so far, the only helpful thing about this crime.

"Chief Inspector?"

Lloyd went downstairs to where the scene-of-crime officer stood in the hallway by the front door.

"This letter was on the mat," she said. "There's a partial shoe print in blood on it, and it's clearer than the others—I think we should be able to confirm whether or not Mr. Waring's shoe made it." She handed him the letter, now encased in polythene, the shoe print preserved. "It's addressed to Dr. Theresa Black."

Things were looking up; possibly useful evidence, and the deceased had acquired an identity at last. Lloyd looked at the envelope, taking out his glasses. It was junk mail; its contents would be of no use, and it had no postmark. But if they were moving out, the letter had presumably arrived this morning or it would already have been picked up, even if it was just to throw it in the bin. It looked as though the postman had been here sometime this morning, and that meant that they had a lead—slender, to be sure, but a lead.

He went to the front door, which still stood open, like every other door in the house. Which was odd, Lloyd thought. "Alan!" he called. "Here, a minute."

DC Marshall, slow-moving, slow-talking, but painstakingly thorough, detached himself from the SOCOs examining the car and ducked under the flapping, snapping tape that cordoned off the porch area where Waring had been found. "Sir?"

"Find out who delivered this, and ask him if he can come and make a statement."

Alan Marshall took the envelope. "They don't think the Alfa was involved in what happened to Waring. Do you want it taken to the lab, just in case?"

They had found the keys to the cottage and garage in Waring's jacket pocket; Lloyd presumed the car would be as safe in the garage as anywhere, since it seemed unlikely to be going to yield any evidence. "No," he said. "I'll get it put back in the garage when the scene-of-crime people are finished in there."

"Something else, sir. An Audi Quattro's been found abandoned not that far from here. It's registered to a Mrs. Lesley Newton at a London address, and it's not been reported stolen, so it seemed a bit strange that someone abandoned it. There might not be any connection, but I've arranged for it to go to the lab, and the Met are going to trace Mrs. Newton for us."

"Did anyone see the driver?"

"A group of boys—these kids that hang about down by the clearing, causing mischief. They saw him running away from the car into the woods. One of them described him as being in his twenties, with short blond hair. No description of what he was wearing, but the lad said he was in a bit of a state."

"I think he's got a bit of explaining to do when we catch up with him."

Marshall assumed the anxious look that his colleagues knew well. "It might be a stolen car, sir—just hasn't been missed yet. He could have abandoned it when he saw all the police cars. It could be a wild-goose chase."

Alan Marshall could always be relied upon to look on

the gloomy side of everything. "I know," Lloyd said. "But I'd sooner be chasing a wild goose than chasing nothing at all. Let's hope the postman has something interesting to tell us. I should be back at the station by about . . ." He consulted his watch. ". . . three o'clock. See if you can get him there for then."

His mobile rang as Marshall left, and it was Bob Sandwell, at the hospital, saying that the hospital had found Ian Waring's donor card, which had been countersigned by one Theresa Black, and that one of the nurses had known him since they'd been in their teens; she said that he had lived in the old woodsman's cottage in Stansfield with Theresa Black, the last she heard. She had known of Theresa rather than known her personally.

"Does anyone know her at the hospital?" Lloyd asked. "She seems to be a doctor."

He heard Sandwell talk to someone before replying. "No," he said. "She's not a medical doctor—she's got a Ph.D. in something."

Two things occurred to Lloyd as he got that confirmation of the deceased's identity; one was that he had been right about Sandwell's ability to find the right person at the right time, and the other was that Waring must be in a very bad way if they had looked for a donor card, and that wasn't good. He was beginning to feel as upbeat and optimistic about this as Alan Marshall.

"I'm on my way back to the station to take charge of the incident room, unless you want me for anything else," Sandwell said.

"No—you carry on. I'll be there at about three."

Lloyd went back through the kitchen into the utility room, to find Freddie supervising the removal of the body, and beckoned him into the less oppressive kitchen.

"Well?"

"Well. You don't need me to tell you that she was hit

several times with a heavy, blunt instrument. And that's about all I can tell you."

"Time of death?"

"From what your officer said about the temperature of the body, and the readings I've taken, I'd say you found her well within an hour of her death." He turned back toward the utility room. "Was the light on in there when your lads found her?"

"Yes. Why?"

"The body's been disturbed since it happened. Not much—turned over on its back from lying on its side, I'd say. I'd have said it was perhaps someone checking to see how badly hurt she was, but if the light was on . . . well, there wouldn't really be any need, would there?"

"No," said Lloyd, with some feeling. "Was it definitely the doorstop that was used?"

"It seems to have been something of that general size and shape, and the doorstop has what looks like blood on it, so I'd say yes, it was."

Lloyd pointed through to the utility room. "And it definitely happened in there?"

"Unless you've got another body with its brains bashed out somewhere, because someone's blood and brain tissue has been splashed all over the utility room, and, simple soul that I am, I'm inclined to believe it belongs to the dead woman found in there. *Is* there another body with its brains bashed out?"

"Just the one so far, thank goodness. And they were good brains, apparently. She was Theresa Black, Ph.D., before this happened to her."

Freddie nodded seriously, then smiled, the sudden smile that completely altered his naturally somber features. "So Dr. Black was killed in the utility room with the doorstop, was she? The question obviously is: Where was Professor Plum?"

Lloyd had to assume it was how Freddie coped. "Very funny, Freddie," he said as his mobile rang again.

"Marshall here, sir. The post office say the postman should be back in the depot any minute, and they'll send him to the station for three o'clock."

"Good."

"And the guy I spoke to says the house has been up for sale, and was empty for the last few weeks. But the post office wasn't given a forwarding address, so they were still delivering mail."

Lloyd tapped his mobile gently against his temple as he thought. The house had been empty? Now it seemed that they must have been moving in, but Sandwell's contact said that Ian Waring had lived here for years. So *he* must have been moving out, and that meant—

"Sir? Do you want me back at the cottage?"

Lloyd gave his attention to Marshall again. "Nothing can be simple, can it?" he said. "No. Report to Bob Sandwell—I'm sure he'll have plenty for you to do." He terminated the call and sighed. This new information meant that the victim was quite possibly whoever Waring had sold the house to and needn't be Dr. Black at all. That would upset the Clue-themed jokes that Freddie was doubtless working on even now.

"What have I told you about theories?" Freddie said, when he told him, and strode past him to the door. "I'll be able to do the postmortem this afternoon!" he called as he disappeared down the hallway. "Half past four, sharp. Don't be late." There was a moment's pause; then his head appeared round the door again. "Maybe by then you'll have detected who the victim is—then you can move on to the trickier question of who actually murdered her."

Lloyd pulled a face.

*   *   *

*". . . the baby was abducted from Malworth's Riverside
Park at a few minutes after eleven o'clock this morning.
Police say they are anxious to trace a woman seen in the
vicinity just before the abduction, in order that she may
be eliminated from their inquiries. She is described as
around thirty years old, with a slim build, shoulder-
length brown hair, and wearing a pale yellow sleeveless
summer dress.*

*"Superintendent Ewan McArthur spoke to Jim Bol-
solver a few minutes ago, and this is what he had to say:*

*" 'We would like to interview this lady, both to elimi-
nate her from the inquiry and as a potential witness. We
think she may have vital evidence which would help us
reunite baby Emma with her parents, who are, as you
can imagine, totally distraught. Obviously, if anyone
thinks they may have seen this lady, or was in the park or
anywhere in the Riverside area this morning and thinks
they may have seen something—however insignificant—
we would like to hear from them. And if the abductor is
listening to me now, I would ask you to think of what
Emma's parents are going through, and please get in touch
with the police.' "*

Theresa sighed a little as she reached into the back of
the van for the bundle of ironed bed linen she was about
to deliver. Bad news seemed all wrong in weather like
this, somehow.

She wondered, as she delivered the ironing and found
change for the twenty-pound note she was offered, what
it was that drove women to that. She and Ian had never
really discussed children, which was probably just as
well, in view of how they had ended up. Of course, they
might not have grown apart if they had had a family; she
would never know now. But why would being unable to

have a baby assume such terrible proportions that you would steal someone else's?

She got back into the van, and to the background of Radio Barton's pop songs she made her deliveries. She was halfway through when the two o'clock bulletin came on. It led with the baby, but instead of the minor news items that had followed the one earlier, this time there was more bad news.

"Reports are just coming in that police were called this morning to a house in the Byford Forest area of Stansfield, where they found the body of a woman and a man they described as 'seriously injured.' The man is undergoing emergency surgery at Barton General Hospital. No further details have been released."

And that news was very close to home—Byford Forest wasn't a forest but a housing estate. It got its name from the woodland that had once covered that whole area, and it included Brook Way Wood. Whoever these people were, they had been, technically, her neighbors. Not that she would know them; the cottage was too isolated for that. But even so, it made her give a little shiver. Had he murdered his wife and then tried to kill himself? Probably. And she wondered what drove men to that.

It was odd that the genders favored one type of crime over another. Men rarely became obsessed with babies, and women rarely reached that sort of murderous despair. It might be an interesting academic study; she had been trying to think of what she would like to do.

The baby's head was warm against Kayleigh's face as she walked along the dusty path toward the cottage, her heart beating faster and faster.

She came to the edge of the woods and could see the corner of the house; she walked slowly toward it, unsure of what to do. But the decision was taken out of her hands; as soon as she had rounded the corner to walk to the front gate, she was met by a uniformed policeman.

"Sorry, love, but you can't go in there, I'm afraid. Did you have business with the people who live here?"

"*I* live here. Well, sort—"

"Could you wait there a moment?"

He was calling someone else over, but Kayleigh didn't wait there; she walked farther along until she was at the gateway and she could see the cars and vans and people wearing white overalls and policemen everywhere. A man came up to her then; he was perhaps a bit older than Phil and had even less hair.

"My name's Lloyd," he said, and showed her a card. "I'm a detective from Stansfield Police. What's your name?"

She licked her lips. "Kayleigh Scott."

"Kayleigh. That's a nice name. How old are you, Kayleigh?"

"Fourteen."

"And what's the baby's name?"

"Alexandra."

"Is Alexandra your sister?"

She looked over at the cottage and frowned. Someone she didn't know was driving Ian's car into the garage, and her mother's car wasn't there. Where was it? Where was Ian? She didn't understand what was happening. "Where's Ian?" she asked. "Who's that driving his car? What's happened?"

Chief Inspector Lloyd smiled, but it was a sad smile. "Kayleigh—would you mind if Julie here looked after Alexandra for a few minutes while you and I had a little chat?"

Kayleigh gave the baby to the policewoman and allowed herself to be steered to one of the cars. Lloyd opened the rear door of one and invited her to sit down.

He didn't get into the car with her; he just crouched down to speak to her.

"Are you related to Ian Waring?"

She shook her head. "He's my mum's boyfriend."

He took a short breath. "Is your mother called Theresa Black?"

"No." She frowned again. "That was who Ian lived with before he came to live with us."

He looked puzzled. "And you live here?"

"Sort of. It's Ian's cottage." She looked over at it again. "We're moving in today."

"Oh, I see." He thought for a moment before he spoke again. "Something very bad has happened here, Kayleigh. I'm afraid Ian's been badly hurt. He's in hospital."

Kayleigh stared at him, her head shaking.

He took a deep breath before he carried on. "And someone has been killed. I'm very, very sorry to have to tell you this, but I think it could be your mother. Can you tell me what she looks like?"

"She's got fair hair, and she's slim. Smaller than me." Kayleigh watched his face as she described her mother. "Is it her?"

He gave a little nod, and his voice was gentle and sad when he spoke. "I think it must be. But we need someone who can tell us for sure, and I don't want to ask you to do it—is there someone who can help us? Someone who can perhaps look after you and Alexandra? Do you have grandparents somewhere?"

She shook her head. Her mother had been brought up by Dr. Barnardo's—that was why she had wanted to adopt her, give her a real home. It didn't matter how good a children's home was, she said; it wasn't the same. And since he'd died, her mum hadn't had much to do with Richard Newton's parents, who Kayleigh supposed were legally her grandparents. She didn't even know where they lived.

"Is there anyone we can contact? Your dad, maybe?"

She didn't know where he was. She didn't answer, just stared at the cottage and all the activity, trying to understand what had happened.

"Well, don't worry. That doesn't matter." He looked across at the cottage, then turned his attention back to her. "Was anyone else here this morning?"

She couldn't answer him.

"When you left with Alexandra, was it just Ian and your mum who were here?"

She couldn't *answer*.

"I am so sorry." He straightened up. "I'll tell you what we'll do. We'll get you and Alexandra somewhere to stay, and maybe we can talk later?"

Maybe. Once she understood what had happened.

CHAPTER SIX

It was like being back on the beat; they had been walking up and down the streets and alleyways of Riverside for over two hours and were now once again following the Andwell along Bridge Street. It was half past two and Judy thought it was a lost cause, but Tom still hadn't given up hope that she might spot their quarry. And he hadn't given up selling child care to her, either, which puzzled her a little.

"But if you employed a nanny, she would be the real McCoy."

"Have you any idea how much they cost?"

"I mean she would be a grown woman—she wouldn't be seventeen. And she wouldn't be going off back to her car instead of watching Charlotte."

"I know. But I still think maybe I should stay at home."

Part-time work had occurred to her; on their first walk along Bridge Street, she had seen again the young woman she had seen that morning, picking her baby up from the Riverside Nursery. They had acknowledged each other again, but still Judy hadn't asked her about the nursery. This time, she had been carrying a briefcase; she had presumably reached the compromise of part-time work, Judy thought, but she doubted if Bartonshire Constabulary had many part-time posts that they would be prepared to give someone of her rank. Not that it would have to be police work at all, really. She could do something else. But it would still mean leaving Charlotte with strangers.

Besides, she had watched the girl put the baby in the pram, and something about her attitude, about the impression she gave, bothered Judy. She didn't want to turn into someone to whom the baby was an inconvenience. She was probably still projecting her own doubts and fears onto this poor girl, but it bothered her, all the same.

"I don't think I can—" She broke off when, in among the people sitting outside a wine bar in the sunshine, a flash of pale lemon caught her eye. Naturally, a bus came between her and the tables just as she had spotted it and it took an age to drag its length past her, but when it had, the yellow dress was still there, and in it was the woman she had seen in the park. She had held out no hope at all of Tom's idea working, but it had. She touched his sleeve. "That's her," she said, nodding across the road and turning away in case she was recognized. "The couple at the table farthest from us. That's the woman I saw."

Tom looked across at the couple and took out his mobile phone. "What about him?"

"I couldn't swear to it being the same man, but that's the wooden case that was beside the easel." The man was also about thirty and did indeed have a beard but no mustache. Judy always objected to that, for some reason that she couldn't explain. He and the woman were ostensibly eating a late lunch but were in fact engrossed in serious, possibly confrontational conversation.

She looked at Tom. It might still have been a waste of time. "Where's the baby?" she asked. "Maybe they've got nothing to do with it."

Tom pressed the short code for the incident room. "Or maybe they were stealing her for someone else," he said, his voice grim. He got through and asked for Superintendent McArthur.

No. No, it was bad enough that something like this had happened in Malworth without it being a criminal, rather than a desperate, act. But Tom could be right, she reluctantly conceded, because the man and the woman certainly didn't seem to be together in the park and now they were.

Tom spoke briefly and put the phone away, leaning back on the wall, smiling at her as though he were making small talk. "We're to watch them, follow them if necessary."

Judy leaned her arms on the wall, facing the river, her back to the couple. "Why are they just sitting there? Wouldn't you want to get as far away as possible?"

Tom nodded. "But I think we've got a falling-out, by the looks of things. They're definitely arguing about something."

"Why come out in the open to argue, rather than stay in the wine bar? And what's his role in the setup?"

"I think they might have targeted Emma," Tom said. "That she was always going to be snatched, whatever Andrea had done. Andrea takes her to the park most mornings—he was there to watch for her, and as soon as she arrived, he contacted the woman, and packed up his easel for a quick getaway. Perhaps Andrea was going to be distracted by him, and Emma snatched by her."

"And Andrea just happened to make it easy for them?" Judy doubted that. If they had snatched the baby, she thought that Andrea's story should be examined rather more closely than it had been. And where had the baby gone? "We should check out the wine bar," she said. "They must have been in there the last couple of times we passed."

"Here we go," said Tom. "That was quick."

Judy looked away from the river to see one squad car

approach from one end of the street and an unmarked car and another squad car from the other end. The two squad cars waited, and the other car pulled up beside Tom and Judy.

Superintendent McArthur wound down the window. "So which of that lot are we after?"

Judy indicated the couple, and, accompanied by two officers, McArthur approached the wine bar. There was an earnest shaking of heads, a display of puzzled innocence, then apparently ready compliance; in moments, the two were being taken away in separate cars and McArthur was on his way back to Judy and Tom.

"They went voluntarily to give statements as possible witnesses. They didn't seem too worried. Anyway—whether they had anything to do with it or not, that was good work, both of you. Let's hope we're as quick at finding the baby."

Tom and Judy had been watching the wine bar throughout the muted drama; no one had left. McArthur agreed that Tom should make a discreet search of the place.

"I don't want to spook anyone if the baby is still there. Just get a good look round—if there's a baby on the premises, I'll take it from there."

McArthur and Judy waited, with McArthur, less harassed than the last time they had met, making baby noises at Charlotte, who beamed at him, as she did at everyone who took the trouble to talk to her. If Judy did get Malworth CID, McArthur would be her boss, and she thought that she could live with that. She sighed, wishing there was an easy way out of her dilemma. After about five minutes, Tom came out, indicated that there was nothing of interest, and Charlotte's new best friend left.

As McArthur's car drove off, Tom walked back across the road toward Judy, shaking his head. "I checked everywhere," he said, joining her. "Told them I was from Trading Standards. And I asked if anyone ever brought children or—" He broke off as his eye was obviously caught by something on the river behind her.

Judy turned, but she didn't know where he was looking. She turned back to see him running along the pavement, leaning over the wall, shouting to people on the opposite bank. She pushed Charlotte along to where he stood, his hands on his head, his face white. "What is it?" she said. "What's wrong?"

He spoke in an appalled whisper. "A baby's body, Judy. I saw a baby's body caught up in those reeds."

Judy stared at him, at the river, then back at him. "Are you absolutely sure?"

He nodded. "I shouted, but they couldn't hear. It was a baby's body, Judy. There was nothing I could . . ." He closed his eyes. "It was dragged under."

Dean opened his eyes, disoriented and aching all over, the sound of shifting branches overhead. Where the hell was he? Gradually, he became aware that he was sitting on the branch of a tree, leaning against its trunk, and remembered, his heart plunging.

His mouth was dry and he couldn't think very clearly, but at least he wasn't wringing wet anymore. But he should be; he hadn't been asleep that long. His mind began to clear a little, and while he might not be a country boy, even he could see that the sun, which had been climbing, was now on its way down the sky, and he accepted that he must have been asleep for at least a couple of hours. Maybe he really could stay here until dark, he thought, then shook his head. He couldn't do that; the pain was even worse, and he had a feeling he ought to be seeing a doctor or something. He had to start walking and make his way back to the bus station somehow.

He pushed himself up from the branch, his arm across his chest. As long as he took it slowly, he would be all right. Just keep walking, he told himself. Find a path, follow it, and get to civilization. How difficult could that be? It wasn't the Black Forest; it was just a wood. He stumbled as he set off, as though he'd had too much to drink, and he steadied himself, his hand on a tree. He wished his thinking processes were a bit sharper; he had to think up some sort of story to account for how he looked if anyone asked, and he couldn't seem to concentrate on that.

He still hadn't found a path, but the trees were thinning a bit and he thought he was probably walking in the right direction to get out of the wood, at any rate. It was just that walking was difficult, because his chest hurt, his head was muzzy, and he felt as though he were moving through treacle. In fact, he felt very strange. Weak. He held on to another tree as the giddiness claimed him. If he could just get his head clear, it wouldn't be so . . .

He sank to his knees as his legs gave way, and everything went dark.

"Thank you for coming in, Mr. Keyes."

Lloyd sat down opposite the man who was the nearest thing he had to a witness, apart from one deeply shocked teenage girl who was having to wait at the police station until Social Services found her and Alexandra somewhere they could be together, because it was thought by everyone concerned that they should not be separated if at all possible. He had sent for the police doctor to have a look at Kayleigh.

And her arrival on the scene had thrown up infinitely more puzzles than answers. She had to have been wandering around in the woods for almost three and a half hours, so she had to have seen something that had made her pick up the baby and run away, but she was too shocked to speak at all now and Lloyd just had to hope that the postman had some information that would help him get to the bottom of all this.

"I understand you delivered mail to Brook Way Cottage this morning?"

"That's right." Keyes, a stout man with tanned skin and sandy hair, narrowed his eyes a little. "Has something happened there?"

Lloyd nodded. "When were you there?"

Keyes blew out his cheeks. "I get there about twenty past, half past ten usually. So I guess that's when it would—" He broke off, snapping his fingers. "No—no, I tell a lie. It was just after twenty minutes to eleven, because I knew I was running pretty late, and I checked my watch just as I turned into Brook Way." He sat back. "Between twenty minutes and quarter to—and that's definite."

Lloyd smiled. He was glad something about this case was definite.

"I can't say I'm surprised you got involved. They were going at it hammer and tongs when I was there."

Lloyd leaned forward a little. "You heard an argument?"

"Not half. A man and a woman. He was yelling at her about how she had no right to take his daughter out of the country—she was saying he wasn't the father and I don't know what all."

Lloyd could never have hoped for this. "Did you see them at all? Or hear any names mentioned?"

Keyes shook his head.

Ah, well. That was reaching for the moon, he supposed. "Did you see any vehicles there?"

"There was a car in the garage, but don't ask me what kind. I'm not into cars. I'm a bike man, myself. That's partly why I became a postie. Wanted to give me a van a while back—I said no thanks, two wheels and pedal power's quite good enough for me."

"Do you know what color it was?"

"Red, I suppose," said Keyes.

Lloyd frowned. "You suppose?"

"Well, it's the post office color, isn't it?"

"Ah . . . no." Lloyd smiled. "Not the van. I was wondering if you noticed the color of the car in the garage."

"Oh—no. Dark, that's all."

Not the Alfa, then. "There wasn't a car on the forecourt?"

"No. Just the one in the garage. Are they the new owners, or what? The FOR SALE sign came down a couple of weeks ago."

Lloyd didn't answer. "Has the house always been empty the other times you've delivered mail since it's been up for sale?"

"For the last month or so, yes, I think so. The curtains were always drawn."

"And before that—do you know anything about the people who lived there?"

"A couple. I don't think there were kids—I certainly never saw any."

"Did you know them by sight?"

"Don't know him. But I saw her once or twice. Dr. Black, her name is."

"Can you describe her?"

"Late thirties, I'd say. Tall, dark. Quite a big girl. But she wasn't pregnant; I'm sure of that. So I didn't think it could be them having the argument about who the father was. I thought it must be whoever had bought the place."

That seemed to Lloyd to be a reasonable supposition. And Dr. Black definitely wasn't the victim, who was five-foot-two, slim, and blond, like Kayleigh's mother. Dr.

Black could, however, be the murderer; he didn't suppose she would have taken too kindly to Waring moving his fancy woman into what had been her home. But that wouldn't explain the argument.

He tipped his chair back slightly as he thought. Without knowing the setup, it was perfectly possible that the argument had been between Waring and Kayleigh's mother, but the postman hadn't seen Waring's car and the two victims certainly hadn't caused each other's injuries.

But the postman *had* seen a car in the garage that wasn't there now, and they still hadn't found the young man seen abandoning the Audi. As Marshall had pointed out, they didn't know that the Audi had anything to do with what had gone on in Brook Way Cottage at all; it was perfectly possible that this Mrs. Newton had parked her car wherever she worked and wouldn't know it was gone until early evening. But Lloyd doubted it. The Audi was involved; he was sure of it.

Lloyd thanked Mr. Keyes for his time and went to what it pleased them to call the rape suite, the room they had had furnished and decorated with the comfort of victims in mind and where it had seemed best to put Kayleigh. He knocked and raised his eyebrows at the doctor, who came out.

"Can I speak to her?"

"She seems quite calm. But I think that's because she can't take it all in, so I doubt if she'll give you any answers."

Lloyd hoped that she might start speaking, now that he knew a little more about what had been happening. He and the doctor went back in, and he smiled at Kayleigh. "How are you feeling now?" he asked.

Her eyes followed him as he sat down, but she didn't answer.

Lloyd switched on the fan. This part of the station, part of the extension that had been built on, was supposed to have air-conditioning, but it had broken down and despite the stiff breeze, the extension—mostly glass—was heating up like an oven. Fans had been begged, borrowed, and, for all he knew, stolen in order to cool the occupants down a little in the heat wave.

He sat down. "Kayleigh, believe me, I wouldn't be asking you all these questions if it wasn't really important," he began. "But I've just been speaking to someone who was at the cottage this morning, and who overheard an argument between a man and a woman. Do you know anything about that?"

Kayleigh shook her head.

Lloyd was certain that she did and carried on as though he had been given confirmation rather than a denial. "We think the row was over Alexandra. Someone didn't want your mother taking her abroad."

Kayleigh's eyes widened a little.

"*Was* your mother thinking of going abroad?"

She nodded.

Well, at least he'd got something other than a shake of the head. It had to be regarded as progress of a sort. "Were you there while the argument was going on, Kayleigh? Did you take Alexandra away because of that?"

She still didn't speak, but she frowned a little. And then the frown went, and Lloyd saw her eyes widen again, just for a moment. It was as if she had realized something, something she hadn't understood and now she did. Lloyd tried, gently, to capitalize on that.

"Did someone come to the cottage? Have an argument with your mother?" He paused, to give her time to speak, but she didn't. "Did you take Alexandra away because you were afraid?"

But the brief moments of communication were over; Kayleigh's face was impassive, expressionless.

"Would you excuse us for a moment?" Lloyd said, and took the doctor back out into the corridor. "Am I harming her with these questions?" he asked.

"I don't think so. But I don't think she's going to say anything until she's ready, so you're probably wasting your time."

Lloyd nodded. "I'd like to ask her just a few questions more."

Kayleigh could hear the whispered conversation but not what they were saying. She was in a room with sofas and magazines and a coffee table; she didn't know they had rooms like that in police stations.

She was glad Lloyd had put the fan on; her sweatshirt was sticking to her in the heat. She and Andrea had each bought one, like they did most things, and Andrea had been wearing hers when Kayleigh had seen her that morning; she wondered if Andrea was all hot and sticky, too. The sweatshirt had been all right walking about outside in the cooling breeze, but it was too hot to wear inside.

Kayleigh had been pleased to have the day off school and not to have to wear the awful uniform dress with the flowers on it, but she wished she had one of them now; at least they were cool. She had the clothes that she had put in her case, but she had left it behind in Malworth and she wasn't telling them about Malworth, not now. She wasn't going to tell them anything, because there was only one answer to who could have been at the cottage having a row with her mother.

She had thought at first, when Chief Inspector Lloyd had told her about the argument, that maybe it was

Ian—he didn't want to go to Australia, and maybe whoever had overheard it had got the wrong end of the stick.
But Ian didn't have noisy arguments with her mother; he
discussed things with her, quietly, endlessly, and use-
lessly, because he always did what she wanted anyway.

It was Phil who got noisy, Phil who shouted, Kayleigh
had thought, and then she had realized. Maybe it *was*
Phil. If he had found out about Australia, maybe he had
come to see her mother. So she wasn't going to say anything to them at all, not if it was going to get Phil into
trouble. As long as they kept on believing that her mother's
name was Scott and that Alexandra was her sister, they
wouldn't find out about Phil.

Lloyd and the doctor came back in, and Lloyd gave
Kayleigh a little encouraging smile, sitting down opposite her again. "Ian was conscious when we got to the
cottage," he said. "He told us he had seen an intruder.
Do you know who that might have been?"

Phil? Maybe, thought Kayleigh. Ian didn't know Phil,
not as far as she was aware. So if he'd found him there,
he would think he was an intruder, she supposed.

"We think that's who ran him over."

Phil ran Ian over? Kayleigh couldn't make sense of any
of this. She was just very thankful that she hadn't told
them about her mother's car being missing. If Phil had
taken it for some reason, she didn't want the police looking for it.

"We think that might have been a young man," Lloyd
was saying. "Blond hair, in his twenties. He was seen
driving an Audi Quattro—does that mean anything to
you?"

Dean? That had to be Dean. It wasn't Phil who had
taken the car; it was Dean. Oh, my God. Dean. Had he
gone to the *cottage*? Surely not. She had told him that her

mother would be there—she had said that she would meet him at the bridge. Why would he have gone to the cottage? But he must have been there, if someone saw him driving her mother's car. They didn't *know* it was her mother's car, she told herself, and it could take them a long time to find out, as long as she said nothing. She closed her eyes. It didn't make any sense. None of it made any sense. Until it did, she was saying nothing. Nothing at all.

"Kayleigh?" His voice was still gentle, but she could hear the urgency. She had given herself away about the car. "Is that who came to the house? Is that who had the argument with your mother?"

No, no, no, thought Kayleigh. That had to have been Phil.

"Kayleigh, I think you left the cottage with Alexandra because something was happening that frightened you. And I know you're still frightened, and confused, and I don't want to make it any worse for you than it already is, but if you can tell us anything, it really will help both of us."

No, it wouldn't help. It would just make everything even worse.

It came on the three-thirty news bulletin.

"Police say they are treating as murder the death of a woman in the Byford Forest area of Stansfield. She was found shortly after eleven o'clock this morning when officers responded to a nine-nine-nine call to a house in Brook Way in Stansfield."

The van slowed to a halt as Theresa stared at the radio. There was only one house in Brook Way.

"They have not yet released the name of the victim, or that of the injured man also found at the address, who is

presently undergoing emergency surgery in Barton Gen-
eral Hospital. Police are appealing to anyone who was in
Brook Way at or before eleven o'clock this morning to—"

The hospital. She had to get to the hospital. Theresa
put the van in gear.

Phil's train had arrived, on time, and now he was back in
his flat, wishing he had never left it.

If only he hadn't gone. If only he had taken some time
to get over the initial anger. He had told himself, all the
way down on the train, that he must not lose his temper,
that he must just talk to Lesley, point out the unreason-
ableness of what she was doing, make her understand
that it couldn't possibly be the right thing to do from
Kayleigh's point of view.

But you couldn't just talk to Lesley. He couldn't, at any
rate. Once she had made up her mind, she developed tunnel vision; whatever anyone said or did made no difference. Right or wrong, Lesley had decided, and her decision
was final. But that had never stopped him from trying,
and sheer frustration would make him lose control of his
temper.

It hadn't always been like that; toward the end she had
gone on at him to take one of these anger management
courses, but he didn't lose his temper if there was nothing to make him lose it, and despite the odd row, the first
few years of their life together had been good, even better
once Luke came along. They hadn't tried to have another
baby after Luke, so it had remained just him and Lesley
and Kayleigh, and even that had worked.

And it had worked because Phil had worked at it, tried
hard to be what Kayleigh needed and Lesley wanted, and
he had thought he had succeeded, at least as far as Lesley was concerned; he had always felt that Kayleigh

needed more than he or Lesley could offer, but Lesley had disagreed.

He *had* succeeded with Lesley, for as far as it went; she'd told him that today. Because what she had wanted then was someone older, someone who could take charge, someone who would help sort out her life, shattered when her husband had died so suddenly and tragically, and Phil had done that; he had been her strength when she needed him. It had never been a bed of roses; Kayleigh had problems, and Lesley was Lesley. There had always been rows, and they had started to become more frequent, until Luke. But Luke's death hadn't shaken their relationship; if anything, it had strengthened it, and the rows stopped altogether for a long time.

It was only after that, as she had slowly pieced her life back together after Luke, that Phil had discovered that the woman he had fallen in love with wasn't Lesley at all. He had met someone who had been knocked back on her heels, and Luke's death had occurred before the recovery process was complete, delaying it. But, in the end, the real Lesley had surfaced, and she had begun to want not someone to take charge but someone to take orders. And that wasn't Phil.

And she was being the real Lesley with a vengeance today; nothing he said would make her see reason, see that what she was proposing wasn't going to do Kayleigh any good at all. So he had lost his temper, in the face of Lesley's unmovable resistance, within two minutes of arriving there.

He didn't want to stay here; for one thing, the police might well be looking for him, and for another, he really didn't want to be alone. There was somewhere he could go, somewhere there would be no questions asked. Well, he amended, yes, there would be questions asked, but no

answers would be expected. His mother's sister, his aunt
Jean in Worthing.

Time to throw a change of clothes into a bag and con-
sult the railway inquiries people again.

Ten to four. It was almost an hour since he'd seen it. Tom
stood on the riverbank, at the spot where he had seen the
baby's body, and wished that the divers would hurry up
and get here. Not that time mattered; what he had seen
had been naked and lifeless. But it could still be caught
up in the weeds below the water level. If it wasn't found
soon, it might never be found.

There was nothing he could have done. Even if he
could have got into the river from where he was, he
could have done nothing to save her, because there was
no way that the baby he saw was alive. And yet he felt so
guilty.

He had persuaded Judy to go home; her still-fragile
nerves, trying to recover from Charlotte's birth and her
father's death within two months of each other, had
taken enough of a battering today without witnessing
this. And he felt guilty about her too. He had argued
with her about nannies, and he wasn't sure if in putting
up those arguments he had been reassuring her or trying
to make sure that his promotion prospects didn't take a
nosedive by her deciding to stay at home to look after
Charlotte herself. He had a horrible feeling it was the
latter.

Today, which had started so well and promisingly, had
turned into the worst day he could remember. And it
would get worse still, because one way or the other,
someone would have to tell the Crawfords. Not him,
thankfully. An officer had been assigned to them to keep
them informed of progress, and it would fall to him or
her to break this news. Naturally, it had not yet been

communicated to them, but they would have to know sooner or later. And better that the divers found the baby than that the Crawfords had to spend any time hoping against hope. But Tom felt that he would have visited it on them, just by having seen it.

None of this business made any sense. Whoever had done that had to be deeply disturbed, not criminally or commercially motivated. But who could be so disturbed as to do a thing like that?

The woman and the artist turned out to be husband and wife, and they were having problems. He had stormed out of the house early in the morning and she had waited for him to come back, but he hadn't. He had taken his painting equipment, so she had known where she was likely to find him and had gone to the park looking for him. He'd seen her approaching and had packed up his stuff, not wanting to talk to her, but she had caught him up on Bridge Street, and they had gone into the Riverside Inn for a drink and to talk things out. Eventually, they had decided to have a late lunch and had taken a table outside.

They were still at Malworth Police Station, but if they did have anything to do with it, no one had got anywhere with them. And why would they do a thing like that? What earthly reason could they have? Unless there was something in the Crawfords' background that the police didn't know about and it was some sort of sick revenge, but that seemed very unlikely. The Crawfords were just an ordinary family whose lives had been blasted by what had happened.

So why in God's name *had* it happened?

CHAPTER SEVEN

He hadn't been unconscious, not really. Just not quite conscious, he supposed. He had been aware, as if in a dream, of a dog sniffing him, barking; if Dean had been fully conscious, he would have been alarmed, because he had the healthy mistrust of dogs acquired by postmen and sneak thieves. As it was, the sensation of the cold nose examining his face and the pungent breathing close to his own nose had brought him to the state of semiconsciousness that he had remained in until now.

He had been aware of people, of urgency. Of being lifted onto a stretcher. He had thought then, for a few moments, that he had been hurt playing football; that was the only other time he had been on a stretcher, despite his sometimes-violent way of life. He had always been walking-wounded before, even after the severe going-over in prison. He had been aware of the journey to the hospital and the ambulance crew talking to him, asking him his name. He had been conscious enough to dredge it up from somewhere, like trying to remember a film star's name. And he had been aware of people working on him, putting strapping on his chest, discussing his injuries.

Now, he was lying on a bed, and he opened his eyes to see plastic curtains and a middle-aged man feeling his pulse.

"Ah, Dean, you're with us. I'm Staff Nurse Dixon. Call me Paul. How do you feel?"

"Terrible."

"I'm not surprised. You've cracked a couple of ribs, and taken a nasty blow to the head, amongst other things. What happened to you?"

"I fell."

"Oh, yeah?" Paul grinned. "Are you sure? It looks more as though you were in a fight. Did some woman give you those scratches?"

Dean was used to not being believed. He just wasn't used to telling the truth, and he wasn't sure how to do it convincingly. "No," he said.

"So where did the blood come from? It isn't yours, is it? The scratches didn't bleed that much."

Dean didn't answer.

"Does anything else hurt besides the ribs and the head?"

"Everything." Dean closed his eyes.

"Don't go to sleep on me, Dean. I want to check your eyes."

He allowed Paul to shine a torch into his eyes and then closed them again. If he was asleep, he couldn't answer any more questions, could he?

It was five past four when Theresa at last found a parking space on the sprawling Barton General grounds and made her way to Reception.

"Are you a relative?"

"Well, I lived with him for twelve years, if that counts." She was startled to hear the anger in her voice, and she didn't know whom she was angry with. Except that her first thought on hearing that news bulletin had been that someone had murdered his wife and tried to kill himself and she had been seeing it as a suitable subject for academic study, an interesting aspect of human nature. Now she was having to come to terms with the notion that Ian might have done something like that.

"Oh. Sorry. I'll show you where you can wait."

After about five minutes, a nurse came in. "Miss Black?"

"Yes. How is he?"

"Holding his own."

"I never know what that means. It doesn't *mean* anything, does it? Like everything else you people say. Stable. Comfortable. As well as can be expected. Meaningless."

"In this case, it means he's got a fighting chance," said the nurse.

Theresa bit her lip and blinked away the tears. Why was she giving this woman a hard time? "Sorry. Please— what happened to him?"

"We think he was hit by a car."

Theresa would never have believed she could hear those words and feel relief above all else. Whatever had happened, Ian was the victim, not the perpetrator.

"When can I see him?"

"Well, he's out of theater now, but he's in intensive care, and still unconscious. You can sit with him if you like, but he really won't know you're there."

"Yes, I'd—I'd like to sit with him. Just—you know."

"Sure."

Theresa was taken to where Ian lay, with tubes and wires attached to his body, little screens monitoring his vital signs, and a machine breathing for him.

"Don't let that worry you," said the nurse. "He'll be able to breathe for himself soon. But he may not regain full consciousness for a while."

"What happened?" Theresa asked. "How did he get

run over? They said on the radio he was found outside
his own house."

"Nobody's very sure. The police might know more
than we do, of course."

Detective Superintendent Case, big, bluff, with thick
gray hair that Lloyd envied, came into his office without
knocking and looked bleakly at Lloyd.

"I've just been to the murder scene," he said. "And,
correct me if I'm wrong, but we seem to have a dead
woman, a man whose organs are being eyed up for har-
vesting, and a teenage girl with a baby, and we still don't
know who the hell they are, whether they were moving
in or out, or even where they were coming from or going
to, never mind who actually caused all this mayhem.
Right?"

Lloyd managed a smile. "We're a little bit further forward than that. We know the man is definitely Ian Waring, and we believe the murder victim is a Mrs. Scott, but
I'd much rather not ask Kayleigh to identify her if we can
get someone else to do it. And we know that they were all
moving into that cottage, which is owned by Ian Waring,
though he seems not to have been living there for the last
few weeks."

"And he's the father of this baby, is he?"

Lloyd shrugged. "According to the postman, that's a
matter for debate. At quarter to eleven, someone was
there shouting the odds about taking her out of the country, and whoever that was claimed to be the father, but
was told that he wasn't."

"Mr. Scott, presumably."

"That's the premise we're going on. Waring said the
intruder was male. But the man seen abandoning the
Audi sounds too young to be Kayleigh's father, so it
might be more complicated than that."

Case frowned. "I thought the Audi was registered to a Mrs. Newton somewhere in London."

"It is. But the postman saw a dark-colored car in the garage at the cottage that isn't there now, and it's my guess that it was the Audi, or it's a pretty odd coincidence."

"So who's Mrs. Newton? Coincidence or not, her car might have nothing to do with it. Have the Met found her yet?"

"No. Apparently she moved from that address at the end of January, beginning of February, and the neighbors don't know where she's gone. The car still hasn't been reported stolen—perhaps the driver is Mrs. Newton's son or husband or something, and he was visiting the cottage."

"Maybe." Case looked unconvinced. "But if this car the postman saw was parked in the garage, that's not likely to be a visitor's car, is it? Visitors don't drive into the garage."

"True."

"Anyway," Case said, "the uniforms are looking for him. *Our* first priority is finding this Mr. Scott, if for no other reason than that we've got two children here who need him."

Lloyd knew that. But every alley he turned down was blind. He wanted very much to know where the Scotts were living before they moved into the cottage, and he was currently engaged on trying to find Dr. Black, and not just because she was on his list of suspects; if he could just find out something about these people, it would make the murder that much easier to solve, without red herrings muddying the water. He found himself wondering if red herrings *could* muddy water and was brought back to more immediate concerns by Case.

"What's happening about the baby and the girl, anyway?"

"Social Services are looking after Alexandra, and Kayleigh is here with a social worker, pending a suitable placement for them both. They think they might be able to accommodate Kayleigh in the children's home in Barton that's currently looking after the baby, but we're waiting for confirmation from the director. The doctor thinks Kayleigh will talk when she's ready, but until we know where they were moving from, finding Mr. Scott is a little difficult."

"But what's really bothering you?" Case asked. "I know you. You're not happy about something."

Lloyd stood up and looked out of the window at the car park, thinking of the positive mountain of little puzzles he now had. He wasn't happy about a lot of things, and he wished Judy were here; he didn't like having to work them out with other people. But this one was urgent. "I'm having problems with this baby. She doesn't seem to fit into the picture." He didn't have to look at his superintendent to see his reaction; he knew exactly what expression was on his face.

"You always want to complicate things, don't you, Lloyd? It seems nice and straightforward. Mr. Scott left Mrs. Scott, Waring moved in, and in due course Mrs. Scott had a baby. They decide to go and live in his cottage, probably once his ex-partner vacated it. Scott reckons it's his baby, comes to claim it, but she says he's not the father. They have a row during which the mirror gets smashed; she tries to get away through the utility room; he kills her before she makes it; Waring arrives there, finds her body, rings us. Then he sees Scott driving off, runs outside, and gets knocked down. What problems?"

"You mean apart from why did Scott so kindly give him time to phone the police?" Lloyd turned to look at Case.

"He didn't want to kill anyone else—he just wanted to get away."

"So why do what he did to Waring? Waring didn't put himself in the path of the car—he was by the front door when he was hit. Scott could have got away without doing that to him. It was deliberate."

Case sighed extravagantly. "Waring had stolen his wife. Was claiming to be the father of the baby he believed to be his—he'd been driven to murder over it! Damn it, Lloyd, he'd lost his reason—he just did it. You said it was the baby that was bothering you."

Lloyd nodded. His bachelor boss didn't know about babies. "Babies do *not* travel light," he informed him. "Every time Charlotte goes anywhere, we have to lug along a huge zipper bag with nappies and clothes and toys and sterilizing units and formula milk—there's nothing like that in the cottage. And there's no cot, no pushchair . . . nothing in any of the packing cases to suggest that a baby was going to live there. No baby food, no feeding bottle. Kayleigh was apparently wandering round for hours, and yet according to Mrs. Spears—she's the director of the children's home—the baby still isn't hungry, so she must have been given a feed very shortly before she left the house. It doesn't add up."

Case came into the room properly then and sat down. "And a baby's gone missing in Malworth." He took out the cigarettes he had been trying to give up ever since Lloyd had known him, lit up, and shook his head. "Oh, come on. Are you saying this kid happened to steal a baby the same day someone killed her mother? And wouldn't that mean that the row was about some other baby altogether? That's what I call a coincidence. Have you ever considered just taking things at face value?"

"I *am* taking things at face value. They seem to be intending leaving the country according to the argument,

and it's clear that they weren't moving in there for long—
they took exactly what they were going to need, and no
more. Three knives, three forks, three spoons. No spoon
for the baby, but she's probably being weaned. Two sets
of bedding for each bed—no cot blankets. If a baby was
moving into that house, there should be some sign of it."

Case shook his head. "Not necessarily. She might not
be on solids. She might be breast-fed. And she might
sleep in her mother's bed, for all you know. I did."

Lloyd was impressed; he had, it appeared, been under-
estimating Case's knowledge of babies.

"And all those packing cases weren't moved in a
sports car, were they? There must have been some more
practical vehicle there at some point, and we know there
was another car in the garage—which is much more
likely to have belonged to someone who lived there than
to someone who didn't—and it could still have had the
baby's things in it, for all we know. The murderer could
have driven off in that car, taking the pram and everything else connected with the baby with him."

That sounded plausible. Lloyd frowned. He had imagined Kayleigh, frightened by the row, picking up the
baby and leaving the house. That was why the lack of a
pram or a cot or food had been so inexplicable. But perhaps the baby and her equipment had never made it into
the house. He really should have had more sleep—it was
a poor do when Case had to outline scenarios for him; he
was the scenario man.

"Do you think they had just arrived?" he said. "That
Kayleigh was taking the baby from the car when her
mother went into the utility room from the garage and
began unpacking? That whoever did it was waiting in
there for her, and Kayleigh actually witnessed the attack
from the garage, and ran away while it was going on?"

"Well, no, not having your fertile imagination, I just

thought that the baby's things could have been in the car that's disappeared. But yes—that's quite possible. I prefer it to your last theory."

So did Lloyd. It would certainly explain a lot of things that had been puzzling him about Kayleigh. But who was having the row, in that case? And was it incidental to the murder? Lloyd was inclined to think that it could be, so Case's scenario sounded good to him.

"And if I'm right," Case went on, "then not only is the baby who Kayleigh says she is, but the Audi *is* a coincidence, because there wasn't anything at all in it. And it's a damn sight more likely than your coincidence."

True. But plausible or not, it was still just a theory, and Freddie was right; theories always came to grief. Lloyd's own theory about Emma and Alexandra being one and the same would doubtless go the way of all theories, but he was pursuing it, just in case. "You're probably right, sir. But I've told McArthur that we've got a mystery baby, I'm getting Freddie to check if Mrs. Scott really did have a baby in the very recent past, and I'm going to get a photograph of Emma and take a very close look at Alexandra."

Case looked worried. "I don't like it when you remember that I outrank you—it means you're serious. And it seems unlikely, Lloyd."

"I know. But it won't hurt to make certain."

Case got up. "All I'm saying is, don't go raising the Crawfords' hopes."

As if he would. Lloyd had only found out when he'd spoken to McArthur that Judy was so involved in the kidnap and that it was Emma Jane Crawford, of all babies, who had been stolen. It wouldn't be doing Judy any good; he knew that—he'd like to see how she was. As Case left, he glanced at his watch; it was almost half past four and he was already very late for the postmortem, so he couldn't really go home even if he had his own transport, which, of course, he hadn't. Anyway, Judy wouldn't like it if he went home, however much it had affected her; she didn't much care for being regarded as a damsel in distress.

He picked up his jacket, walked along the corridor, and popped his head round the door of the CID room. "Can someone ask the kidnap incident room to fax through a photograph of baby Emma? I'm just off to the p.m., if I can cadge a lift."

It wasn't easy; most of the cars were out. Eventually, he was grudgingly given a car and driver, and at twenty past five he arrived in the mortuary.

"What time do you call this?" was Freddie's greeting.

Lloyd held up his hands in an apology. "Extenuating circumstances. I don't have a car, for one thing."

"Your baby theory's looking good, because the answer is that she has definitely not given birth in the recent past."

Lloyd wasn't at all sure if he was relieved or worried by Freddie's answer. It strengthened his belief that Alexandra and Emma were one and the same, but that was leading him down a path that could cause the Crawfords even more heartache if he was wrong.

"So what can you tell me about her death? Could a woman have done it?"

If the row really was about some other baby altogether, it might have no bearing on the murder. A vengeful Dr. Black could indeed have been lying in wait for her victim. Most compelling of all: she could have a key to the cottage.

"I think the victim was stooping over the carton, which gave the attacker a considerable height advantage. Bring something that heavy down from a height onto someone's head, then repeat often enough, you'll get the job done, whether you're male or female."

"Did she put up a fight? Is her attacker likely to be marked?"

"She has no other bruises," said Freddie. "Nothing under her fingernails. I think she would have been out cold after the first blow—no chance to fight back. Whoever did it would in all likelihood be splashed with her blood, but other than that . . ." He shook his head.

Blood. Blood was producing a great many of Lloyd's puzzles. "Waring's clothes had blood on them," he said. "And it wasn't his."

If Ian Waring had been hale and hearty when Lloyd had arrived, he would have been the prime suspect; it was sometimes grossly unfair, but it was a fact. The suspicion had already been there in the voice of the girl in Dispatch when she had sent the car. And Lloyd wasn't convinced that Waring's hospitalized state exempted him from prime-suspect status.

Freddie shook his head when Lloyd said that. "The man didn't drive a car into himself, Lloyd."

"No, but what did he do? If he came home and found her as he said . . . did he pick her up and carry her, or what? How come he got blood on his clothing? And we've had confirmation that he left the footprints in the kitchen and hallway."

"Well, I did tell you the body had been moved slightly. He might have tried to see if she was still alive—if he got close to her, he could have got blood on his shoe. And if he turned her over for any reason, the blood would come off on his clothes."

"If she was still *alive*?" Lloyd shook his head. "I know we ordinary mortals don't have medical degrees, Freddie, but some conditions are pretty obvious even to the layman. He couldn't possibly have thought she was alive. Her brains, as you pointed out, were visible. You said yourself that no one would have had reason to examine her closely if the light was on, because it was all too obvious that she was dead."

"Even so, there are several innocent explanations of how her blood could have got onto his clothes. People react in all sorts of ways when confronted with violent death. He could have cradled her in his arms, for instance. Forensics should be able to tell you how he got it, anyway—whether it splashed or dripped onto him or whether it just came off on him."

Lloyd knew that. The room was having to be sealed off until all the blood had dried in order that Forensics could work out exactly what sort of blood patterns they were dealing with. But he also knew that whatever one expert said, you could always find another to say just the opposite. He didn't like relying on esoteric discussions of blood patterns when he took a case into court. He liked witnesses, and he thought he might have one.

"Come to that, there's no reason to suppose her assailant stepped in the blood at all. Most of the blood on the floor would have seeped out after the attack."

"Why was this assailant still there?"

"How should I know? That's for you to work out, not me."

"Indulge me, Freddie. Theorize for a moment—I won't tell anyone; I promise."

"Very well," said Freddie, raising his eyes to heaven. "Presumably, he had just finished the job when Waring came home."

Lloyd nodded. "But he must have heard Waring's car arriving. And his car—or at any rate, the car he got away in—was in the garage. So why would he wait until Waring had come in, walked through the house, found the body, and summoned the emergency services before he even got into it? What was he waiting for? Not to kill Waring, or he would have used the same weapon."

"I give in. I don't know. What's your theory this time?"

"I think the other person wasn't an intruder at all, but a witness. He came in by the garage, saw the body, got into the car, and drove out. Then he saw Waring coming out of the front door with blood on his clothes and ran him over before he ended up the same way. He used Waring's phone to call the police."

"But where is this person who called the police? Why didn't he just stay there?"

"For the same reason as he gave Waring's name. Because he didn't want us to know he'd been there."

Freddie abandoned theorizing and took Lloyd on an unpleasant tour of the injuries, explaining exactly how he had drawn the conclusions he had, which weren't really any different from his conclusions at the cottage, except that he could now demonstrate that the doorstop was undoubtedly the weapon used.

"And there's no evidence of sexual assault," he concluded. "Know who she is, yet?"

"Not exactly. Just that she's almost certainly Kayleigh's mother." Lloyd glanced at his watch. "While I'm here, I'll check up on Waring—see if there's any likelihood of his ever being able to talk to us."

"Do you really think he did it?"

"No. But it's a possibility, and I'm taking nothing for granted."

The girl on Reception tracked down a doctor that Lloyd could speak to, and they now seemed a little more optimistic that Ian would recover.

"When he regains consciousness, barring any postoperative complications, he will be able to speak to you, but you certainly won't be able to question him for any length of time. A few moments—no more. And, of course, he probably won't remember anything about what happened to him."

Oh, wonderful. A murderer who had genuinely forgotten that he'd done it. That was all Lloyd needed.

The doctor turned to go and then turned back. "Oh—he has a visitor, I believe. I thought you might be interested."

A visitor? Someone who knew him? Knew his circumstances? Would they just have kept that to themselves if Lloyd hadn't happened to be here? He bit back the angry words that rose to his lips. Once he would have told the doctor exactly what he thought, but his years with Judy had, as it were, tempered his temper. He reminded himself that the doctors weren't aware of his fruitless efforts to find out exactly who these people were and where they had come from; they were just trying to save Ian Waring's life and seemed to be making a rather better attempt at their job than he was at his.

The gods had decided to smile on him again; in the intensive care ward he found an attractive dark-haired woman, tall, as the postman had said, slightly overweight, as the postman had said, sitting by Waring's bed. He correctly assumed that it was Theresa Black.

"DCI Lloyd, Stansfield CID. Would it be possible to have a word with you?"

"Of course." She came out into the corridor. "Can you tell me what happened at the cottage?"

Lloyd had two choices: treat her from the start as a suspect, take her to the police station, to an interview room with taping facilities, caution her and question her, or simply talk to her. He led her to a bench, and they sat down. "Quite frankly, Dr. Black, we don't know what happened. In fact, we really know very little. I'm hoping you can shed some light on it all."

"Me?" She shook her head. "All I know is what I

heard on the radio. They said a woman was dead. Is it Lesley?"

Lloyd sat back. "Who's Lesley?"

"Ian's new . . . whatever. Partner. Significant other. Whatever silly name you want to—" She pursed her lips. "Sorry, sorry. I seem to be angry with everyone, and I don't know why."

"Oh, that's all right. It's a very unpleasant business."

She took a moment to compose herself, and Lloyd didn't hurry her. He had waited all day for some information; he could wait a little while longer.

"Ian and Lesley were moving into the cottage this morning. *Is* it Lesley who died?"

"We're not certain who it is. At first, we thought it was you. Now, we think it's a Mrs. Scott. Does that name mean anything to you?"

"Scott?" She shook her head. "No." But as she spoke the word, a tiny frown appeared, and she thought for a moment. "Wait . . . yes. Yes, it does. Lesley's daughter's name is Scott. Kayleigh Scott. They didn't change it when they adopted her."

"When who adopted her?" asked Lloyd.

"Lesley and her husband. Late husband. She's a widow."

Kayleigh was adopted. So perhaps Freddie's findings were irrelevant, because Alexandra could also have been adopted. But that would make the conversation that the postman overheard a little unlikely, because presumably one knew whether or not one had adopted a baby; there could be no argument about it. Except if her natural father was claiming her, of course. The young man driving the Audi? But why would he murder the woman?

"Is Kayleigh all right? I hadn't even thought about her until now."

"She's had a dreadful shock. That's one reason we're

having problems—she can't, or won't, speak to us. What's Lesley's surname?"

"Newton."

Lloyd felt as though a huge weight had been lifted. Mrs. Lesley Newton was the owner of the stolen Audi. He should have been quicker than that—he should have noticed that the first name was the same when Theresa Black mentioned it. Bloody jigsaw. At least he had been right about the Audi being involved, but the baby's things weren't in it, so that was still a puzzle.

And now the driver of the Audi was officially a suspect. In Lloyd's book he was possibly merely a witness, but he knew this opinion would not be shared by his colleagues. And though the stolen car made it a racing certainty that Lesley Newton was the victim, they still needed someone who could identify her.

"Do you know Mrs. Newton personally?"

She shook her head again. "I've heard about her. That's all."

Oh, well. It would have been a lucky break in a day that had never heard of such a thing. "Do you know anyone who does know her personally?"

"Phil Roddam. She was his—oh, God, I wish they would think of a word for it—his long-term partner until she took up with Ian."

"You don't by any chance know his address, do you? It's very important that we get in touch with him—we really need to get a positive identification."

"Yes—if you have a piece of paper, I'll write it down for you."

Lloyd tore a page out of his diary and handed it to her, watching as she wrote down the address and two phone numbers, a little puzzled by her familiarity with Lesley Newton's ex-partner. "You don't happen to know when Mrs. Newton left Mr. Roddam, do you?"

"Well—they separated a year ago. But he was the one who left. Or was invited to leave, I should say."

"And is that when Mr. Waring left you?"

"No. Ian didn't actually move to London until January of this year. But he'd been seeing Lesley in what he thought was secret since the previous April—I've no idea why he couldn't just move in with her."

"You knew he was having an affair with her all that time?"

"I *guessed* that he was having an affair." She smiled suddenly. "But it's an odd word to use when you're talking about Ian—he's really not like that. And it's not quite how it sounds—there was no acrimony. Ian and I are still good friends."

"It's none of my business," he said, "but you seem very . . . forgiving."

"*Forbearing* would be a better word. He even borrowed my van to move some of their stuff into the cottage."

Case's more practical vehicle—it wasn't the Audi, after all, so the lack of baby things in the Audi might not be a puzzle; they could be in the van. "Do you know where your van is now?" he asked.

"In the car park." She nodded her head toward the window.

"Oh—you've got it back?" Lloyd frowned. "I take it that you didn't find items of baby equipment in it, did you?"

"No." Dr. Black looked puzzled. "Why?"

"We can't locate Alexandra's things," he said, in a deliberately casual reference. "Pram, clothes, feeding bottle, cot blankets—we thought they must be in whatever was used for the move."

She looked even more puzzled. "I'm sorry—who's Alexandra?"

"Mrs. Newton's baby daughter." Lloyd mentally crossed his fingers.

"But she didn't have a baby daughter."

Yes! thought Lloyd. But then again, it wasn't the sort of thing Waring was likely to tell his ex-partner. He could be celebrating Emma's return to her parents a little prematurely.

"Can you be certain of that? We know she didn't give birth to her, but we think she might have adopted her in January—at least, that's roughly when we believe the baby was born." Using the official-sounding "we" lent his surmises an authority that they didn't deserve, but being apparently confident about your facts was one way of eliciting the actual information. "And I know that regular adoption agencies probably wouldn't allow the adoption to go through if there were domestic problems, but these days . . . well, people go to Romania and places like that for babies, and who knows what checks they make?"

Dr. Black was shaking her head. "If Ian had been talked into adopting a baby, I would have heard all about it, believe me."

Lloyd asked her to excuse him and walked a discreet distance away in order to phone Bob Sandwell.

"So when we find the man who took the Audi, we've got our murderer," was Sandwell's instant response to the information.

Lloyd was less inclined to take things at their face value than his colleagues, as Case had pointed out. "Perhaps," he said.

"Forensics have just phoned through to say that they've found traces of human blood on the driver's seat, which seem to have come off someone's clothing, and that a tire mark on Waring's shoe matches the tire pattern on the Audi. The man's foot was crushed, sir. If the Audi crushed it, I think we can assume it did the rest of the damage."

"Oh, I realize the Audi driver caused Waring's injuries," said Lloyd. "But I'm not convinced he was Mrs. Newton's killer. Maybe he just walked in on a murder, and exacted revenge, or was afraid for his own life."

"Oh." Sandwell managed to pack a lot of doubt into one syllable. "You won't mind, will you, if I just assume for the moment that the Audi driver's our man for both incidents?"

Lloyd laughed. "Be my guest, Bob. He very probably is. And I've at last found someone who can formally identify the body." He gave him Roddam's details. "Has the photograph of Emma Crawford come through?"

"No, sir—I'm afraid there's bad news. They've sent police divers to the river. Tom Finch and DCI Hill were observing a suspect couple when Tom saw a baby's body in the water."

Lloyd took that in but could find no words.

"Sir? Did you want something else?"

"No. No—thanks, Bob."

Lloyd gave himself a few moments to come to terms with what he had been told before he walked slowly back along the corridor toward Theresa Black, his mind no longer on the murder investigation. Was this what the stars had had in store for Emma Jane Crawford? He could see Roger Crawford's face, slightly merry and completely joyful. He had wanted a little girl this time, he'd said. And the labor had been so easy; Lloyd had thought how Judy would envy Mrs. Crawford. Judy would be devastated, and he had to go home now, whether she objected or not.

But he *was* on an investigation, and he still wanted to talk to Theresa Black; there was a lot she could tell him. Besides, she might well have murdered the woman, for all he knew. If he left now, he might never see her again, and quite apart from any considerations of the murder, he had to find out how sure she was that Lesley *hadn't* acquired a baby, because Alexandra existed and she wasn't Emma. She must belong to someone, and just who she belonged to seemed to be an issue.

He saw how he could satisfy both his desire to go home and his desire to continue his investigation and took a gamble, sending a text message to his driver that he could leave without him. Mobile phones were so useful, he'd found. But he sent the message in the Queen's English.

"Dr. Black, I'm so sorry about this, but . . . well, something's come up, and I have to get home to Malworth, I'm afraid, but there are some other things I'd like to talk to you about. If I could see you later this evening, perhaps?"

"Of course. I'll be here."

He turned to go, then tapped his head. "Damn," he said. "I'm an idiot."

"Something wrong?"

"I forgot I haven't got my car." He glanced at his watch. "I'm going to have to get someone to come and collect me."

"I can give you a lift, if you're in a hurry."

"Oh, would you?" Lloyd smiled at her. "That would be a godsend."

Sometimes, he thought, it was just too easy. And if Theresa Black was a murderer, she had chutzpah; he had to give her that.

"Tell me to mind my own business if you want," he said as they walked through the corridors to Reception, "but you seem to me still to be very fond of Ian Waring. Am I right?"

"Quite right. But it's a platonic relationship now, and

had been for some time before he left. I'm a sort of mother-confessor, really."

"Do you think that he would have told you if he and Mrs. Newton had, well . . . unofficially adopted a baby? An illegal adoption? Would he have told you something like that?"

"I wouldn't know if Lesley would do anything like that, but I know Ian wouldn't."

"If she had done it without his knowledge, and he'd found out only when he moved in with her?" The big glass doors at Reception slid open as they approached. "Is that remotely likely? It might explain the delay in his joining her in London, if she wanted to present him with a fait accompli, and didn't want him around while the negotiations were going on. And perhaps that's something he would rather not tell you."

She led the way to her van. "Buying a baby is something Lesley could afford to do, and given that she *would* do such a thing, then doing it without consulting Ian sounds to me entirely in character. But believe me, Mr. Lloyd, there is *nothing* Ian would rather not tell me. I got told this morning all about his problems with Lesley, and they didn't include him suddenly discovering that he had responsibility for a new baby. At least . . ." She trailed off as she thought about something.

Lloyd noted that Ian had had problems with Mrs. Newton but right now was more interested in the baby. "Yes?" he said encouragingly.

"There was one thing he was less than forthcoming about. And if I'm right, he would think that it was none of his business and therefore none of mine." She looked at him. "I think this baby you've got might be Kayleigh's own baby."

That simply hadn't occurred to Lloyd; Kayleigh was no more than a child herself.

*   *   *

They had brought her to the children's home where they had taken the baby and put her in a small sitting room that Mrs. Spears had called "the quiet room," whatever that meant.

Kayleigh had had a fleeting moment of recognition when she had walked into the home; she had never been here, of course, but her very earliest memories were of somewhere just like this.

Social Services had got some sort of child psychologist in to speak to her, but Kayleigh didn't care who asked her questions or what they asked her; she wasn't going to say anything. They'd got it all wrong, but they'd have to sort it out for themselves, because anything she said might get Phil into trouble.

She thought about what she had told them. Just that they were moving into the cottage. She was sure she hadn't said anything else. She didn't understand what was happening, and she didn't know what to do; she had never felt so alone, so frightened, so confused.

The doctor sat back, and she saw him glance at Mrs. Spears before he spoke.

"You told Chief Inspector Lloyd that you were going abroad."

So she had. She'd forgotten that. But that wouldn't help them much. She hadn't even said where.

"Do you want to talk about that? Were you looking forward to it?"

Sooner or later, he'd get it into his head that she didn't want to talk about anything. Period.

Phil was on another train. He hadn't called her to say he was coming; she might be away on holiday, in which case he would book into a B & B for the weekend, but he hoped she was there.

He and his aunt Jean were close, in an odd, blood-is-thicker-than-water way; when he had been a child, she had looked after him as often as his mother had. His father, if he had ever been on the scene, had left it long before Phil was old enough to know him, and his mother and her sister had brought him up between them.

He wondered if that was why he and Kayleigh got on so well; she had never known who her father was at all, and perhaps that shared feeling of rootlessness had given them the bond that undoubtedly existed, as strong as if he were her real father. And something of that bond existed between him and his aunt Jean; their lives had taken separate paths when he had reached adulthood, and even the exchange of Christmas cards had ceased once he'd taken up with Lesley and found himself moving every few months. He still sent Aunt Jean one, but she never knew where to send his.

She might have moved herself, he supposed, but he doubted it.

Judy was sitting on Lloyd's reclining chair, the only piece of furniture he had imported from his own flat, holding Charlotte close, rocking her gently backward and forward. She had long since gone to sleep, but Judy needed the comforting motion. She couldn't let Charlotte go, because nothing could happen to her while she was in her arms—no one could steal her; no one could harm her.

It could have been Charlotte. That was all that was going through Judy's head as she sat and rocked. It could have been Charlotte. And there was no comfort to be had in her overwhelming thankfulness that it wasn't, only a heightened awareness of how Nina Crawford must be feeling.

The world frightened Judy today, in a way that it never had before. She wanted to put bars at the window, to build a fortress round her baby, to keep the world and its wickedness out. On a slightly higher plane, she knew that she couldn't, that it wouldn't be right, because Charlotte lived in this world like everyone else and most people in this rich, healthy, civilized society survived it to old age.

But not Emma. Not Emma, because while the wealth and the health were a reality, the civilization was an illusion, merely cosmetic, and not even skin-deep.

At last, the divers were here, two of them, taking it in turns to go down into the river and search. Tom watched, not wanting to be there yet having to be there. They had been looking for a very long time; he was beginning to think that it wasn't going to resolve anything at all when one of the divers surfaced, and he was holding the baby cradled in the crook of his arm.

Tom's stomach turned over, and then he couldn't believe what he was seeing when the diver gave a thumbs-up. It was their usual signal that they had found what they were looking for, but it was hardly necessary and hardly appropriate. Then the diver removed his mouthpiece and his goggles, swimming toward Tom, and he was laughing.

And soon so was everyone who was there, including Tom, even though the laugh was on him and his laughter was very close to sobbing with sheer relief. No one else had seen what he had seen and no one else had been through what he had been through since he'd seen it, because no one else had been as certain as he was that Emma Jane Crawford had been drowned in that river.

Except Judy, he realized. She had trusted the evidence of Tom's eyes, as he had himself. He couldn't get away, not yet, and he couldn't just telephone her. She had been deeply shocked by what he'd told her he had seen, and a telephone call simply wouldn't do. He'd go there as soon as he was through here, confess face-to-face. She might never speak to him again.

CHAPTER EIGHT

Kayleigh still hadn't spoken a word. The doctor had left, and after a few minutes another woman had come in with the baby and Mrs. Spears had left. The new woman had asked Kayleigh if she wanted to change Alexandra; when Kayleigh hadn't replied, she had done it herself and then had sat with the baby in her arms. She said the baby had been fed, that she didn't think she would be due another feed for a couple of hours, and would Kayleigh like to feed her next time? Kayleigh hadn't answered, and eventually the woman had taken the baby away, saying that Kayleigh would get fed herself soon.

That was why, when Mrs. Spears came back, Kayleigh thought she had come to tell her that her meal was ready, but she hadn't.

"Kayleigh? The police have just rung to say that they're going to contact someone they think you'll be pleased to see. Someone called Phil Roddam?"

Kayleigh closed her eyes briefly. How? How had they got on to Phil? It wasn't anything she'd said.

"And . . . the hospital rang. Mr. Waring has had his operation, and they seem quite hopeful about him now."

That was something, Kayleigh supposed. The first good news she'd had.

*   *   *

Theresa told Chief Inspector Lloyd everything she knew about Lesley and Kayleigh, which wasn't a great deal, but it did seem to add up. The crisis with Kayleigh that resolved itself in January; the unsuitable relationship that so worried Lesley that she was dragging both Ian and Kayleigh off to Australia, though neither of them had any desire to go; keeping their whereabouts secret from Phil. Was that what it had all been about? Kayleigh had got involved with some boy and had had a baby, and Lesley didn't want Phil to know? Ian would have been sworn to secrecy as far as she was concerned, of course, in case it got back to Phil through her.

"So you know Mr. Roddam quite well?"

"No. I don't actually know him at all. I've only spoken to him on the phone. But—well, yes, I suppose we have got quite close that way." They had; she felt as if Phil and she were old friends.

"But you haven't rung to tell him what's happened here?"

"I couldn't—I had no idea what *had* happened. I didn't want to make him think Lesley was dead if she wasn't. And . . . well, as I said, I had honestly forgotten about Kayleigh. I should have told him—he'll want to be with her, and she'll want him here; I'm sure she will. I suspect that if anyone can get her to tell you what happened, he can."

She had been too busy worrying about Ian to think about Kayleigh. But the doctor had assured her that Ian was still holding his own and that the prognosis was now good.

Lloyd sounded thoughtful when he spoke again. "You said that Mr. Waring had been having problems with Mrs. Newton?"

Theresa brought her thoughts back to the here and now and frowned. She might be giving the man a lift, but he was still a policeman and there could only be one reason that a policeman was interested in Ian's domestic troubles. "You surely don't think *he* killed her, do you? He almost died himself."

"I still have no idea what happened. At the moment, there are a number of people who could have killed Mrs. Newton, and Mr. Waring is one of them. You said you saw him this morning? When was that?"

"I saw him twice. He came at about seven to borrow the van, and he brought it back again."

"He borrowed the van this morning? And then took it all the way to London just to come all the way back?"

My God, when he said he had no idea what had happened, he meant it. They really didn't know anything. "Malworth," she pointed out. "They lived in Malworth, until today. He was only in London for a couple of weeks before they moved here."

"Dr. Black, I'm very glad you turned up. Though I have to confess I'm not sure whether you're clearing up a lot of puzzles or creating a whole lot of new ones."

She flicked her eyes toward him to see him run his hand over the strip of thin hair that still grew on his scalp.

"Where did they live in Malworth?" he asked.

"Riverside. In one of those big town houses on Bridge Street."

Lloyd gave a whistle.

"She's wealthy. Was wealthy."

There was a little silence before he spoke. "Right. Let's take one thing at a time. What time did Mr. Waring bring the van back to you?"

"I think he came at about twenty to eleven or so. And he stayed for a few minutes, chatting."

"About his problems."

She smiled a little reluctantly. "Yes. He really didn't

want to go to Australia any more than Kayleigh did. But he'd hardly murder Lesley because of that."

"It would seem a little extreme. When did he leave?"

"I can tell you that exactly, because I was leaving to go on my rounds. He left at five minutes to eleven." She realized from Lloyd's reaction that the time was important and took her eyes off the road again to glance at him. "When did all this happen?"

He looked as though he was going to get official on her, but if he had been going to, he changed his mind. "He made the emergency call just on eleven o'clock, and we arrived within five minutes of that call."

Theresa relaxed. "Well, there you are. He couldn't have done it—it takes five minutes to get from my flat to the cottage. You can't do it any faster than that because of the speed bumps. So he could hardly have packed in killing Lesley *and* getting half killed himself before you got there, could he?"

"No," Lloyd agreed. "He couldn't." There was a heartbeat before he asked his next question. "Do you go from your flat to the cottage often?"

She smiled. "Not to meet Ian in secret, if that's what you're thinking. I've been doing it every day to pick up the mail, because I keep forgetting to tell the post office my new address, and poor Ian hasn't been in one place long enough to decide what his address is, so his mail still goes there, too."

"Could it have been later than twenty minutes to eleven when he brought the van back?"

"I don't think so. But I expect the security cameras in the garage area at the flats will tell you exactly." It took Theresa a moment to work out why he wanted to know. "Because he could have done it before he left the cottage, is that what you're saying? You think he killed Lesley and then calmly brought the van back to me?"

"I deal in possibilities, Dr. Black, and that is a possibility. I'd be delighted to cross Mr. Waring off my list of suspects; believe me I would."

Theresa sighed. "I wish you'd call me Theresa. I don't call myself Dr. Black anyway. And how do you know I could if I wanted to?"

"The mail. You didn't pick it up today. Just one letter. It's at the forensic lab, but you'll get it in due course."

"No need. It's just junk mail."

"How do you know that?"

"Because," she said patiently, despite the implication that she was lying about not being at the cottage today, "they're the only ones addressed like that. They get the lists from professional organizations that I once belonged to."

"And why didn't you pick the mail up as usual?"

She sighed and indicated the left turn off the dual carriageway. "I didn't want to risk running into Lesley. Forbearance goes just so far."

"I'm sure it does."

"Am I on your list of suspects?" she asked. "I was shopping from about half past nine." She gave him a list of the shops she had gone to, before he asked. "And then I went to the bank, where I stood in an enormous queue, and I posted some letters at the town center post office. I got home at about half past ten, I think. You can probably track my movements on a dozen security cameras."

"I'm afraid that at the moment everyone is on my list of suspects, though I'm inclined to believe that it was someone closer to Mrs. Newton than you are."

"In other words, Ian. Despite what happened to him?"

"Including Ian," he said. "But not exclusively Ian."

"You don't know him. Even if he *had* resorted to murder as a means of getting out of going to Australia, he could never have carried it off like that. He'd have confessed what he'd done as soon as he'd seen me."

She pulled up outside the greengrocer's as instructed, and Lloyd got out. "Oh," he said. "Can I ask—did you have a heavy cast-iron doorstop in the cottage?"

"A doorstop? No."

"Not necessarily a doorstop, though that's what it is. It could be thought of as an ornament. It's shaped like a cat."

"I didn't have a heavy cast-iron anything."

He smiled. "Thanks. I might see you at the hospital tomorrow—I'll want to talk to Mr. Waring as soon as they let me. And we might need to talk to you again."

"If the security cameras don't bear me out?" She smiled. "I'll be either at the hospital or at home. Feel free to talk to me anytime you like."

She had finally put Charlotte in her cot, but she still hadn't left her, couldn't leave her. She stood in the shaded nursery, her arms folded on the edge of the cot, watching her sleep. She heard Lloyd's footsteps on the stairs, heard the front door open, heard him come into the nursery, but she didn't look round; she couldn't take her eyes off Charlotte. Lloyd came and stood beside her, his arm round her shoulders, his head touching hers. He didn't speak, just held her, and she felt safer with him there.

"Is this what maternal instinct feels like?" she asked, her voice hoarse.

"Sometimes, I suppose."

"I don't like it."

"Instinct's a very primitive thing," he said. "It frightens us."

In that moment, as in many previous moments, she knew why she loved him. He knew what was frightening her better than she knew herself. That it wasn't what had happened so much as her reaction to it, because it wasn't just disturbed, sick, unbalanced people who reverted to the untamed state. Judy knew now that she would kill to protect Charlotte, and that realization of her own lack of civilization was what had frightened her so much. And it frightened her a little less now that Lloyd had put into words what she had merely felt.

Lloyd straightened up the cot blanket that his sister had made, and the movement momentarily woke Charlotte. Then her arms went up beside her head; she gave a little sigh and fell asleep again. Lloyd kissed her, straightened up, and put his arms round Judy.

"I couldn't get here any sooner," he said, kissing her, too. "And I have to go back to work."

She nodded. She didn't know which variant of wickedness he was having to deal with, and right now she didn't want to know. Wicked enough for him to have to carry on dealing with it regardless of the time. But she was very glad he was here now.

"I've time for a sandwich," he said. "I'll make you one."

Her automatic protestation that she had no appetite was silenced by his finger on her lips.

"You have to eat. And I'm sure Charlotte wishes we would get the hell out of her bedroom and let her sleep."

She took another look at Charlotte, then allowed herself to be propelled gently out of the nursery and into the kitchen.

"A lioness protecting her cubs still finds time to grab the odd impala." Lloyd reached into the bread bin as he spoke. "And so can you."

The doorbell rang, and they looked at each other.

"Tom," she said. "I made him promise to tell me what happened."

"I'll go."

Judy didn't leave the kitchen, not until she heard Lloyd's voice echoing up the stairwell.

"A *doll*? How the hell could you mistake a doll for a baby?"

She went back out to the hallway as Lloyd and Tom came upstairs. "A doll?" she said, uncomprehendingly, when they arrived in the doorway. "Did I hear you say it was a doll?"

"Judy, I swear to you, it looks exactly *like* a baby. Well—not really when it's close to, but from a distance, in the water—I made them bag it up, so you could see it for yourself."

"I don't want to see it for myself!"

"I'm sorry." Tom looked helplessly at Lloyd. "I'm so sorry. I would never have—"

"Nothing to be sorry for," said Lloyd briskly. "It wasn't a baby—that's the main thing. I'm just about to make some impala sandwiches. Do you want some?"

Tom looked a little puzzled.

"Private joke," said Lloyd. "Irritating, aren't they? I don't know what will be in the sandwiches until I look in the fridge, but it probably won't be impala. Do you want some?"

"Yes, thanks, I'd love a sandwich, even if it is impala. I'm starving." Tom looked at Judy. "That's if I'm welcome."

Judy's maternal instinct was running riot now; she looked at poor Tom, all pink and worried and upset, and she wanted to cuddle him, too. She contented herself with smiling at him. "Of course you are," she said, and followed him and Lloyd into the kitchen. She felt guilty for having snapped at Tom, but sheer relief had prompted that reaction. "It wasn't your fault. And thank God it wasn't Emma."

Judy found out what Lloyd was working on, as he quickly and efficiently made enough sandwiches to feed the entire Bartonshire Constabulary, and he and Tom proceeded to demolish them. Her ravaged emotions had done nothing for her appetite.

Lloyd told them that he had thought at one point that he had found Emma, but now he thought it might possibly be Kayleigh's own baby. "But if it is, I still don't know what happened to all the baby things, so I'm keeping an open mind about that."

"And do you really reckon this Waring bloke did it himself?" asked Tom.

"He's fast becoming my favorite, but they're all still on the list, including Kayleigh herself. I'm crossing no one off but Alexandra." His mobile rang, and he sighed. "Oh, well, that's my meal break over."

Judy smiled. "Maybe it's a breakthrough."

"Maybe. Hello—Lloyd." He smiled. "I think your sister should be on a retainer." His face grew serious as he listened. "No—I'll go. I'll update you when I get back."

"*Is* it a breakthrough?" Judy asked.

"It could well be." He stood up. "Could I have the keys to your car? Mine's run out of petrol, would you believe, and now I don't even know where the petrol can is. I think I probably left it in a panda car."

Judy gave him the keys, and he was gone. When she and Tom were alone, he apologized again.

Judy shook her head. "I was overreacting. I wasn't being very professional about it, was I?"

Tom smiled. "You're off-duty, and you've had a lot to cope with recently. You get to overreact. But you're always professional."

It was funny, Judy thought. Someone, somewhere, would be very upset, because these dolls that looked almost exactly like real babies cost a lot of money and it had presumably been lost. But it wasn't a real baby, and that put the loss of an expensive toy into perspective.

And her mistaken belief that Emma was dead had put her disappearance into perspective, too; it seemed somehow less hopeless. Everything was relative.

"That couple look as though they must be kosher. They were interviewed separately, and they both saw Andrea with the baby in a pram but said they didn't see the baby on its own. And the husband saw a couple of other people while he was there painting, but . . ." He shrugged. "He says they weren't still around by the time the girl arrived. He saw you, and gave a good description, so I think he's quite reliable."

Judy didn't ask what the description was; she felt she'd rather not see herself as others saw her.

"We've got security camera videos of the Bridge Street car park, and they picked up Andrea taking the baby out of the car and putting her in the pram. There didn't seem to be anyone taking any interest in her, and no one followed them from the car park."

Judy pushed the remainder of the sandwiches over to him. "Do you think Andrea could be involved?"

"You've thought that all along, haven't you? What makes you think she is?"

"Two things, really. One is the way she was acting. She said she didn't see anything, but I felt as though she knew more than she was saying, and she seemed so calm about it all, even though she'd just been screaming her head off."

"And the other thing?"

"It was what you said earlier. About the only person who saw the baby left unattended having stolen her. If you think the couple had nothing to do with it, that makes five people in the immediate area who all saw the girl with the baby, and yet no one noticed the baby on her own." She shrugged. "It just seems odd."

"It does, doesn't it? But she did go back to her car

for her phone—the security video confirmed that as well. All the same, I hadn't thought about that. I'll see what McArthur thinks about leaning on Andrea a bit."

"If he agrees that we should," said Judy, "see if he'll let you do the leaning."

"Why?"

She once saw an angelfish on a wildlife program. There it was, swimming along, gently opening and closing its mouth, looking as though it thought only beautiful thoughts and longed for nothing more than universal love and world peace, when it turned its pretty head toward the fellow marine creature swimming by its side and, without breaking its aquatic stride, ate it.

She smiled. "Just because."

"Well, well, well. If it isn't the prodigal nephew."

She looked older, he thought, as he pecked her on the cheek. But then, she would. He hadn't seen her for a long time. How old was she now? Seventy? Seventy-five? He knew she was quite a bit older than his mother, but he wasn't sure by how many years. He smiled. "Can I come in?"

"How long for this time?" she asked, standing aside to admit him. "Ten minutes or ten weeks?"

"The weekend, if it won't put you out too much." He followed her through to the living room and put his overnight bag down on the trendy wooden floor. Not for his aunt the time capsules that so many solitary elderly people made for themselves. She had acquired a wide-screen telly, he noticed. One of his aunt's prouder boasts was that she had never needed a man to provide for her. She had had a good job with a good pension and she had invested her savings well and wisely, which was why she could afford to retire to her seafront bungalow. She wasn't short of a bob or two.

"No, it won't put me out."

She sat down, but he stood by the window, looking out at the sea. When he was little they had come here on holiday; he used to stand on the shore and imagine how one day he would go to sea. He was going to join the navy and see the world, his mother would say. But he had become an accountant, and he still regretted that just a little. No one wrote rousing drinking songs or romantic adventure stories about accountants. No accountant had ever had his likeness put on top of a 185-foot monument. Accountancy did not inspire poets to stirring lines of verse. Home is the hunter, he thought, home from the hill, and the accountant, home from the office. Ah, well. At least he'd seen some of the world now.

"What wound are you licking this time?" she asked.

He turned. "What makes you think I'm licking a wound?"

"Because the last time your wife had left you. And the time before that you had been made redundant."

He sat down then and thought about that. "Do I really only come to see you when I've got problems? I hadn't realized." He smiled. "Shows you how few problems I've had in my life, doesn't it? I promise I'll come and see you some time when everything's going great."

"I'll get us some tea." She went through to the little kitchen, and he heard the kettle being filled.

He noticed another acquisition. "When did you get the computer?" he called through to her.

"Oh, a couple of years ago. I thought it was time I found out what the information superhighway was all about."

He grinned. "And do you surf the Net often?"

"When I want to find things out," she said, coming in with cookies and little cakes. "And I like E-mail. It's a lot cheaper than the post, for one thing."

"What, are all your cronies on-line, too?" He followed her into the kitchen and plucked mugs from the tree. No china tea services for Auntie.

"I don't write to my cronies." She put tea bags in the pot and poured on the boiling water. "What would I want to write to them for? I see them every day."

"Who then?"

"Whoever I feel like writing to."

"I'll have to give you my E-mail address. Then we can keep in touch. Have you got a mobile phone yet?" He picked up the tray on which she had put milk, sugar, and the teapot, complete with cozy, the only old-fashioned touch he'd noticed, so far. She had always been practical; no sense in letting the tea get cold just to be modern.

"Not yet, but I'm thinking about it. I should keep one on my person at all times, according to the advice sheets. You never know, at my age—I could fall and break my hip."

Lesley had kept hers on her person at all times; clipped to her belt or in her pocket. Organized, well-meaning, infuriating, misguided Lesley. Phil sighed as he set the tray down on the coffee table.

Jean sat down as he poured the tea. "What have you been up to, Phil Roddam?"

"Nothing very clever." He put her mug down in front of her. "You wouldn't want to know."

And the wonderful thing about his aunt Jean was that she would accept that nonanswer and inquire no more deeply into the circumstances.

Bob Sandwell had put out a description of the Audi driver, and his sister, coming in for her night shift, had discovered that Barton General had a patient answering that description whose clothes had been stained with someone else's blood. The staff in the accident and emergency department had been debating the ethics of telling the police; she made their minds up for them and phoned Bob.

Fletcher's police record had been brought up on the computer, and Bob, resourceful as ever and a great believer in the six degrees of separation theory, had rung a friend of a friend of a friend until he had spoken to someone in the Met who had actually worked on the investigation into the sexual offense for which Fletcher had been imprisoned. According to him, Fletcher had found Kayleigh through an Internet chat room, arranged to meet her, cynically and systematically abused her over a period of several weeks, then claimed that she had misled him.

"I put him in here," the doctor said, stopping at a side room off the main ward. "We're keeping him in overnight because of the blow to the head. And I can only let you see him for a few minutes. He's really very tired."

Lloyd nodded and went in. "Dean Fletcher?"

The young man lying on the bed nodded wearily. His mouth was swollen; his arms had masses of tiny cuts and scratches on them. His ribs were strapped up.

"My name is Lloyd. I'm a detective chief inspector with Stansfield CID." He showed Dean his warrant card. "Can I ask where you were at around eleven o'clock this morning, Mr. Fletcher?"

"In Stansfield."

"What brought you to Stansfield?"

"I went there to meet Kayleigh Scott."

Lloyd nodded. "Would you like to tell me how your clothing came to be stained with blood?"

Fletcher sighed. "I fell over a dead body."

Lloyd walked round the little room, glancing out of the window, opening the door of the cupboard beside the bed, picking things up. His purpose, if it could be called that, was twofold; one, it tended to unnerve people when he did it and gave him the chance of catching them off guard; and two, he wanted to give himself a moment to try to assess Fletcher. To Bob, he represented the prime suspect, and Lloyd could hardly disagree; he was there, objecting to their taking Alexandra to Australia, and he ran away. But Lloyd couldn't see how that argument would lead to his battering Kayleigh's mother to death, and Fletcher could just as easily fit the description of the witness shy of giving his name to the police.

All Lloyd knew right now was that Fletcher had broken the conditions of his parole in order to come to Stansfield and that was very stupid, very brave, or very calculating. Already Lloyd had discounted the first possibility, because even tired and in pain, there was an alertness in the eyes that simply wasn't present in truly stupid people. But either of the other two could apply, and while the picture painted of Fletcher by Sandwell's contact suggested the latter, Lloyd wasn't convinced.

"You fell over a dead body." Lloyd put on his glasses and looked at the chart at the end of the bed. It meant nothing to him; he just liked having props. "Where?"

"In a cottage in the middle of a wood."

"And what were you doing there?"

"I told you. I went to meet Kayleigh. But she wasn't there. And I tripped and fell as I went in. I landed on a dead body."

"And is that how you cracked your ribs and banged your head?"

"No. I did that when I fell over the branch of a tree."

Lloyd looked at him over his glasses. "You seem to have been particularly unfortunate."

"Yeah, well. It makes a change. I'm usually lucky, apparently."

Lloyd could hear the bitterness in Fletcher's voice. "A man answering your description was seen abandoning an Audi Quattro, and running into Brook Way Wood. Was that you?"

"Yes. I took the car from the garage."

"In that case, Mr. Fletcher, I'm arresting you for the attempted murder of Ian Waring." He noticed but didn't comment on the show of innocent puzzlement from Fletcher, at odds with his candid answers. "You will be taken to a designated police station as soon as the hospital releases you into our custody, where you will be questioned about these events. I will be removing your clothes in order that they may be forensically examined. You will be given suitable clothing to wear while yours are being examined." He cautioned him, informed him of his right to free legal representation. "Do you understand?" he asked routinely.

"I understand the caution. I don't understand what you're arresting me for."

A male nurse appeared, and Lloyd left, without further enlightening Mr. Fletcher, and headed back to Stansfield.

There wasn't much they could do on the murder during the night, but Lloyd didn't want vigilance relaxed even though they had apprehended the prime suspect. He wanted every call to the incident room followed up until it was too late to do so, every statement cross-checked, and he wanted Phil Roddam found.

Fletcher hadn't mentioned Alexandra, and though it was becoming more and more unlikely, there was still a possibility that the baby was Emma, because they still hadn't found anything at all to suggest that a baby was moving into the cottage. Lloyd had no sooner thought that than PC Sims, on attachment to CID on Tom's recommendation, knocked and put his head round the door. "Alan Marshall found a pram dumped in Brook Way

Wood this afternoon, sir. He's downstairs with it—he says he thinks you'll want to see it."

Downstairs, Lloyd found Marshall, standing as proudly by the pram as any brand-new father. "It's been dusted for prints," he said. "Just in case. It was in a clearing where people do fly-tipping, but it's far too good to have been thrown out, so I think it must have come from Mrs. Newton's car. And I found a handbag—probably Mrs. Newton's, since hers is missing. I think the car was looted by those kids as soon as it was abandoned."

Lloyd was impressed. "What made you think of searching the woods?"

"He did." Alan Marshall jerked his head toward Sims.

PC Sims looked a little bashful. "I asked the lab to take a look at the Audi to see if it had fixings for a baby seat—it occurred to me that if Alexandra had been transported in it, it should have had a baby seat in it."

And why hadn't it occurred to anyone else? thought Lloyd. More specifically, why hadn't it occurred to him? Because, he thought, he had been so convinced that Alexandra was Emma.

"And they confirmed that there are fixings, and since the baby seat had gone, I told Alan I thought the car might have been looted."

"Very good." Lloyd looked closely at the pram. "It's a collapsible pram, isn't it?" he said.

The other two agreed that it was.

"Did you find it like this?"

Marshall nodded.

A puzzle, thought Lloyd. "So why wasn't it collapsed? Surely it would be easier to transport that way?"

"The kids probably used it to wheel away anything they could sell, and then dumped it," said Marshall.

Sometimes his little puzzles didn't last very long. Lloyd was a bit surprised that the boys who stripped the car hadn't been a little more enterprising, because prams were expensive, as he had recently found out, and it would certainly have a secondhand value. But the missing baby things had ceased to be a puzzle, and Alexandra wasn't Emma. Tom had been right; Sims would be an asset.

Lloyd brought the baby-snatch team up-to-date, and now he could concentrate fully on the murder. Tomorrow he would have everyone's background thoroughly researched, Theresa Black's movements checked, and the times that Waring was at her flat confirmed by the security cameras in the garage area. This case, he felt certain, was far from over, whatever everyone else thought.

But tonight, Lesley Newton was in the mortuary, Ian Waring was in intensive care with Theresa Black by his side, and Dean Fletcher was in Casualty with an officer right outside the door, well aware of his charge's history of absconding. With almost all the major players tucked up, one way or another, in Barton General, Lloyd really could go home, this time with a clear conscience.

"No, mate, sorry. No one like that."

Tom was back to square one, now that Lloyd's mystery baby was almost certainly no longer a mystery. McArthur had said that he could interview Andrea Merry tomorrow; as his last job tonight, he was trying the bus drivers, but he was down to his last one.

Judy had been suggesting that Andrea herself had taken Emma, but that wasn't borne out by the video camera evidence. All the same, Tom thought, it *was* odd that no one saw Emma in the pram on her own. And while it was true that they all saw the baby with a girl, they might not, it seemed to him, all have seen the same girl; the clothing was hardly distinctive. They had been thinking in terms of an older woman, but it could have been a young girl who had taken Emma. So he asked if they had seen anyone carrying a baby, especially a youngster.

"Most of them are youngsters," said the one he was speaking to now. "Never heard of contraception, these kids."

"Was there one who had the baby in her arms, rather than in a carry-cot or whatever?"

"No. I mean, you notice. You see them making their way down the bus with a baby, and you know you're going to be there for ages while they find the pushchair or the wheels or whatever it is they've got, and get it out and all that—sometimes you've got to get out and help them or you'd be there all bloody day. If one got off the bus with a baby in her arms and didn't pick up a pushchair . . . you'd notice."

It had been the same story from the taxi drivers. Pushchairs and folding prams were bad news—they always held things up. Besides, a baby who wasn't in a carry-cot or one of those pouch things—you didn't see that very often, not in the middle of town. You'd remember if you picked up someone with a baby in her arms, wouldn't you?

And, so far, no one had reported seeing anyone at all walking with a baby in her arms. They had had one or two calls from neighbors who reckoned that they had suspect babies next door, but so far they had turned up nothing.

If it had been a professional snatch, the baby could be anywhere by now, Tom thought gloomily, especially if Andrea was in their pay. And if that was the case, he had to hope that he could gain her confidence enough for her to get cocky. Just one slip, that was all they would need, and McArthur could be relied upon to put the fear of God into her, Tom was sure.

He drove home to his own children, safe and well with their expectant mother, and hoped that this last throw of the dice would be successful and that the hunt for Emma didn't turn into the kind that made national headlines.

It hadn't surprised Dean when the cop had appeared; he had known, as soon as he was put in a side ward, why he was getting VIP treatment.

It hadn't surprised him when he had been arrested; that had been going to happen the minute he had fallen over the branch. He had known there was no way he could avoid capture, because those kids had seen him and he couldn't run, not this time.

He had declined the nurse's offer of something to help him sleep, but now he wished he had taken him up on it, because in addition to being in pain and scared about what was going to happen, he was completely baffled, and that was what was keeping him awake. Because what *had* surprised him was what he had been arrested for.

Who the hell was Ian Waring, and when was he supposed to have attempted to murder him?

CHAPTER NINE

Judy opened her eyes to the early-morning sunshine, wondering, just for a second, why the dread in the pit of her stomach. And why the silence?

The dread was for Emma. The silence was because this was the first time Judy had woken of her own accord since the eighth of January.

She got up and padded quickly through to the nursery, smiling when she saw Charlotte, like her father, soundly, deeply, earnestly asleep. Judy had slept like that once, but her ability to sleep through anything but very sunny mornings hadn't been able entirely to withstand Lloyd's habit of staying up until all hours before coming to bed, had been further eroded by pregnancy, and had been destroyed altogether by the living alarm clock in the cot.

If only they had found Emma, this would have been a pleasant change, solitary Saturday morning moments when no one was demanding her attention. But Lloyd's mystery baby seemed to belong to Kayleigh, so that ray of hope, never exactly brilliant, had faded away.

She pulled on a robe and went into the kitchen, wondering if she dared try to make herself breakfast. She always used to have a cooked breakfast, but she had found it too difficult after Charlotte's arrival; a plate of bacon and eggs would make her feel a whole lot better about life, she was sure. Lloyd would feed Charlotte if she announced that she was hungry while Judy was still eating. He hadn't been home until late and he had to go in to work, so it wasn't very fair to expect him to do that, but she risked it anyway.

Charlotte graciously allowed Judy to make and eat her own breakfast before she demanded to know where hers was, and Lloyd, showered and shaved, came into the kitchen to find Charlotte being burped. He reached for his coffee—all he ever had in the morning—with one hand and with the other seized the digital camera that he had bought before Charlotte was even born.

"I wish you wouldn't do that! I must look awful. You're never going to look at them all anyway."

"Yes, I am. You can do all sorts of things with them once they're on the computer. If you look awful, my love, I can make you look radiant. I can even turn you into someone else altogether, if that seems preferable."

The man who once positively backed out of a room with a computer in it had discovered that they Did Things, and that was all he needed to know. Lloyd loved gadgets. Judy shook her head. "Are you going to need a lift to a petrol station? Because if you are, you'd better put that thing down and get dressed. You said you were going to Barton to see Kayleigh before you went to work."

"Oh—yes. I'd forgotten about the car." He drank some coffee and disappeared again while Judy got herself and Charlotte ready.

"We're going to the garage," she said to Charlotte. "Where we have to buy not just petrol, but a whole new petrol can, because Daddy's left his somewhere, and he's not sure where. Then we have to go and put the petrol in Daddy's car, because he let it run out. He's had to leave it on a road in a business park, and it will probably have been vandalized, if not stolen. And he lectures me."

Charlotte beamed at her, and Judy felt guilty about

having what Nina Crawford had lost. And about wanting to go back to work, especially now that she knew she might be going to run Malworth CID. It would be a challenge; it was hard to win back the trust of the community when it had been lost. But it would be a challenge that she would relish, and she had liked what she had seen of McArthur, so that hadn't put her off.

But that young woman with her Gucci shoes and briefcase and her old pram had. Charlotte meant everything to Judy, she knew that now, and she didn't want ever to think of her as a chore, a burden to be off-loaded, as coming second. But Judy did want to go back to work, so did that make her just the same as Ms. Gucci? She would see what Lloyd thought, when he wasn't so busy. For now, all he could think of was his murder investigation.

And despite Dean Fletcher having come on the scene, Lloyd still seemed to suspect Ian Waring, Judy found out, as she drove him to the petrol station. "But why would he do that?" she asked. "Surely you don't think he murdered the woman because he didn't want to go to Australia?"

"Because she was rich, perhaps."

"Does he get her money?"

Lloyd shrugged.

"Anyway—didn't you say he was with his ex-partner when the postman heard the row going on?" She was watching the car behind her in the rearview mirror; he was a little too close for comfort. She had become very aware of that since having Charlotte in the back. "He couldn't be in two places at once."

"Why does everyone assume that this row was with Lesley Newton?"

"Because she's the one who was found dead." The driver behind her turned off, much to Judy's relief. She wondered about one of these stickers telling people there was a baby in the back, but she decided against it.

People always thought they could stop in time and would whether there was a sticker or not. Besides, she had always hated the stickers before.

"We have rows," Lloyd pointed out. "Nobody finds battered bodies lying around as a result."

"Not yet." She signaled the turn for the service station.

"Isn't the row more likely to have been with Kayleigh herself? Who else could tell Fletcher with any authority that he wasn't the father?"

That seemed reasonable. "Do you think that's true?"

"I doubt it. I'm still having trouble accepting that Kayleigh had relations with one man, never mind more than one. I suspect he came causing trouble, and she told him that purely to get rid of him."

"But if Waring had already killed Lesley before he took the van back to Theresa Black," Judy said when Lloyd had returned with his new petrol can and was filling it up, "that means Kayleigh and Fletcher were having this argument with Lesley's dead body in the house."

"Yes," said Lloyd thoughtfully. "It does, doesn't it? And it wouldn't surprise me. Fletcher says he fell over a dead body, and perhaps he did, because I think Kayleigh knew her mother was dead before I told her. She seemed to know something had happened to her, at any rate. And she was anxious to know where Ian was."

"Of course she knew something had happened to her mother—the police were all over the place. And she wanted to know where Ian was because she needed to see a friendly face."

"I'm not convinced his was a friendly face." Lloyd went off to pay for the petrol, and Judy realized what else was wrong with Lloyd's theory.

"Don't you think Theresa Black would have noticed the blood on Waring's clothes, if he'd done it before he left?" she asked when they were under way again.

"He had other clothes there. He could have dumped the ones he was wearing, and changed."

"Where did he dump them? No one's found any bloodstained clothes, have they?"

"Well, no, not unless you count the ones Mrs. Newton was unpacking, and that would mean he was wearing a size ten floral print summer dress when he did it, so all right, he didn't dump the clothes. But he could have been stark naked, for all we know."

"Why? Or are you saying it was planned?"

"Oh, I'm sure it was planned."

He obviously wasn't going to tell her why he was so sure, which meant it was something he had yet to prove. But Waring *did* have blood on his clothes, which seemed to negate what Lloyd had just said. Judy pointed that out.

"So he did," he conceded. "And yet, whatever way you look at it—whether he murdered her or not—there doesn't seem to be any good *reason* for him to have blood on his clothes. So it's a little puzzle, isn't it?"

It wasn't really a puzzle, Judy thought as she drove to where Lloyd had left his car. Just because seasoned police officers, used to the aftermath of violence, used to dealing with road accidents, recognized death when they saw it didn't mean that Waring did—he could have tried to revive Lesley, however useless the attempt. Or could simply have held her in his arms, unwilling to believe what had happened; Freddie was quite right—there was no right way to react to sudden and violent death.

But Lloyd was into his theorizing stride. "So let's say that Waring has done away with Lesley, and has left the cottage. Kayleigh comes back from wherever she's been—Waring got rid of her on some pretext or another—and she's on her own with Alexandra when Dean Fletcher arrives. He argues with her about taking Alexandra to

Australia, and she tells him he's not Alexandra's father to get rid of him."

Judy nodded.

"But he doesn't give up, so Kayleigh, carrying Alexandra, tries to leave by way of the utility room. She's still in the kitchen when she puts the utility room light on, and she sees her mother's body. She comes back out of the kitchen just as Waring arrives home. She realizes that he must have killed her, and runs out of the house, into the woods, and stays there until she feels brave enough to come back."

"OK."

"No objections yet? This must be a record." He thought for a moment before carrying on. "Meanwhile, Waring and Dean are left in the house. Waring can't trot out his story about having found the body, so he has to dispose of the witnesses, starting with Dean. He hopes to deal with Kayleigh later."

Now poor Ian Waring was turning into a would-be multiple murderer, but Judy still didn't raise any objections. Theorizing was how Lloyd disposed of his little puzzles, and their disposal made the big puzzle easier to solve, according to him. He was very often right.

"Yes. . . ." Lloyd expanded on his theme. "Waring fought with Dean, and the fight took them into the sitting room, where Dean was pushed into the mirror, getting covered in cuts from the broken glass. Possibly was attacked with that little table, getting the blow to his head, cracking his ribs."

Judy smiled. "Why didn't Waring just use the doorstop again? It would have been more effective."

"Because it was still in the utility room. And Dean Fletcher *is* covered in cuts, which is more than anyone else is—he must have got them somehow. And the cracked ribs."

"Perhaps he fell over the branch of a tree, like he said. He was found in the woods, wasn't he?"

Lloyd ignored her mundane solution. "He managed to get away, and ran through to the kitchen, with Waring following. In the utility room, they struggled again—disturbing the body, and each getting the victim's blood on their clothing—until Dean finally got away from him and ran into the garage."

"Intrepid, isn't he?" Judy pulled into the curb ahead of Lloyd's car, which had remained unmolested during the night. "He's got cracked ribs and concussion, but Dean wins through."

"He didn't have concussion," said Lloyd in defense of his story. "Just a bang on the head. He was woozy, but not concussed. Anyway, Waring runs out of the utility room via the kitchen and hallway—leaving shoe prints—arriving at the front door as Dean drives out. And Dean runs the car into him."

"Why?"

"To stop him doing anything to Kayleigh."

"And then he kindly stopped to ring the police?" She undid her seat belt. "Are you going to put that petrol in your car, or what?"

They got out, and Lloyd unlocked his petrol cap. Judy checked Charlotte, who had predictably fallen asleep, and felt again a pang of guilt.

"No reason why he shouldn't ring the police. He wouldn't want the man to die, because it would make it more difficult for him if he got caught." Lloyd emptied the contents of the petrol can into his tank as he spoke. "But, obviously, he had no intention of getting caught—he didn't even want us knowing he'd been there, since that would land him in trouble, so he gave Waring's name; then he drove off, and abandoned the car." He put the empty can in the boot and slammed it shut. "Well? Does it pass muster?"

It accounted for the shoe prints and the blood on Fletcher's and Waring's clothes. It accounted for Kayleigh wandering round carrying a fourteen-pound baby for three and a half hours. Judy couldn't see anything immediately wrong with it, except that it was nonsense, but Lloyd knew that already. She watched him drive off, then got back into the car and drove Charlotte home, firmly putting the missing Emma and her own shortcomings as a mother out of her mind and concentrating on Lloyd's investigation instead.

Lloyd didn't believe his wild theories; they were just possible answers to the questions thrown up by an investigation, until they could be disproved. He wanted them to be challenged, to have the holes in them pointed out, so that he could see the facts more clearly. Judy hadn't been able to find much in the way of elimination that time, so she probably hadn't helped very much; it wasn't as easy when she was having to work on his puzzles secondhand.

But she had a little puzzle of her own, because while Lloyd didn't think for a minute that all that had gone on exactly as he had outlined it, he really did seem to suspect Waring of this murder, and it was for no reason at all that Judy could see.

It was DCI Lloyd, Mrs. Spears said, and once again Kayleigh found herself in the quiet room. She had discovered that it was a room that you had to have permission to go into; if someone was in there who wanted to be alone, you couldn't just barge in on her. But the system didn't seem to work with Kayleigh; she hadn't been alone in it for five minutes.

DCI Lloyd smiled his serious smile and she and Mrs. Spears sat down, but he didn't; he walked slowly round the room, looking at the pictures on the walls—drawings that the children had done, mostly. "I'd like to talk to you about Alexandra," he said.

Kayleigh's heart gave such a dip that it hurt.

"I think I was mistaken," he went on, "when I assumed that Alexandra was your sister. She isn't your sister, is she?"

Kayleigh shook her head, waiting to see what was coming before allowing herself to speak.

"And last night, I spoke to Dean." DCI Lloyd wasn't looking at her; he was putting his glasses on to read the names of the children who had done the pictures. He glanced at her as he said Dean's name.

They'd got Dean. She still couldn't understand why he had gone to the cottage. And why did he take her mother's car? That must be how they found him.

"Was it you and Dean who were having the argument about Alexandra?"

She didn't know what to do. But if she said that it was, then they might not work out that it must have been Phil, arguing with her mother. She swallowed and nodded.

"All right, Kayleigh." He gave her shoulder a little pat. "I'll leave you alone now." He walked to the door and turned back. "We haven't been able to get hold of Mr. Roddam yet, but we'll get him here as soon as we can. Do you think you might feel able to talk to him?"

Kayleigh nodded again. If she could talk to Phil on his own, it might make things a bit easier.

They had given him trousers and an open-neck shirt, old but clean; he was clearly going to be here for some time, or it would have been paper overalls. Now he was in an interview room, watching while they set up the tape. He had waived his right to have a solicitor present. In his experience, solicitors just complicated things, and what he was going to tell them was very simple.

"You know why you're here, Mr. Fletcher?" said Chief Inspector Lloyd.

"No."

"Well, for one thing," said the man who had called himself Acting Detective Inspector Sandwell, "you've admitted taking and driving away a car without the owner's consent."

"Fair enough." Dean turned to Lloyd. "But you arrested me for trying to murder someone I've never even heard of."

"Ian Waring," said Lloyd. "Who owns Brook Way Cottage. He's in intensive care at Barton General Hospital, having been run down in his own driveway, and our laboratory has confirmed that the car you've admitted taking and driving away is the car that was used to run him down."

Dean didn't understand. He hadn't run anyone down. Why did they think he had? Ian Waring must be the guy at the cottage. But . . . it didn't make sense. If that's who he was and they found him in his driveway, then who *had* run him down? And when? Dean thought about those desperate moments in the garage and felt himself grow pale as he realized what must have happened. Just like when they had interviewed him about Kayleigh, he was discovering that he *had* done what they were accusing him of doing, and once again, he hadn't known he'd done it. "Oh, Jesus," he said.

"Go on, Mr. Fletcher."

"Oh, God. Oh, look—I swear to God, I didn't know I'd hit anyone. I just backed out as fast as I could, and there was all this stuff piled up in the back, you know? I couldn't see where I was going. I just turned the car left so I could drive out of the gates frontwards, and I knew

I'd hit something, but I swear . . . I didn't know it was him!" He couldn't believe it; of all the things that had happened yesterday, he had thought that taking the car was the least of his troubles.

"And if you had known you'd hit someone," Sandwell said, his voice heavily sarcastic, "you would of course have stopped and rendered assistance?"

"No, I'm not saying that! I wanted out of there, and I'd probably have just carried on—but I *didn't* know I'd hit anyone. I thought I'd banged into one of those pillars. It wasn't deliberate, for God's sake!"

Lloyd stood up then; he started wandering round, like he'd done last night in the hospital. Dean watched him for a moment.

"All right," said Sandwell. "What were you doing at the cottage in the first place?"

"I thought Kayleigh would be there." Dean prepared himself to tell his story, but as far as he could see, Lloyd wasn't even going to listen, never mind believe him. "I didn't get an answer when I knocked, but I could see there was a side door off the garage into the house, and it was open, so I went in that way. But it was dark, and I tripped over something heavy."

He glanced at Lloyd, who was looking out of the clear pane of glass at the top of the frosted window, as though anything and everything was more interesting than listening to him.

So he addressed himself to Sandwell, telling him that he had picked himself up after falling on the body and had then heard a car pulling up. He had frozen for a few moments, panicking, then had hidden behind the car in the garage. He saw the utility room light go on and heard someone dialling 999, asking for help, and tried to get away before he got the blame, but he was seen. The keys were in the ignition of the Audi; he got in and reversed out. He had not realized that he had run anyone over.

Sandwell had asked the odd question—did he know whose body it was, did he see the man who had called the police, did he see anyone else there, that sort of thing. His answers were that he thought the body looked like Kayleigh's mother, no, he hadn't seen the man who had called the police, just heard him, and no, there had been no one else there to the best of his knowledge.

Lloyd had got tired of looking out of the window; now he was perched on the edge of a low cabinet, leafing through some booklet.

"How did you find out where Kayleigh lived?" Sandwell asked.

"Hasn't she told you?"

"Just answer the question."

He explained about her writing to him in prison.

Sandwell made a disbelieving noise. "And why would she do that? She was the one who had you put away— why would she want to get in touch with you?"

"Look, I know what it sounded like in court, but it wasn't like that."

"It doesn't matter what it was like," Sandwell said. "She was a thirteen-year-old child."

"I know that now, but she didn't *look* thirteen. She told me she was eighteen, and she *wasn't* a child. When I finally did ring her she told me she had had my baby in December, before the trial." He gave up on Sandwell ever believing him and looked at Lloyd, who now seemed to be reading with great interest the notice that gave advice to people in custody. "She had my baby," he repeated. "Doesn't that *prove* she wasn't a child?"

Lloyd ignored him, and Sandwell was still unimpressed. "She was barely thirteen years old," he said again. "Baby or no baby. And why would she tell you about it now? She didn't mention it at the trial, did she?"

"But she *did* tell me. And she said she wanted to see me."

"It didn't sound to our witness as though she wanted to see you."

"Witness?" repeated Dean, baffled. "What witness? And what is your witness supposed to have witnessed?"

"All in good time, Dean. How did you really find out about the baby? How did you know where she lived?"

Dean looked down at the table. He didn't have any proof that Kayleigh had wanted to see him, and for some reason, she hadn't told them that she did. He wondered, then, if something had happened to her. "Is Kayleigh all right?" he asked.

"She's fine."

Then why hadn't she told them? They thought he'd come looking for her, and that would make it all even worse than it already was. He supposed she thought she should keep quiet about him being there at all, since he was breaking the conditions of his parole. "She told me," he said wearily. "How else *could* I have found out?"

"Prisons have grapevines. If you wanted to know where she was, there are people who can find out for you."

"Oh, yeah, like I was one of the lads." He looked up. "No one would give me the time of day, never mind Kayleigh's address. *She* told me. And she wanted to see me."

"I don't think so," said Sandwell. "You wanted to see her, though. You heard that she'd had your baby, and that she was going to take her to Australia, and you didn't like that, did you?"

Dean blinked at him. "Australia?" he repeated, shaking his head. "I don't know what you're talking about."

Sandwell sat forward. "You were overheard, Dean. Someone heard you shouting at her that she couldn't take your daughter to Australia."

Dean stared at him. "I never even saw her or the baby! They weren't there. I don't know anything about Australia, and I didn't have an argument with anyone."

"All right—let's say I believe you. She asks you to meet her, and despite the fact that you say she lied to you about who she was and how old she was, despite the fact that she then reported you to the police and made you out to be an Internet pedophile, despite the fact that you could find yourself back in prison if you were seen with her, you agreed to meet her?"

Put like that, it sounded crazy. It had been crazy, he supposed. But though he had done many things in his life before thinking them through, that hadn't been one of them. "To start with, I said no, but she really wanted me to do it, and I thought maybe it was the least I could do."

"Wanted you to do what?"

"She wanted a photograph of me holding Alexandra," Dean said. "She wanted Alexandra to have it. So that she would know that her father had seen her, and held her. I said I'd do it." He looked up again at Sandwell, not expecting to be believed, and he wasn't disappointed.

"You came to have your photograph taken? Do me a favor, Dean."

"Yes, I came to have my photograph taken. Because I knew that she had a real hang-up about not knowing who her father was. I think it really screwed her up—I think that's why she got involved with me in the first place, why she told me all these lies about herself. I didn't want the baby to be screwed up like that because of me. If this photograph would help, then I was prepared to do it."

Sandwell raised his eyes to heaven. "Did you do a psychology course in prison?"

Dean ignored the sarcasm. "It didn't seem much to ask, and she said she could make sure no one saw me."

"Oh, yes?" Sandwell's face was like stone.

It didn't matter, Dean told himself, if they didn't believe him. Kayleigh would confirm it once she realized that there was no point in keeping quiet about it. He described how she'd told him to wait on Brook Way Bridge and that she would come and meet him.

"She said to watch for a white van, because they'd borrowed it for the move and it had to go back to its owner. Once it had gone, she would tell her mother that she was taking Alexandra out for some fresh air, and she would meet me without the risk of anyone seeing me with her, because her mum would be in the cottage and her mum's boyfriend would be driving the van." He grew tired of Sandwell's disbelieving expression and turned once again to Lloyd. "But she hadn't turned up, so I went to the cottage." He was talking, of necessity, to Lloyd's back, since he seemed to be reading the instructions for the fan that sat in the corner of the room.

"What time was she supposed to meet you?" asked Sandwell.

"No particular time—anytime after the van passed, she said. I don't know what time it was."

"What made you think she wasn't coming?"

"I didn't."

"Then why didn't you wait for her? Why did you go to the cottage? I thought you didn't want her mother to know were there."

"I thought Kayleigh would be on her own. I thought her mum must have taken the van back instead, because I'd seen the van go past, and then I saw her mum's boyfriend leaving."

That got Lloyd's attention. He looked up from the fan instructions. "You saw him leaving? In a vehicle, or on foot?"

"On foot."

"How do you know her mother's boyfriend?" asked Sandwell.

"Kayleigh told me about him. And he came to the trial, sat with her mother."

"Describe him to me."

"He's in his late forties, early fifties, maybe. Not a lot of hair. Not fat, but he doesn't exactly work out a lot."

Lloyd shook his head and went back to the instructions, apparently not in the least interested in that.

"Sorry, Dean," said Sandwell. "Nice try. But her mother's changed boyfriends since the trial. That one doesn't live with her anymore."

He had known they wouldn't believe him. "I saw him," he repeated. "So I started walking back through the woods to the cottage. I thought I'd either meet Kayleigh on her way to the bridge, or see her at the cottage. But when I got there, no one answered the door. And everything happened after that the way I've already told you."

The fan whirred into life. Lloyd examined it closely, pushed in a button, and the blades sped up.

"There's just one problem with that," said Sandwell.

Dean, fascinated by Lloyd's activities, brought his attention back to Sandwell with some difficulty. "What problem?"

"Kayleigh's confirmed that you and she were the couple having the row."

He felt as though he'd been punched in the stomach, and he closed his eyes, almost in physical pain. "No," he said. She couldn't be screwing his life up again, not again. Why? Why would she lie? Why would she *do* that? He opened his eyes and looked at Sandwell. "No!"

he shouted. "I don't care what she's saying. I wasn't arguing with Kayleigh or anyone else. Kayleigh wasn't there. The baby wasn't there. I fell over a dead body, and now you tell me I ran someone over, and I'm sorry about that, but it was an accident. That's what I did. And it's all I did."

Sandwell was entirely unmoved. "She told you that you weren't Alexandra's father—did that upset you?"

Dean stared at him. What was all this? Was Sandwell making it up? Was his so-called witness? Was Kayleigh? It made no sense, anyway. "Why would she tell me that? She got me here *because* I'm Alexandra's father!"

Sandwell nodded, his face thoughtful. "All right—I'll accept that. But you went to the cottage, instead of waiting for her where she'd told you to wait, and you were wrong about Kayleigh being there on her own, because her mother was there. So was it her mother who told you that you weren't the father? Was that who you had the row with? Did she find out about your tryst with Kayleigh, and put a stop to it?" His eyes widened slightly as another solution presented itself to him. "Did *Kayleigh* kill her? Is that why you keep saying she wasn't there?"

Dean didn't even bother to answer. Lloyd pushed another button, and the fan began to oscillate slowly. He moved the fan experimentally, presumably trying to gauge the best position for the even distribution of disturbed air.

"Just tell us the truth, Dean," said Sandwell. "I'm tired of playing guessing games."

"I've told you the truth. I've told you a dozen times."

The fan's configuration finally met with Lloyd's approval. Now he came and sat down opposite Dean. "From the top," he said.

Dean frowned. "What do you mean?"

"It's an informal musical expression, Mr. Fletcher. It

means to repeat what you have just done, from the beginning. In your case, I want you to tell me your story again, from the beginning—by your reckoning, for the thirteenth time. By mine, for the second time."

"You mean right from where Kayleigh wrote to me in prison?"

"I do. You can, of course, refuse. That is your right."

Dean shook his head wonderingly. "No, I don't mind. But if you listened the first time round, you'd find your interviews would go a lot quicker."

And tiredly, a little self-consciously, he began all over again.

Theresa had stayed all night, despite the attempts of the hospital staff to make her go home. He was breathing for himself now, and the doctors were very pleased with his progress—they said that his level of consciousness had improved considerably, and they really seemed to think he was going to be all right. Except, she thought, as she looked at his peaceful, blank sleeping face, Chief Inspector Lloyd believed he had murdered Lesley. It seemed ludicrous. But then . . . he had never been bullied before. And perhaps . . .

No, she told herself, that was nonsense. He could never have been so calm, so ordinary, if he had just done something like that. But at the back of her mind she knew she had heard those words, read those words, in the accounts of murder trials. People who murdered and then went to the pub as usual, people who murdered and went to work. Everyone saying how normal they had seemed.

Not Ian, though. Not Ian. She had known Ian all her adult life; he never lost his temper. He would put up token resistance and then just go along with people, like he was going along with Lesley about Australia.

Phil—well, by his own admission, he flew into rages.

He said he'd never been violent toward another person, but Theresa didn't *know* that he hadn't. And he had been very angry when she'd told him about them going to Australia. She had tried to ring him several times, but all she got was the answering service, on his home phone and his mobile. He did seem to have disappeared. Oh, but surely not. Surely he wouldn't have done something like that.

She tried not to think about it, because if he had, it was all her fault.

Fletcher was telling his story again, still looking perplexed about why he was being asked to do it.

But Lloyd always found it best to let people talk, and then go over what they had said. That way, he could find out if it had been rehearsed—people tended to use exactly the same phrases, tell the story in exactly the same order, if it had. And he could seek clarification of any points that concerned him with the benefit of having already heard the whole story. So far, Fletcher was passing his tests; Lloyd hadn't had to interrupt him at all.

But he couldn't understand why Fletcher was so anxious to keep Kayleigh out of it. As he had pointed out, if she had brought him here purely so that the baby could have a photograph of her father holding her, telling him when he got here that he *wasn't* the father would seem a particularly perverse thing to do. And yet Kayleigh had confirmed that she was the one having the argument, so someone was lying. It was much more likely to be Fletcher, much more likely that Kayleigh hadn't told him about the baby at all, that he'd heard about it from someone else and had gone there to make trouble. The problem was that Lloyd believed Fletcher and didn't believe Kayleigh. Fletcher was convincing; even Bob Sandwell seemed to be coming round to that way of thinking.

When Dean had finished, Lloyd pulled a bundle of papers toward him. "I had this faxed through," he said. "It's a transcript of your trial."

Dean rubbed the back of his neck. "Look—I know you think I'm some sort of creep who looks in chat rooms for underage girls, but I'm not."

"She said that she was nervous of being there with you and wanted to leave, but you persuaded her to stay and got her drunk so that you could have sex with her. That afterward you told her not to tell anyone or you'd get into trouble. That you gave her presents to let you, to use her words, 'do things' with her."

"It wasn't like that."

"Did you stop her leaving?"

Dean looked uncomfortable. "Well—yes, I suppose. I thought she had just got cold feet because she'd never done anything like that before, but neither had I, so we were in the same boat. I mean, I just said she couldn't run out on me, not after all the stuff she'd been writing to me. I was on a promise—that sort of thing."

"Did you buy alcohol?"

"Well—yes. A half bottle of vodka. She suggested it. She said it would steady her nerves."

"Was she under the influence of the vodka when she finally did let you have sex with her?"

Fletcher sighed, nodded. "A bit. But she wasn't drunk."

"Did you say anything about getting into trouble?"

"I—well . . . I knew she had sneaked out to meet me, that she wasn't being completely straight with me. So I said I hoped she'd keep me out of it if she got found out, because I didn't want to get any bother about it. But I meant with her boyfriend or husband or whatever. And, yes, before you ask, I bought her presents! Didn't you ever buy your girlfriends presents?"

"No lies, then."

Dean looked down at the table. "Not lies, exactly. But she made it sound . . . I don't know . . . dirty. And it wasn't. I didn't abuse her! We made love. Both of us."

"She was thirteen years old," Bob Sandwell said for the third time.

"She told me she was eighteen."

"We've seen Kayleigh," Sandwell said. "Spoken to her. Even if she did tell you she was eighteen, you must have known it wasn't the case. You just didn't care. It amounts to the same thing."

Sandwell was right, of course, thought Lloyd. Fletcher couldn't possibly have believed she was old enough. But as for the rest, the truth could be stretched to breaking point without actually committing perjury. It didn't lessen the offense, but it did put a different complexion on it.

Dean sat back. "Has Kayleigh told you all this about Australia and me having a row with her about Alexandra? It isn't true."

"She's told us very little," said Lloyd. "Which is why I'm inclined to believe you."

Dean sighed. "Is this where he's the aggressive cop and you're the sympathetic one? There's no need for all that. Just ask me what you want to know."

Lloyd did have sympathy for Fletcher, but not because he and Bob had worked out some interviewing strategy. Kayleigh's youth was what made the relationship illegal, but hardly unnatural; Lloyd was inclined to agree that anyone sexually mature enough to give birth was no longer a child. After all, he thought, Judy was thirteen when he was twenty-three; he hadn't known her then, but what if he had? He would have had the sense not to get involved with her, but he might well have fallen for her. He couldn't voice any of that, of course, but yes, he did have sympathy for Fletcher.

"Look—all I want is for you to stop thinking of me as

some sort of child abuser, because I'm not. We met over the Internet. Hundreds of couples have met that way—I didn't think anything of it. And I've had it up to here with being treated like some sort of monster, like one of those sickos who get their kicks doing it with kids, because I'm *not* one!"

"You sound very bitter about it," Lloyd said.

"Of course I'm bitter about it! I've got to notify the police of every address I use. Even if I go for two weeks to Blackpool! And what happens? You tell me. What happens if some kid goes missing in Blackpool while I'm there?"

"You would be routinely brought in for questioning."

"That's right. And I'll be routinely spit at when I leave. And routinely hounded out of my own home if it gets out that I'm on the register. You'd better believe I'm bitter, but because that's *not how it was*!"

"You can't have it both ways," said Sandwell. "You want us to believe that she told a pack of lies to send you to prison, and yet you also want us to believe that you came running when she called."

"It wasn't her fault—I told you, I think she got screwed up somewhere along the way, and that's why she told me all these lies about herself. And I added to her problems, even if I didn't know that's what I was doing. She probably resented that. Resented me, for making her pregnant. So if coming here meant I could make things better . . ." He shrugged.

"Oh, spare me," said Sandwell.

"It wasn't how it looked! We had a real relationship." Fletcher looked down, his face reddening slightly. "It sounds strange now I know how old she is, but I loved her." He looked up defiantly. "I still do. That's why I did what she asked. Because I once told her I'd do anything for her, and I meant it."

Did he now, thought Lloyd. Did that include covering up for her when she dispatched her mother with the doorstop? Or, perhaps, covering up for her when she tried to murder Waring in revenge for what he had done to her mother? Kayleigh could have found her mother, as he had suggested to Judy, but rather than running into the woods had run to the safety of the car, locked herself in, leaving Dean to fight off Waring. Dean joined her in the car, drove out . . . and perhaps Kayleigh, seeing Waring, had grabbed the wheel, driven the car into him. Perhaps that was why he kept denying that she was there at all.

"How did you get the swollen mouth?" Lloyd asked. "The cracked ribs and the cuts? Were you in a fight with someone?"

"No. I got the cuts when I ran through a load of greenery in the woods. And I told you how I cracked my ribs. I fell over a low branch at the base of a tree. That's how I got the smack in the mouth, too."

"You can take me to this aggressive tree, can you?"

"Of course I can't! I don't know where the hell I was."

At ten forty-five, Lloyd terminated the interview and was summoned to Case's office as soon as he had got back into his own.

"Roddam finally rang Sandwell—he's on a train to Stansfield."

At least now they would get a positive identification of the body. "I'll meet him at the station," said Lloyd. "Take him to Barton General myself—I want his help with Kayleigh, so we can go to the children's home afterward."

He turned to go, wondering why Case couldn't have vouchsafed this information on the phone instead of dragging him all the way upstairs—why, indeed, he hadn't left it to Sandwell to tell him. But he didn't have to wonder long.

"Why didn't you arrest Fletcher for Mrs. Newton's murder? Why just the attempted murder?"

Lloyd turned back and looked at his boss, knowing that his face held the slightly mutinous expression that would cause Judy to give him the Look. "Mainly because I don't think he did murder Mrs. Newton," he said.

Case reached for his cigarettes, a sure sign that this was a complication he could do without. "I know better than to dismiss your theories out of hand, so I won't." He lit up. "But everyone else thinks he murdered her. Why don't you?"

Lloyd sat down. "I can't work him out."

Case released cigarette smoke. "What's to work out? He's a violent offender who abuses little girls."

That was certainly how it looked on paper, and Lloyd was having a problem with it. "Does that strike you as someone who would give a damn what happened to Alexandra?" he asked.

"Ownership. It wouldn't matter if it was Alexandra or a microwave oven. If he owns it, he claims it."

Lloyd shook his head. "And murders for it?"

"Like I said, he's violent." Case shrugged. "She said he wasn't the father, so he picked something up, hit her—realized he'd better finish the job."

"So you think that the row the postman heard was between Fletcher and Lesley Newton?"

"Yes, Lloyd, oddly enough, I do." Case took a long drag of his cigarette, expelled the smoke, and looked at Lloyd through the haze. "Since she's the one who's been murdered."

That was what Judy had said, but Lloyd thought they were both wrong about that. "I think that Kayleigh said it to get rid of him. And I can't see it being something that her mother would say even for that reason."

"I expect he was rowing with both of them." Case

ground out his cigarette, only half-smoked. "When it turned nasty, Kayleigh took Alexandra away from it, like you said all along."

Lloyd smiled to himself. Case was hoping that admission that he had been right in the first place would appease him, but it wouldn't. There was something all wrong about this.

Case sat back and looked at him. "You," he said, after long moments, "think that Waring did it. Without a scrap of evidence. And why? All right, so Lesley Newton has money—so what? He only went to live with her January— they haven't married. Her money probably goes to this Roddam bloke and Kayleigh."

"Very probably. I'd be happy to entertain either of them as suspects. Fletcher says he saw Roddam leaving the cottage just before he got there."

"And you believe him?" Case's voice was incredulous.

"Not necessarily—he obviously thought Roddam still lived with Lesley Newton, and he was possibly just trying to shift suspicion onto someone else." He gave Case the bare bones of Dean's statement. "But I'll certainly ask Roddam where he was yesterday morning, because regardless of her money, Lesley Newton had taken up with Waring, so he had a motive, as you yourself pointed out."

"So had Fletcher, and he's got a record of violence going way back."

Lloyd frowned. "What motive?"

"Anger is a motive, Lloyd. All right, you believe him that Kayleigh brought him here—fair enough. The way I see it is that Kayleigh wanted him to see the baby, and her mother found out. She was waiting for him at the cottage, and she told him he wasn't the father in the hope that he would go away. He lost his rag, picked up the first heavy object he could find, and battered her with it.

Kayleigh grabbed the baby and ran away when it got violent."

Lloyd considered that. It sounded plausible. It was more or less what Bob Sandwell thought. But he didn't think that Fletcher had tried to cure Kayleigh's problems by murdering her mother.

"And there's the little matter of evidence," Case said. "He's the one who deliberately ran down Ian Waring. He's the one who abandoned the car and ran away, who has Mrs. Newton's blood all over his clothes—"

"He says he ran Waring down accidentally." Lloyd told Case what Fletcher had said about the car. "And if the baby's things were in it, that could be true, too. But he keeps insisting that Kayleigh and the baby weren't there at all and we know that they were, so he could be covering up for her. She could have caused what happened to Waring in revenge for what he had done to her mother. Or she could have murdered her mother herself."

Case sat back and looked at him, his mouth slightly open. "You're happy to—how did you put it?—ah, yes, you're 'happy to entertain' Waring and Kayleigh and Phil Roddam as suspects, but not Fletcher? Am I missing something here?"

"I haven't crossed anyone off. But Waring's my favorite, and Kayleigh's my second favorite. Roddam's odds could shorten or lengthen—it depends. And as far as I'm concerned, Fletcher is the rank outsider."

Case ground out his cigarette and swiveled his chair round to look out of the window for a moment before turning back. "You know what I feel like around you? I feel as though I'm playing one of those namby-pamby parlor games, where everyone's in on the joke but me. 'Mrs. Newton loves butter, but she doesn't like cream.' " He employed a high-pitched, camp middle-class voice for his example; then it dropped back to its usual gruffness. "I never could get the hang of them, and I never can get the hang of you."

Lloyd smiled.

"Am I supposed to *guess* why he's the odd one out? You only suspect people whose first names have an *i* in them?"

Case wasn't that unfamiliar with namby-pamby parlor games, thought Lloyd, still smiling. "Not quite that off-the-wall. But it wouldn't stand up in court."

Case shook his head. "To hell with court. You don't think it would stand up in this *office*!"

True. And he hadn't felt sure of it enough to tell Judy, so nothing would induce him to tell Case what it was. But it was more than that; he believed that Fletcher *had* fallen over a dead body and that he hadn't deliberately attempted to kill Waring.

And, despite having advanced the notion to Case, Lloyd felt that covering up for Kayleigh seemed unlikely, because he even believed Fletcher when he said that he hadn't seen her, hadn't had an argument with her or her mother. And Lloyd believed him not because he had Waring down for the murder, but because he liked to think that he knew when someone was speaking the truth. Kayleigh—even though she hadn't spoken—was not, in his estimation, being entirely truthful, and if Fletcher had not been having the argument with her, then perhaps there *was* someone else who was claiming to be the father of her baby.

"Tell me," said Case. "I know Theresa Black's alibi checked out, but if it hadn't . . . would she have been on your A-list?"

"That's an impossible question to answer." Lloyd smiled again, knowing just how much he was about to irritate his superintendent. "It's because she's *not* a suspect that I've got an A-list at all."

*   *   *

Tom Finch wasn't looking forward to his interview with Andrea, because she was still living with the Crawfords. He would have preferred the station, but McArthur was very big on interviewing people at home unless and until it was necessary to take them in for questioning.

A tear-stained, tight-lipped Nina Crawford opened the door to him. She had known to expect him and he immediately told her that he had no news, but he hadn't been able to stop the hope rising and dying in her eyes. He introduced Sarah, the WPC—not that he called her that, of course, not being in any way sexist—who had come to chaperon the visit, since it would take place in Andrea's bedroom, and was invited in.

"No news," said Mrs. Crawford when her husband jumped up from where he sat, and he sat down again, his face tortured.

"I was surprised to discover that Andrea was still with you," said Tom. "In the circumstances."

"She's under notice," said Mrs. Crawford. "But I won't throw a seventeen-year-old girl out on the street. I have to give her time to find somewhere to live."

Tom nodded. Why did things like this happen to good people?

"What do you want with her?" asked Roger Crawford.

"Oh, just details," said Tom. "Sometimes people remember things afterward—she may have seen something that she didn't recollect in the shock of finding Emma gone."

"Is *anything* happening?" Crawford's question sounded like a plea. "Have you been told anything at all that you can go on?"

"I'm sure Mr. McArthur would have let you know if we had anything concrete," said Tom. "But it is a fact that babies taken in this way are almost always found, and returned unharmed."

"Almost always," repeated Mrs. Crawford, her voice flat.

"I'd be lying if I said always, Mrs. Crawford. But believe me, every lead is being checked. Everything that can be done is being done." It was cold comfort; he knew that. But it was all he had to offer.

Upstairs, they found Andrea sitting on her bed, looking, if anything, even more devastated than the Crawfords. Once again, Tom had to say that there was no news, and once again, he had to try to reassure someone who was in near despair.

"She's not coming back, is she?" Andrea said, rocking slightly on the edge of the bed. "She's not coming back."

"I've just told Mrs. Crawford," said Tom, "that stolen babies are almost always found. And they've usually been very well looked after."

"No. No—she's gone. Something's happened to her. Something must have happened to her, or why hasn't anyone brought her back?"

Andrea had had direct responsibility for Emma, Tom thought. That was why she was feeling even more wretched than the baby's parents and wasn't allowing herself the luxury of hope, as she dissolved into tears of desperation.

It seemed impossible that the distress was manufactured, but he had to question her again, just in case. As soon as Sarah managed to calm her down.

Phil Roddam nodded. "Yes. That's Lesley."

That morning he had taken a long walk along the promenade, blown away some of the demons that had haunted him in the night, and then had come in to the heartiest breakfast he'd had in years, courtesy of Aunt

Jean, who might never have needed a man but knew how to look after one.

She wanted to see his mobile phone, she said. If he explained to her how they worked, she might get one. Not in case she broke her hip, but in case she broke down. It would be handy, being able to ring from the car.

The phone had informed him, as he was showing her how it worked, that he had seven messages. He couldn't remember the last time seven people had wanted to get in touch with him, so he presumed that it was one person who wanted to get in touch with him very badly.

He tried to ignore the messages, but in the end, she made him listen to them. The first was from Acting Detective Inspector Sandwell of Stansfield CID, and Phil groaned quietly. Sandwell wanted him to ring him; he left his direct line number and his mobile number. The others were all from Theresa, wanting him to ring her.

He hadn't rung Theresa, because he had rung Sandwell first and had caught the next train out of Worthing. Now he was with Detective Chief Inspector Lloyd in the hospital mortuary, looking down at Lesley's dead body.

Lloyd took him out into the fresh air; he suddenly felt very light-headed. They sat on the low wall that bounded the car park.

"When did you last see Mrs. Newton?" asked Lloyd.

Phil wiped the cold beads of perspiration from his forehead. "Last January," he said. "I went to see her in the hope of a reconciliation, but she had found someone else."

"Ian Waring?"

"Yes."

"He was very badly hurt during the incident. Someone drove a car into him."

Phil stared at him, trying to make sense of that. "What was it all about? Who did it?"

"We know who was driving the car, but we don't know that he was responsible for what happened to Mrs. Newton. We're hoping Kayleigh can tell us."

Phil was immediately alarmed. "Was Kayleigh there when it happened? Did she see something?"

"Quite possibly. She has been very badly shaken up, and she won't speak to us. Literally. She might nod or shake her head, but that's it. She indicated that she would speak to you, and we'd be very grateful if you could try to get her to tell us what happened."

Poor little Kayleigh, thought Phil. More upheaval, and more and more.

"I believe you haven't seen her for a while?"

"I saw her in January, too. Not under the best of circumstances."

"At Dean Fletcher's trial?"

"Oh, you know about that, do you? Yes. But I haven't seen her properly since last June."

"In that case," said Lloyd, clearly preparing him for something he wasn't going to want to hear, "I think perhaps you won't know that she's had a baby."

Oh, Lesley, Lesley. Phil closed his eyes, shook his head slightly. "I thought I'd won that one, at least."

"What's that?" asked Lloyd sharply.

"I said she should have a termination, and Kayleigh was quite happy about that. Lesley didn't believe in abortion, but I thought I'd persuaded her that it was the right thing to do."

He supposed that had been a naive thing to think. And Lesley had seen how she could solve two problems at once; if she threw him out, she could go her own sweet way about Kayleigh's pregnancy and clear a space for Waring while she was at it. Sensible, organized Lesley, who simply wouldn't face facts. And, of course, the baby would be due mid- to late December. That was why Kayleigh was mysteriously on holiday at Christmas.

"It's a girl. Alexandra."

Phil wished he could feel happy about it, but he didn't suppose Lloyd expected him to be popping champagne corks, so it probably didn't seem strange to him that the news simply made him anxious. He took out cigarettes. "Do you mind? I'd given up, but what with one thing and another . . ."

He'd bought them that morning, at the station, and he had only four left now. He had needed something to make him able to face identifying Lesley's body. As a crutch, it was better than booze, he supposed. Perhaps not much better for the consumer, but a lot better for those who had dealings with him. But then, no one wrote wistfully soulful songs about chain-smokers. They wrote them about drunks and winos and drug addicts, but chain-smokers were unromantic. He thought he'd better resign himself to the fact that he was not the stuff of story and song.

"Did you speak to Kayleigh during the trial?"

"Oh, yes—she and Lesley and I had meals together, that sort of thing."

"And neither of them told you about the baby?"

"If I'd seen Kayleigh on her own, she'd have told me, but Lesley was always there." He flicked the ash from his cigarette onto the ground. "Kayleigh's not . . . not mature enough to look after a baby," he said. "That was why a termination seemed the sensible solution. What happens about this sort of thing?"

"Social Services have got it in hand."

"Will they let me visit Kayleigh? I mean—I'm not officially anything to her, but . . . well, I'd like to help."

"Oh, I'm sure you'll be able to sort something out." Lloyd looked at his watch. "Well, Mr. Roddam, I think we should get you and Kayleigh reunited, now that you know what to expect. It would be extremely helpful if you could get her to—"

"Chief Inspector?" A young woman was crossing the grass toward them. "Mr. Waring's come round," she said. "The doctor says you can have five minutes."

It had been an odd sensation, not really like waking up, because he felt, in a way, as though he had been awake all along. As though he simply hadn't been paying attention. It took him a moment to make out Theresa's features; gradually, he realized he was in the hospital. He had absolutely no idea why. It hurt if he tried to move at all, and he felt physically tired. But mentally, apart from not knowing why he was there, he felt as though he'd had a good night's sleep. He asked what he was doing there, and his voice was weak.

"You were hit by a car," said Theresa.

"When? Where?"

"Yesterday morning. At the cottage. While you were moving in."

He remembered then that it shouldn't be Theresa at his bedside. Not now. Lesley wouldn't like it if she knew. "Where's Lesley?" he asked. "Was she hurt, too?"

Theresa nodded. "I'm afraid she was." And she told him, gently, that Lesley had died.

He stared at her. "Died? Lesley's dead?"

"I'm so sorry, Ian."

He blinked. Lesley was dead.

"They said I shouldn't tell you. But I wasn't going to let you believe she was alive. I didn't think you'd like that."

Ian nodded. Theresa knew him better than anyone else ever had. He couldn't really react to the news; he didn't know how. He felt detached, a little unreal.

The nurse came in and told him that a Chief Inspector Lloyd would like to speak to him. "You can say no. But if you do see him, I'll throw him out after five minutes, so don't worry."

"I'll see him. But I don't—" Ian looked back at Theresa as Chief Inspector Lloyd came into the room, assuring the nurse that he wanted only a few moments with her patient. "How did it happen? Where's Kayleigh? Is someone looking after her?"

"Kayleigh's fine," said Theresa. "And the baby."

Ian frowned. He couldn't raise his voice above a whisper; he couldn't move without pain; he couldn't remember the accident, and he couldn't really grasp that Lesley was dead. He felt a little as though he were watching all this being played out on a stage, but he did know how many beans made five.

"Baby?" he said. "What baby?"

CHAPTER TEN

Ian hadn't been expecting the astonished reaction he got to his question; he followed Theresa's apprehensive, questioning look toward the chief inspector.

"Mr. Waring?" The look on Lloyd's face mirrored Theresa's. "Are you saying that Kayleigh didn't have a baby?"

Ian licked dry lips. "Of course not," he said. "She only turned fourteen in February."

"But if the baby isn't Kayleigh's . . ." Theresa said.

"You're absolutely certain?" Lloyd was speaking through the rest of what Theresa was saying. "Your memory could be—"

Ian sighed. It was quite tiring, trying to talk, especially when he couldn't make himself heard. He had no idea what they were talking about, but they were both speaking at once, and he waited for them to stop. When they did, they were looking at him, apparently expecting some sort of explanation from him, but he could only tell them what he'd already said.

"I don't remember how I ended up like this, but I remember everything else. Of course Kayleigh doesn't have a baby."

Lloyd came and sat by the bed. "Mr. Waring, how much do you remember of yesterday morning?"

Ian thought. His last clear memory was of driving the

Alfa back from Theresa's new flat. He remembered everything up until then; indeed, he was finding it hard to believe that it *was* yesterday morning. He felt as though it
was just a quarter of an hour ago that he had called up to
Lesley, told her where he was going. He told them that.

"Where was Kayleigh?" Lloyd's voice was quiet but
urgent. "Was she at the cottage with her mother?"

Ian felt even more alarmed. Why couldn't Kayleigh tell
them herself what they wanted to know? He turned his
head slowly, painfully, to look at Theresa. "What's happened to Kayleigh? Is she all right? Has she been hurt,
too?"

"No, she's not been hurt. But the police think she
could have seen what happened, and is too shocked to
tell them."

They didn't know what had happened, either? Someone must know. Theresa said Lesley was dead. And he
was . . . he tried to remember, but there was nothing. He
was driving the Alfa home and then . . . nothing.

"*Was* Kayleigh at the cottage?" Lloyd asked again.

"Not when I left." Ian's mouth was dry. "Can I have
some water?" Theresa poured some into a glass and held
it for him as he sipped it; it was the most delicious drink
he had ever had. "But she could have come back while I
was gone."

"Where was she?"

"She stayed behind at the house." He saw his visitors
exchange glances.

"She was in Malworth?" said Lloyd. "On her own?"

Ian nodded. "Lesley couldn't find the keys. . . ." He
stopped. Theresa had said Lesley was dead. He didn't
understand, and he turned his head again to look at
Theresa. "What happened to Lesley? Why is she dead?
Was she in the accident, too?"

Theresa shook her head, and Lloyd sat forward a little.

"Just one more question, Mr. Waring, and I'll leave you and Miss Black to talk."

Ian nodded tiredly, frowning with concentration as Lloyd asked his question.

"I understand that Mrs. Newton was going to Australia to get Kayleigh away from some man she was involved with. Was that Dean Fletcher, or was there someone else?"

Ian's frown grew deeper. He didn't know what Lloyd was talking about. Who was Dean Fletcher? There was no man. "Man?" he repeated uncomprehendingly.

"A boy, perhaps?"

"What?" Ian didn't understand, and it was frustrating, not being able to talk above a whisper.

Theresa touched his arm. "You said that Kayleigh was in a relationship that Lesley didn't like. That's why she wanted to go to Australia."

"Oh—no, no—not a man." At last, something Ian understood. "It's a girl—don't think it was . . . you know, but Lesley was worried about it. She . . . she said Kayleigh was . . ." Words were beginning to escape him as the tiredness took hold. ". . . too involved with this girl. She was worried. Really worried. Never . . . never with anyone else, she said. Her name's Andrea."

He'd done it again. Suddenly Lloyd jumped up and was dialing out on a mobile, much to the annoyance of the nurse who had come in.

"You can't use that in here. We've got sensitive equipment monitoring Mr. Waring's condition."

"Just this one call," said Lloyd. "It's very important."

"Whatever it is, it can wait until you're outside." She bundled him out of the room as she spoke. "You, too, Miss Black. Mr. Waring must be allowed to rest now. No more talking, Mr. Waring. That's an order."

Ian turned his head and smiled tiredly at Theresa, then remembered again what she had told him about Lesley.

She was dead, and he didn't understand. He caught her hand. "Theresa? Please . . . tell me what happened to Lesley."

"As soon as they let me back in again," she said. "I promise."

The nurse was fixing his pillows, checking the equipment, making notes, asking him if he needed anything.

Yes, he thought. He needed Theresa.

Tom had waited until the girl had calmed down a little, and then had gone through her movements with Emma from when she had left the Crawfords' house until the moment she went back to the car park for her phone, but he was barely listening to her, because what she had said before he'd even asked her any questions kept repeating itself in his head. It had been a very strange thing to say: something must have happened to Emma, or someone would have brought her back.

If she had somehow taken Emma herself, it made no sense at all, and if someone else had taken her, why would she imagine anyone would have brought her back? There seemed to him to be only one answer to that. She *knew* who had taken Emma. "Who did you think would have brought her back?" he asked.

"What?" She looked up at him, her face streaked with tears.

"You said that if she was all right, someone would have brought her back. What did you mean? Who would have brought her back?"

"I—I don't know."

"She's been snatched, Andrea. No one's going to bring her back. People don't bring back babies they've abducted. They keep them." He could see Sarah's face, startled by his brutal statement. And it was brutal; he had intended it to be. "And she was snatched because you left her unattended."

The girl began to cry again, and Sarah was looking anything but happy with him; it had taken her forever to calm Andrea down.

"Except that you didn't leave her unattended, did you?"

The sobs stopped; Andrea looked at him with a mixture of fear and relief. And Tom knew he was right.

"Who did you leave her with, Andrea? Who did you think was going to bring her back?"

"Kayleigh," she whispered. "Kayleigh Scott."

Lloyd had been right, too. But then, as he was fond of pointing out himself, Lloyd was always right. "Does Kayleigh have a baby of her own?" he asked.

Andrea shook her head.

"Then I think there's a good chance that Emma is safe, Andrea. Safe and well."

Now the relief was entirely evident; Tom could see for the first time the girl the Crawfords had employed.

"Suppose you tell me what really happened."

She looked worried, uncertain. She was still wondering where her loyalties lay, Tom presumed. He would help her out there, if she needed it, because there was no way he was letting her clam up on him now. But he saw her come to a decision.

"I took Emma to the park." She wiped the tears with the back of her hand as she spoke. "I'd just got the carrycot back on the wheels and had started walking along by the river when Kayleigh came over the bridge. It was her last day in Malworth—she said she'd come for a walk with us, but she ought to phone her mum, because she'd told her she was getting the next bus to Stansfield."

The words were tumbling out, now that she was telling someone what she had been keeping to herself since it had happened, and Tom had to listen carefully to catch it all.

"There's a phone in the car. I just leave it there, because I never use it, but the Crawfords got it so that I could get help if I ever broke down or anything. And Kayleigh asked if she could use it—she said she'd look after Emma while I went back and got it. She wouldn't have been able to find the car, you see, so I had to go myself, but I thought it would be all right, leaving her with Kayleigh."

"And when you came back, they were gone?"

"Yes. The pram was where I'd left them, by the willow tree. And I looked round for them, but they were nowhere. I panicked—I screamed. But then when the policewoman asked if I'd seen anyone, I couldn't tell her about Kayleigh. I didn't want to get her into trouble, and anyway, I thought she would bring her back; I really did."

"Why didn't you tell anyone once you realized she wasn't going to bring her back?"

"I thought . . . she's got to go home, and someone's bound to bring Emma straight back. But . . . but no one brought her back, and I thought maybe Kayleigh *hadn't* taken her home. But no one was looking for Kayleigh, either, or they'd have asked me, because I'm her best friend, and then I didn't dare tell anyone, because I thought something must have happened to Emma, and . . ."

No names had been released in the murder inquiry; Andrea had had no way of knowing why Emma hadn't been brought back, thought Tom. She must have been frantic with worry. He took her back with him to the station, telling the Crawfords they needed her to give them more details of her movements, and left her making a statement while he reported back to Superintendent McArthur, who nodded grimly.

"DCI Lloyd's just found out that there was no baby.

Kayleigh *was* pregnant, but she probably had a termination, or miscarried or something."

"She's Andrea's best friend." Tom shook his head. "If we'd only mentioned her name to the Crawfords—"

"We'd have got it all sorted out by three o'clock yesterday afternoon." McArthur stood up and ushered Tom to the door, walking with him down the corridor. "Ironic, isn't it? The one thing we didn't want them to know was that Lloyd had a mystery baby, in case it raised their hopes. And they'd have known straightaway that it had to be Emma."

"So what happens now, sir?"

"Well—Kayleigh's being taken to Highgrove Street for an interview, and I'm on my way there now. I want you to make sure Andrea's kept here until Emma's safely with the Crawfords—I don't want her telling them that Emma's been found until we've definitely got her back. Then advise her that there might be charges, and make sure she goes back to the Crawfords' place, even if she doesn't want to—I don't want to find myself looking for her next." He stopped at the top of the staircase. "Lloyd's on his way to Highgrove Street—he's got Kayleigh's sort-of stepfather with him in the hope that he can help, because apparently she hasn't spoken at all so far."

No wonder, Tom thought, thinking of her troubled background and what had greeted her when she got to the cottage. Which was, of course, where she had taken the baby in the end, as Andrea had thought. She must have known that she couldn't keep her, unless . . .

"You don't think she really believes it *is* her baby, do you, sir?"

McArthur raised his eyebrows. "Who knows? But Andrea's statement will make the interview a whole lot simpler than it might have been, so it shouldn't be too long before we can pack up the incident room." He turned to go downstairs, then turned back, with a grin. "I think this almost makes up for the baby-in-the-river fiasco."

Tom was never going to live that down.

Phil had followed Lloyd back into the hospital, to the intensive care ward, and waited in the corridor while Lloyd went in to talk to Waring. The next thing Phil knew, Lloyd had come out and walked straight past him, heading toward the exit. He supposed he should have followed him back out, but he had seen the tall, dark woman who had left Waring's room with Lloyd, and heard her speak to the doctor. He was listening, not to what she was saying but to the rise and fall of her voice.

She turned to go back into the room, and Phil approached her a little diffidently; he felt as though he knew her really well, but she might not be of the same mind. "Excuse me. I—I think I recognize your voice. It is Theresa, isn't it?"

She smiled. "Phil?"

She didn't look the way he'd imagined her; he had seen her as smaller, slimmer—more like Lesley, he supposed—and he wondered what her mind had conjured up for him. He was probably a grave disappointment to her, but he liked the friendly, intelligent face he saw and very much hoped that he wasn't.

They shook hands a little self-consciously.

"It's hard to take it all in." Phil wished he could have thought of something more original, rather than what had to be the lamest understatement of the day. He felt a little shy, now that he was face-to-face with her, and not for the first time wished that he were smoother, more self-possessed, or at least something more appealing than an unemployed accountant who had taken up smoking again. "Do the police have any idea what happened?" he asked.

"I don't think so. And Ian can't remember anything. I'm . . . I'm very sorry about Lesley."

Yes. So was he. There wasn't much he could say; he just nodded acknowledgment of her condolences.

"I'm just going back in to sit with Ian. He wants me to explain what happened." She looked troubled. "And I can't. I only know what I heard on the radio. I don't even know how she died."

Phil did. He closed his eyes briefly, trying to rid himself of the image of her in the mortuary.

"Mr. Roddam?" Chief Inspector Lloyd came along the corridor. "I've been looking for you. If you could come with me? We have to speak to Kayleigh, and I'd like you to be there."

"Yes, of course." Phil ducked his head a little shyly as a farewell to Theresa. "Maybe . . . ," he said haltingly, "maybe we can meet for a drink or something?"

Theresa smiled. "Yes, I'd like that. You've got my mobile number, haven't you?"

Well, he might not be smooth and the circumstances might be far from ideal, but he'd got a date, and he was looking forward to it.

On the way out of the hospital, Phil listened, disbelieving, as Lloyd told him what had been happening with Kayleigh.

"You . . . you think she *stole* this baby?"

"I think she must have."

Phil made an involuntary sound, a cross between a sigh and a groan. "At least now she'll get professional help," he said.

Lloyd looked at him sharply. "Now? Has she a history of this sort of thing?"

"In a way. Lesley wouldn't hear of taking her to a

doctor—thought she could handle it on her own. Whenever there was a problem, she just moved away from it. You have no idea how many times we've moved house—Lesley had it down to a fine art. She'd do a recce at the new house, work out exactly what was going where, what we needed to take, what we could sell with the old house. It was like being in a traveling circus or something. But running away from the problem was never going to work—I *knew* something like this would happen in the end. I tried to tell her—I tried."

"What exactly is the problem?"

"Kayleigh's obsessive. Really obsessive. Lesley would never admit it, never use the word. She used expressions like 'forming attachments' or 'becoming very involved,' but it's much more than that. Things consume her, take her over, and nothing is as important as whatever or whoever it is while she's in its grip. It isn't her fault—she can't help herself."

"Has she done anything like this before?"

"No." He sighed. "And I don't understand why she did it."

"I imagine she did go through with the termination. The loss of her own baby . . . emotional confusion—it's not that uncommon. And it happens to people with more stable personalities than Kayleigh's."

"No, I don't mean that." Phil took out his cigarettes and then remembered he was in a nonsmoker's car and put them away again. "It's just—well, Kayleigh's not stupid; in fact, she's anything but. She's got a very high IQ, and . . . this is going to sound terrible, but . . . well, she's quite calculating when she's out to get whatever it is she wants. Like the business with Fletcher. I mean, you have no idea of the complex lies she told us so that we didn't wonder where she was." He wondered if they would ever have found out if Kayleigh hadn't got pregnant and had to tell someone. "What I don't understand is what she intended doing, once she'd got the baby. Kayleigh's usually got a plan."

"This seems to have been spur-of-the-moment. The girl went off and left Emma—the park is right across the road from where Kayleigh was living in Malworth. If she had become very attached to Emma, she might simply have seen her opportunity."

Phil nodded his agreement, but he wasn't convinced. And Lloyd was doing it, too; Kayleigh hadn't become "very attached" to Emma. She had become obsessed with her. There was a big difference, one that Lesley had always refused to accept and which Lloyd didn't appreciate. A silence fell then, as Lloyd drove through Barton's busy streets to the police station and Kayleigh. When Lloyd spoke again, Phil's heart skipped a beat.

"Mr. Roddam, we have a witness who overheard an argument at the cottage shortly before we received the nine-nine-nine call at eleven o'clock yesterday morning. He heard a man telling a woman that she had no right to take his daughter out of the country, and the woman telling the man that he wasn't her father."

Phil didn't speak.

"We assumed that this argument was between Kayleigh and Dean over Alexandra, and Kayleigh allowed me to believe that it was. I think she did that to protect you."

Oh, God, what a mess; Phil still didn't say anything.

"We also have a witness who claims to have seen you leaving the cottage shortly before we received the emergency call. Did you see Mrs. Newton at the cottage yesterday morning?"

There was no point in denying it, not if he had been seen. "Yes. I'm—I'm sorry I lied to you."

"I will want you to come to Stansfield Police Station

with me when we've concluded our business at High-grove Street."

"Yes. Of course."

He got to have his cigarette when they arrived at the police station, standing outside the big double doors, talking to Mrs. Spears while Lloyd liaised with Superintendent McArthur. Phil was pleased to discover that he liked Mrs. Spears, and hoped Kayleigh did, too. Then McArthur and Lloyd brought him into their discussions before he, Mrs. Spears, and the two policemen joined Kayleigh in a small interview room.

Kayleigh jumped up and hugged Phil when she saw him, but she still didn't speak; now she was sitting looking at them, her face pale and frightened, her hands clasped in her lap, and he didn't feel much better. All these people ganging up on her, poor little Kayleigh looked lost as she was cautioned, told that the interview was being taped. McArthur had agreed, reluctantly, that Phil could, at least to start with, ask the questions. And Phil knew what did and didn't work with Kayleigh; pussy-footing around was not the way to get a response.

"Kayleigh," he said. "Whose is the baby that you took back to the cottage yesterday?"

He saw Lloyd and McArthur look at each other apprehensively, but Kayleigh looked, if anything, relieved. Finally, she spoke.

"It's Mrs. Crawford's baby." Her voice was slightly hoarse, and she cleared her throat. "It's Emma."

"Why, Kayleigh? Why did you take her?"

"Because I didn't want to go to Australia and leave her."

There was more to it than that, Phil was certain. The name, for instance. She had given the baby a name. "Why did you tell the police that her name was Alexandra?"

"Because that's what I was going to call her. She's a little bit younger than Alexandra, but not much. Alexandra was born on the twentieth of December, and Emma was born on the eighth of January."

Phil, who had once again credited Lesley with the sense she was born with, realized that once again he had been wrong. "Are you saying you *did* have the baby? You didn't have a termination?" His mind was racing. If she had had the baby . . . where was it? He didn't dare even ask.

"Mum said it would be better if I had the baby, and then let her be adopted, like I was. She said that it was wrong to kill babies before they were born."

Adopted. The baby had been adopted. On the one hand, Phil was deeply, deeply relieved. On the other, he was toweringly angry with Lesley.

"I didn't mind, not then. I didn't have to go to school, because she got someone to teach me at home. And she said not to tell you, because you would make a fuss. But then . . . after I'd had her, I wanted to keep her. But Mum . . ." She trailed off. "She . . . she said I should give her away. They said they'd ask the people who took her if they would call her Alexandra, but I don't know if they did."

Phil felt impotent rage boil up and had to work very hard to keep it under control. He could, when Lesley wasn't there, reasoning with him. How could she have thought that was the right thing to do? No wonder Kayleigh had resorted to stealing someone else's baby.

"I'm told that you didn't go with your mother and Mr. Waring to Stansfield," said McArthur, taking over the questioning. "Why was that?"

Kayleigh answered him readily enough. Too readily. "Mum couldn't find the keys to lock up, and she couldn't phone Ian at the cottage because he'd lost his mobile phone, so I said I'd wait behind while she went to the cottage to get them. Then I found them, and rang Mum to tell her. I said I'd lock up and get the bus to Stansfield, because they had to unpack the van."

"And when did you see Emma?"

"When I was leaving the house. I saw Andrea go into the park with Emma, and I just wanted to be with her for a little while longer. So I had to ring Mum, tell her that I would get a later bus, and Andrea went to get her phone for me. I was alone with her, and . . . and . . . I just took her."

"What were you going to do, once you'd got her?"

That was what Phil wanted to know, but Kayleigh just shrugged. "I don't know. I took her home, played with her. I knew really that I couldn't keep her. But I could see all the police in the park, and I was frightened to take her back."

No, Phil didn't believe that. He knew Kayleigh much too well to believe that she had acted on impulse; that wasn't how it worked. Why was she alone in Malworth, instead of going to Stansfield with Lesley and Waring? Because the keys to the Malworth house had gone missing. And who had found those keys, used them to let herself back into the house with Emma? She stole a baby on an impulse, and as luck would have it, she had access to an empty house directly across the street where she could secrete herself and the baby within seconds of taking it? No, Phil thought, Kayleigh had had a plan.

As it turned out, McArthur had something more than instinct to go on; he had evidence. "When you brought Emma to the cottage, she wasn't wearing the same clothes that she'd been wearing when she went missing. Those clothes were found in a waste bin in Malworth. Can you explain that, Kayleigh?"

Kayleigh's face once again assumed the closed look that it did when questions got too difficult for pat answers.

"Kayleigh." Phil's voice was sharp, making Kayleigh start a little. "This is very serious. You have to answer Mr. McArthur's questions."

"I bought new clothes for her."

"When?"

"About two weeks ago." Kayleigh wasn't looking at anyone as she spoke; she sat, eyes cast down, her hands clasped.

"Are you saying that you planned to abduct Emma Crawford?" asked McArthur.

"Yes."

"Did you deliberately get yourself left alone with the keys to the house? Did you deliberately trick Andrea Merry into leaving you with the baby?"

Kayleigh didn't answer, and Phil put his arm round her. "Kayleigh—whatever you were going to do, it's over. The baby is going back where she belongs. But you must tell us the truth. Did you have the keys to the house all along?"

Kayleigh still didn't look at anyone. "Yes," she said, her voice sulky. "And I put Ian's phone in the glove compartment of his car, so he wouldn't have it, because he was lending the car to his friend. That way Mum wouldn't be able to phone him about the keys, and she would have to go and get them. Mum nearly spoiled it. She told him he'd probably left his mobile in his car, but it was all right, because he'd lent it to his friend by then."

"Do you still have the keys?" asked Lloyd.

Kayleigh went into the pocket of the jacket she was wearing, and drew them out. "The estate agent's supposed to have them."

Lloyd took them. "I'll see they get there," he said.

"Why did you do it, Kayleigh?" Phil asked.

Her shoulders moved slightly.

"Kayleigh, I know . . . I understand . . . how you felt

about the baby. And I know that you don't mean to do bad things, that you get carried away. I'm not blaming you. I just want to know what you intended doing once you'd got her. Did it have something to do with Dean Fletcher?"

But this time even he got the silent treatment, and he felt that shock tactics would have to be used. "I know he was in Stansfield, Kayleigh. He was on that little bridge over the stream that runs along by the road. I saw him when I left Lesley."

Kayleigh's head shot up when he said that, and Phil gave her a little hug of reassurance. "The police know I was there. I didn't want your mum taking you off to Australia, and I lost my temper, but I only broke a mirror. I didn't have anything to do with what happened." He felt Kayleigh relax a little and wished that he could.

"What was Dean Fletcher doing in Stansfield?" Lloyd asked.

Kayleigh's head went back down, but this time she did answer the question. "I wrote to him in prison and got him to ring me. I told him Mum had made me tell the police and say all those things about him in court."

"Kayleigh!" Even Phil had a tolerance level and Lesley might have been misguided and pigheaded, but what Kayleigh had said in court was exactly what she had told him and her mother. "That's not true!"

"I had to tell him that, or he wouldn't have done what I wanted!" She looked up, her eyes blazing. "I wasn't going to go to Australia and leave Emma!"

"And what did you want him to do?" asked Lloyd.

"I said I wanted a photograph of him holding Alexandra. So she would know who her father was. I thought if I could get him to meet me, I could persuade him to take us away with him, and I wouldn't have to go to Australia and leave her behind."

"Take you away where?" asked Phil.

"We could live in his camper van, and no one would find us. They didn't find us before, not till I got pregnant and had to tell Mum."

She would probably have succeeded, Phil thought. Kayleigh could be very persuasive, and she was always one step ahead of everyone else.

"Did you tell Dean all that?" asked Lloyd.

"No!" Her voice was impatient; Lloyd wasn't keeping up, a position in which Phil had often found himself with Kayleigh. "He wouldn't have come if I'd told him what I really wanted." She looked down again. "But it all went wrong."

It certainly did, thought Phil.

"Andrea didn't come to the park for ages. I thought she wasn't coming at all. But then she did come, and I did it. I took Emma to the house, and I put the new clothes on her, and fed her. And then I dumped the Winnie-the-Pooh clothes, and took her to Stansfield on the bus. But I was an hour later than I'd said, and when I got to the bridge, Dean wasn't there."

"Did you see Dean at all on Friday?" Lloyd asked.

"No. I waited in the wood, where I could see the bridge, but he didn't come, so in the end I took Emma to Mum, because I didn't know what else to do. I thought she'd sort it all out." She looked up at Lloyd. "But you were there, and—" She swallowed. "I was scared. I didn't know what to do. Then you said someone had been arguing with Mum, and I knew it must have been . . ." She glanced at Phil. "I thought if I said who Emma was, they would work out that you must have been there. So I didn't say anything."

"When did you decide to steal Emma?" asked McArthur.

Now perhaps Lloyd understood what he was dealing

with, Phil thought as he saw him sit forward a little, listening intently to Kayleigh now that she was talking at last, finding out just how detailed, how intricate, a plan it was. How long it had been in preparation. How she had used Andrea, and her mother, to bring it to fruition.

McArthur put Kayleigh under arrest and arranged for her to be released on bail, then, after he and Lloyd had spoken briefly, he left to take the baby back to her parents, and Mrs. Spears waited at the door of the police station for Kayleigh.

"Aren't you coming with us?" Kayleigh asked.

Phil explained that he and Lloyd had some business to attend to, and Kayleigh looked troubled.

"Go on, love," said Phil. "I'll ring you."

Reluctantly Kayleigh went off back to the children's home, and Phil walked with Lloyd to his car. "What'll happen to her?"

"That'll be up to the court. But obviously, they'll take her circumstances into account."

Neither he nor Lloyd said much on the drive to Stansfield, where Phil was taken to an interview room.

DC Marshall set up the tape, cautioned Phil, and, the formalities observed, Lloyd sat in contemplative silence for some time before speaking. "Tell me about the row you had with Lesley."

Phil sat back a little. "Well, as your witness said, it began with me telling her she had no right to take my daughter out of the country without even consulting me, and Lesley very quickly put me in my place, reminding me that Kayleigh was *her* daughter, not mine." That was presumably all that their witness had heard; no wonder he had thought it was about this baby Kayleigh had turned up with. "And I said that was beside the point. Kayleigh thought of me as her father, and what she was doing was wrong. She said she was doing what was best for Kayleigh. I'm afraid I got very angry."

"Why?"

"Because she *never* knew what was best for Kayleigh—she never understood Kayleigh at all. She was abandoned because her mother couldn't cope with her when she was two and a half! But Lesley saw her as a challenge." He screwed up his face in disgust at himself as he heard his own voice, and felt obliged to retract what he had said. "No—no, that's not fair. She really wanted to help her." He explained about Lesley's own underprivileged background and her desire to use the money and influence that she had acquired to help other underprivileged people. "She really wanted to help . . ." He held his hands out in an all-embracing gesture. ". . . everyone, anyone who needed help."

"What was wrong with that?" asked Marshall.

"Nothing. She was very well-meaning. Kindhearted. But she never really understood other people—she could never put herself in someone else's shoes. She thought she could . . ." He searched for the right word; Theresa had called it bullying, in one of their telephone conversations, but that was too harsh. ". . . could . . . impose her will on everyone. And she would never accept that some things were beyond her. Kayleigh was way, way beyond her."

"And that made you angry?"

Phil didn't know if he could make these men understand the complex nature of Lesley's personality. She would never have adopted a child who hadn't come with a health warning; that would have been too easy. And when she had discovered that he, too, was a flawed human being, that he was given to flying into a rage, she wasn't worried or alarmed; she was *interested*. Lesley had interests, and Kayleigh was one of them.

"She had no *idea* what went on in Kayleigh's head. And she wouldn't face up to the fact that she was seriously disturbed. She would just take her away every time anything happened. She would never have gone to the police about Fletcher—she would just have moved again. She meant well, but all she was doing was allowing Kayleigh to get worse and worse. And this time she was dragging her off to Australia!" He shook his head. "She thought it was this girl that Kayleigh was obsessed with—she didn't even get that right."

"Kayleigh went to considerable lengths to make her believe that," said Lloyd.

Phil nodded. He was being unfair again; he knew that. But Lloyd hadn't known Lesley. "I'm telling her that Kayleigh should be getting help, and she's blithely telling me that Australia isn't really that far away, I can always come and visit. I just . . . just saw red."

"And what did you do," asked Lloyd, "when you saw red?"

"I picked up the table and threw it at the mirror."

"Why the mirror?" asked Marshall.

"Because I could see Lesley's reflection in it."

"So, in effect," said Marshall, slowly, "you were throwing the table at Lesley?"

"In effect. It's how I manage my anger, as Lesley would say. I direct it at inanimate objects. And Lesley's image happened to be in that particular inanimate object, yes."

"Why did you lie when I asked you when you had last seen her?" asked Lloyd.

"You know why. Because I was there, yelling at her and smashing mirrors, and I knew what you would think. I don't blame you—I'd think the same thing if I was in your position. Even Kayleigh thought I might have done it, and she knows that I would never have hurt Lesley or anyone else."

Lloyd looked at the weekend bag that sat at Phil's feet. "Are the clothes you were wearing yesterday in that bag?"

"Yes. You want to take them, is that it?" He pushed the bag over to Lloyd's side of the table. "Help yourself. My aunt washed and ironed them, I'm afraid, so they might not be of much use to you. Maybe you could leave me the underpants."

"Your aunt washed the clothes you were wearing." Marshall was instantly suspicious. "Why would she do that?"

Phil smiled. "If she sees something that isn't hanging up or folded up it goes straight in the machine."

Lloyd looked at him for a long time again; Phil was uncomfortably aware that he was being appraised, his statement evaluated, checked against the facts, against Lloyd's experience of other people in other situations.

"Why did you drop out of sight immediately after this row?"

Phil opened his mouth to say that he hadn't dropped out of sight, he had merely gone to visit his aunt, but that would have been factual rather than true. He had dropped out of sight. "Because I thought the police would be looking for me, and I needed to cool down before I dealt with that."

Lloyd raised his eyebrows.

"I'd committed criminal damage or something, hadn't I? When I did it, she said she was getting the police this time, because it wasn't her house and it wasn't her mirror. She was phoning them when I left. That's *why* I left."

"Well, if she was, she must have changed her mind," said Marshall. "We didn't get a call about anyone committing criminal damage at the cottage." He paused. "Just a triple nine to report a murder."

Phil sighed. "She probably just pretended to phone to get rid of me."

Lloyd was frowning slightly. "What phone did she use?"

Phil failed to see the significance. "Her mobile." He smiled sadly. "Lesley was never without her mobile—she was involved in so many things that people rang her all the time, day and night. She had it clipped to her belt yesterday, I remember."

"Clipped to her belt?" Lloyd looked thoughtful, but he didn't ask any more questions.

"Are you going to arrest me?"

"No, I'm not."

That startled Phil; he thought he was bound to be the prime suspect.

"But I'd be happier if you could find somewhere to stay in Stansfield until the investigation's completed, or you've been eliminated from the inquiry."

"I'll be in Stansfield for the foreseeable future—I don't want to leave Kayleigh facing the music on her own."

Lloyd sat back a little and regarded him again. "You're very fond of Kayleigh, aren't you?"

"Yes." It occurred to him that Lloyd might well wonder why, and he smiled a little. "You're seeing her at her worst. Come to that, you're seeing me at my worst. I've always had a temper, but—well, I didn't go overboard, not like that, not until I lived with Lesley. And the rows were always about Kayleigh, because we both loved her, but Lesley wouldn't face the facts, and I couldn't make her see reason. I'd boil over." He sat back again. "Sheer impotence. That's what made me smash the mirror."

Lloyd nodded. "Just one more thing, Mr. Roddam. Did you see Mrs. Newton's car when you were at the cottage?"

Phil was a little puzzled by the question. Lloyd seemed

to be taking a very keen interest in Lesley's possessions. "Yes. It was in the garage."

"You didn't happen to notice what was in it, did you?"

"It was full of stuff that they were moving into the cottage, I suppose. The back was piled up with all sorts of things."

He told them as much as he could remember about what he'd seen in the car. "And her handbag was on the front seat," he added.

"And . . . which way was the car facing?"

"It was in the garage nose first. Why?"

"The car was stolen, and found abandoned. A handbag was found nearby. Perhaps you wouldn't mind identifying it?"

Phil realized then what had happened. "It was *Lesley's* car that was driven into Waring?"

Lloyd didn't confirm or deny that; Marshall was dispatched to get the handbag that had been found.

"The fixings for a baby seat seemed to confirm that the baby was Kayleigh's," Lloyd said. "Or we might have arrived at the truth sooner."

"We had a little boy," Phil said. "He died."

"I'm sorry."

The handbag was brought in, and Phil confirmed that it was Lesley's. She'd had it for years, a big black leather handbag that she could use with whatever she was wearing. She had a small one that she took with her to the sort of function where she had to dress up, and that was it. Lesley hardly ever bought anything new for herself.

Phil was shown out of Stansfield Police Station by DC Marshall, who pointed along the wide pedestrianized street directly ahead, across the road. "At the far end, you'll find the Derbyshire Hotel," he said. "There are cheaper places, but it's handy, if you've not got transport."

Phil set off for the Derbyshire. He'd ring Kayleigh

when he got there. And Theresa. He needed company, and he hoped she did, too.

Dean was lying on the bunk, staring up at the ceiling of his cell, when he heard the custody officer check up on him. It wasn't time for a check; he swung his legs over and sat up as the door was unlocked and DCI Lloyd came in, the custody sergeant hovering anxiously outside.

"Kayleigh has confirmed that she did ask you to come to Stansfield. And we now know that you didn't see her or the baby while you were at the cottage, and that you were not the man overheard having an argument. I thought you'd want to know."

Dean let out a sigh and leaned back, weak with relief, but it was short-lived.

"You're very far from being off the hook."

"But you know I was telling the truth! What about the guy I knocked down? Has he told you it wasn't deliberate?"

"No, because he has no memory of it. But . . ." Lloyd paused. "I have been given information which supports your contention that it was an accident."

"So *why* am I not off the hook? It's her mother's boyfriend you want—the one Kayleigh calls her dad!" He looked at Lloyd's face, and his shoulders slumped. "You don't believe me about seeing him, do you?"

"Oh, yes. We know you told the truth about that, too. The problem is that he says he left Mrs. Newton alive, and you say you found her dead."

"And you believe him."

Lloyd sucked in his breath. "Well, Dean, you have to look at it from our point of view. He didn't steal a car and run away from the scene. He didn't knock the only witness down and almost kill him. He doesn't have Mrs. Newton's blood all over his clothes."

Dean closed his eyes and bumped the back of his head on the wall, trying to knock the impossibility of his situation out of his mind and concentrate on trying to make Lloyd believe him. "She was dead when I got there," he said, repeating it with every bump, but Lloyd was talking through him.

"You, on the other hand, have spent months in prison enduring the sort of treatment that's handed out to sex offenders, and will spend ten years on the sex offenders' register—you told me yourself what that means. And Kayleigh told you who you had to blame for that."

Dean opened alarmed eyes and sat up. "Hang on a minute—" Kayleigh had said that her mother had made her say those things, but he hadn't believed her. Her mother couldn't have made her put on that performance for the jury—that was Kayleigh's own doing.

"And she arranged to meet you. Only you didn't wait for her, did you?"

"I've told you why! I thought she'd be on her own in the cottage!"

"Perhaps. But perhaps, once you saw the van on its way, you knew that Waring would be otherwise engaged, that Kayleigh would be on her way to meet you—and that her *mother* would be alone in the cottage. Perhaps you didn't come here to have your photograph taken with Alexandra—perhaps you just played along with Kayleigh in order to take revenge on Lesley Newton."

Dean felt the blood drain from his face. "Are you going to charge me?"

"Not yet. I have some further inquiries to make. But I strongly advise you to reconsider legal advice."

Lloyd left, and the custody sergeant slammed and locked the door.

Dean scrambled off the bunk before he closed the hatch, putting his mouth close to the little opening. "All right!" he shouted after Lloyd. "I'll get my brief down here. But you keep on inquiring! Because every time you do, you find out that I'm telling the truth, don't you?"

"Yes, Mr. Fletcher," Lloyd's voice came floating back to him from along the corridor. "I do."

Lloyd reported back to Case, who looked heartily relieved to discover that Lesley Newton had been alive and well after Waring left the cottage.

"At least we can cross him off at last." Case picked up a typewritten document and handed it to Lloyd. "But Theresa Black just rang Sandwell about Mrs. Newton's personal papers. She wants Waring's private medical insurance. And he's found this."

It was a copy of Lesley Newton's will. As Case had suspected, Waring wasn't even mentioned. Some of her money went to Roddam, most to a trust for Kayleigh, and the rest to various charities. Lloyd wondered if he should have been so ready to let Roddam go, in view of his financial incentive, however minor. People had been known to murder for less.

"That's why I'm not insisting that you charge Fletcher. But it's the only reason—so as soon as you find anything that clears Roddam, this case is closed."

Lloyd went back downstairs, only to be waylaid by Sandwell.

"I think you'll want to see this, sir."

Lloyd followed Sandwell into the IT room, where they had all the high-tech equipment needed for police work these days.

"It seems a taxi driver picked up a fare from the station yesterday," Sandwell said. "Took a man to Brook

Way Cottage. He came in this afternoon while you were in Barton, and saw Gary Sims."

Lloyd smiled. Sims had presumably used his initiative again. He wasn't at all unlike how Sandwell had been at that age.

"The description wasn't up to much, so Gary took him to the railway station and got him to pick his fare out on the security videos. He spotted him getting off the London train, and Gary thought it was worth taking a look further along the tape to see if he made a return journey, and he did. He brought the tape to me in the incident room five minutes ago."

He played the video, and Lloyd saw Phil Roddam, dressed in the open-neck short-sleeved shirt and slacks that were in his weekend bag, pacing up and down the little platform, glancing over at the exit now and then. The station clock and the video itself gave the time and date as eleven-thirty yesterday morning.

"Same clothes as he was wearing when he got off the train, and no bloodstains. Even before his aunt washed them." He handed Lloyd a copy of the taxi driver's statement, which gave as much detail as Sims had been able to persuade out of him. "I think that removes the final question mark, doesn't it, sir?"

Maybe he should hand the whole investigation over to Gary Sims, Lloyd thought as Sandwell left and he remained looking at the paused video.

He had been wrong about a lot of things, not least about Waring. But he'd been right about the baby. He had known, all along, that the baby wasn't right, that Kayleigh's nods and shakes of her head weren't truthful. Case had said that it would be too much of a coincidence, Kayleigh stealing a baby the very day someone killed her mother, and that, more than anything else, had been why Lloyd had doubted himself.

But Dean Fletcher, already drowning under the weight of circumstantial evidence, had now been revealed to have had both motive and opportunity, and that removed the element of coincidence almost completely; Kayleigh had brought him here in order that he would take her and Emma away with him, and he had used the information she gave him in order to murder Lesley Newton.

Even so, thought Lloyd. Even so. Phil Roddam, unlike Fletcher, had lied in the first instance. Kayleigh had thought him capable of it, or she wouldn't have stayed silent all that time. He had more than enough motive; Lesley Newton had cheated on him, thrown him out, was taking Kayleigh away from him, and he came into a bit of money now she was dead. Even his desire to get treatment for Kayleigh could constitute a motive.

His clothes would go to the lab if Lloyd could persuade Case of the necessity; there could have been microscopic bloodstains on them and they might still be detectable, even if the clothes had been washed. Come to that, Freddie had said merely that the attacker was *likely* to have been splashed with blood, so Lloyd still wasn't crossing Roddam off, whatever Case said.

And tomorrow, once the incident room in Malworth had been packed up, he would have Tom Finch back; he had already detailed him to go through all the statements first thing to acquaint himself with the murder inquiry. He could send him to talk to Roddam's aunt, see if she was the kind of woman who might help a blood relation evade the clutches of the law.

He switched off the video recorder and put the tape back in its box. For now, he was going home. Or so he thought, but when he left the IT room it was to find that Mrs. Spears was in the front office, wanting to know if she could get into the Malworth house to pick something up.

"Kayleigh had a small case packed," Mrs. Spears explained. "For running-away purposes. It had her personal things in it, and her favorite clothes, that sort of thing. She intended taking it with her when she left the house, but once she actually had the baby with her, she realized she couldn't carry them both, so she left it there. I wondered if I might be allowed to pick it up for her? We've found clothes for her, but she'd obviously be happier with her own things, and I believe all her other clothes are still with the police."

"I don't see why she can't have it," Lloyd said. "I'll let you in myself—I live in Malworth, and I'm just about to call it a day, anyway."

Lloyd had taken the keys in order to have a look round the house tomorrow, just in case it yielded any clues to which of his suspects had actually killed Lesley Newton. It was possibly the longest shot ever, but he had to be able to tell himself that he had left no stone unturned before he charged what he believed to be an innocent man with murder. The lab hadn't been able to get any prints from the murder weapon, and he was fast running out of options.

The house was indeed directly across Bridge Street from the park; it would have taken Kayleigh about thirty seconds to lift Emma from her pram and run across the road into the house, and then she simply had to get on a bus to Stansfield before McArthur had even marshaled his troops, before Tom and Judy had started their walk, before members of the public were aware that anything had happened. No wonder no one had seen her.

"That must be it," said Mrs. Spears, picking up a black leather case.

"I'd like to take a look in it, before you take it."

It contained exactly what Kayleigh had said it contained, considerably more expensive clothes than the ones Mrs. Spears had found for her to wear, some keepsakes, and her toilet bag, plus a feeding bottle, an opened packet of formula milk, and some jars of baby food.

Lloyd smiled sadly at the pathetic little collection. Kayleigh had thought that by now she would be on her way to wherever, to set up her idyllic life with Dean in his camper van, living on fresh air and kisses, presumably. At least the baby would have been fed. He closed the case and wondered just how alarmed Dean would have been if he'd discovered why he'd really been brought to Stansfield. Going back to prison would have seemed preferable, Lloyd was sure.

He saw Mrs. Spears off the premises and conducted a search that revealed nothing of any interest at all. It was like a show house, with its tasteful furniture and fittings and no character whatsoever. That, if it had ever existed, had been removed with its occupants.

The door to the kitchen was a swing door; it pushed open from either side and closed itself again. But on the hallway side there was a little mark, about fifteen inches from the bottom of the door. As though, Lloyd thought as he crouched to examine it, the door was normally propped open and whatever propped it open had marked it. A doorstop, presumably, one of the same height as the cast-iron cat and one that had been there since long before Mrs. Newton bought the house: that mark had been made over years. He got up again and pushed the door to and fro as he thought.

Some of the witness statements were more easily doubted than others. The time of Phil Roddam's visit to Lesley was fluid; they knew the train had arrived at five past ten, but there had been no taxis on the rank. Roddam had had to wait for what had seemed to him to be half an hour or so, and when young Sims had inquired, the taxi driver had said that he picked Roddam up at some time between twenty past ten and twenty to eleven.

And one white van looked very much like another. Dean Fletcher had no idea what time he had seen Roddam, only that he'd seen him after he had seen the van, which was why he had thought Kayleigh would be in the cottage on her own. But he could have seen another van altogether.

Other evidence wasn't so easily dismissed. If only Phil Roddam had found Lesley dead, rather than infuriatingly alive. If only the security cameras at Theresa's flat hadn't confirmed that Waring had indeed driven the van in at twenty minutes to eleven, in person, in full color. If only the very definite postman had heard the argument just a little earlier.

Lloyd's eyes widened. But perhaps he had, he thought. Perhaps he had.

What Theresa liked best about Phil Roddam was what she had noticed the very first time she had spoken to him; his disarming frankness about himself.

They were in the lounge bar of the Derbyshire Hotel, where he had booked in, having been advised not to leave Stansfield. It seemed strange, sitting over drinks, with music playing softly in the background, discussing all these dreadful happenings.

"So that's it. I thought you ought to know." He sounded desperately weary. "I find out that Lesley's dead, then that I'm suspected of murdering her, and Kayleigh has been arrested for abducting a baby. Apart from that, I've had a great day."

"It surprises me a little that Lesley didn't consider bringing up Kayleigh's baby herself," Theresa said. "If she was so keen for her to have it."

Phil swallowed hard, and she could see that he was suddenly fighting tears as well as fatigue; she had been in his company for about twenty minutes, and already she had put her foot in it.

"Oh—I'm sorry. I didn't mean to—"

"No, don't apologize. I'll tell you why she didn't. It might help you understand why feelings were running so high about Kayleigh."

"Well, only if you think . . ." She felt a little flustered; she was supposed to be giving him moral support, not jabbing an insensitive finger on a raw nerve.

"After Lesley and I had been together for about five years, she became pregnant, and we had a little boy. Luke." He blinked away the tears. "Sorry. I never quite know who I'm crying for. Myself, I suppose."

"Phil, I really didn't mean to bring up anything that upsets you. You don't have to—"

"I'd like to tell you." He cleared his throat. "When he was born, Kayleigh couldn't do enough for him—it was a problem, as usual. She wanted to do everything for him, got angry if anyone else touched him."

He took out a new packet of cigarettes, tearing off the cellophane, his hand shaking slightly. He was having trouble getting a cigarette out, so Theresa took it out for him and put her hand round his to hold the lighter steady as he lit it. He drew deeply on it before he carried on.

"When Kayleigh gets obsessed about something, it takes her over. Then suddenly, she loses interest. Except that she doesn't just lose interest—she resents whoever or whatever it was for having . . ." He moved his hands, as though he were grasping something, as he searched for the right word. ". . . possessed her, I suppose. She turns on them—well, she turned on Dean Fletcher, for instance. And maybe he deserved it, but not everyone does."

He took a moment, then, to compose himself, smoothing the ash on the end of his cigarette on the rim of the ashtray. Theresa didn't speak.

"After a few months she'd had enough of Luke. She ignored him, took nothing to do with him. Until one evening, when she was upstairs getting ready for bed, and Luke was in his cot, and he started crying. Then we heard a bump, and Kayleigh screaming, and went out to find Luke lying at the bottom of the stairs. She said she was bringing him downstairs to us when she missed her footing, and dropped him. He died."

Theresa closed her eyes.

"Everyone chose to believe it was an accident. The hospital, Lesley, me . . . everyone. Perhaps it *was* an accident. But we couldn't take the risk of letting her keep this baby, and fortunately—I thought—she didn't seem interested in keeping it. I'm certain that if Lesley had just let her have the termination, she would have taken it in her stride, but . . ." He shook his head. "To Lesley, abortion was murder. So she talked Kayleigh into adoption. It was an incredibly stupid thing to do, but there was no third choice—she couldn't have let Kayleigh keep the baby. She really couldn't."

"Oh, Phil—I'm so sorry."

He took a sip of his cold beer. "I just thought you ought to know."

That was twice he had said that. There was, of course, no reason at all that she ought to know any of his business, except that there was: their relationship thus far might have consisted only of telephone conversations of the most platonic nature, but they had become close, as she had told Lloyd. Very close. And what had happened yesterday had thrown them together in a way that they couldn't have imagined.

She could, of course, be sitting having a drink and a heart-to-heart with Lesley's killer, but she wasn't sure that she would run screaming from the room even if she found that she was. Obviously, she didn't know Lesley's side of the story, but she knew secondhand of her intransigence, and now that she knew about Luke, she understood how desperate Phil had been to get help for Kayleigh. If his frustration had led him to that—well, she could understand that.

"I don't know if Kayleigh can ever really be straightened out." He stubbed out his half-smoked cigarette, looking at what he was doing, not at her. "But I feel about her the way I would about my own daughter, and I won't desert her. I should have adopted her when Lesley and I were together, and if I can, I intend to adopt her now." He looked up then. "I think you ought to know that, too."

His cards were well and truly on the table; the word had not been mentioned, but Phil was saying love me, love my daughter. And, impossible though it seemed, after a long-distance courtship of which neither of them had been aware, Theresa knew that she did love Phil, and that he felt the same about her.

Kayleigh was glad that Emma was back with her mother now. She hadn't known what to do when she found out what had happened at the cottage, and just when she wanted to tell them who Emma really was, Mr. Lloyd had told her about the argument.

She was still worried about Phil; his assurances that they knew all about his being there, as though he'd sorted it all out, seemed a bit unlikely when they wouldn't let him go with her. But they hadn't arrested him or anything; he had telephoned her and told her that he would be staying at the Derbyshire Hotel.

She still didn't understand why Dean was at the cottage or why he'd taken her mother's car. And had he really run Ian over? She was going to see Ian in the hospital tomorrow; they said he was going to be all right, except maybe for his foot. He might be able to tell her what had happened. But it looked as though Dean must have been the intruder he'd seen.

She hadn't spoken to Andrea yet; she thought it best to leave it until she'd got over it a bit. She wanted to tell her how sorry she was, explain to her why she had done it, but common sense told her that this wasn't the time. Andrea would be very angry with her, but she would make it up with her.

The knock at her door turned out to be Mrs. Spears, bearing the case with her clothes in it, and Kayleigh smiled her thanks to her. It was nice of her, going all the way to Malworth for it.

Kayleigh wasn't sure what was going to happen to her, but she hoped that they would let her stay in Bartonshire.

When Lloyd told her that Emma was safely back with Nina Crawford, Judy felt almost light-headed with relief. Then she listened, her eyes widening, as he told her Kayleigh's plan.

"Kayleigh and Andrea would buy clothes together, and wear the same things on the same days," he said. "According to Tom, Andrea thought it was because Kayleigh saw her as some sort of role model—hero-worshiped her. He thinks Andrea was quite flattered by that, and I think Kayleigh did feel like that about her, to some extent. But she engineered the business about the clothes so that she could steal Emma."

Judy shivered. Tom had been right that Emma had been targeted, but she would have preferred the criminals they had thought they might be dealing with to this.

"That way, she could make her mother believe it was Andrea she was obsessed with, rather than the baby.

And wearing the same clothes as Andrea meant that she would just disappear when witnesses were asked about who they'd seen in the park, because the descriptions would match, and it would look as though everyone had seen Andrea."

Judy shook her head. "But when did she plan all this?"

"She had been going to take Emma from the moment she saw her, and she was always going to do it when her mother moved house again, which she knew she would do sooner or later. She just didn't know exactly how, until the temporary move to Stansfield provided the solution." He shook his head, almost in admiration. "In Tom's words, she's nuts, but she's clever."

He was, of course, happy that Emma was back where she belonged, but he was ruefully reflecting on how easily he had been swayed from his original belief that Alexandra was Emma.

"When Alan Marshall found this practically new pram on the rubbish tip, we thought we'd got it all worked out. These kids looted the car, and the baby's stuff was in it—our finely honed detective instincts told us that." He smiled. "But there you are. The boys did help themselves to what was in the car—once we knew what we were looking for, we recovered some of it—but there was no pram in it, because there was no baby. And someone did throw the pram away, however profligate that might seem to Alan and me." He smiled. "Theories always come to grief, like the man said."

"Speaking of babies," said Judy, wrinkling her nose and holding Charlotte at arm's length. "Yours needs changing."

Lloyd took her. "All right, Chaz, let's get you presentable, shall we?" He put his face close to hers, making her laugh.

Judy watched him, finding it hard to believe, even with

the evidence of her own eyes, that Lloyd really didn't mind changing nappies at all. And he did it quickly and efficiently, like he did so many things that she found difficult.

"Who's Daddy's gorgeous girl? Maybe Mummy will find you more socially acceptable now." He sat with Charlotte on his knee, playing This Little Piggy with her.

Judy smiled at them. She could enjoy this much more than she had now that Emma was home. But there was still the problem of work versus Charlotte. Judy wanted to be Malworth's DCI, but she put that to the back of her mind. "What do you think will happen to Kayleigh?" she asked.

"And this little piggy cried 'wee, wee, wee' all the way home!" Charlotte smiled, and Lloyd shrugged. "The courts are usually pretty understanding about mental illness." He played absently with Charlotte's feet as he talked. "And perhaps it's an ill wind. At least it's brought Kayleigh's problem to other people's attention, and no harm done to Emma."

"And how's the murder investigation going?"

"Well—on the one hand we have Phil Roddam, who had a violent row with the deceased and a positive embarrassment of motives, but who, half an hour later, was waiting for a train, his clothes innocent of bloodstains, and who came to us of his own accord, and on the other we have Dean Fletcher, who believed Lesley Newton to be the author of his misfortune, who knew she would be alone in the cottage, whose clothes have her blood on them, who stole her car and drove it into Waring before going on the run, and who was captured only because he passed out while trying to evade arrest."

"Don't tell me; let me guess. You think it was Phil Roddam."

"Well . . ." Lloyd smiled. "No."

Judy's eyebrows rose. "Do you mean you're going

along with the majority?" She gave a little sigh. "I'm glad you don't think it was Roddam—that would be the last straw for Kayleigh."

"Either way, it wouldn't be good. If it was Fletcher, it's her fault for bringing him to Stansfield, and if it was Roddam, she loses her dad as well as her mum."

Lloyd didn't use tenses loosely; if he thought it had to be either Roddam or Fletcher, he would have said that it *wasn't* good, not that it wouldn't be good. She frowned. "You don't think it was either of them, do you?" Then her mouth opened slightly. "You don't still think it was Waring!"

He looked like a child who wanted to stay up and watch television when he was being told to go to bed.

"Lloyd, you know it can't be him. He was with Theresa Black when Roddam was at the cottage. And Lesley Newton was still alive."

"Well . . . that depends."

"On what?"

"On when Roddam was at the cottage. You see— we've been assuming that it was around quarter to eleven. But what if it was earlier than that? Say fifteen or twenty minutes earlier? It could have been, according to the taxi driver. That way, Waring would still have been there when Roddam arrived, and he would have stayed out of the way—what they were discussing was none of his business, was it? So Roddam thought Lesley was alone. Then, when Roddam leaves, Waring kills Lesley and takes the van back to Theresa Black."

"So how did he end up with blood on his clothes? Does he still have the fight with Fletcher in this scenario?"

"Ah—no." Lloyd smiled. "I think that has a much more down-to-earth explanation. He used Lesley's phone to call the police—he had to, because Kayleigh had hidden his. He would have to turn her over to get it, because she had it clipped to her belt. That's how the blood got on his clothes."

Charlotte had grabbed both his thumbs; he was moving his hands, making her look as though she were sending semaphore signals; she was giggling.

"I'm pretty sure that's what happened whether he genuinely found her or not. It also explains why there was blood on the phone itself."

Judy was relieved to hear that he was still allowing for the fact that Waring had probably simply found Lesley dead. "Anyway," she said. "Why would Waring want to kill her? Does he get money in her will?"

"Not unless she changed it from the copy we found, and she's very organized, so I doubt it."

"So what motive did he have?"

"Well . . . I saw him today with Theresa Black—the man's still in love with her; I'm sure of that. And he was being dragged off to Australia with this woman and her mad daughter—he could have decided that doing away with her was the easiest way to get out of it."

"But he didn't know Kayleigh was going to be left behind in Malworth. He'd hardly plan to murder her mother with her in attendance, would he?"

"He was going to get rid of her somehow. She just made it easier for him."

Judy gave him the Look.

"All right," he conceded, with some reluctance. "I think I must be wrong about it having been planned, though I don't see why Lesley would—" He shook his head and didn't finish what he was saying. "I suppose it's just another theory come to grief."

Judy smiled. "Does that mean that Waring is no longer your prime suspect?"

"Probably," Lloyd conceded. "But even if he didn't plan it, it could still have been him. It isn't impossible that he did it *because* Roddam was there causing trouble, and would be a perfect fall guy."

There was one big flaw in this scenario. "I thought you said the postman was very definite about the time he heard the argument."

"Yes, but why was he definite? Because he was running late and he checked his watch." He picked Charlotte up, held her face close to his again. "But what if he wasn't running late?" he asked her. "What if he only *thought* he was running late?"

"Ba-ba-ba," said Charlotte.

"Charlotte wants to know why he would think he was running late if he wasn't," said Judy.

"Elementary, my dear Charlotte." Lloyd beamed at her. "Because his watch was fast."

Judy laughed. "Don't you think he might have mentioned it to you when he found out?"

Lloyd conceded that it was a little unlikely. "But the fact remains that we've been taking what he said as gospel, and we shouldn't—there's nothing to corroborate it. And as far as I'm concerned," he solemnly told Charlotte, "this is still a three-horse race with two favorites and one outsider."

An outsider who was, of course, everyone else's favorite, Judy thought. But she wouldn't bet against Lloyd.

CHAPTER ELEVEN

Phil opened his eyes to the semidarkness of the hotel bedroom. The thick, lined curtains kept out the morning light except at the very top, where a band of sunlight made its way in, and the shapes around him resolved themselves into recognizable objects. The TV, the wardrobe, the drinks cabinet, the dressing table, Theresa.

Last night had happened so naturally, so inevitably, that he hadn't given a thought to the morning after; now, as he looked down at Theresa sleeping beside him, he reviewed how it had happened. Had he made the first move? Had she? He couldn't remember either of them suggesting it, openly or obliquely; they had had a meal and then had come up to his room.

He hoped she didn't think that was why he had asked her to come to the hotel, because nothing had been further from his thoughts when he had rung her; he had felt so weary, so defeated by life, that it was a miracle that anything had happened at all. He smiled. It hadn't exactly been earth-moving stuff, but then he had never claimed any particular expertise in that department and he was not at his best. He wondered then if he had disappointed her, as he had wondered when he met her, and hoped, once again, that he hadn't been too much of a letdown.

It was a strange situation to be in; he thought he might, in his youth, have slept with someone he had just met, but it wouldn't have been someone like Theresa, and anyway, he didn't think he had. And it hadn't been overwhelming desire for each other; it had just seemed the right, the natural, thing to do. At least, it had to him and still did; he felt as though they had been together for a long time, that they knew each other, that they belonged with each other. And he didn't feel defeated any longer. He could get through this, especially if Theresa was with him.

But she might not feel the same way; she might want to cut and run, and he wouldn't blame her for that. He lay back and watched the band of sunlight creep slowly over the ceiling. He mustn't get ahead of himself, mustn't make Theresa feel that he expected any more of her than she was prepared to give.

She had already given him hope and confidence and love. He couldn't ask for more than that.

Tom was packing up the incident room, listening to the tape of Kayleigh's interview. Lloyd had told him some of it, but he had wanted to hear for himself what Kayleigh had to say. A fourteen-year-old kid had put the Crawfords, him, Judy, Andrea—even the couple who had originally come under suspicion—through an emotional wringer, and he wanted to know what made her tick.

McArthur came in as he was filing the witness statements, trying not to think of the work that would be involved in preparing the case for the Crown Prosecution Service, because he didn't suppose he would escape having to do some of it.

"Thanks, Tom—you were a great help."

Tom shook his head. "I think she would have told you all that without my flash of inspiration. She was just trying to keep her dad out of trouble—once he was there, there was no point in keeping quiet."

"Maybe. But it was good work, all the same."

Perhaps he really had redeemed himself in McArthur's eyes. He certainly hoped so. He switched off the tape. "What'll happen to her, sir? She's had a bit of a raw deal, one way or another."

"Well, I can't concern myself with all the other things that are going on in Kayleigh's life—that's for the courts to worry about. All I could do was charge her, and release her on bail into Mrs. Spears's custody. I expect she'll have to have some sort of therapy in the end."

"Who?" asked Tom with a grin. "Mrs. Spears?"

"It wouldn't surprise me," said McArthur, laughing. "I know I'd sooner have Kayleigh for a week than a fortnight."

Tom left Malworth and headed for Stansfield and all the paperwork on the murder that Lloyd wanted him to read. He hoped the reorganization did spread the load a little more evenly; Liz had hardly seen him for the last three days.

Lloyd came into the CID room while Tom was working through the statements, and sat on his desk, impatient for him to finish.

Tom looked up when he got to the end of the transcript of Fletcher's interview. "Seems to me that Fletcher saw this guy Roddam after he'd seen Waring driving the van back," he said. "Roddam says he left Lesley Newton alive, and Fletcher says he found her dead. They both had motive—so it's down to the physical evidence. And that all points to Fletcher."

Lloyd's face held the obstinate look that it sometimes did. "I know. But it doesn't make sense."

"Ten years of being branded a pedophile to look

forward to, and he thought it was all her fault it ever came to court? It makes sense to me, guv."

But it wasn't Fletcher's motive that Lloyd was querying. His argument was that if Fletcher used Kayleigh's information and came to Stansfield with the sole intention of murdering Lesley Newton, he couldn't have been intending to do it with the cast-iron doorstop that just happened to be there.

"Well, maybe he's telling the truth as far as it goes," Tom said. "He really did think Kayleigh would be alone in the cottage, and he did go there expecting to meet her on the way. But when he got there, he found Lesley Newton, and a blunt instrument. The temptation was too much."

Lloyd looked thoughtful. "Could be. That would make more sense. But I'd like to get proof one way or the other. I hope to persuade our revered superintendent to detain Fletcher without charge for another twelve hours for further inquiries to be made."

Tom looked at the statements again. He was probably missing something; he hadn't been in on it from the beginning. He worked best when things were tangible and he could employ his senses. Words on paper were never quite the same as hearing and seeing people when they talked to you; the description of the murder scene wasn't the same as being there. But they had all the evidence they needed, and Case would be quick to point that out. They were obliged to charge Fletcher or let him go, and they weren't about to do that. "What further inquiries, guv?"

"I want confirmation that the murder weapon really did come from the Malworth house, and I'd like you to talk to Roddam's aunt."

Tom felt that if Roddam's aunt had calmly washed her nephew's blood-spattered clothes, she would be unlikely to break down and admit it now. And there might be an easier way of resolving this. He picked up Roddam's statement and glanced through it again. "It says here that Lesley was phoning someone when he left."

"The police," said Lloyd. "But she wasn't, was she? So perhaps she wasn't phoning anyone at all. Perhaps she was too dead to phone anyone."

But perhaps she wasn't, thought Tom, and perhaps she really did phone someone. "Have we still got her phone, guv?" If he could find out who, it might cross Roddam off, and he could get home in time for Sunday lunch.

"Yes, and last number redial gets you nine-nine-nine— but that's from when Waring had to use it. We know it was the phone he used—we just didn't know then that it was Lesley Newton's phone."

Tom nodded. "I just thought I'd see which numbers she's got short-coded—if Roddam thought she was phoning the police, maybe that was because she only punched a couple of numbers. I can find out if she made a call before the nine-nine-nine was made, and when she made it."

"There you are." Lloyd stood up. "Further inquiries. You can be getting on with that while I go and sweet-talk Case."

Tom retrieved Lesley Newton's phone from the evidence room and very soon discovered that Phil Roddam had not exaggerated about the number of calls she made and received; there were dozens of numbers in its memory and about thirty short-coded ones. And Roddam was probably right—she had probably just pretended to phone the police so that he would go away.

But then again, it was true that Roddam had just caused a great deal of damage in a house that wasn't hers. And she didn't seem too fond of letting the police sort out her domestic problems, but she might have thought there was a case to answer this time. So surely if she *had* rung anyone, she would have rung Waring, to see if he wanted to take the matter any further, if he wanted her to get the police?

And according to Kayleigh, Lesley had assumed that Waring's phone was in his car; he had gone to pick his car up, so she might well have tried his mobile. But if she had, he thought, he hadn't answered, because he obviously still hadn't found his phone by the time he got back to the cottage. So it was probably not going to be of any help, but—the motto he would have on his coat of arms if they ever made him a peer of the realm—it was worth a try.

He found Ian Waring's full mobile number and used his own phone to dial it out. It rang four times before Ian Waring's voice spoke.

"Hello, I'm sorry I can't speak to you right now, but if . . ."

Tom hung up, his face thoughtful. Then he took his jacket from the back of the chair and went in search of the keys to Ian Waring's garage.

Ian had had a good night's sleep and no longer needed to be closely monitored; he had been moved into a private room. He had felt a little shy about saying anything to the doctors, but he had told Theresa that he was in a private patients plan, and she had sorted it all out, getting the appropriate paperwork from the police, ringing the insurance people.

It was like being in a hotel room; TV, radio, phone, power points for a computer, if he wanted, when he felt well enough, because he was going to be here for a while. It was, he supposed, very quiet and restful, and since Lesley, horrified to discover that he had, up until that moment, been happy to rely on the health service, had gone to the trouble of getting him medical insurance, he thought he ought to do what she would have wanted. But he would really have preferred to be on the main ward, with other people to talk to.

He was beginning to accept that Lesley was dead, though Theresa hadn't been able to tell him much. It seemed inconceivable that someone had murdered her, but the police seemed quite certain of that, and they thought he had witnessed something, had been knocked down by the murderer in an attempt to kill him as well. If he had, he had no memory of it whatsoever. He remembered everything else quite clearly, right up until the moment he had driven up to the cottage.

His first visitor of the day wasn't Theresa, as he had hoped, but Kayleigh, and he really didn't know what to say to her. Theresa had told him about the baby they had all thought was Kayleigh's and about the baby who had gone missing. Four did seem to be the inescapable result of adding two and two, and Ian really didn't feel capable of dealing with that.

"We waited until the supermarkets were open," she said. "So I could get you something." She put a small basket of fruit on the cabinet by the bed.

"Who brought you?"

"Mrs. Spears. She runs the children's home. She's really nice. But she says I probably won't stay there. She thinks they'll try to get me foster parents."

"Kayleigh, I'm sorry. Please forgive me."

She frowned. "What for?"

He wasn't sure. He just felt somehow responsible. "I don't know if I could have stopped it, or if I tried to stop it—I don't know. They say I rang the police, that I found her like that. That I saw an intruder—but I can't remember, can't even give them a description. Maybe if I'd been there . . ." And he knew as he spoke why he felt responsible. Because he had been with Theresa and he hadn't wanted to go back to Lesley. And someone had come in while he was away and murdered her. It felt like a judgment. "Maybe . . . maybe it wouldn't have happened."

"They think it was Dean."

Dean . . . Dean . . . the chief inspector had said something about someone called Dean.

"Dean?" he repeated.

"Did Mum never tell you about Dean?" And she told him about Dean and Alexandra and about taking this other baby, in an almost matter-of-fact way. "I've to appear in court on Wednesday. I'm seeing a solicitor tomorrow."

Ian could hear Theresa's voice telling him to watch his step, that he didn't know anything about the problem daughter. As usual, she was right.

"They think Dean stole Mum's car, and ran you down with it. So they must think he killed Mum. I just wondered if—well, if you remembered anything, because I don't understand what he was doing there."

Ian shook his head. "I'm sorry, Kayleigh. I really don't."

"My dad was there as well. He found out about Mum taking me to Australia. I think he had a big row with her, but the police didn't arrest him or anything, so they can't think it was him, can they?"

Ian couldn't believe that so much could have happened in the twenty-five minutes he was away from the cottage, but it had. Theresa must have told Phil where to find Lesley—she really shouldn't have done that. What if it was Phil who killed Lesley? But this Dean character seemed a lot more likely. "No," he said, "I'm sure they don't think it was your dad."

A nurse came then, to tell him that Chief Inspector

Lloyd wanted another word with him, if he was up to it, and Ian agreed that he was, though what he could possibly tell him he didn't know.

Kayleigh offered to leave when Lloyd came in.

"No, no—I'll only be a moment. In fact, you might be able to help me. I'd like to know if either of you can tell me anything about a cast-iron doorstop in the shape of a cat."

"Oh, that was in the Malworth house," said Ian, by now used to being asked very strange questions by Chief Inspector Lloyd, and not even asking why he wanted to know. "It was used to prop open the kitchen door. We didn't know why, at first, so we took it away, didn't we, Kayleigh? Only then we discovered that if someone was in the kitchen trying to get out and someone was in the hallway trying to get in, it was . . ."

He felt tears coming then, the first he'd cried over Lesley. Remembering a silly incident like that. The laughter, when he and Lesley realized they had each been silently, determinedly, pushing a door they believed to be stuck. Lesley had been going to get the door replaced, but they had decided to move to Australia before she had got round to it.

"I'm sorry," Lloyd said. "I didn't mean to—"

"No—no, I'm just being . . ." Ian took as deep a breath as he could, which was deeper than he had been able to yesterday, so he must be getting better. "I'm all right."

"Do you have any idea what happened to it?"

"Isn't it still there?"

"No—we found it in the cottage."

"Lesley must have taken it with her." Ian smiled, but he could feel the tears pricking his eyes again. Lesley was so organized, so aware of using every minute of her time

wisely. "She had moved house a lot. She knew all the pit-
falls. She and Kayleigh came to the cottage and sorted
out exactly what was what. I expect she found some
door that wouldn't behave itself."

Lloyd looked over at Kayleigh. "Did she mention it to
you?" he asked.

"No. But I was outside most of the time. It's boring going with her to houses. All she does is measure up and
things. This time she was seeing what was there already
and what we'd have to bring. She probably brought it to
keep a door open while she carried stuff in."

Lloyd nodded and looked back at Ian. "I take it you
haven't remembered any more than you had?"

"No, sorry. I was just explaining to Kayleigh."

"Well, I'm pleased to see you looking so much better.
Sorry to have interrupted your visit, Kayleigh."

And he was gone, leaving Ian with Kayleigh once
more. And he still didn't know what to say to her.

They were having a late breakfast, having slipped in under the wire just as they were going to stop serving.

"That's two man-size breakfasts I've had in two
days," Phil said. "I'll never be able to go back to a slice of
toast and a cup of tea after a few weeks of this."

She had woken to the sound of Phil showering and
shaving; he had come out of the bathroom, they had
found themselves making love again, and still neither of
them had actually said anything about what they intended
doing.

"It would be silly to stay here," she said. "Your money
will run out very soon if you do that, and you might not
get a job straightaway."

"Especially if I'm a murder suspect." He spread mar-
malade on his toast. "I'll look for somewhere to rent, I
suppose."

Was that what he wanted to do? Or was that what he thought she would want him to do? Or what other people would think he should do? If they carried on like this, they would be old and gray and still wondering about each other. Making love twice in the middle of the biggest crisis of either of their lives didn't count as a lifelong commitment, but she felt as though they had been sitting across the breakfast table from each other for years, and coyness seemed out of place.

"There's my flat. I'd like you to stay there. As a lodger, if you'd prefer that—there's a spare room. Or as a couple. It's up to you."

He smiled. "I feel as if we're a couple."

"So do I." She could see one possible cloud on the horizon and thought it best to mention it now rather than later. "Will Kayleigh mind?"

Phil shook his head. "I think she'll be pleased. But it's too bad if she's not, because I've got my own life to lead. Don't think you'll be playing second fiddle to her, because you won't—I just think she needs someone that she can rely on, at least until she can stand on her own two feet. And that's me."

And now, Theresa thought as they got up from the breakfast table, the waitresses eager to clear away and set the tables for lunch, she would have to tell Ian, and Phil would have to tell Kayleigh, in a complete reversal of how all this had started.

She hoped—no, she was sure—it would have a happier ending.

"So I fetched his phone from his car," said Tom. "Listen."

Lloyd took the phone, and listened as it informed him he had a message.

"Ian—I don't know if you'll hear this, but just in case

you do, I think you should get back here now; you might want to get the police. Phil's just been here, and he's smashed the mirror in the living room—just picked up that little table in the corner and threw it at it. I'm not hurt, so don't worry. But please come back." There was a pause. "And if I'm right that this 'mate' you borrowed the van from is Theresa, please tell her not to interfere again."

Lloyd gave the phone back to Tom. Lesley Newton had been alive, well, almost heroically polite, and very understandably cross after Phil Roddam's visit, and therefore it hadn't been Phil Roddam who had murdered her.

"I rang the mobile company," said Tom. "The call was timed at eleven forty-six."

And she had been alive and well when Ian Waring was demonstrably somewhere else altogether.

". . . but it may harm your defense if you do not mention now something which you later rely on in court. Do you understand the charges?"

Dean nodded dumbly, his solicitor having advised him to say nothing more. This wasn't happening. It couldn't be happening. He hadn't murdered anyone. And what had happened to Waring was an accident. Reckless driving, OK, yes—he had shot out of there backward when he couldn't see out of the rear window. But he hadn't murdered anyone, and he hadn't attempted to murder anyone.

Possibly for the first time in his life, he had told the police the absolute, unvarnished truth, and look where it had got him.

Kayleigh finally rang Andrea; at first she was angry, as Kayleigh had known that she would be, but she explained why it had happened, and Andrea had begun to be a little less hostile, had begun to understand. Then Kayleigh told her about Dean taking her mother's car, about what had happened to Ian.

"And my dad was there as well."

By the time she had explained about Phil, Andrea wasn't angry with her anymore, and Kayleigh felt much happier. "Are you going to get into trouble over Emma?" she asked.

"The police said they might bring charges. But Mrs. Crawford's been really nice about it, now that she knows I didn't leave Emma all on her own. She said it was wrong of me not to tell them straightaway what had happened, but she's letting me stay—I just can't be on my own with Emma, not until I'm older and wiser, she said." There was a pause before she spoke again. "And she said that you wouldn't be welcome in the house anymore."

No, Kayleigh didn't suppose she would be. But she hadn't thought for a moment that Andrea would be able to keep her job; she was really happy for her, and relieved that Andrea had forgiven her for putting her through all that. And if Mrs. Crawford was being like that about it, maybe the police wouldn't prosecute Andrea for not saying anything.

Andrea had heard on the radio that someone had been charged with murdering her mum and trying to murder Ian, and that had to be Dean. Kayleigh still didn't understand why he hadn't just waited for her at the bridge.

But at least it wasn't her dad; he had been to see her, to tell her that he would be moving in with Theresa Black. She hadn't realized that he even knew her, and she wondered what Ian would think about that; she thought he might be a little jealous.

Lloyd had come home early, having thought that he was going to have to put in a full day, but far from being pleased at having Sunday at home, he had been unnaturally quiet and withdrawn, and even Charlotte at her beaming best hadn't been able to cheer him up much.

Judy's suggestions as to what they might do with this unexpected free time had met with a shrug of the shoulders, so they hadn't done anything. He had watched an old film in the afternoon, and in the evening he had bathed Charlotte and put her to bed. Apart from that, he had sat lost in thought, answering when he was spoken to but otherwise silent.

Judy could hear the rise and fall of his voice as he told Charlotte a bedtime story, something he had done since the day Charlotte had been brought home, on the grounds that the more she heard the language, the quicker she would learn it, and the sooner she would love it.

Judy hoped that might make him feel better, because she had a proposal to put to him and she wasn't sure whether she should while he was in this mood, one with which she was, despite having known him so long, unfamiliar. But time was getting short, and if he didn't like the idea, she would have to know now.

"I've been thinking," she said when he came back in.

He sucked in his breath. "Oh, you don't want to do that. It's bad for you. Much better just to accept everything, and think about nothing."

Oh, great. "Yes, well, anyway. I've been thinking that my mother's in London, on her own, and for all I know she's having a high old time, but I doubt it. My father was the one who made friends, really. She isn't nearly as outgoing as he was—I think she might be quite lonely. And we need someone we can trust to look after Charlotte." She paused, trying to gauge his reaction, but she could never do that at the best of times. "So what do you think? She might not want to do it, of course. But . . . what do you think about asking her?"

He looked at her the way she had seen him look at suspects. A slight frown, his head to one side, as though he was deciding whether or not she was a genuine van Gogh or a fake.

"You mean what do I think about having my mother-in-law living with me twenty-four hours a day, seven days a week?"

Judy had hoped, since he got on so well with her, that he might not mind that aspect of it. "Oh, well," she said. "We'll forget that."

He grinned and joined her on the sofa, putting his arm round her. "I asked her on Friday morning before I even told you that I wasn't getting early retirement. She said she'd be here like a flash if you wanted her, but I had to let you make up your own mind what you wanted to do, because she didn't want you thinking you had to ask her."

She smacked him. "One day I'll know when you're doing that to me." At least he was in a good mood again, even if he was being irritating.

"Never. It gets you every time." He kissed her. "You do realize it means we have to find a proper house to live in—one with a granny flat or something, so as your mother can have her own space. I promised her that."

"Yes, dear."

"And that means you have to make a commitment. Sign on a dotted line."

"Yes, dear."

"And that you do actually have to move. That is, take your possessions from here to there, and . . ." He sighed.

"What's the matter?"

"Sorry. I'd managed to put it out of my mind until I started talking about moving house."

"Why has it got to you like this?"

"I think we've charged the wrong man." He rubbed

his eyes tiredly. "I know he's a villain, as Tom would say. And I know that at the very least he took advantage of Kayleigh. But I believe that what happened to Waring was an accident, and I don't believe he murdered Lesley Newton."

"Why are you so certain that he didn't?"

"Well, you know yourself you get a feel for whether or not someone's lying. But it's more than that." He pulled away a little and looked at her. "He asked me to keep on making inquiries, because, he said, every time I did, I found that he was telling the truth. And he was right—he told the truth about everything that I was able to check. But my prime suspects all have perfect alibis. I think someone's getting away with murder, and I don't like it." He sat back and closed his eyes. "But what do I know? I was working on the wrong little puzzles all along."

"Were you?" It wasn't like Lloyd to do that. His interpretation of them was free-ranging, but he usually homed in on what mattered.

"Oh, yes. Right from the word go." His eyes were still closed as he went through the things that had misled him. "When we went into the cottage, and saw that they were in the middle of a move, I thought they were moving out, because why would Lesley be unpacking clothes in the utility room? But they were moving in. I thought that Kayleigh was there when it happened, because why else would she ask where Ian was rather than her mother? But Kayleigh was in Malworth. I thought it had to have been premeditated murder, because Theresa Black told me that the doorstop didn't belong to the cottage, and she wasn't a suspect, so she had no reason to lie about that. Ergo, someone had to have taken it with them."

"That's bad grammar, as you never fail to remind me."

He opened his eyes and squinted at her. "It's slowly becoming accepted usage, to denote a person of either sex.

A plural word being used as a singular does have a precedent in English grammar."

"Does it?" Judy frowned. "What, like *media* and *phenomena*?"

"No, *not* like *media* and *phenomena*, which are plural, and are wrongly used as singulars with the singular form of the verb. I mean like *you* rather than *thou*. A plural word, taking the plural verb form, but used as a singular. As such, I have admitted *them* as a singular to my vocabulary."

"Oh, good. Can I admit it to mine?"

"If you employ it only when you wish to be non-gender-specific."

"I'm not sure I'd know whether I did or not." She smiled. Lloyd wasn't so bothered by this business that he couldn't lecture her. "So why should someone taking the doorstop with them constitute a puzzle?"

"Because I was in that house with every door standing open, on a breezy day. If ever any of them was going to close of its own accord, it would have been then—she couldn't have found a door that wouldn't stay open. And the more I found out about Lesley Newton, the more of a puzzle it became. Why would someone as organized as she was take an inessential doorstop with her? Especially one that had a very specific use in the house it did belong to?" He shook his head. "That was why I was convinced that she hadn't taken it and that was my theory. That someone else must have taken it, with the intention of murdering her with it." He sighed. "But she had taken it. And if she hadn't, she might not be dead."

"If a thing's not there to be picked up . . ." said Judy, with a smile.

"Well, it's true! The reason America has so many murders by shooting is that guns are around to be picked up.

If they weren't, a lot of people would still be alive—
including the ones that did the shooting. And that
damned doorstop was around for no good reason that I
could see."

"She might have wanted it as something other than a
doorstop. To weigh something down, perhaps. Like you
said, it was breezy. She might have wanted to stop something blowing away."

He looked a little fazed by that. "I never thought of
that. So, there you are," he said with a shrug. "I got that
wrong as well. The only thing I got right was that the
baby was Emma, and I talked myself out of that when we
found the pram, because I thought no one would throw
away a perfectly good pram. But they had. All my puzzles turned out to be just that—the puzzling things that
people do, and nothing more. What qualifies me to think
I know best about Fletcher mystifies even me."

"Maybe there was a real intruder, one that nobody
saw."

Lloyd nodded. "It's possible, in theory. As far as we
can work out, there was ten minutes between Fletcher
seeing Roddam leave and arriving at the cottage himself.
So she was alone for about fourteen minutes all told.
Someone could have come through the woods, gone into
the house, and killed her. But they—still using it in its singular sense, I presume—would have had to do it straightaway, and then leave. And why? There wouldn't be time
to have a violent quarrel. Nothing was stolen. She wasn't
sexually assaulted. It makes no sense at all."

Judy smiled sympathetically. Lloyd's theories almost
always came unstuck, but his little puzzles usually
pointed him in the right direction, even if he had no idea
what direction that was. This time, they had let him
down, and he had been taken in by a plausible liar. His

pride was hurt. He wanted it to have been anyone at all but Dean Fletcher.

She kissed him. "Cheer up," she said. "Maybe it was the postman."

CHAPTER TWELVE

Dean lay on his bunk, reading a paperback, inasmuch as his eyes were scanning the pages, but his mind was on his forthcoming trial. Last time had been bad enough, but this time he was being accused of murder, and even he felt that the prosecution had a watertight case. He closed the book and stopped pretending to read. This was what he had been doing exactly a year ago today, he realized. For all he knew, it was the same paperback.

On the first of August last year, he had been picked up for skipping bail, and he had been remanded in custody to await trial; it had been the end of May before he'd seen the outside world again. Two weeks of freedom, and he'd found himself back in prison, but this time . . .

Dean felt sick. This time, there was a real possibility that the outside world would become nothing more than a distant memory.

His solicitor and barrister had once again told him, in effect, that he should admit it; they would plead diminished responsibility. Not that they gave that defense much chance of succeeding, but it might just work, they said, given a liberal jury and a fair wind; if it did, the resultant verdict of manslaughter would give the judge some leeway when it came to sentencing. They held out little hope at all for a straight not-guilty plea, in view of the evidence, and if the verdict went against him, it was automatic life imprisonment. And he had told them, once again, that he had no intention of pleading guilty to something he had not done.

He would be found guilty—apart from anything else, there seemed to have been no one else who *could* have done it. But unless his responsibility for his actions was truly diminished, to the extent that he had no recollection whatever of doing anything other than falling over the woman's body, he had *not* done it, and therefore someone else had. The lawyers said they believed him, but it was professional belief, and Dean couldn't really blame them for being skeptical.

They were doing their best for him, as they were obliged to do; they were trying to find out if anyone else had been seen in the area, if there was some way in which suspicion could be if not actually directed at someone else specifically, then at least lifted from him, if any of the evidence against him was tainted or otherwise inadmissible, if any of the witnesses could be proved to be lying or mistaken. But Dean knew it was a hopeless task. He knew because he had been there and, apart from the man he had inadvertently run down, there had been no one else in that cottage, the witnesses were telling the truth, and there was no challenge they could make to the physical evidence. Either his explanation as to how it got there would be accepted or it wouldn't.

Plenty of people *had* been at the cottage, all those people the police had lined up to explain exactly how Dean could be proved to be the only person who was there at the material time and leave the jury to come to the inevitable conclusion that in the few minutes at his disposal Dean had murdered Lesley Newton, stolen her car, and attempted to murder the sole witness. Even if the motive the police ascribed to Dean were to be deemed inadmissible, it would make no difference; the prosecution were under no obligation to prove motive.

He might study law during all those years he would have at his disposal; petty criminals always had a head start in matters legal, knowing exactly which laws they had broken and which they had not, which defenses were valid and which were not. He certainly hadn't needed a solicitor to tell him he was in the shit.

He wondered what they were doing now, all those people who would not be spending the rest of their lives in prison. Because that, though his mind flinched away from the enormity of it, was what it amounted to; eventual release on license was given only to lifers who finally admitted their guilt, accepted responsibility, and felt remorse for their offense, and Dean would never, never do that, because he hadn't murdered anyone. Thus guilty men went free and innocent men stayed behind bars.

So how were all these people with whom he had become involved one sunny weekend in June spending their Saturday morning? What were they doing right now?

And what was the real murderer doing?

"This place in which you are now met has been duly sanctioned according to law for the celebration of marriages." The superintendent registrar's voice was quiet and clear. "And before you are joined in matrimony, I have to remind you of the solemn and binding character of the vows you are about to make."

They looked at each other and smiled a little.

"A marriage according to the law of this country is the union of one man with one woman voluntarily entered into for life to the exclusion of all others. But it is more than just that. Marriage is the desire of two people to share with one another the ups and downs, the joys and sorrows, that come into every life, to offer help, encouragement, and support to one another in moments of adversity, and to appreciate and enjoy one another's good fortune. You are here to witness the celebration of this marriage, to hear the vows that will be made, and to share in the joy of this union."

She dropped her voice a little. "Are you, Philip Jeremy Roddam, legally free to lawfully marry Theresa Anne Black?"

"I am."

Phil had whispered to her, as they had walked from the registrar's office into the marriage room, that she still had time to change her mind, but she knew the commitment she was making and she was prepared to make it. Everyone thought she was mad, of course, especially her brother.

She and Phil had talked to each other, to social workers, to lawyers, to adoption agencies, they had gone into every existing and potential problem that anyone could think of, and she had seen no reason to change her mind. The marriage was necessary if Phil was ever to be allowed to adopt Kayleigh, and Kayleigh was a commitment he had made nine years ago, without the need for vows to be made. It was a commitment that Theresa was quite prepared to share. She wasn't Lesley; she didn't have a burning desire to sort out Kayleigh's or anyone else's world. But it wasn't a compromise—Theresa wasn't accepting Kayleigh as the downside of her relationship with Phil. If she had felt like that, she would have backed off.

The registrar turned to her, then, and she, a little self-consciously, certain that she sounded as though she had a string of bigamous marriages behind her, agreed that she was legally free to marry Phil.

Kayleigh was still awaiting trial, but she was now receiving psychiatric treatment; Theresa didn't know her well enough yet to know how successful the treatment was likely to be, but she knew that its success or failure mattered to Phil only inasmuch as he wanted to see Kayleigh well. If nothing could be done for her, it wouldn't make any difference to how he felt. And it wouldn't make any difference to how Theresa felt about Phil.

The registrar turned back to Phil. "Please repeat after me. I promise that I will try to keep our . . ."

Tommy is a bright and capable student, but an aversion to written work has marred what could otherwise have been excellent academic progress. He is popular with both staff and fellow students, and cannot be faulted on enthusiasm and effort when a subject interests him. Provided he curbs his tendency to avoid (or at best pay lip service to) whatever he perceives as boring, he could and should succeed in whichever field he chooses to pursue.

"Tom? What are you doing up there? We're going to be late! Have you found it?"

"Yes, I've got it. Won't be a minute."

Tom, crouching under the roof beams, balanced precariously on the joists, closed the end-of-term report on his final year at the Liverpool comprehensive that had concluded his formal education, and put it back in the box of family treasures. Quite why it qualified as a treasure he wasn't sure, except that it so accurately summed him up; Judy Hill had said virtually the same thing at his last assessment. He smiled to himself. Now that his crown of golden curls had grown back to its full glory, he even looked virtually the same as he had then; the last fifteen years had seen little change, and all his irredeemable, sometimes inconvenient, characteristics remained firmly in place.

But that didn't matter, he thought as he lowered himself down through the hatch, feeling gingerly with his foot for the top step of the ladder, because by the time the Lloyds came back from their honeymoon and he had done his preappointment course, Tommy Finch would be Detective Inspector Tom Finch, Malworth CID. Providing he didn't break his leg getting down from the loft, that was.

"I thought you'd gone to sleep up there," said Liz as he safely negotiated his way down to the landing. "Oh, look, Tom! You've got dust all over your trousers." She swatted at him as she spoke, handing him his jacket when she was satisfied that the dust was all gone. "The ring's in the pocket—don't lose it."

"You look terrific in that," Tom said, shrugging on his jacket, belatedly realizing that Liz was no longer wearing the dressing gown in which he'd last seen her, on his way up to the loft. "Is that one of the outfits Judy gave you?"

"It's *the* outfit—the one she was going to be married in last time round. It's got this clever buttoning arrangement so it fits you whatever size you are. Not that I'm that much smaller than she was in her last month. It's brand-new—never been worn—but she wouldn't take any money for it."

"Well, there you are," said Tom, with a grin. "We're quids in already. Who says they're expensive?"

The baby had turned out to be twins. Only after they had found out did Liz's mother remember that one of her aunts had had a twin sister who had not survived, or they might have been prepared for the possibility. The babies were due in December, and now that he and Liz had got over the shock, they could hardly wait.

Life was being good all round at the moment—on Friday, the LINKS project had been formally inaugurated and Tom had collected a cool hundred quid on his bet, thanks to Bob Sandwell, who had already transferred to

Highgrove Street in Barton, where he was duty inspector, which suited him perfectly; his wife already worked in Barton, and they were buying a house there. Judy had indeed got the DCI post at Malworth, starting right after her honeymoon, and Lloyd was moaning that everyone he worked with had been scattered to the winds, but he had Stansfield CID to organize however he chose and today he was finally getting married, so he was happy, too.

"Are we ready to go now?" said Liz. "We're supposed to get there quarter of an hour before the ceremony, and we're running very late."

Tom gasped. "Whose fault's that?"

"I thought it would take you a few seconds—you were up there for ages." She looked into their son's bedroom, but it was empty. "Bobby? Bobby! Are you back in the bathroom? Get him out of there, Tom."

Nine years old, and he spent hours making himself beautiful. Tom couldn't believe it. When he was nine, it was only the Shirley Temple comments that forced him to get his hair cut at all, but Bobby always knew exactly how he wanted his hair, which was never the same two visits running; he had to keep up with whatever was in fashion, and making it look exactly as it should involved much gazing at himself in the bathroom mirror while he carefully applied hair gel. Tom had somehow sired a miniature cool dude, which mystified him. Bobby had inherited Liz's dark, straight hair, for which he was truly thankful. Chloe, on the other hand, looked just like Tom and behaved just like her mother; at six, she had golden curls and much more common sense than Tom or Bobby ever would and regarded her older brother with something approaching disdain.

The bathroom door opened as Tom was about to knock—one didn't walk in on Bobby's preparations—and he emerged, looking cool. "Wicked," he said to his mother as he passed her on the landing, so Judy's taste in pregnancy outfits had passed muster. Bobby was a man of few words; his reaction to the news that there was to be not one but two additions to the family had been a thoughtful nod and then "Cool."

"I'm getting into the car." Liz started back downstairs. "I'm going, even if no one else is."

"Don't you want it now I've got it?" asked Tom, holding out the garter.

"Oh, yes!" She grabbed the frilly blue garter from him and put it in her shoulder bag.

He smiled. "I gave you that for our wedding."

"It's all right; she's only borrowing it. That's the whole point."

Judy didn't know yet that she was borrowing it; she had steadfastly refused to pander to tradition in any way, vetoing a hen night, pooh-poohing the idea of her and Lloyd spending the night before the wedding apart, refusing to countenance wedding presents, insisting that between them she and Lloyd already had everything they needed and that anyone who would have bought them something should instead send the money to charity.

The garter had been a last-minute inspiration, and Liz, a believer in tradition and more than a tad superstitious, intended putting Judy in a position where she couldn't refuse to wear it without being impolite, and had reasoned that since her bridal outfit was bound to be new, the garter would at a stroke fulfill the rest of the rhyme's conditions.

". . . take you, Theresa Anne Black, to be my wedded wife."

Phil hadn't looked at Theresa once during the actual ceremony; some things still made him feel shy. They had known each other for months, really, but they had spent just over six weeks in each other's company, and he was still afraid of disappointing her. He had wanted to learn by heart the vows they had chosen to make, but he hadn't been able to do it. The registrar had said he could repeat them after her instead and he had felt that he had let Theresa down a little, but she had just laughed at him when he said that.

He still couldn't quite believe that she was doing this for him; he had thought that the mention of adoption would put paid to any chance he had with her, instead of which she had spent the night with him. After her subsequent offer to marry him, he had told her exactly how difficult Kayleigh was, but it hadn't put her off, and now, here she was, going through with it.

During all those weeks when all he had done was speak to her on the phone, he had daydreamed about meeting her and had often thought of asking her up to London to see a show or whatever but had been too bashful to suggest it. Somehow, meeting her under the dreadful circumstances of Lesley's death had made it easier, made him bolder, made him brave enough to grasp the daydream, because he had fallen for Theresa Anne Black before he'd ever met her. And now the wildest part of his daydream was coming true; she was in the process of becoming his wife.

Kayleigh had been sent to foster parents in Malworth—he and Theresa had met them informally, and they seemed like pleasant, capable people. And Kayleigh seemed to enjoy being with them, especially since Andrea had forgiven her and was best friends with her again.

Kayleigh and Andrea were Theresa's bridesmaids, if that was the appropriate term when everyone was in civvies, rather than gowns and morning suits, and had been looking forward to today for the last three weeks—

once the decision had been made, they had given notice of their intention to marry at the earliest possible date in order to get the adoption procedure under way. Almost the earliest possible date—they had picked the Saturday so that Theresa's brother could make it back from holiday.

Lesley had left Phil a bit of money, with which he would be able to set up on his own once the will went through probate, but it was a risky enterprise in a town where he had no reputation and at the moment he was still jobless, so he wasn't spending what he had left on anything other than necessities. The wedding was a low-key affair: a handful of guests, and a small party in the flat to celebrate.

The witnesses were Theresa's brother and his aunt Jean, and the guests were those of Theresa's friends able to come at such short notice. His on-the-road existence with Lesley meant that he had lost touch with everyone with whom he might have become friends, but he and Ian had been for a drink together a couple of times and got on pretty well, despite the way they had met.

Phil could see why Lesley had picked Ian; he was someone who did as he was told, basically. But he was a nice guy, and Phil couldn't see the point in not becoming friends with him. Both he and Theresa had wanted Ian to come to the wedding, and he had got out of the hospital just in time. He was sitting at the end of a row, his plastered leg sticking out, his crutches on the floor.

Theresa's brother had thought it very strange, inviting Ian to the wedding—stranger, if anything, than he had found Theresa's decision to marry Phil in the first place and being prepared to adopt Kayleigh—but Phil knew that Theresa wouldn't have dreamed of not inviting him; Ian was her friend and always had been. And, he thought, if Theresa could accept Kayleigh as part of the package, then he could surely accept Ian.

"Now you, Theresa. I, Theresa Anne Black . . ."

Kayleigh was really glad about Phil and Theresa; she seemed much more likely to make him happy than her mother ever had, even if it was all very sudden. Not that Phil and her mother had been unhappy, but they had had rows all the time, because of her, and she hadn't liked that.

". . . to be my wedded husband."

Phil kissed Theresa now that they were man and wife, a little peck on the lips. He had always been shy of showing his feelings in public, and Kayleigh smiled as she saw his face grow pink. He was all right once everyone started signing the register and he had stopped being the center of attention.

Theresa had said that if they could, she and Phil would adopt her, and then she would be able to live with them instead of with her foster parents. They were all right, but it would be much better to be at home with her dad again, and now that he and Theresa were married, it might happen.

Kayleigh hoped it would.

Judy hadn't felt anything like as nervous as this the first time round; she had married Michael without any of the jitters she'd been subject to over the last few weeks as the date approached. And the silly thing was that she had known that she and Michael were all wrong for each other, whereas she and Lloyd were and always would be right together. Perhaps, she thought, it was because this time really mattered.

"We're going to be far too early," Lloyd said. "It's only half past ten now."

"I know. But I'd rather be there than sitting waiting at home."

Home was still her flat, with her mother sleeping in a single bed in the nursery, but if their offer was accepted, it would soon be a stone-built detached house—with a garden in which Lloyd could pretend he would grow strawberries—in the old village of Stansfield, just a couple of streets away from where Lloyd had had his flat.

Judy hadn't been able to believe her luck when she had been scanning, with no great enthusiasm, the property supplement in the local paper and had found it up for sale. She really liked the old village; she never knew whether it was the village itself or her association of it with the moment when she and Lloyd finally consummated the love affair they had begun when she was twenty years old, but a house becoming available there made the thought of moving so much easier than it might have been.

They were having to get a much bigger mortgage than they had meant to, even with the sale of their respective flats, and it didn't yet have the self-contained living accommodation that Lloyd had promised her mother, but it did mean she would have her own room, and a loft conversion was being planned, on the in-for-a-penny principle.

Her mother had been dressing Charlotte as they left, glad, Judy was sure, to see the back of her nerve-racked daughter and to be left to her own devices with her granddaughter. Charlotte now had two bottom teeth, of which Lloyd had to have taken two thousand photographs, and these days the conversations were two-way affairs, with the odd lisped sibilant; Charlotte still spoke gobbledygook, but she did it in sentences now, if not paragraphs, and got cross if Judy didn't seem to be listening. Judy had a dreadful feeling that Charlotte was going to be just like Lloyd as soon as she did get the hang of the language.

"Have you actually been struck dumb, or are you just having second thoughts?"

She smiled at him. "Neither. I was just thinking how we've turned into a family. And I like it."

Theresa posed with Phil on the steps of the Civic Centre and laughed as the confetti swirled in the breeze that was playing havoc with the hair that had been so carefully styled that morning.

Ian knew that it hadn't been her choice; Theresa had told him that her hairdresser had said that she must have something special for her wedding day and had proceeded to build her hair into a style that made her look like someone else. The wind was turning her back into Theresa; a good thing, in Ian's opinion.

He and Theresa had never discussed marriage; he supposed if they had, they would have done it. And then Lesley would never have happened. He didn't know why a piece of paper would have made a difference, but he knew that it would have. It had never occurred to him to ask Theresa to marry him because he and Theresa had always really just been friends, not lovers, and while he would have liked to return to the status quo, he knew it was never going to happen. So he was glad she had found someone she was happy with.

It had been very sudden; they seemed just to have met when they were announcing their intention to marry. But then, he had felt like that about Lesley, so he understood. His brief interlude with Lesley seemed almost unreal now; there were moments, memories, that could give him a stab of pain, but mostly he felt a little as though someone he had known in passing had died, not someone with whom he had intended spending his life.

"Ian, can you manage a camera with your leg?"

Ian smiled at Kayleigh. "Not with my leg, no, but I can probably manage it with my hands."

"Oh, funny man."

He laid the crutches down on the low wall and stood with his legs slightly apart, his weight on his good leg. He could achieve relative stability that way. His leg had suffered a clean fracture and was healing quickly; it was the foot that had given him all the problems, all the pain. They had thought for a while that they might have to amputate it, but they had operated instead. And they thought now that he might not need any more operations, so things weren't as bad as they might have been. He would have a limp, but it could all have been a great deal worse.

"Oh, good, thanks. I want one of Dad and Theresa, the witnesses, and the bridesmaids."

He watched as she and Andrea shepherded Phil's aunt and Theresa's brother a step up from the bride and groom, one to either side, then took up their own flanking positions on the step up from them.

She hadn't said much about Lesley when she'd visited him in the hospital; Ian couldn't tell how badly or otherwise it had hit her. She seemed just to have accepted it, but so much more went on in Kayleigh's mind than anyone ever suspected that it was difficult to tell.

"Move in a bit closer," he said, looking into the viewfinder. "Lovely. Now, smile!"

They all smiled just as a gust of wind lifted up the bride's dress and the carefully posed tableau fell into laughing disarray. Ian took the photograph anyway; it would be better than the posed one.

Lloyd glanced at Judy as he stopped at the zebra crossing just before the registry office, put there so that people getting off at the bus stop didn't get mown down as soon as they tried to cross the road. She had said that if Lloyd wanted to get married, that was all right by her. If he wanted to spend a fortune on a reception, fine. But, she had said, she was not going to behave like a virgin bride—he was not going to stay somewhere else the night before, because of some ridiculous superstition. They would drive to the registry office together, or they wouldn't go there at all.

"I had no intention of spending the night anywhere else," he had said. "How would I know you would turn up?"

He had, of course, had every intention of sticking to tradition; he had been going to stay with the Finches. But it didn't bother him; he didn't think it could ever be bad luck to see Judy. This morning she was very nervous, slightly flushed, and she looked wonderful. She was, he had told her that morning, the second most beautiful woman in his life. The first most beautiful was being brought by Judy's mother at something more like the time of the ceremony.

He pulled into the car park and backed into a space without having to search for one; no bad luck yet, he thought. They were much earlier than they needed to be, and he watched, smiling, as Judy anxiously took the makeup mirror from her bag and made minute adjustments.

"Stop staring at me."

"Sorry." He amused himself instead by looking at the people posing for photographs in the stiff breeze that had got up. After a few moments, they ceased to be an anonymous wedding party and resolved themselves into people that he knew. He wound down the window to get a better look at them.

"Well, well, well," he said. "Fancy that."

He got no reaction, so he tried again.

"Who would have thought it?"

Still nothing.

"They were quick off the mark. I feel a bit like Cupid, since I was the one who brought them together, as it were. If I hadn't taken him to Barton General, they might never have met. I was there when he made their first date."

She was, of course, ignoring him on purpose, so he began all over again.

"Well, well, well. Fancy that. Who would have—?"

"Well, well, well, what?" she asked, a mite crossly for his bride-to-be. "What are you going on about? Stop being mysterious."

"Romance would appear to have blossomed. That bride and groom—do you know who they are?"

Judy looked across, shaking her head.

"Theresa Black and Phil Roddam. And the man with the crutches and the two young women is Ian Waring, ex-partner of the bride and ex–fancy man of the groom's deceased wife."

Judy looked at him, her brown eyes suspicious. "Are you making this up?"

He laughed. "No, honestly. The entire wedding party is composed of my murder investigation. It's a wonder Dean Fletcher hasn't been given compassionate release to attend."

Judy was clearly still not convinced that he was telling the truth; she went back to plucking invisible hairs from her eyebrows as Lloyd watched his onetime suspects arrange themselves in various groups until they had been photographed in every conceivable combination. The thought crossed his mind that Phil Roddam had been left some money by Lesley, but it was hardly an amount worth murdering for, even if it hadn't been conclusively proved that neither he nor his new bride could have murdered her. Lloyd's eyes widened as he realized who one of the young women was, and he sighed, still unhappy about the outcome of his murder inquiry.

"And there's another thing Dean Fletcher was telling the truth about," he said. "I don't know about looking eighteen—she looks about twenty-five in that getup. I didn't recognize her."

"Who?"

"Kayleigh—that's her, with the camera."

Judy looked across, without much interest, just as Lloyd saw the Finches' car pulling in, then went back to her activities with the tweezers before her head swiveled back in a perfect double take. "That's Kayleigh Scott?"

"It is. But she doesn't normally look like that—no one believed Fletcher that she *could* look like that." Lloyd was beginning to wonder just who had taken advantage of whom in the Dean/Kayleigh relationship. "I don't know the other girl."

"That's Andrea Merry." A slight frown was bringing her carefully plucked eyebrows together.

"Is it? I wouldn't have thought Andrea would be too keen on staying friends with her after what she did to her."

"Are you *sure* that's Kayleigh?"

"Of course I'm sure!"

Tom, Liz, and their children were coming over to them, but Judy didn't seem terribly interested in that.

"But I saw . . ." she began, and her voice trailed off. "And I know that was before ten, because . . . and it wasn't until after eleven that . . . and that bus stop means that she would just have to—" She broke off completely then, as the Black-Roddam wedding party made its way toward the car park.

"Why have you suddenly become incoherent?" he

asked, looking back at her, and closed his eyes when he saw her face.

She couldn't possibly be looking like a gundog. Not now. Not today. She hadn't even worked on the investigation—how could she be looking like a gundog? But she was.

Suddenly she was scrambling out of the car. "Tom," she said, her voice urgent. "Do you recognize that girl with Andrea Merry?"

Tom looked at Kayleigh, at first shaking his head, then nodding vigorously as the group of people came closer to him. Lloyd saw the girl half smile, her face slightly puzzled, and the girl he now knew to be Andrea Merry caught her arm. The two of them started discussing something, casting glances over at Tom and Judy.

Lloyd looked at Liz and shrugged. "Sorry about this," he said. "I don't know what's going on, either."

"Lloyd?" Judy bent down to talk to him through the window, her voice quiet and apologetic. "I think you're going to have to arrest them."

Lloyd stared at her. "What? No—no, absolutely not. We came here to get married, and that's what we're doing. They're on their way to a wedding reception, for goodness' sake. Phone the station if you want them arrested. They're not going to run away."

But Judy was shaking her head. "I think that's just what they are going to do. She's recognized me and Tom—Andrea's telling her right now who Tom is, and she's putting two and two together, just like I am. Look at them!"

"She's right, guv," said Tom. "If ever anyone would have a contingency plan, it's Kayleigh."

It was all too obvious that both Judy and Tom knew something that he didn't know and that he wasn't going to be able to ignore it. The girls were still in tense discussion, and his bride and his best man were standing by, waiting for him to make a decision.

It was his wedding day; he had guests. His father, his mother-in-law and his baby daughter, his sisters, his son and his wife, his daughter and her current boyfriend, Freddie and his wife, his friends, his colleagues . . . they would all be arriving any minute now. The girls were getting into their car, but you didn't just drop everything and arrest people on your wedding day, especially other people's wedding guests. He was sure that all wedding etiquette books would agree that it was the height of bad form.

"I mean it, Lloyd—if you want to get Dean Fletcher out of prison anytime soon, you're going to have to arrest them. Quick—box them in before they drive off!"

He looked helplessly at the other car and back at Judy.

"Lloyd? Now would be good."

It *was* bad luck to see the bride before the wedding, Lloyd thought, and he knew when he was beaten. He fired the engine and drove out, stopping the car across the bows of the other one as it tried to reverse out of the parking space.

He got out of the car and went to one side of the girls' car as Tom went to the other. "This had better be worth it," Lloyd said as Judy ran up to join them.

"It is." She was ringing the station as she spoke. "I'm still piecing it together, but if I'm right, then all your little puzzles were spot-on."

She'd be right. His gundog was never wrong.

CHAPTER THIRTEEN

"What do you mean, I can't see her? She's fourteen years old! She's got to have an adult present if you're going to interview her!"

"I know that, Mr. Roddam, and there will be an appropriate adult present when we do interview her. But for the moment, I'm afraid you can't talk to her."

"Why not? Have you got her locked up in a cell?"

Constable Sims remained as maddeningly reasonable as Lesley always had. "No, sir, she isn't in a cell—we prefer not to keep juveniles in cells if we can help it."

"Then why don't you interview her now, and get her out of here one way or the other? I'm present." He jabbed his own chest. "I'm an appropriate adult."

The constable smiled sympathetically. "I'm afraid you're not, Mr. Roddam. One of Kayleigh's foster parents will be here when we interview her."

Phil felt himself grow red with frustration. "But she's my d—" He broke off. No. He mustn't say that. The constable would simply remind him, as Lesley had, that she wasn't. "As good as . . . my daughter," he said. "I should be with her."

"Where possible the appropriate adult should be someone with current care and control of the child," said Sims. "And you're a witness in the investigation into Mrs. Newton's death, even if that wasn't the case. It really *wouldn't* be appropriate. I appreciate how you must feel, but there honestly is nothing I can do."

Phil accepted that the young man was just doing his job and that he was right; they probably wouldn't have let him see Kayleigh even if he were her natural father. But he couldn't help worrying. "Is she all right? Has she asked for a solicitor?"

"Yes, sir. And one is on his way."

The truth was that Kayleigh didn't need him, not for this. She needed lawyers and doctors to help her now. What she needed him for was to understand why she had done it, and he thought he did, just. He understood that Andrea had become more important to her than anything or anyone and that Andrea had felt the same about her, just as Lesley had said; like two cars colliding head-on, the impact was at double the speed at which they were individually traveling. Lesley had known Kayleigh better than he had given her credit for and had tried, in her own way, to steer Kayleigh out of the path of the oncoming vehicle.

But it had been much too late.

"If this clears up the murder inquiry and proves that you were right about Dean Fletcher, will I be forgiven?"

Lloyd didn't look as though he was in a forgiving mood. "I've told Tom just to take everyone across to the Derbyshire and have the reception without us. At least the food won't go to waste."

"Good."

Lloyd sat back. "Well? Have you pieced it together now?"

She nodded. "I think so." She had no notebook to refer to; she felt a little lost about where to start without being able to leaf through mounds of notes, ticking them off. But she had had time to think now, and she thought she knew the sequence of events.

"Things are becoming clear, at last," she said. "Like Andrea Merry, screaming one minute, calm the next, and then practically suicidal by the time Tom saw her." She smiled. "And do you remember Kayleigh's running-away suitcase?"

"Yes," said Lloyd.

"Was it black leather?"

"Yes."

"I bet I can tell you what was in it. A lilac Versace trouser suit and a navy-and-lilac striped top that probably cost the best part of three hundred pounds on its own."

Lloyd smiled. A reluctant smile but a smile nonetheless. "I wouldn't know the price. But even I could read the label. Yes, amongst other things, that's what was in it."

"One of the other things being a mobile phone."

"Am I going to get an explanation of this in due course? Or do I have to become a member of the Magic Circle before you can divulge your methods?"

"And the pram that was too good for someone to have thrown away." Judy was enjoying herself now. It was usually Lloyd who was mysterious. "You have still got it, haven't you?"

Lloyd nodded. "We got fingerprints from it. We never did anything with them, because it didn't seem to have anything to do with it. I take it that you think it has?"

"Oh, yes. Do you remember I told you about that girl I saw going to the nursery? The one who didn't seem to have much time for her baby? That was Kayleigh."

Lloyd's eyes widened. "Are you sure?"

"I'm one hundred percent sure. I've thought about her over and over again—you know I have. And the pram she was wheeling is the one Alan found in the woods. I know that without seeing it."

"But—" Lloyd frowned as he thought about that. "But you said it was an old, shabby pram. The one we found is in perfect condition."

Judy had thought about that, too. And, as she had told herself not so very long ago, everything was relative. "A pram that looks old and shabby when it's being pushed by someone in Versace turns into a practically new one when it's found on a rubbish tip," she said. "All either of us meant was that it looked out of place. But not so out of place that we couldn't just accept it."

Lloyd nodded, but his face still held some doubt. "Are you saying it was Emma that she had in this pram?"

"Yes. And she left her at the Riverside Nursery well over an hour before she was supposed to have been stolen."

"But you saw Andrea Merry with the baby. So did half a dozen other people."

"No. We saw what we took to be a baby—why would we think it was anything else? Tom thought it was a baby, too, when he saw it in the river. He said it didn't look like a real baby close to, but from a distance . . ." She leaned forward, her arms on the desk. "We all saw it from a distance. Surveillance cameras watch from a distance. It was a doll, Lloyd. A lifelike doll that looks just like a baby until you take a closer look. No one was allowed a closer look—Andrea made sure of that."

Lloyd tipped his chair back as he thought. "So . . . Kayleigh contrives to get left in Malworth on her own. She puts on makeup and designer clothes to make herself look older. And Andrea leaves the Crawfords' house with Emma, saying she's taking her shopping . . ."

". . . but instead goes straight to Kayleigh's," Judy said. "Where they give Emma a different set of clothes and put hers on the doll. Then Kayleigh pops Emma in the pram and takes her to the nursery."

"Then what?"

"Then she goes home and changes again. She puts her designer clothes into a case, along with her mobile phone and the doorstop. And she takes out of the case, and changes into, what she wore when she murdered her mother. A size ten floral print dress. You were right about that, too, even if it was just a joke."

The floral print dresses, Lloyd had discovered, were the summer uniform of the exclusive girls' school in Malworth at which Kayleigh was a pupil. Should he have begun to wonder then about Kayleigh? She was, after all, the only person in the whole drama who could entirely remove the coincidence to which Case and he had objected.

"Andrea must have driven Kayleigh to Stansfield, dropped her somewhere she could walk to the cottage— probably at the bus stop by the Civic Centre. She would walk through the woods, and watch for Waring leaving with the van. And Andrea drove back to Malworth, parked in the car park by the shops, and went to Riverside Park with the doll masquerading as Emma. That's why she went to where the willow tree would screen her from other people."

"And meanwhile, Kayleigh killed Lesley," said Lloyd.

And Lloyd had been right about the ultraorganized Lesley, Judy thought. Of course she hadn't been unpacking clothes in the utility room; why would she? She just happened to be in there, and she was going to be killed wherever Kayleigh had found her. Kayleigh had taken the packing case to Lesley, got her to look in it, Judy supposed, since that would give her the height advantage that Freddie had mentioned . . . then she had put her bloodstained dress on top of the ones that had spilled out and become stained when it had got knocked over during the murder.

Lloyd's chair moved back and forth as he thought aloud. "And then she changed back into the designer gear, used the mobile phone to tell Andrea that it was done, and went back through the woods to the town center, where she presumably got the bus to Malworth." He let the chair fall forward. "And when Andrea got the message?"

"She removed the Winnie-the-Pooh all-in-one and dropped the doll in the river. Then she went back to the car park, stuffing the all-in-one into a waste bin on the way, and apparently got her mobile from the car. Came back and started screaming."

"And all the time everyone was looking for Emma, she was safe and well in the Riverside Nursery," said Lloyd. "Being fed—which is why she wasn't hungry until late afternoon. And when Tom worked out—or thought he had—that Andrea had left the baby with Kayleigh, we thought several people had actually *seen* Kayleigh in Malworth five minutes after the murder had taken place in Stansfield."

Judy nodded. "That's why they wore the same clothes. Not so Kayleigh could disappear—so she could *appear*. But only Andrea was there, just like we thought in the first place."

"And when Kayleigh got back to Malworth, she picked Emma up again from the nursery."

"Yes. I saw her then, too. That's when Tom saw her. I thought it was a briefcase she had with her."

Then she had taken the baby back to the house, removed the makeup, changed yet again—back into the clothes she had been wearing in the first place, the ones that matched Andrea's—and put the designer clothes in the case with the mobile, filling it up with other clothes and personal things to give credence to its being a case packed for running away with Fletcher.

She smiled, a little reluctantly. "She even realized that walking about with a change of clothes in a suitcase might seem suspicious, so she left the suitcase in Malworth, and then *told* Mrs. Spears what was in it, once she'd planted the running-away story, because by that time, there was nothing suspicious about it. It was just slightly pathetic."

"My thoughts exactly," said Lloyd. "The baby-food touch was nice."

"And then she went back to Stansfield, with the baby in the pram," Judy went on, "which is why the bus drivers didn't notice anyone without one. She was going to be traveling on that bus after everyone knew a baby had gone missing—she didn't want to be carrying one in her arms. She walked through the woods, dumped the pram, and carried Emma the rest of the way to the cottage."

The pram hadn't been there when those boys had looted the car, Lloyd thought. That was why they had failed to notice its secondhand value. That was a puzzle he hadn't even voiced.

"And when she arrived at the cottage with Emma," Judy went on, "she thought that Ian Waring would be there, and that as soon as he saw the baby, he would want to know where it had come from. She would confess what she had done, her alibi would be in place, and the Crawfords would have Emma back safely within three hours of finding out she was missing. That was why she was anxious to know where Ian was. You were right about that, too."

"Yes," said Lloyd absently. "I noticed the puzzles, but I misread them."

"Andrea knew that was the plan, which is why she

didn't seem to be that concerned to begin with. But when it didn't happen, she genuinely believed that something must have happened to Emma. No wonder she was frantic when Tom saw her. Killing Mrs. Newton was one thing—but an innocent baby . . . a baby she really did love, unlike Kayleigh—the thought that something had happened to Emma was too much for her to bear."

Lloyd frowned. "But why didn't Kayleigh tell us herself about Emma?" he asked. "When she realized Ian wasn't there?"

"How could she tell you herself?" asked Judy. "By saying, 'Oh, by the way, I just stole this baby'?" She shook her head. "No—she hadn't bargained for Ian not being there, and she had no idea what had been going on in the cottage. She needed thinking time, and that's what she gave herself."

"And then I told her about the row," said Lloyd. "And she knew that Phil Roddam must have been there. She hadn't meant him to come under suspicion, so she just clammed up altogether and hoped we wouldn't find out about him. She didn't mean anyone else to get the blame— not even Fletcher. She had no idea he'd been to the cottage."

He loosened his tie slightly, giving up his effort to look smart now that he wasn't getting married after all. Judy smiled; she liked him better crumpled.

"Fletcher was just part of the smoke screen," she said. "She had to have a reason for taking the baby. Pretending it was Emma she couldn't bear to leave and that she had planned to steal her and run away with Fletcher was as good a reason as any. It didn't matter that Fletcher would never have agreed to such a thing—it didn't even matter if he failed to turn up at all. All that mattered was that he would confirm that she had asked him to be there, and that we *believed* that was what she intended doing." And they had believed it, she thought. They had believed it all.

"She knew the court would be understanding about the baby snatch," Lloyd said. "They usually are, and she had been through several traumatic experiences."

"Certainly more understanding about that than they would be about her murdering her mother," said Judy.

Lloyd sighed. "It's like the old joke about the man who murdered his parents and asked for clemency because he was an orphan."

"And she's a juvenile—nothing would appear in the papers that could identify her, so no one at the Riverside Nursery would be able to put two and two together. And whatever the court did—wherever she ended up—Andrea could join her."

A silence fell while they both thought about how it had so very nearly succeeded.

"You know," said Lloyd, "I wished all the time that you were working on the investigation with me, but if you had been, we'd never have known. It was only because you were at the Riverside Nursery when she was there and saw her again today that she was caught. Sheer coincidence—not detective work."

Judy was very well aware of that. "I know. So you might not forgive me for scuppering the wedding, because I'm not sure how much hard evidence we've actually got."

"Well, you and Tom are eyewitnesses. And the Riverside Nursery staff might be able to recognize Kayleigh or Emma, or both. There's the pram—someone's prints are on it, so let's hope they're Kayleigh's. And the lab will take a closer look at the bloodstained clothes and the photographs of the utility room—they might be able to prove that one of the dresses was placed there after the murder. I don't suppose the doll will be of much use—"

Judy hadn't thought about the doll. "Oh, but it could

be," she said. "They're quite often limited editions. If we can trace the people who made it, they might know who they sold it to."

Lloyd smiled. "Well, there you are. And we can get experts to tell us where and when the doll had to have entered the river to be seen where Tom saw it—"

"Even so. Like Tom says, Kayleigh will have a contingency plan."

"She very probably had one for running away with Andrea if we got too close for comfort," said Lloyd. "I'm sure she would have worked out how they could just disappear. But I doubt very much if she had one for actually getting caught. This was all or nothing. She was taking a huge risk—any one of the people who went to the cottage could have caught her in the act." He stood up. "Well, we can't interview her until her foster father gets here. But Andrea can be talked to now. And without Kayleigh pulling the strings, I don't think Andrea will hold out for very long."

Judy brightened when she realized that. Andrea didn't have nerves of steel, as Tom had discovered.

"We're going to be here for a long time yet," Lloyd said. "You'd better ring Tom and tell him not to expect us at the reception."

"Right," said Judy, dialing his mobile number. "And I'll get him to organize transport for those who need it." She waited until the door closed before letting it ring and was relieved to get Tom immediately. "Tom," she said, employing her very best wheedle, "do you think you could do something for me?"

"Are you sure you're all right?" asked Theresa.

"Yes, of course," said Ian.

She felt sorry for him because his new house was less than welcoming at the moment. The cottage would be going back on the market as soon as the police said that it was all right to have the utility room sorted out, and he was renting a small semi-detached. It needed a bit doing to it, but as soon as he could get about without crutches, he would set about making the place more like home.

"I can do everything except walk properly." He was worried about her, rather than thinking she should be worried about him. "What are you going to do?" he asked.

"About what?"

"About Kayleigh—you know perfectly well about what. You're not going to carry on trying to adopt her, are you?"

"If Phil wants to, and I'm sure he will." Theresa, who had been on the point of leaving, sat down on the sofa. "What's so strange about that?"

Ian gave an unamused laugh. "Theresa, the police didn't arrest her and Andrea on a whim. They murdered Lesley." Poor Lesley, he thought, remembering his baffled response to her worries about Andrea. She had been right, and the unhealthy relationship had become even more destructive than she could have imagined.

No wonder Dean what'shisname had got out of the cottage as fast as he could. He had already been on the receiving end of Kayleigh's machinations, and Ian could well understand that he had not wanted to get involved in any more of them. And since Dean hadn't murdered Lesley, Ian doubted very much that what had happened to him had been deliberate; if he could get the police to drop the charge of attempted murder, he would. It seemed to him that those who got involved with Kayleigh had enough to contend with.

"She was calmly letting that ex-boyfriend of hers take the blame," he added. "And if he hadn't turned up, it could have been Phil himself who was being charged. Do you think she would have let that happen, too?"

Theresa's eyes filled with tears, and her hand went to her mouth. "Poor Phil," she said.

"Poor Phil? He can walk away from it—Kayleigh's got nothing to do with him now!"

She looked at him exactly as she had when he had told her he was going to Australia, with disbelief and a hint of anger. "She has everything to do with him. He's been trying to get her treatment for years—it's Lesley's own fault that she's dead! She should have listened to what Phil was telling her. The child is ill."

"Even so—"

"Even so, nothing. If she was Phil's real daughter, then I'd be her stepmother whether I liked it or not, and that's what I'll be, if that's what he wants. She needs his help, and he needs someone to help *him*."

Ian held up his hands in surrender. He admired Phil Roddam for what he was prepared to do, but he thought Theresa had taken leave of her senses. He remembered thinking that Kayleigh would be much better off with Theresa and he still believed that, but he didn't think that Theresa would be better off with Kayleigh. She was one hell of a responsibility.

And ashamed though he would be to admit it to anyone—even Theresa—the little part of him that cut through all the layers of half truths, manufactured emotions, and assumed airs was telling him that he should really be grateful to Kayleigh for making certain, before it was too late, that she was never going to be *his* responsibility.

Kayleigh listened to what Chief Inspector Lloyd was saying, her solicitor on one side, her foster father, looking perplexed, on the other. Andrea had told Lloyd everything, of course, but that didn't matter. There wasn't really any way back from here.

It was a shame that woman had seen her at the nursery, because even with all these things happening that she hadn't bargained for, it had worked. No one had seen her the first time she had gone to the nursery with Emma, when she had arranged, a month in advance, to leave her there for a few hours while she kept a business appointment. And that had been far more risky; her mother and Ian were both in Malworth that day and could have happened by at the wrong time. When she actually left Emma there, they were safely in Stansfield; it hadn't occurred to her that there was any risk at all.

The plan had worked. She had thought, from the moment her mother had said they were going to Australia, that there was only one way to stop it, but she hadn't been able to work out how she could do it without getting caught. It had been when she and Andrea had been walking in the park with Emma that she had begun to realize that she could give herself an alibi.

She had been wishing that her mother had never adopted her, and that had made her think about Alexandra and about how desperate some people were to have babies. They adopted them, they had test-tube babies, they used other people to have them for them, and sometimes, she had thought, sometimes they even stole them. And the thought of substituting one crime—one that people understood and barely even thought of as a crime—for the one that she intended carrying out had come to her. After all, she had had to give her baby up for adoption, and wasn't that just the sort of thing that made people steal babies?

She and Andrea already dressed alike, so the idea of making people believe that they had seen her in the park when she was in fact somewhere else altogether had presented itself almost instantly. The other things were easy; she had bought the doll from America, over the Internet, and had given Andrea the money to buy the baby clothes and a secondhand pram, which she had kept in the boot of the car until it was needed.

All of that was in place before she had any idea of how she was actually going to do it, but then the people who were buying their house had come to her rescue. Ian had taken them to the cottage, told her how he used to play in the woods, how you could walk to the town through them. While her mother had been in the cottage seeing what was what, Kayleigh had explored, and by the time they were on their way back to Malworth she had known exactly what she was going to do. She had worked out a way of doing it, believing that it would be a removal van that would take their stuff to the cottage; when Ian had suddenly insisted on doing it himself, she had been worried. But as it turned out, that had worked out even better.

In fact, the whole thing had worked far better than she could have hoped; Andrea had told her that she hadn't even had to tell the police that she had left Emma with her, because Sergeant Finch had told *her* that she had. The police had worked out her alibi for themselves. And once Andrea realized that Emma was safe and well, she had told the story that they had rehearsed together.

But when Kayleigh had seen that woman this morning, with Chief Inspector Lloyd, of all people, and then the man with the curly blond hair, who turned out to *be* Sergeant Finch, she had known it was over, unless they could get away. And they couldn't.

So she had told the solicitor the truth, and she had admitted killing her mother when Lloyd had asked her the straight question.

"Do you want to tell me your side of the story?"

"My client doesn't want to make any further comment at this point," said the solicitor. "Except to say that she is

currently receiving psychiatric treatment, which could, of course, have a bearing on her defense."

"Was Dean Fletcher in any way involved in the conspiracy to murder Mrs. Newton?"

"No. No one. Just me and Andrea."

"Very well, Kayleigh, interview terminated at thirteen-twen—"

"Wait. I want to say something else."

All three of them looked at her, their faces alarmed at what she might be going to say. But it wasn't anything awful, just something she thought she ought to say. She regretted, in a way, what she had done to Dean before all of this. He had been quite brave, coming to Stansfield to see the baby like he had, to have his photograph taken with her. She hadn't meant him to get charged with the murder. And there was one way she could make amends.

"I lied at Dean's trial," she said. "I said I told him my real name and how old I was. And that I thought he was a boy of my own age. But I didn't. He did believe I was eighteen. I did know how old he was when I went to meet him. And he really didn't know who the police were talking about when they asked him about me. It wasn't the way I said." She looked at Lloyd, at her solicitor. "Can he appeal or something? I'll tell the truth this time. And I'll let them see me dressed up, if that'll help. Because he shouldn't be on that register."

Lloyd nodded slowly. "Since he was only twenty-three when it happened, believing you were sixteen or over is a valid defense," he said. "It might be worth his while to seek leave to appeal, if you're now saying that you did mislead him. Why did you do that?"

People were very slow, Kayleigh felt. Always wanting explanations for things that were perfectly obvious. "Because he wouldn't have had anything to do with me if he'd known how old I really was."

"Why did you lie about it?"

That was a question that didn't have an obvious answer, because Kayleigh wasn't sure why she had done that. She had wanted to be with Dean more than anything in the world, and then . . . well, then she hadn't. Not because of the pregnancy—that hadn't meant much to her one way or the other. Just because. She didn't know why, but she had felt angry, and she had wanted to make him pay for . . . for something. Like Luke. She didn't know why she'd done that, either. She had loved him once, too. And her mother. She didn't know now why staying with Andrea had seemed so important.

"I'm not sure why I do anything," she said. "But I wish I didn't."

Theresa parked the van and let herself into the flats. Now, she had to set about reassuring Phil that she was just as prepared to go ahead with trying to adopt Kayleigh as she had ever been.

The truth was, she admitted to herself, as she went up the stairs, that she was considerably happier about it than she had been, because whatever happened now, Kayleigh was going to be under someone else's roof—preferably a secure one—until she had reached and passed the age of majority and would not, after all, be coming to live with her and Phil. So, she thought with a sad little smile, she wasn't just as mad as Ian thought she was or just as self-sacrificing as Phil thought she was.

And she was relieved that the dark thoughts she had harbored about each of them, prompted by Chief Inspector Lloyd's certainty that someone close to Lesley had killed her, had been completely wrong.

Lloyd, however, had been right, and looking at it from a purely selfish point of view, if anyone had to have mur-

dered Lesley Newton, Theresa was glad it had been Kayleigh.

"Visitor."

Dean looked up, startled. No one ever visited him. Please God, don't let it be Kayleigh, he thought as he followed the guard. He was let into the visitors' room, its tables empty except for one, at which sat his solicitor.

Dean sat down wearily. "Now what?" he asked.

"You remember I told you that you were lucky?"

Dean raised his eyebrows slightly. "Oh, yeah," he said. "Lucky Dean."

"Well, I've just had a call from the police in Stansfield."

Thirty seconds later, the whoops and hollers echoed in the big, empty room and the guard rushed in, thinking someone was being murdered.

But Dean wasn't a murderer, and now, at last, they believed him about that. And with any luck, he wasn't going to be a sex offender for much longer. Unless, of course, such offenses included kissing a solicitor without his consent.

"She does know," said Liz, "that she has to come into the ladies' room as soon as she gets here?"

"Yes, she knows." Tom had agreed to try to do Judy's favor for her and it had been very hard work, but he'd done it. Liz had produced the condition as soon as she knew what was happening.

"Don't tell her why," she had said. "Just tell her. She has to promise on her honor to go to the ladies' room before she does anything else, or the deal's off."

Lloyd made his way back to his office, rubbing the tension out of the back of his neck. Phil Roddam had told him that Kayleigh always had a plan, but no one had realized how grand or how ruthless a plan it had been.

Judy still sat there, still looking cool and calm and uncreased, unlike him. "Right," he said. "I think that's it, and as far as I can recall, I'm on holiday now. It was going to be a honeymoon, but my bride-to-be turned into a gundog."

Judy smiled and got up. "The car's still at the Civic Centre."

He walked with her through the shoppers to the other side of the town center. First Charlotte, four weeks early. Then an arrest. What would Judy manage to do next time he tried to marry her? Though he wondered if there would be a next time. She could put it off forever now.

"We could see if the registrar's still there," she said.

That startled him, until he realized that she was only offering because she knew the registrar would have gone long ago. "They close at one," he said. "It's nearly two o'clock now."

"You never know. They might still be there."

Lloyd shrugged. He supposed she was trying to make up for what had happened, but it was a waste of time. "You do know that it's legal as long as it's before six?"

Judy frowned. "Yes. Why?"

"Oh, I just thought you were perhaps thinking of a way to marry me and get out of it later." He stopped when they got to the Derbyshire. "Let's go in and see if we can get something to eat. I don't know about you, but I'm starving."

"They'll have stopped serving lunch."

"Then let's go home and get something to eat." He crossed the road to the car park, empty save for his Rover and a couple of other vehicles in the spaces reserved for the staff, and pointed the remote at the car, unlocking it.

"We might as well try the registry office first," she said as she arrived.

He didn't understand this. She knew they'd missed their chance for today. "Why?" he demanded. "It's closed. It's pointless. Even if she is still here, she won't do it. Why do you want to try?"

"Because I don't want to go through more weeks of waiting for the wedding—I don't like it. If we can get it over with today, I'd much rather do that. And these cars must belong to someone."

Get it over with. There wasn't an ounce of romance in her.

"Even if the registrar is here and is prepared to do it, Tom and Liz aren't. We need witnesses."

"There'll be cleaners, or something."

That wasn't at all what he had had in mind. But it was true that the whole thing made her very nervous, and if there was any chance at all of marrying today, it would be better, from her point of view, to get it over with, as she so delicately put it.

"All right," he said, locking the car again. "Let's go and find out. But she'll have gone home hours ago."

"I'll just pop to the ladies' room."

Lloyd frowned. "Why didn't you go when you were at the station?"

"Won't be a moment."

She wasn't gone long, and, as it turned out, the registrar hadn't gone home, and she even agreed to do it. Her staff were still there, she said, so she and her assistant would conduct the ceremony, and the other two could be witnesses.

Two people he didn't know. Still, at least he was getting married after all, and even if it wasn't the romantic occasion he had planned, it was, he supposed, as the pre-ceremony formalities were gone through, better than nothing.

"If you'll follow me into the marriage room."

He made to set his tie straight, but Judy stopped him. "Leave it," she said.

Puzzled, he left it and followed Judy, whose cheeks were glowing a faint pink as they always did when she was excited or nervous, into the marriage room. But he couldn't really share the excitement—this was all too matter-of-fact for him. It was one thing agreeing to a virtually anonymous wedding when she was eight months pregnant, but now . . .

He stopped at the door, blinking slightly. Everyone was *there*. Tom, Liz—his dad, Charlotte, Bob Sandwell and his wife, what seemed like half of the rest of Bartonshire Constabulary—everyone. The room was packed. Judy and the registrar were looking very pleased with themselves, and Tom gave Judy a little thumbs-up sign.

"It was a great reception," said Case. "You should have been there."

"The car park's empty. Where are all the cars?" Lloyd asked, ever the vigilant detective.

"Distributed all over the town center," said Judy. "Tom's been working very hard organizing everyone and everything."

"Your detective sergeant is a very persuasive young man," said the registrar, beaming at him. "I don't usually work on Saturday afternoons *or* conspire to trick my customers, but I somehow found myself doing both."

Now that he was standing in front of her, Judy at his side, Tom and Liz flanking them, his friends and relations behind him, Lloyd, too, felt nervous and excited, and not just about getting married.

"This place in which you are now met has been duly sanctioned according to law for the celebration of marriages. And before you are joined in matrimony, I have to remind you of the solemn and binding character of the vows you are about to make."

They didn't need reminding, and they didn't need vows. They had chosen the simplest of ceremonies, not because of Judy's lack of romance but because Lloyd had decreed that extra promises were redundant.

Almost the simplest of ceremonies, he amended. The simplest was simply to answer, "I am," when asked if you were free to marry, but he had vetoed that when he had seen the split infinitive and had been unable to persuade the registrar to unsplit it.

He knew now that he should have got Tom to launch a charm offensive on her, but he hadn't known that at the time, so he was about to make a declaration. Not to Judy—she already knew what he was about to declare. Not to his father or his sisters or his two older children. They knew, too. But everyone else in this room was about to find out.

"I do solemnly declare," he said, "that I know not of any lawful impediment why I, Desiré Daniel Lloyd, may not be joined in matrimony to . . ."

He could hear a little whisper of reaction as his name was repeated for those who had failed to catch it. Tom was grinning, and Liz was frowning at him for grinning, as Judy declared that she, too, was free to marry.

And now the contract. "I, Desiré Daniel Lloyd, take you, Judith Cornelia Hill, to be my wedded wife." She hated her middle name, come to that, and that made him feel a little better, but not much.

Judy's voice shook a little. "I, Judith Cornelia Hill, take you, Desiré Daniel Lloyd, to be my wedded husband."

Tom gave him the ring; Lloyd slipped it on her finger and, with a deep sense of relief, kissed his wife. His *wife*. He couldn't believe it.

Outside, in a swirl of confetti, they posed for photographs, just as the Roddams had done, but no one came and arrested any of their guests. Well, not yet. There was time . . . policemen who were already merry on free booze had been known to get a little rowdy. But the high complement of wives would probably ensure that decorum was observed, even though they had spent hours in the Derbyshire already and had every intention of returning there as soon as this bit was over.

Liz Finch was taking dozens of photographs. The happy couple, Lloyd and his dad, Judy and her mum, Judy on her own, lifting her skirt to reveal the frilly blue garter she was wearing. "Old, borrowed, and blue," she said. "To cancel out seeing me before the ceremony."

Charlotte was being passed from one set of arms to the other and loving every minute of it. Lloyd and Judy posed with her as a threesome; then his son, Peter, stood beside Judy and Linda joined him; Judy's mother and his father completed the group.

Lloyd removed a circlet of paper from his tongue and smiled at Judy. "Are you regretting it yet?"

Judy smiled back, the strain of waiting over, her eyes shining with what Lloyd liked to think just might be tears.

"I'll never regret it. And that's a promise, whether you need one or not."